CW00485429

Lily LeBlanc isn't versed in the art of casual sex, but after seven years in an on-again, off-again relationship, she's definitely willing to give it a shot. And who better to try it with than her best friend's boyfriend's best friend? What could possibly go wrong?

NHL player, Randy Ballistic, lives up to his last name on the ice and in the bedroom. His best friend and teammate has recently given up the puck bunnies and traded them in for a real girlfriend. And she just happens to have a seriously feisty, extra-hot best friend on the rebound. Randy's more than happy to be Lily's spring board back into the dating scene.

But casual sex is only casual until those pesky things called emotions get involved. Once that happens, someone's bound to get pucked over.

PRAISE FOR HELENA HUNTING'S NOVELS

"Characters that will touch your heart and a romance that will leave you breathless."

-*New York Times* bestselling author Tara Sue Me

"Gut wrenching, sexy, twisted, dark, incredibly erotic and a love story like no other. On my all-time favorites list."

-Alice Clayton, *New York Times* bestselling author of *Wallbanger* and The Redhead series

"A look into the world of tattoos and piercings, a dash of humor and a feel-good ending will delight fans and new readers alike."

-*Publishers Weekly* (on *Inked Armor*)

"A unique, deliciously hot, endearingly sweet, laugh out loud, fantastically good time romance!! . . . I loved every single page!!"

–*New York Times* Bestselling author Emma Chase on *PUCKED*

"Sigh inducing swoony and fanning myself sexy. All the stars!"

-*USA Today* bestselling author Daisy Prescott on The Pucked Series

"A hot rollercoaster of a ride!"

-Julia Kent, *New York Times* and *USA Today* bestselling author on *Pucked Over*

"*Pucked Over* is Helena Hunting's funniest and sexiest book yet. SCORCHING HOT with PEE INDUCING LAUGHS. All hail the Beaver Queen."

-T. M. Frazier, *USA Today* bestselling author

TITLES BY HELENA HUNTING

PUCKED SERIES

Pucked (Pucked #1)
Pucked Up (Pucked #2)
Pucked Over (Pucked #3)
Forever Pucked (Pucked #4)
Pucked Under (Pucked #5)
Pucked Off (Pucked #6)
AREA 51: Deleted Scenes & Outtakes
Get Inked (A crossover novella)

THE CLIPPED WINGS SERIES

Cupcakes and Ink
Clipped Wings
Between the Cracks
Inked Armor
Cracks in the Armor
Fractures in Ink

STANDALONE NOVELS

The Librarian Principle
Felony Ever After
Shacking Up
Getting Down (novella)
Hooking Up
I Flipping Love You (May 2018)
The Good Luck Charm (August 2018)

HELENA HUNTING

Published by Helena Hunting

Pucked Over is a work of fiction. Names, characters, places and incidents are all products of the author's imagination or are used fictitiously. All references to the NHL are fictitious and that there is no endorsement by the NHL. Any resemblance to actual events, locals, or persons, living or dead, is entirely coincidental.

Cover art design by Shannon Lumetta
Cover font from Imagex Fonts
Cover image from LoveNBooks and Franggy Yanez
Back cover image from @Zametalov at Depositphoto.com
Formatting by CP Smith
Editing by Jessica Royer Ocken
Proofing by Marla at Proofing with Style

First Edition:2016

ACKNOWLEDGEMENTS

Each time I write another book, the list of people I'm grateful for grows.

Thank you to my family who make this dream possibly every single day. Mom, Dad, Mel and Chris, thank you for backing me up, for supporting me and for being proud.

Deb, one day we'll write side by side in Florida.

Kimberly, you're an amazing agent and I'm so glad to have you in my corner. Nina; thank you for being amazing in all ways. Jessica, thank you for helping me wrestle this one into submission. Shannon, you're a genius at the pretty. Marla, thank you for catching all the wrongs!
Teeny, you're such a generous soul. Thank you for showing me the way. I'm learning all the things.

Sarah, you rock my PA world, I couldn't find my head if it wasn't for you. Hustlers, you know how much I love you. I can't even begin to tell you how important you ladies are. Thank you for getting behind me. <3

Beaver Babes, you're incredible. I love sharing my brain with you!

Ellie, thank you for Franggy, and text messages, and floating hearts. Franggy, thank you for taking the most amazing selfies, and for being so incredibly talented.

Kelly, Christina, Susi (round two), Julia, Olivia and Deb, thank you for being the first set of eyes on this and for helping me slap this one into shape. I love you ladies!

Heather, you're the best stalker, I can't wait to see you and your hair again.

Kandace, you're the most amazing kind of human being.

To my Backdoor Babes; Tara, Meghan, Deb and Katherine, you ladies rock my socks. Thank you for all the support and more importantly, friendship.

To my Pams, the Filets, my Nap girls; 101'ers, and Indies, Tijan, Vi, Penelope, Susi, Deb, Erika, Katherine, Alice, Shalu, Amanda, Leisa, Kellie, Vicki, you are fabulous in ways I can't explain. Thank you for being my friends, my colleagues, my supporters, my teachers, my cheerleaders and my soft places to land.

My WC crew; thank you for celebrating this journey with me. I'm lucky to have such amazing people on my side.

Colleen, thank you for The Bookworm, for being an inherently good person, and for being such an inspiration.

To all my author friends and colleagues; thank you for all the amazing things you do and share, for celebrating each other's successes, for sharing the platform and for making this such an amazing community to be part of.

To all the amazing bloggers and readers out there who have supported me from the beginning of my angst, to the ridiculousness of my humour; thank you for loving these stories, for giving them a voice, for sharing your thoughts and for being such amazing women. I'm honoured and humbled and constantly amazed by what a generous community you are. And to my Originals; my fandom friends who started on this crazy journey back in 2008, thank you for sticking with me, and for being the reason I'm here, doing this thing, and loving it.

DEDICATION

Hubs and mini; you're the reason for everything.

PUCKED
OVER

PROLOGUE

DAMN YOU. MEMORIES

LILY

"I have a brown belt in karate."

"And I have a black belt in kick your fucking ass."

These are the words that keep repeating in my head, over and over. Along with Randy's promises: "*I can take your mind off your problems if you want.*" And "*I bet a few orgasms'll make you forget all about that dickface ex of yours. Wanna find out if I'm right?*"

I drag my palm over my face and check the clock. It's four in the morning. I've been trying to sleep for the past five hours. Between two and three I managed not to stare at the ceiling or my clock, but I woke up with my hand in my damn underpants. Again.

I cram my head under the pillow, as if it'll act as a barrier between my brain and the memories. I'm unsurprised by my lack of success. So I give in. If I stop fighting the fantasies, maybe I'll be able to manage seeing him tonight. I roll over onto my back, close my eyes, and let the images come. I'm instantly transported back in time.

Okay, that's not even remotely true, but I recall, with startling clarity, my introduction to NHL superstar Randy "Balls" Ballistic, the newest addition to Chicago's team.

I'd been camping in the northern Canadian wilderness with Benji, my jerkwad boyfriend; Sunny, my best friend; and Kale, Benji's best friend and Sunny's ex. The experience had not been all that pleasant. After seven days with no running water, I'd been desperate to disappear the forest on my legs and bask in the wonders of a hot shower at Sunny's brother's cottage in Muskoka. I also needed to tackle the mess that was my fur burger.

Before the trip I'd canceled my appointment with my waxer. She was expensive, and I needed the money to buy groceries for the trip. I was also angry with Benji, so I let my bush grow in to spite him. He had grown a horrible, patchy, ugly beard, so I'd done the same between my legs to see how much *he* liked it when I rubbed it all over his damn face. Not that he gave me the opportunity to do so very often.

Anyway, as I was about to tackle the hairy muppet living on my cooch, the door to the bathroom flew open.

I fully expected Sunny, or maybe dickhead Benji, to be the one busting in on me. It was neither.

Instead I stared at a man—a broad, well-built, superhot man—with his hand in his shorts. His dark hair was pulled back in one of those stubby little man-bun things, and his eyes were the color of honey. He sported a somewhat ungroomed beard, but it was lush, and it worked for him. The hand down his pants was attached to an arm with a full tattooed sleeve.

I screamed, as seemed appropriate, considering the superhot guy I'd never seen before in my life—apart from on TV during hockey games, but this was out of context so I didn't recognize him—standing in the bathroom doorway. His massive, muscular frame blocked my only way out. Also, I was completely naked, covered in shaving lotion from ankle to thigh, and my crotch was extra furry.

His eyes dipped and widened, taking me in. "You should probably lock the door."

"Who the fuck are you? Get out! What are you doing here?" I nabbed my towel to cover all my bits.

He took a step back, hands raised as if in apology, but his smirky smirk said he wasn't all that sorry. "Settle down, honey. I was just looking for a bathroom." He moved away from the door, chuckling.

I was furious. Embarrassed and not completely rational, I covered myself with the towel and searched the bathroom for a weapon. The toilet paper holder had a blunt end if I needed to club the sexy intruder. For some reason, instead of staying in the safety of the bathroom, I'd chased after him, wielding my makeshift weapon, and managed to flash him my overgrown vagina yet again. His amusement was infuriating.

As if that wasn't bad enough, less than an hour later I found myself trapped in the kitchen with him. Alone. Sunny and her current boyfriend, Miller "Buck" Butterson, had disappeared into the woods to "work things out." Randy was Miller's friend and NHL teammate. So there I was, forced into close proximity with a hot, insanely cut hockey boy. Despite the earlier embarrassment, being trapped with Randy was preferable to ending up alone with Benji, who had gone from being my boyfriend to my ex over the course of the past week and still hadn't taken the hint and left.

He and I had been fighting nonstop while we'd been camping—a trip that was supposed to be relaxing. The situation had been escalating for a long while, but it had finally reached unmanageable. I was done in so many ways. After seven years, Benji's persistent needling and negativity had become an anchor, weighing me down, keeping me tethered to a history that no longer felt good.

While I wallowed in the aftermath of my poor life choices, Randy had sat at the table, eating bowl after bowl of Corn Pops and reading the sports section of the newspaper. Benji had followed me around the house, pushing every single one of my buttons. Heedless of our audience, he wouldn't give up. I'd told him in no uncertain terms that we were done, but sometimes he was thickheaded. Or he thought it was a game. We had broken up before. Several times.

And then he called me a bitch.

It felt like a verbal backhand. And it was humiliating in front of a bystander.

Randy had dropped his spoon in his bowl. Milk splattered the table and his shirt. "The fuck you say to her?" he'd asked as he pushed back his chair. It toppled over, clattering to the floor. He wiped his mouth with the back of his tattooed hand.

And then he'd stalked over to Benji and threatened to kick his ass—even though I'd come after him with a toilet paper holder earlier.

So I did what any hot-blooded Canadian woman would when a hot man—hockey player or not—threatened extreme violence on her behalf: I grabbed his face and stuck my tongue in his mouth.

I played it off as though I'd done it to make Benji jealous. But I hadn't. Mostly I wanted to kiss Randy's face for what he'd done. Play a little tonsil hockey with him. Plead insanity for a minute.

His beard was soft where it touched my lips and chin. His mouth tasted like Corn Pops. His tongue—oh God, his tongue.

Despite my unexpected assault, he'd kissed me back. Benji's freak-out had become mere static in the background. Sunny and Miller must have returned from their "walk in the forest" somewhere between Benji's insult and my jumping Randy, because when I opened my eyes, there they were, witnesses to my attack.

Mortified, I locked myself in a bedroom at the cottage for the rest of the afternoon. I told Sunny I needed to be alone. During that time, I relived the kiss over and over, wondering if it was so electric because Randy had defended me, because I was angry with Benji, or because Randy was so damn hot.

I promised myself I wouldn't attack him like a starved lion on steak again. But by dinner, Benji had taken off, his raging texts cementing my conviction that we were now as over as we were going to get. Calling me a "flat-chested, cheating whore" wasn't much of a point-winner in my book.

And still here was Randy. Gorgeous. Cocky. Chivalrous. Maybe a little arrogant. An excellent kisser and an absolute flirt. I needed a distraction, and he seemed like a good one. We ended up dry-humping in the kitchen. Later he came to my bedroom with promises of fun and orgasms. No obligations. No strings. Just a casual fling. Inhibitions loose from drinks and hormones raging from all the flirting, I couldn't say no. I didn't want to, either.

Randy followed through on his promise to distract me from my problems. The orgasms were out of this world. Intergalactic.

But we didn't have sex.

He was okay with being a rebound lay, but he drew the line at revenge fuck. I didn't ask what the criteria was for one or the other, but as the receiver of plenty of non-penetration-related orgasms, I could hardly complain. At the time. Regrets came later.

I thought he was so sweet. Until he and Miller went to a charity car wash the next morning, leaving Sunny and me at the cottage. The guys were only going to be gone a couple of hours, and Randy promised more orgasms upon his return. I had plans to make them the sex kind.

Then things got complicated. Before they even got back, pictures of Randy and Miller with what appeared to be topless models went viral.

I got a little ragey.

Pissed that I'd been hoodwinked, I deployed a black permanent marker with the wrath of a thousand PMS-ing women on a full moon. I defaced every pair of Randy's underwear with the same message: TINY DICK INSIDE. It was a lie. A fabrication. Based on what I'd felt the night before—it was too dark to see—he was packing a substantial stick in his pants.

I gave his T-shirts a similar treatment, decorating them with ASSHOLE, so he knew how I felt about the bullshit he'd pulled. Like I would let him give me any more orgasms after some bunny'd been all over his dick, probably riding it because I wasn't allowed to.

Rolling over in my bed, I sigh and blink away the memories. Turns out it was all a misunderstanding. But by the time I got the real story, it was too late. The damage had been done. I couldn't take back the clothing destruction.

It's been a month since all this went down. A month of reliving the hours spent in that bed with him. A month of embarrassment over my overreaction. A month of being horrified that I let the whole situation happen in the first place. Tonight there's a charity exhibition game, and Randy's playing. Sunny's forcing me to go with her because her boyfriend, Miller, set the whole thing up. So I have to see Randy again. I'm not sure what's worse: my residual mortification or the fact that at least twice a week I wake up on the cusp of an orgasm, with Randy's stunning face and body burned into the back of my lids. My body is clearly interested in receiving the pleasure he generously provided again. And again.

And again.

But that's too bad because I hate him. Smug bastard.

I hate him more because I can't get my body on board. He was supposed to be a distraction. A fling. Screwing around for the sake of gratification and nothing else. He's the last man I should want. He's a player. He lives for the game. On ice, off ice, it's all the same. And I don't want to make the mistake of ramming my tongue down his throat yet again. I've already embarrassed myself enough when it comes to Randy Ballistic.

1

RUN. RUN. RUN

LILY

The game is over, and Sunny—formally known as Sunshine Waters—my best friend since grade one, is currently projected on the Jumbotron for the entire arena to view. Miller is mauling her while "Walking on Sunshine" blasts through the sound system in celebration of his team's win. Actually, the real winner is a twelve-year-old boy named Michael and his family. Proceeds from this charity event are going toward his treatment. He has a brain tumor.

Miller and Sunny's overly affectionate display would be cute if I wasn't such a jaded bitch. Right now I hate everyone in happy relationships, including Sunny.

Okay, that's not entirely true. If anyone deserves someone to love all over her, it's Sunny. Prior to Miller, her boyfriends were sucky.

He, however, is a great guy. I didn't think so at first, but like mold, he's grown on me. I look away from the screen when they kiss, surveying the rink and the players milling around off the ice. I'm seeking out one player in particular, just to torture myself.

I spot Randy about twenty feet away from them, his helmet under his arm. His beard is lush and magical, and his grin is the prettiest thing I've ever seen. He runs a sweaty hand through his hair, pushing it back off his face. It's wet. Probably sweat-soaked. I should find that gross. I don't.

Instead, a backbeat starts up in my clit—full percussion. It's like a deejay made a home in my underwear, and my vagina's where all the bass resides. *Fuuuuuck.* Why does he have to be so hot? Why was I such an asshole last time I saw him? The tiny flutter in my stomach turns into a tornado of hummingbirds. Heat lasers from my vagina through my body, exploding in my cheeks.

"Come on, Lily!" Daisy Waters, Sunny's mom and my "Momma Two," as I've come to refer to her over the years, tugs on my arm. "Let's go upstairs to the bar and get ourselves a drink before everyone gets there!"

I look away from the insane hotness, shutting down my memories before I melt into the floor and lose the ability to speak.

"Can I have pop? And can I order some food?" Brett, my thirteen-year-old cousin asks. He's endlessly hungry, and he's with me tonight because he's friends with Michael—and he'd say Miller and Randy as well—after going to the hockey camp they volunteered at this summer.

"There's tons of food! Don't you worry!" Daisy ruffles his hair.

He ducks out from under her hand and hurriedly rearranges his 'do. In the past month he's gone from wearing jogging pants and not caring what he looks like to spending forty-five minutes in the bathroom, fixing his hair and using far too much body spray. It could be worse. He could smell like most preteen boys: more goat than human.

Daisy links arms with me, chatting away about the engagement party she's throwing in two weeks for Sunny's brother, Alex, and his fiancée, Violet. She rambles on about how excited she is. This party has been a constant topic of conversation over the past month. It's pretty much all anyone's been talking about—that and this fundraiser.

Sunny's older brother also plays professional hockey. Alex is center and team captain for Chicago, the team Miller and Randy also play for. Violet, Alex's fiancée, is actually Miller's stepsister. It's a weird circle of love—almost like a soap opera, but with athletes and without inter-dating.

I spent an excessive amount of time at Sunny's house as a kid, and she and I annoyed the hell out of Alex on the rare occasions when he was home. He spent most of his life at the arena. He's a little strange, and I knew him before his hockey fame, so I'm well aware of his nerd status in high school. I guess he's hot, but I can't see him as anything other than a surrogate brother who used to help me and Sunny with our homework.

Daisy's still talking, but I'm not paying attention. I'm too preoccupied with the fact that we're about to pass all the players, and Randy's still there, a smile on his gorgeous, sweaty face.

"Of course you're coming with us. Can you get the weekend off work?" Daisy asks.

"Oh yeah, for sure." I nod absently.

"That's wonderful news! Sunny wasn't sure you'd be able to manage it. I know you have such long hours with two jobs and all, but we'll take care of your ticket to Chicago. Alex has plenty of room in his house, so you can stay there with us. It'll be a great weekend!" She squeezes my arm. "Oh! There's Miller and his parents and Alex and all the boys! Let's go say hi! Sunny's there with them. Come on!" She starts dragging me toward the group of players, which contains Randy.

I dig my heels into the rubber flooring and pry her fingers off my arm, scrambling for a reason not to go with her because I have the feeling my body is going to go rogue the first chance it gets. She knows about the Randy situation—or at least she knows the toned-down, PG version of it—but I can't explain this to her. "Oh... uh... I need to use the bathroom. I'll meet you upstairs in the bar."

"We're just going to say hi, sweetie," Daisy gives me one of her knowing-mom smiles.

"I really, really need the bathroom, Momma Two."

"Aw, come on, Lily. Michael's over there," Brett whines in his pitchy, almost-changing voice.

"You come with me, Brett." Daisy puts a hand on his shoulder and winks at me. "We'll meet you up there."

I nod vigorously. "Sure. Great! See you in a minute!"

I've spent most of my life figure skating in this arena—Alex used his connections here in Guelph to get the space for the exhibition game—and now I work here, teaching skating lessons. I know where all the best bathrooms are, including a secret one not far from the bar where the afterparty's being held.

I don't know what I was thinking when I agreed to come to this. I can't deal with seeing Randy. I have too many conflicting emotions—like lust and embarrassment and self-preservation, if that's an emotion. I bypass the crowded elevator and hit the stairs. I take them two at a time and go right, instead of left toward the bar, at the top, heading for the hidden bathroom at the end of the hall.

I open the door, flick on the light, and lock myself in, exhaling a long breath. Turning on the tap, I shove my hands under the cold spray, hoping it will cool down the rest of me. Randy fucking Ballistic is a goddamn problem.

There are a million things in my life I regret. Staying with Benji for seven years is one of them. Not having Randy fuck the living hell out of me while I had a decent excuse to do so is another. Now, I can't be sure that's what would have happened, had things progressed differently, but I'm guessing.

The worst part is, I threw myself at him—offered up my body on a platter, which is totally not my thing. I'm responsible. I stay safe and comfortable. And then he refused to have sex with me because I was emotionally "vulnerable." He more than made up for the lack of penetration, but that doesn't negate my embarrassment, particularly since I went apeshit on all his clothes and proved I'd gone from "vulnerable" to unstable in a matter of hours. Nor does it temper my regret. That man can eat a pussy like nobody's business. And his fingers, and his mouth, and—*Jesus* I need to stop thinking about him mostly naked and touching me.

I groan and stare at my reflection. I look like absolute crap. I almost never wear makeup, and the only stuff I have is meant for figure skating competitions. I thought about putting some on tonight, but I didn't want to look like a street-walking clown. Also, the powder crap makes my skin itchy. My hair is flat, and so is my chest. I glance down at my pathetic cleavage. I need to gain five pounds, in my boobs. There's nothing I can do about my sad little barely B-cups.

I rummage through my purse, searching for something beyond lip balm. Anything with a hint of color would be better than the look I'm rocking now. I bet Momma Two has an endless supply of sparkly tubes in her bag. She wears an insane amount of makeup. And hairspray. She's worn her hair the same way for as long as I can remember. I'm not sure if she just loved *Dallas* and can't let it go, but her hair is a special kind of fashionably unfortunate.

I find a tube at the bottom of my purse. The top has come off, and there's all sorts of gunk stuck to the lipstick. Snatching a few squares of toilet paper from the roll, I remove the dirt and flakes of old granola bar before I rub it over my lips. It's a bright, obnoxious shade of pink. I blot it with the toilet paper, but all I do is smear it over my mouth.

"Damn it." I grab a paper towel from the roll. Running it under the water, I pump some foam soap onto it and scrub at my lips, trying to get the pink off. The soap gets in my mouth, the chemical taste making me gag.

Someone knocks on the door. Almost no one knows about this bathroom.

"I'll be out in a minute!" I shout over the running water. All the scrubbing has left redness around my mouth. Now I have to hide in a dark corner until my skin calms down. I slather my lips in a shiny clear gloss that's also lurking at the bottom of my bag, turn off the water, and open the door.

Sunny's standing on the other side with her arms crossed over her chest. She's effortlessly beautiful. She can roll out of bed with her perfect blond hair a matted mess, and she still looks ready for the runway. She's currently dressed in a huge hockey jersey, a pair of black yoga pants—from lululemon, of course, because that's what her brother buys her—and a pair of flats. She's modelesque. If I didn't love her, I'd hate her.

Violet, her soon-to-be sister-in-law stands beside her. She only comes up to Sunny's shoulder. She's a tiny thing with huge boobs and this amazing long hair that's not brown or red, but somewhere in between. Her eyes are a fabulous shade of green. Neither one of them is wearing a stitch of makeup, as far as I can tell, and both of them are gorgeous. Next to Violet is another girl. I've met her once before, but I can't remember her name.

She's also stunning. It's a whole squad of them.

"I knew you'd be hiding in here." Sunny flips her hair over her shoulder.

"I'm not hiding."

Sunny raises a brow.

"What happened to your face?" Violet asks, leaning closer. "It's all red."

"I got something on it. I was trying to rub it off, and I made it worse."

"What'd you get on it?" Violet gets even closer; she's right inside my bubble.

I've met her a bunch of times now. She's kind of crazy, in a good way, but I'm used to people being a little less in my face. That's probably because I give off a bitchy vibe or whatever. Violet seems immune to it.

"Just …" I flounder around for a second, trying to come up with a lie. I don't want to tell them I was putting on lipstick because Sunny'll know I'm trying to get pretty for Randy. "… stuff."

"Stuff?" Violet asks.

"It's not important. We should probably get to the bar before it's super busy."

"Was there a guy in there with you? Do you mean jizz stuff?" Violet brushes past me and opens the bathroom door.

The girl whose name I can't remember shakes her head. "Just ignore her. She's lost it."

"I have not lost it, Char! That's a totally legit question." She looks to me as though I'm going to confirm the legitimacy of having a reaction to jizz on my face. At my silence, she continues her explanation. "Sometimes, when Alex eats too many suicide wings, his jizz makes my chest red."

Sunny cringes, because Alex happens to be her brother, I

assume. “I think I need a mojito.”

“Ohh! Good plan!” Violet threads her arm through Char’s and leads her down the hall. “Come on, ladies, let’s drink too much and share jizz stories.”

“Is she always like this?” I mutter.

“She’s stressed about the engagement party. She’s been drinking out of a flask the entire game, according to Charlene.” Sunny twirls a lock of hair around her finger. “I’m concerned about her.” She turns her attention back to me. “How about you? Are you okay? I thought you said you’d be fine to see Randy.”

“I am fine. It’s fine. No big deal.” I wave my hand around in the air a little hysterically. “We fooled around. It’s nothing.”

She tilts her head. “Lily.”

“Really, Sunny. It’s cool. I should probably make sure Brett’s doing okay and not bugging the players.”

“Are you wearing lip gloss?”

“What? No. Let’s go.” I turn my head to the side and wipe my mouth with my sleeve as we follow Violet and Charlene to the bar.

This is different than the scene after real games. There are loads of kids running around because this is a family event. I’ve been to a few Toronto games with Sunny. The usual afterparties can be loud and overwhelming. There are always a million skanky girls trying to get next to the guys. It’s not like that tonight.

I follow Sunny to the bar and order the same thing she’s having. Because she’s Miller’s girlfriend, they want to run a tab for her, but she refuses, passing over a twenty. I know she won’t let me give her money, so I’ll buy her next drink to make it even.

I move with her, drink in hand, staying a little behind her so I can hide if necessary. She’s oblivious to my anxiety, stopping to chat and introducing me to everyone she knows, which is a lot of people. I stay quiet and sip my drink. It's delicious. Minty and limey and the perfect amount of sweet.

I glance around the room, taking in all the well-dressed, attractive people. It's easy to understand why women hang all over these guys. A lot of them are carrying seriously padded wallets. Some of them are hot. Miller reminds me of a Ken doll, but he's attractive.

And then there's Randy. I sigh-groan-cough just thinking about that full sleeve covering his solid, well-built arm, and that deep V of muscle, and those abs… I make an awful slurping sound, which startles me out of my thoughts.

"Ha! I must've been thirsty." I hold up the empty glass, certain my face is on fire. "I'm gonna get another drink. So parched! Want a refill?"

"I'm good for now." Sunny holds up her mostly full drink.

I leave her with her friends and head back to the bar. More people have come in, and the players arrive in a pack. I slide down to the end of the bar and put in an order for another mojito. I keep my head down, letting my hair fall in my face. It only comes to my chin, so there isn't much to hide behind. Every so often I peek up, watching those huge, well-built boys greet everyone with friendly smiles. Tonight none of them seem to care whether they were on the winning or losing team.

"Hey! There you are!" Violet bumps her curvy hip against mine. She's wearing the same shirt I am, the same shirt as most of the people at this event, except she fills it out way better than I do in the chest area. She throws her arm around my shoulder. She's a little sweaty. "Let's get shooters!"

"I don't really—"

"How about slippery nipples and screaming orgasms?"

"I'm down for those!" says Charlene, scooting in beside her.

"Having fun yet?" Violet asks.

I nod. I'd have to yell to speak.

"So Buck tells me you and Randy had a thing. How was that? I've heard all kinds of things about that guy. I mean, more than what a great player he is, how he's going to take over Alex's position, and all the other shit people say."

She waves her hand around and pokes me in the ear. She's definitely drunk. I don't think it impacts the things that come out of her mouth, though.

"Anyway, I've heard he lives up to his name, if ya know what I mean? Wink. Wink. Right?"

"I, uh …"

"There you are!" Alex comes up behind us and puts an arm around both our shoulders. He gives me a squeeze. "Hey, Little Lily! How're you? It's been too long!" I hate that nickname. It makes me feel twelve.

"I'm fine. Good. Nice game tonight. I'm sorry you lost to Miller."

"S'okay. It's all for a good cause."

"I'll make you forget you lost later, baby." I don't think Violet means to say this as loudly as she does.

Alex laughs. "Shh. We don't need to tell everyone who's going down later."

"Me!" She raises her hand. "*I'm* going down later."

He puts a finger to her lips, still laughing. "How much have you had to drink, Violet?"

"Just one."

He looks at me, as if I know something he doesn't. I shrug. Which is the exact moment the bartender sets two rows of shots in front of us. Alex snatches Violet's before she can and downs them. I do mine to keep Violet from stealing them. I try to pay for my drinks, but Alex gives me a look. I don't fight him. He's far too aware of my family's financial situation. It's just my mom and me, and sometimes that's tough. Every so often, I'll find a few thousand dollars deposited in my savings account. I know it's him. He never mentions it, and neither do I. It hurts my pride, but it helps when things get tight. Like last year when we needed a new car.

I remember I've got my little cousin with me, so I excuse myself, not that it's necessary since Violet's moved on to trying to grope Alex, and he's busy keeping her hands from going places they shouldn't in public.

I clutch my mojito, keeping to the edge of the room, as I search for Brett. I find him exactly where I don't want him to be: with Randy and Miller and Michael—the boy Miller set up this fundraiser for—sitting at a table surrounded by heaping plates of food. They're smiling and laughing and Miller has his arm on Michael's shoulder. He's got a personal connection to Michael's situation; his own mother died when he was a kid from an inoperable tumor.

I was a real bitch to Miller when he started dating Sunny. Media reports were highly unfavorable; he was traded to Chicago last season for screwing his previous coach's niece in a bathroom stall. I was worried for her. But ever since the post-camping weekend at Alex's cottage, I've seen a much different side of him—one the media hasn't been privy to. He's so in love with Sunny, he'd do anything for her. Like name a foundation after her. The shirts everyone's wearing tonight? They say Project Sunshine.

According to Sunny and the media, Randy, who happens to be Miller's best friend, helped organize this event. Randy's involvement doesn't change how I feel about him, though. Just because he's good to Michael doesn't mean he isn't a manslut player. Yet pathetically, I still want to ride him like a rodeo bull.

Deep down, I don't believe Randy's a bad guy. In fact, I'm

inclined to say the opposite. A player? Definitely. Manslut? One hundred and ten percent. But I'm the one who threw myself at him, not the other way around. What bothers me most is that despite knowing this, I don't regret what happened at the cottage, apart from not having sex with him. Which I regret. The no-sexing part. And I hate that I regret my regret, because it makes me feel like a puck bunny, which I never want to be.

I should be glad my actions over the past month have ensured nothing else is going to happen between Randy and me. Not only did I write terrible things all over his clothes in permanent marker, I've avoided him both times he called. He didn't leave a message, so I have no idea what he wanted to say.

Why all the conflict over a hockey player? It goes back to my conception. My dad, who I've met a total of zero times, played professional hockey. He knocked my mom up when she was eighteen and then went back to his nice life: traveling the country, slapping a puck around on the ice, and banging puck bunnies who stupidly spread their legs for him, leaving my mom to raise me alone.

Ironically, my mom fit into the puck bunny category for a very short time. She never dated another hockey player, and she beats me over the head with a proverbial stick about not falling into the same trap. She does, however, seem to be good at finding guys in other lines of work who don't stick around. It's been a revolving door of unstable jerkoffs my entire life. I'm not cynical at all, though.

I scare myself again when all I get is air out of my straw instead of mojito. I glance down at my glass, frowning at the lack of liquid. How do these disappear so quickly? I look back over to Brett. *Oh, shit.* Randy's noticed me.

A smug grin pulls up the corners of his sexy mouth. He says something to Brett and pats him on the shoulder, then pushes his chair back. I pretend to be involved in my phone. I feel seasick with how often I glance from the screen to their table to the screen.

Oh God. He's on his way over here. I'm not ready for this. I scan the room frantically for Sunny. I can't see her anywhere, so I do the most logical thing in the world: I hightail it across the bar, away from Randy. There's an exit door I'm not supposed to use on that side. The alarm has been disconnected for forever. It'll get me out of here and on my way back to the bathroom where I hid out earlier. I can lock myself in there and figure out how to manage this.

I burst through the fire doors, relieved the alarm is still disconnected, and speed-walk down the hall. I make a quick right. Goddamn it. He's following me. What could he possibly want? To smirk at me some more? Running away should be a sure sign I'm not interested in any kind of confrontation, or discussion, or even getting naked—on the off chance that's on the table. Okay, the last part I totally want to do. Which is why I should keep running.

"Hey, Lily!" he calls. "Wait!"

My knees almost buckle at the sound of his voice. What does he want? I slide on a wet patch and barely avoid landing on my ass. He's right behind me now. I clutch the bathroom door handle and skid to a stop, nearly falling again. Wrenching it open, I throw myself inside. It's extra dramatic with a side of drama fries. But before I can pull the door closed, Randy manages to slide his massive, muscular body in the gap.

"What are you doing?" I screech as the door closes behind him, sealing us in darkness. "I can't see anything!"

He chuckles. The light flicks on, and I blink against the sudden brightness. "Didn't you hear me calling you?"

I plant my hands on my hips. "Didn't you see me running

away from you?"

He laughs again. It's a beautiful sound. "Uh, yeah. I figured maybe you really had to use the bathroom."

"I did. I do. Now get out, or I'll pee right in front of you!" I'm shouting. It's high-pitched and totally unnecessary, seeing as I'm standing about four inches away from him. I might be spit-talking at his chest. His extra-muscular chest.

His sleeves are rolled up to his elbows, leaving all the tattoos on his right forearm on display. He even has one on the back of his hand. It's almost three-dimensional in the way it's been put on his skin: a stunning flower beaded with dew, with a tiny, intricate skull inside the falling droplet. It's so badass. I remember how amazing it looked when the fingers attached to that hand, which is attached to the arm covered in ink, were inside of me, pumping away until I came. I make a strangled sound.

"Did you moan?"

"What? No." My eyes shoot up to his.

That infuriating smirk makes his eyes crinkle. Even his eye crinkles are hot. "I think you did."

"It was a groan. That's very different from a moan."

He leans against the door, blocking my exit. "Oh yeah? Wanna explain that to me?"

"I don't have to explain anything to you. Now get out so I can use the bathroom! In private. Alone." My voice is still super squeaky. I need to stop acting like an idiot. I also need him to get out of the bathroom before I do something I should regret, but probably won't. He doesn't seem nearly as opposed to that as I'd thought he would.

I push his shoulder in an attempt to get him out of the way. He moves maybe a fraction of an inch. He smells fantastic, like he's freshly showered and deodorized. His arm is so solid, nothing like Benji's was. I keep pushing, and I might give his biceps a little squeeze.

"What's with you and busting in on me in the bathroom?" I say, not quite shouting now.

I feel my face heat at the memory of him barging in on me at the cottage with my girl parts on display and his hand in his shorts. Damn it. Now I'm thinking about the near-sexing we did, again.

Randy's still smiling like a jackass. I think he said something and I missed it, too busy being mortified. And turned on.

"What?" I ask.

His tongue sweeps across his bottom lip. He has great lips. They're full and soft and great for kissing. He brushes the hair out of my face, fingertips skimming my cheek. All my muscles clench. I'm pretty sure I could come just thinking about the things he's done to me. Which is crazy, because I've always believed reactions like that are total bullshit.

"I was just saying that the last time we were in a bathroom together, you were wearing a lot less." His gaze roams over me and his eyes—the color of honey, or a sandy beach, or who the fuck cares—drop below my waist. He points at my crotch. "How's your waxer doing these days? You get your situation sorted out down there?"

My mouth hangs open. I close it quickly, then open it again, waiting for some sassy quip of retaliation, but nothing arrives. I don't have a good comeback, or anything to say to that, because the honest answer is *no*. I haven't had a chance to sort it out.

I've been stuck waxing my own girl parts for the last month. I'm not very good at it. I keep missing spots, and I have to go over them with a razor. My vag constantly has patches of five o'clock shadow.

"Wouldn't you like to know!"

"Wanna show me?"

"You're a pig!"

In reality, I kinda do want to show him, even if it's not the best waxing job in the world. Actually, I'd like to get him on his knees, drop my pants, hike a leg up on the edge of the sink and shove his face right in there so he can have an up-close-and-personal view of the hell I have to go through in order to make my vagina presentable for no one, because I'm the only person who sees it.

I think I might need to have sex soon. With something other than my vibrator.

"I hate your perfect face!" I hiss. Literally, I sound like a snake. I grab the lapels of his button-down shirt. Then I shove my tongue in his mouth.

Shit. This is the opposite of what was supposed to happen.

2

WHAT HAPPENS IN THE BATHROOM STAYS IN THE BATHROOM. OR NOT

RANDY

I find myself pressed up against the door, the handle jabbing into my lower back as Lily rams her tongue down my throat. She breaks the kiss—if you could even call it that—and shoves away from me, but she's still holding my shirt. Her nostrils flare a little, and her eyes—a shade of brown so dark I almost can't see where her iris ends and the pupil begins—are glazed.

I have no idea what I thought was going to come of following her into this bathroom. My only plan was to have some kind of discussion, since the last time we had words they included her calling me an asshole, as well as a slew of other creative insults, and she won't answer my calls. She also wrote all over my clothes in permanent marker. I sort of deserved it. I like that she's my kind of crazy.

She shakes her head and smoothes away the dark, chin-length hair that's fallen in her eyes. Her chest heaves with every breath. She looks hot tonight. Her jeans accentuate the fine, lean lines of her body. Her event T-shirt is tied at the side to accommodate how large it is on her narrow frame.

She's pretty much panting. It reminds me a lot of the way she sounded when I ate her pussy at Waters' cottage. That was weeks ago. I haven't stopped thinking about it. I don't know why. I mean, I can eat pussy anytime I damn well please—not that I do. Going down is intimate, and bunnies have usually made the rounds. I'm not putting my mouth where a million other dicks have been.

Hypocritical? Not at all. I don't let the bunnies put their mouths on me either… for a variety of reasons. But Lily's not a bunny, and she needed to be taken care of. Properly. So I went down on her. I drew the line at fucking her, though, because I didn't want to feel guilty if she only let me bang her to get back at her asshole ex.

It was the right thing to do, but I still have regrets. Especially since I know she hasn't gotten back with that dickwad. Not that I've asked or anything. Miller offers up the information. And now everything between her and me seems to be sideways. Or it did until about thirty seconds ago. Anyway, having had my fingers inside Lily, I can say, without a doubt, the sex would be stellar. She's one tight little firecracker.

She drags my mouth back down and pauses when our lips are almost touching. I feel around behind me for the lock and flip it. I don't want any interruptions right now. I pull her against me, trapping her hands between us. Then I brush the end of my nose against hers, all soft-soft.

She lets out this tiny little whimper. It's barely a sound; she tips her chin up, and her hips press forward. She's got to be able to feel my hard-on. It'd be impossible not to. I run my tongue across my lip, over the scar from a stick I took to the face a long time ago. She tracks the movement. When she lifts her gaze, I take her mouth.

This time when she tries to push her tongue past my lips, I force it back with my own. Her hands leave my shirt, fingers closing around my wrists as she fights to get inside my mouth. Not gonna happen. Not yet. It's hard to kiss and smile, but I manage.

She runs her hands through my hair. Yanking out the tie, she tosses it across the small room. I have no idea where it lands, but I sure won't be picking it up off the bathroom floor.

I spin us around so she's against the door and work a knee between her legs. Then I start basically dry-fucking her. I don't know what's wrong with me. This is a charity event. There are families, and kids. And here I am, locked in a bathroom with a girl who wrote TINY DICK INSIDE over most of my boxers. I'm wearing a pair tonight because I half-hoped I'd see her and this would happen.

I cup her ass, squeeze tight, and lift her. She's maybe five-six, five-seven at best, and I'm almost six-three, so I've got a lot of height on her and probably a hundred pounds. She's willowy, compact muscle and narrow everything from her hips to her rib cage. She wraps her strong legs around my waist, another one of those strangled moans bubbling up.

If it were possible for one human being to devour another, we'd be doing that now. She lets go of my hair and searches for the hem of my shirt. Her fingernails scratch over my abs. I bite her tongue in retaliation. She wrenches her face away from mine, banging her head against the door.

"You okay?" I ask.

She pinches my nipple, so I bite her neck. "Do it again and I'll suck until I leave a mark," I warn, parting my lips against her skin. It's salty and sweet and so very, very warm.

"You wouldn't."

"Oh, I definitely would." I apply the tiniest bit of suction and she gasps, her hands going back to my hair, fingernails digging into my scalp.

I adjust my grip and grind up on her while I kiss along her throat to her jaw. I'm so hard right now. I wish she were wearing something other than tight jeans. The only way I can feasibly get inside her is to turn her around and take her from behind. It's not my preferred position.

I know exactly what Lily's come face looks like. If I'm gonna fuck her, I want her eyes on mine when she loses it all over my cock. A public bathroom probably isn't the best place for this to go down anyway, even if it's wheelchair accessible and fairly clean. Public washrooms are more of a Miller move, or a Miller-pre-Sunny move, anyway.

I keep rolling my hips and those little noises of hers get louder, so I cover her mouth with mine again.

Her hands turn into fists, gripping my hair so tightly I'm almost concerned she's going to rip it out by the roots. "*Oh my God*," she groans against my lips.

I pull away, checking to make sure she's okay. She throws her head back, hitting the door again with a low thud. We're making an awful lot of noise in here, but at least it's an out-of-the-way bathroom.

I push her firmly against the door with my hips so I don't have to use both hands to hold her up. That way I can stop her head from smacking against the door. If she keeps it up, she's going to have a bruise. If I didn't know any better, I'd think she was coming—which should be impossible since I haven't done anything but rub myself on her.

"Lily?"

Her eyes roll down to meet mine, her shock replaced by ecstasy. Her mouth drops open. "That's not—I can't—"

"Are you coming?" Despite the lack of probability, I have to ask.

She shakes her head furiously and stutters out a no.

Her expression is suspect. I don't buy it. Gripping her ass, I swing around so we're facing the wall. Then I lower her to the ground. Her nails run down the side of my neck, and she claws at my shirt.

"Why are you stopping?" She air humps once and wobbles unsteadily.

I walk her backward until she hits the wall. She immediately starts rubbing her pussy on my thigh. There are way better places for her to do that. She tries to pull my mouth back to hers, but I have other plans. I pull her shirt over her head and hang it on the knob. Her purse is on the floor by my feet, crap strewn all over the place. Not that it matters right now.

Her bra isn't fancy, or lacy, or anything special. It's plain, pale satin. I can see the outline of her nipples through it. I'll get to those later. While Lily rides my leg, I pop the button on her jeans and pull down the zipper. Her underwear matches her bra, more simple, pale satin.

I shove my hand down the front of her pants. She's been taking care of things. I'm met with smoothish skin. But her jeans are so tight I can't get my hand past the crest of her pelvis. I can feel how hot she is, but I can't get to all that wetness. In her defense, my hands are big, so that only adds to the problem.

Lily fumbles with my belt buckle and then my zipper. My erection strains against my boxers. She freezes, her eyes darting to mine in shock. Not because my dick is terrifying, although it kind of is, but because she can read the TINY DICK INSIDE she wrote on the hot pink material in neat block letters with black permanent marker.

She bites her lip and makes a face, like she's not sure if she should laugh, be embarrassed, or apologize—or maybe all three. She skims the waistband like she's thinking about sticking her hand inside. "Why do you still have these?"

"They're my favorite pair."

"But—" She palms me through the fabric and rubs herself on my leg at the same time. Her eyes roll up, and she shudders again.

"I think we're both well aware that this is false advertising." I move the hand covering my cock away and step back. Then I drop to my knees and yank her jeans over her hips, along with her panties, which are damp. It's like they're damn well glued to her body.

"What're you—"

I slide a hand between her legs, cutting her words short. I glide over her clit and push two fingers inside her. I want to find out if I'm right about the spontaneous, untouched coming. She falls back against the wall and tries to part her legs, but her stupid tight jeans make that impossible. Her entire body trembles, and she cries out when I curl my fingers. That's when I feel it: the pulse around my hand.

"You're coming." I look up at her, shirtless, the strap of her bra hanging off her arm instead of sitting on her shoulder, her palms flat against the wall behind her.

"No shit," she gasps.

"I barely even touched you."

"I'm as confused as you are."

"Bend your knees and spread your legs," I order.

"Wha—"

I move my hand from between her thighs, eliciting a despondent sound. Gripping her by the waist, I duck under her knee and shove my head through the narrow gap so I'm face to face with her pussy. It's not easy, but I manage. Then I lift her so she's sitting on my shoulders with her legs hanging over my back.

I hold onto her left thigh and slide the other hand up her stomach and under her bra. Her breasts pop out the bottom, nipples tightening as I brush my thumb over one. I cover the soft swell with my palm, squeezing as I hold her against the wall. I don't have much room to move, but she's already worked up enough as it is, so I suction my mouth to her clit and circle it with my tongue.

"Holy fuuuuuuu—" Her legs tighten around my head. I abandon her boob and cover her mouth. I don't think she has the ability to control her volume right now, or any other part of her, considering the way she's flailing around. I don't know that I've ever been with a girl who can come as fast and hard as she can with so little contact. Last time she came a lot, but it wasn't like this. Maybe it's because we're in a public place and she's into the exhibitionism thing.

Whatever the reason, I'm all over making it happen again. She moans my name into my palm and bites the fleshy part, writhing against my face. The shuddering starts all over. It's followed by a noise that sounds almost like a sob.

I raise my head, my beard rubbing against her clit. I'm gonna need to shampoo the fuck out of it later. A violent, whole-body tremor shoots through her. "Lily, baby, you okay up there?"

Her head lolls forward, her breath coming in short bursts. All she does is make a sound. Her eyes are droopy and glassy. She looks high as a kite.

"Wha?"

"You doing okay?"

She shakes her head and blinks a bunch of times, like she's trying to clear the fog. "So much coming." It's kind of garbled.

I'm about to go back to eating her pussy so I can make that

happen again, when a knock on the door startles us.

"Lily? Are you in there again?" It's Sunny, Miller's girlfriend. She and Lily are best friends. This is an interesting situation.

Lily's eyes go wide, her panic comical. "I'll be out in a minute!"

She struggles to get off my shoulders, nearly taking us to the floor. It wouldn't be so bad if we weren't in a bathroom. It's clean, but not that clean. I grab her hands and bite the inside of her thigh, sucking hard on the skin.

"Ow!"

"Is everything okay in there?" Sunny asks.

"It's fine. I'm fine. I just stubbed my toe!"

I raise an eyebrow, and she mouths *what?* but she stops making things difficult so I can set her feet back on the floor and duck out from between her legs. She almost loses her balance, but I hold her hips and keep her standing. Before I pull up her panties I press a kiss above the cleft of her pussy, then add enough suction to leave a faint, purple bruise to match the one on the inside of her thigh.

"Stop it!" she whisper-hisses, trying to push my face away.

I'm stronger than she is, though, and she shifts her hips forward even as she pulls my hair, like she's secretly seeking my tongue again. I lick her swollen clit one last time, watching her skin pebble, then carefully shimmy her panties over her hips. She takes care of her suction jeans, getting them up with far less difficulty than I got them down. Lily adjusts her bra so her nipples are covered again and pulls her shirt over her head. Her hair's a sweet mess.

Once all the best parts of her are hidden, I shift my hard, achy dick to the left so I can zip up my pants.

"Oh, God." She reaches out, then stops. "You're so hard. I didn't even—"

"Don't worry." I wink. "That'll get taken care of later."

"I have to take Brett home."

I shrug. "I can wait."

Her mouth drops—that seems to be a reaction I elicit from her often. "Oh my God! You're such a cocky asshole!"

"Didn't you just come three times?"

"Two point five, and I didn't force you to eat my pussy!"

"You're the one who kissed me, and you sure didn't seem to mind me eating you."

She jams the fallen items into her purse and hugs it to her chest. Elbowing me in the ribs, she pushes me out of the way. I don't get how she can go from orgasm bliss to being angry, but then I don't honestly know her that well. Maybe she's got a split personality or something.

"What's the deal?"

She flips the lock and turns to me, panicked. "I gotta go. I need to get away—"

She wrenches open the door and stumbles out into the hall. "Enjoy the rest of your evening!" She motions to my crotch. "I hope your, uh, situation resolves itself!"

"I was still hoping for some help with that." I step out after her, buttoning my pants. Sunny looks from me to Lily and back again. Miller's standing behind her wearing a grim expression.

"Fuck you very much for the orgasms." Lily slaps a hand over her mouth, like she can't believe she just said that.

"That was next on my to-do list." I'm such an antagonistic ass.

"Guess you missed that opportunity. Again." She cringes and mutters something else.

I was being considerate by not fucking her at Waters' cottage. Seems like maybe she didn't appreciate it all that much. "I could fix that if you want to come back to my hotel room." I'm grinning. I can't help it.

"I would so …" Her eyes close for a moment. "I need to find my cousin!" She spins on her heel and rushes away.

"Um… I'm gonna go deal with her." Sunny points in Lily's direction and chases after her, blond hair swishing.

"What the fuck is wrong with you, Balls?" Miller looks put out.

I zip up my pants and inhale sharply, almost catching my boxers in the teeth. Now I want to find her again before she leaves. I haven't resolved anything. The whole point of following her was to talk, not eat her out. "I should go after her."

I take a step in the direction Lily went, but Miller puts an arm up to stop me. "Uh, dude. Not before you manage yourself." He waves to everything above the neck.

I shake my head, frustrated, but go back into the bathroom and check my reflection. I laugh. "Oh, shit." My hair's a mess; like, it's everywhere. My face, well—that's another story. I definitely need to wash it, since Lily came all over it. I can smell her. I also have scratch marks running from the side of my jaw to the collar of my shirt. I search the floor for the hair tie Lily ripped out. I find it beside the toilet. I don't have any other option right now, so I pick it up off the floor and gather my hair back up. I'm gonna need a shower once I get back to the hotel.

"I don't get it, man. You've been off the scene for the last month, and all of a sudden you're back at it. Here of all places? It's a damn fundraiser, Randy, not one of Lance's parties."

"I know that." Lance "Romance" Romero is another one of our teammates. He's notorious for parties full of excess and bunnies. I turn on the tap and wash Lily off my face and out of my beard.

"Really? 'Cause it seems like maybe you forgot. Of all the girls you decide you wanna bone in a bathroom, why's it gotta be Lily?"

"That's not what happened."

He crosses his arms over his chest.

"Seriously. I didn't fuck her in here. I mean, we were messing around, but fucking didn't take place." Then I add, "I just had a little dessert is all."

Miller scrubs his face with his palm. "You better watch yourself, Balls. Lily's super tight with the Waters family. Alex is like a brother, and if he finds out you're screwing her around, you'll be next on his broken-nose radar."

"It's not like that." I shut off the water and turn to face him. "Honestly, Miller, all I wanted to do was talk to her. We're gonna see each other in a couple of weeks at Waters' engagement party. I figured it'd be good to clear the air—"

"By eating her pussy in a bathroom?"

I give him a cheeky grin. "I learned from the best."

Miller shakes his head. "Yeah. Not funny, asshole. I got traded for that shit, remember?"

"I'm sorry. I just—we got carried away." I make some random hand gestures as I try to figure out what I want to say.

"You can't dick Lily around the way you do the bunnies, Randy. It's not cool."

"I'm not gonna dick her around. We're just having some fun."

"I'm gonna go ahead and say I don't think your version of fun and Lily's are the same thing."

"I'll check on her and make sure we're good."

Miller's phone buzzes. He takes it out of his pocket and keys in the password. His eyebrows knit together as he reads whatever's on the screen. Miller's dyslexic, so reading's laborious for him. After a few seconds, he hits the text-to-speech button and a British chick reads the message out loud: "*I can't get Lily to toll me what hipped. She's taking Brett hum.*"

"I'll go find her."

"She's got her little cousin with her, Michael's friend. What're you gonna say with him there?"

"I dunno, but I'll figure it out." I head for the bar. Sunny's standing at the entrance with her phone in her hand, twirling a lock of hair around her finger. "Where's Lily?"

"She's gone." Sunny drops her hair and sighs. "What'd you do to her?"

I don't think honesty is going to work for me here, so instead of saying I tongue-fucked her until she came on my face, I go with, "I think there was a miscommunication."

A kid comes up to me, wearing a familiar look of idolization. "Randy Ballistic?"

I smile. "Yeah, man, how's it going?"

"Can I get your autograph?" He holds out one of those homemade photo books. He's even got one of my rookie cards in a special, protective sleeve taped to it.

"Yeah, sure, of course."

His mom is standing behind him, smiling. "Thank you so much. He loves you. He wants to be just like you when he grows up."

Usually that's something I like to hear, but right now it doesn't make me feel good at all. Not based on what happened in that bathroom.

3

UNINTENTIONAL OVERREACTION

LILY

Okay, so the way I handled that situation could have been better. But his insinuating I was going to take care of his dick later freaked me out—even though I'm the one who brought it up. Because he's right. I would have, had the universe not intervened, even though none of that was supposed to go down. Especially not Randy.

Then there's that whole part where I had an orgasm with only rubbing through fabric. There wasn't even any real touching. Not at first. That's never happened before. I may have had an orgasm even before he started leg-humping my girl parts. It was a baby one—nothing more than a repressed sneeze version—but still. How does that even happen?

I haul Brett out of the arena and call my aunt, who picks us up. Brett's definitely not happy about leaving, but he's thirteen, and it's after ten-thirty, which is later than he usually stays out. I'm totally distracted the entire ride home, which is fine because Brett can't stop talking about how awesome Miller and Randy are and how he totally wants to be a professional hockey player.

My aunt nods and smiles and makes the appropriate positive comments, but when she catches my eye in the mirror, I know this has set him up for disappointment. Brett is one of six kids. My aunt stayed home to raise them, and my uncle has a good job, but it's a lot of mouths to feed. Four of them are boys between the ages of three and fifteen. The grocery bills in that home have to be outrageous.

My aunt and uncle can barely manage the costs associated with Brett's rec hockey. The time it takes to attend all the away games, not to mention the money, will make it impossible for him to go any further. Hockey's an expensive sport. Just like figure skating.

My heart breaks a little. I know his impending disappointment personally. Four years ago I was on the edge of qualifying for the Olympics. It would have meant sponsorship and the opportunity to move forward in that career. Figure skating was the only thing I knew and my greatest love. But my dad, the deadbeat asshole that he is, stopped paying child support. He owes my mom something like eighty grand. He also owes me my goddamn dream back. But I'm not bitter about it. I went to the University of Guelph instead.

By the time my aunt drops me off, I'm not quite so buzzed on mojitos and shooters, and my body no longer feels like it's going to explode. I search my purse for my key and enter the lobby of the apartment building. My mom and I used to live in a little house. It was small, but it was ours. When my dad stopped with the child support, we had to move. The apartment isn't bad. It's in a nice neighborhood, because Guelph is generally a nice town, but it's small, and I miss having a backyard.

I call out when I enter the apartment, but I'm met with silence. My mom isn't home, which may or may not be a good thing.

She has the night off, so she could be over at one of her friends' or she could be on a date.

I head to the kitchen. I need water. Lots of it. I don't drink much. I don't like being out of control, and it doesn't take much to get me that way. Maybe that explains the spontaneous orgasms.

I root through the cupboards for something to eat. I need to get groceries tomorrow. It's slim pickings. I find a bag of extra buttery microwave popcorn and watch it spin around for ninety seconds. Once it's done, I melt some margarine and pour it on top. I have a hard time keeping weight on, so the more fat I consume, the more likely I am to stay where I'm supposed to be.

I tuck the bowl under my arm, refill my glass, nab my purse from the counter, and go to my room. It's small; the double bed takes up almost half the space. I drop down on the mattress and flip open my laptop, which is one of Sunny's old ones. It's really nice. My phone buzzes from inside my purse. I fish it out, and my stomach does some flip-flops as I scroll.

I have several texts from Sunny, which isn't unusual. We're together a lot—except when she's at school, teaching yoga, or volunteering at the animal shelter and I'm not working at one of my two jobs. It's the messages from Randy that make my stomach feel like it's trying to jump out of my throat.

I ignore all of them to test my self-restraint and log in to my computer. As soon as the browser opens, I type in "spontaneous orgasms." I don't get much in the way of helpful information. Mostly it's a bunch of nonsense and hypothetical crap. One article is about a woman who has more than a hundred orgasms a day. It sounds awful, and embarrassing. I can't imagine what it would be like if I had unprovoked orgasms every time I saw Randy. Or maybe I can.

My whole body gets hot and my toes curl at the memory of

his mouth on me. Did I really let him eat me out in a bathroom? In the arena where I work? I'll never be able to use that bathroom again without having some kind of hot flash.

I chug my water and perform another search, this time with "Randy Ballistic" and "girlfriend." I've been cyber-stalking the guy since I ruined his underwear and he ruined my vagina with his fingers and his mouth.

Here are some interesting facts about Randy: he's a serial short-term dater. From the research/stalking I've done, I discovered an online group for girls who have "dated" Randy and been dumped. Four of them have his name tattooed somewhere on their body. The hip seems to be popular. One girl went so far as to have his face tattooed on her boob, except it's a bad tattoo and he looks more like a caricature of that guy from *Sons of Anarchy* than Randy. I'd feel bad for her, but she's a bunny, so it's her own damn fault.

The message is disconcertingly consistent: Randy's awesome in bed. Ballistic is definitely a fitting last name. He has a great sense of humor. He has amazing fingers. He has incredible stamina. His dick is enormous—there could be some exaggeration here. I'm not for sure on that since I have yet to see it. Based on my stroking, it's substantial. They seem to have missed the fact that his tongue is a weapon of sexual mass destruction.

Most interesting is this tidbit: he only has sex with the lights off.

When we were fooling around at Alex's cottage, the light in the bathroom was on, so it wasn't totally dark, but he pulled the covers over us. I thought it was cute because he wanted to keep me warm. In August. Now I have things to ponder, such as *is that a fetish? Is he thinking about someone in particular while getting busy? If so, who? And fuck her.*

There are way too many questions I don't have answers to.

Not that I need them. I'm not getting trapped in a bathroom with him again. At least my *intention* is to avoid that scenario in the future. My lack of self-control is humiliating.

I have two weeks to prepare for Alex and Violet's engagement party. By then I should have gained some will power. Nothing good can come of being a bunny, so here's hoping.

My phone buzzes again. It's Randy.

You still pissed at me?

Silence, huh? You hold a long grudge.
U gotta know the car wash was a misunderstanding.
I meant 2 tell u in the bathroom, but u jumped me, so I didn't have a chance ;)

The winky face annoys me almost as much as being called out on jumping him. And being reminded of the stupid car wash pictures that made me go berserk. I decide to be cheeky.

Who is this?

The humping dots appear right away.

The guy whose face u came on earlier

Every muscle below my waist clenches. Blood rushes to my cheeks and then moves lower, tingles following. I chew my fingernail, unsure if I want to play this game with him. I should brush him off. The trail of emotionally crippled bunnies with his name tattooed on their bodies should be the equivalent of CAUTION tape. But those orgasms…

My phone rings, startling me. I answer it before I can

appropriately weigh my options.

There's no hello, just Randy's deep, sexy voice low in my ear. "Still a little foggy, Lily? Having a hard time remembering? Wanna come by my hotel so I can refresh your memory?"

I bite my knuckles to stop myself from saying yes. Of all the bad ideas, going to his hotel definitely tops the list. I'm guaranteed to make all kinds of bad decisions. Including the one I want to make the most, which is letting him get inside me. I don't know if it's normal to be this attracted to another human being.

I go with snark, because it's safe. "So I'm guessing you didn't find a bunny to ride your dick?

Randy chuckles. "Nope. My dick told me he didn't want a bunny. He's holding out for you."

I roll my eyes, even though he can't see me. "Does that line work?"

"It's not a line. Me and my dick are tight. We had a very serious conversation."

I laugh. "Well, you should tell him not to hold his breath. He'll turn blue."

"He's already blue. You should come by my hotel and see."

"You can send me a picture." I'm almost hoping he does.

"It's not the same. What if I come see you instead?"

I can't even imagine someone like Randy in a bedroom like mine. "You're persistent, aren't you?"

"Is that you saying yes?"

I hesitate for a second, knowing full well if I agree it's a booty call. "I can't. I have to wash my hair."

"Oh, man. The hair-washing excuse? And here I thought we had fun together. Well, if I can't convince you to come to see me, I'm gonna go take care of my own problem. Night, Lily. See you in a couple weeks."

The reminder that we'll be seeing each other at the engagement party is yet another reason I shouldn't keep entertaining this possibility.

"Night, Blue Balls," I shoot back.

"So clever. Not for long. I'll be thinking of you."

Randy hangs up. I send him a meme of an old lady with no teeth with the caption "Let's Make Out."

Ten minutes later, I get one back of his middle finger on the hand with the tattoo. That finger has been inside me recently. He's taken it while lying in his hotel bed with only a sheet covering him from the waist down. His tight abs and the deep, heavily muscled V are captured beautifully. I can see, very clearly, a lump that resembles the shape of his cock under that white cotton. I can also see his blurred reflection in the mirror. His hair is loose and messy, brushing his chin. He's the picture of absolute relaxation.

I don't send a response. Instead I shut down my computer, lock my door, and get out my magic bullet. I pull the covers over my head and get myself off while staring at that damn picture on my phone.

4

WHAT THE HELL IS NORMAL ANYWAY?

LILY

The next morning my phone wakes me up. I feel around for it on my nightstand. It's not there. I find it under my pillow, where I left it after I rolled my marble to Randy's middle finger. Three times. I think I have a problem.

"'Lo?" I mumble.

"Are you still asleep?" Sunny asks.

"Not anymore." Sunny gets up stupidly early even on the days she doesn't have to work. I'm lucky she waited this long to call.

"Great! Get dressed. I'm picking you up in fifteen minutes. I made cinnamon buns, and we're having family brunch. And make sure you bring a bathing suit since all mine fall off you."

"It's freezing out."

"It's hardly freezing, Lily. It's going to be eighteen degrees today."

"That's not pool weather."

"We cranked the water heater. It's like a sauna."

"Wait. What about Randy? Is he going to be there?" My vagina gets all excited by the thought.

"He flew back to Chicago this morning. You *will* be telling me what happened last night. See you soon." She hangs up.

I lie there for a minute and stare at the ceiling, working up the energy to get out of bed and take a quick shower. Instead, I check my messages from last night. Not just to look at Randy's middle finger and naked chest, or the hint of peen under the white sheet. Although that's part of the reason. I have a message from him. It's another picture. It's a close up of his neck and jaw. He's wearing a T-shirt. Red lines travel from his ear and disappear under his collar. It was sent at six this morning.

I'm collecting 4 damages next time I cu.

Oh, man. Those are scratches. From me. I wonder exactly what collecting for damages entails. I don't have the guts to ask, either. I'm certain the answer will make me regret not taking him up on his offer of a visit last night.

I toss my phone aside and roll out of bed. I shuffle to the bathroom across the hall. The apartment is quiet. I get a glimpse of myself in the mirror as I turn on the shower. My hair is sticking up all over the place. On second thought, if Randy woke up next to me looking like this, it'd be the last invite I got.

Less than ten minutes later I'm showered. I open the bathroom door and scream. There's a man standing in the hall in a pair of—*please God why?*—tightie-whities. I'd estimate him to be in his late thirties to mid-forties. He's actually in decent shape, although there's some graying and male pattern baldness. I'm also having a hard time keeping my eyes on his face, because he's tenting the front of his underwear with some morning wood.

"What the shit?" I yell as he stands there, gawking. "Mom!

There's a mostly naked man in the hallway! Is he yours?"

She comes out of her bedroom in one of her satin robes. I try to hold in my gag, knowing she was probably getting the action I should have gotten last night. She runs her hand through her sex hair. "I thought you were staying at Sunny's last night."

"So he is yours." I point at the silent man standing two feet away from me. He's still flag poling, but he's put his hands down to cover it. "Just checking to make sure some half-naked crazy pervert didn't wander into our apartment with a hard-on."

"Lily!"

"What? It's true. And it's happened before."

"Mr. Van Winkle isn't a pervert. He's senile. He forgets where he lives sometimes."

"Yeah, well, he also forgets to wear clothes." Judging from what happens in his saggy underwear, Mr. Van Winkle was probably a hit with the ladies in his day. I turn sideways and slide by my mom's date from last night. Thankfully, I'm skinny enough that I don't have to touch him, since he seems incapable of moving out of the way.

I lock my door and throw on a pair of leggings and a hoodie. I stuff a bathing suit into my knapsack and my clean skating gear, since I have lessons to teach this evening. I'm banking on Sunny being able to drive me to the rink. My phone beeps as I'm running a brush through my hair. It's Sunny letting me know she's here. She knows enough not to come up unless I invite her. My mom's chatty. She can keep us here for hours with tea and lectures about men. Although that's not likely to happen today, what with her man friend.

I open the door a crack and peek my head out. The hall is empty. I tiptoe down it, shove my feet into ballet flats, lift my keys from the hook, and open the door.

"Going to Sunny's and then work. Be back later!" I let the

door close behind me before my mom can stop me with requests for groceries.

Sunny's waiting out in front of my building in her Prius. It was a birthday present from her brother. I don't have my own car. Public transit and my bike are my rides of choice. Guelph isn't big, and I don't live too far from work. Plus, cars are expensive; the one my mom and I share is constantly in need of repair.

I slip into the passenger seat and wait until Sunny pulls into traffic before I check my ringing phone.

She glances at me and then back at the road, her hands at ten and two like they're supposed to be. The GPS is tracking our drive, even though she's been to the apartment at least two thousand times. Sunny's directionally challenged. And she's very diligent about following road rules.

"Who's calling you? Randy? What happened in that bathroom?"

"It's my mom. She probably wants to give me a list of things to bring home. I don't know why she doesn't text." I let the call go to voice mail and shove it back in my bag. "So, get this, my mom brought home her date."

"Last night? Did you meet him?"

"I did this morning."

"No!" Sunny's eyes go wide.

"Yup. He was wearing tightie-whities and showing off his hard-on."

"Oh my God!" Sunny's mortification matches my own.

"So classy, right? Anyway, my mom thought I was at your place, so I guess she figured it would be safe."

"I'm sorry, Lily."

I shrug and make a joke out of it. "I guess the good thing is, there's a low probability that I'll ever see him again."

Sunny doesn't get what it's like to live in a house with a

revolving door of boyfriends. Her parents have been together forever.

I have no idea if my dad was the first professional athlete my mom scored with, but he was the one who got her pregnant. So since then, as long as the guy doesn't play hockey, he's fair game. I think it's kind of insane, because any guy can be a deadbeat, not just hockey players. Still, if I ever came home with a hockey-stick-toting boy, I'd hear about it. Hence the reason my mother will *never* know about my romp with Randy.

"How was the rest of your night?" I ask Sunny after she doesn't respond. I mean really, what is there to say? "The event went so well. Miller did great. How was Michael feeling by the end?" It's definitely not a subtle change of topic, but Sunny doesn't seem to notice, or maybe she doesn't want me to dwell on the unfortunate visual of my mom's date's man rod.

"It was amazing, wasn't it? Michael's such a trooper. He's tired today, though. Miller called him to see how he's doing. He really is wonderful, isn't he? I'm so in love with him. I can't even tell you. Last night he managed to get past Titan so we could get in some alone time. I can't wait until this semester is over." She taps the steering wheel and bounces in her seat.

"How'd he manage to get past Titan?" Sunny's little Papillon is super protective.

"Cookies." Sunny giggles. That's Miller's nickname for her vag. She thinks she's hilarious when referring to actual baked goods.

Sunny's mentioned moving to Chicago more than once since the fall semester began. It makes me nervous. We were supposed to move into an apartment or a little house after we finished college. I received my bachelors in kinesiology this past April, but the jobs in my field aren't the best unless I continue on for a master's degree, which is expensive. I also don't want to give up teaching figure skating, because well, it's been my life since I could walk. Anyway, Sunny switched programs last year, so it's taking her a little longer, but this has been the plan for the past three years.

I don't know what I'll do without her if she goes to Chicago. Especially since I broke up with Benji, and I honestly don't want to get back together with him. We've been apart for more than a month. I've avoided all of his phone calls, aside from the one where I told him I wasn't kidding about being done. He had some very choice words, none of which were nice, and all of which reinforced the reasons why I don't want to be with him anymore. There's nothing more heartwarming than being told I'm a "titless slut who deserves the next loser who fucks and chucks" me.

Anyway, Benji's out, and if Sunny leaves, that's another one of my ties to here severed. I don't want my mom to be the only thing left for me.

"You know, Lily, we could both move to Chicago at the end of the fall semester. Between Alex and Miller, I'll have a placement all worked out for the winter. It'd be the perfect way to start the new year." She glances at me before focusing on the road again. "Alex is looking into buying a little house, and I'll pay him rent or something. He thinks it would be a good investment. He has lots of contacts, and there are all sorts of opportunities in Chicago. You could teach skating to pre-pro hockey kids, or figure skating. Plus you have dual citizenship, so there isn't anything holding you back, especially since you and Benji are done for good, right?"

"I don't know. I can't just leave my mom here." I run my fingertip over a snag in my leggings. It's a lame excuse, but I've never been much for change. Staying with Benji even though he was a terrible boyfriend is a good example of that. Moving to Chicago would be a huge change. Also, Randy's there. My vagina is already aware and excited.

"Your mom can take care of herself. I don't think it would be a bad idea for you to at least consider it. We'd have so much fun."

"Why don't you move in with Miller?" I ask.

"We haven't been dating that long, and I want to live on my own first. I don't want to move into his space and just try to fit in there, you know?"

"But you'll move into his place eventually."

"Probably, but it doesn't need to happen right away. Alex is the one who likes to rush things."

"He's really pushing for this wedding to happen, isn't he?" It's weird. But then, that's Alex.

Sunny sighs. "I think he might send Violet over the edge."

Violet and Alex have been together for nine months, give or take. Ever since he put a ring on her finger this summer, Sunny's mom has been hounding them to set a date. Violet hasn't committed to anything yet. The only thing she's allowed so far is this engagement party I've evidently agreed to go to. Not that I'm complaining. Mostly.

"Anyway, you still haven't told me what happened with you and Randy in that bathroom last night."

"Nothing happened. He barged in on me like the jerk he is and prevented me from being able to pee."

"That's not what Miller said."

"What?" The squeak in my voice is far too telling.

"Come on, Lily. I know something happened in there. It's nothing to feel bad about. I mean, bathrooms are kind of gross, but that one is cleaner than most. As long as you used protection and washed your hands afterward, I'm sure it'll be fine."

"We didn't have sex! Did Randy say we had sex?"

"No. I guess I assumed. I mean with the way you were freaking out—"

"I wasn't freaking out."

Sunny gives me a look.

"Okay, I was freaking out."

She pulls into her parents' driveway. There are five cars in it already. Sunny isn't the best driver. Or parker. She always seems to end up running over her mother's flowers, which is exactly what happens.

"Let's talk about this later." I step over a crushed bloom and head for the front door. Sunny has no option but to follow.

The house smells fabulous; the pungent aroma of cinnamon makes my mouth water. I kick off my shoes, and Alex immediately scoops me up in a hug.

"Little Lily! I didn't get to see much of you last night. I'm glad you're here."

"You're crushing me!" I laugh and hug him back anyway. I miss him sometimes, like I would a real brother. We used to bug the crap out of him when he was a teenager. Me more than Sunny probably. He figure skated with all the boys in the level above me, and some of them were so cute. Slutty, but cute. I was constantly looking for reasons to hang out by the Waters' pool.

Once I made out with one of them. I was only in ninth grade. It was before I started dating Benji. Alex flipped his lid when he found out, and I got a serious big-brother lecture.

My Momma Two comes out of the kitchen in her frilly apron from the eighties. I'm almost positive her blouse has shoulder pads. Her hair is pulled up in a banana clip, and her bangs have been teased so they resemble a bath pouf. I didn't even know they still made banana clips.

I'm pulled into more warm embraces. I'm not actually big on hugging, but the Waters family is. And with Sunny it's more a habit than anything else. She's one of the few people I don't mind having in my personal space.

Miller's in the kitchen, sitting at the breakfast bar with Sunny's dad, Robbie, and Darren Westinghouse—he's Alex's best friend and another Chicago teammate. Robbie has essentially filled the missing father role in my life. He's a serious pothead, but he's brilliant, and I adore him.

The boys are shoving fruit into their mouths and talking about training. Miller spins on the bar stool and opens his arms wide, a huge grin on his face. "Lily!"

I give him a quick back pat and do the same with Robbie. I offer to help with brunch, but everything's already done, so we bring the food out and sit down to eat.

Brunch at the Waters' is always an event. Sunny's a vegan, so there's a selection of food specially prepared for her. The rest of the Waters family loves their meat, so heaps of bacon and sausage and eggs compliment the cinnamon buns, homemade waffles, and chocolate chip pancakes.

Violet and Charlene sit across from me and Sunny, with Momma Two to the right of Violet. She's still talking about the engagement party.

After we stuff ourselves silly, the girls change into bathing suits and head outside. It honestly isn't warm enough, but we're all bundled in hotel-style bathrobes, so that helps. The guys have a tee time at one, so they're packing up the car and getting ready to go. Daisy has plans to join us in a bit, once she's done with dinner prep. That woman could spend her entire life in the kitchen. She's like an eighties edition of June Cleaver.

"Is that steam?" I ask when I reach the pool.

Violet dips a toe in. "This is like a hot tub. I can't even imagine what the heating bill is going to be for this."

"Alex says he's paying for it," Sunny unties her robe and

tosses it on a lounge chair. She shivers and then jumps in. "Oh! Wow! This is great. Come on in, girls!"

Violet undoes her robe and rubs her bare belly. "Look at this! I shouldn't have put whipped cream on my waffles. Now we know what I'll look like three months after Alex knocks me up."

Sunny pops out of the water, catching only the end of the comment. "You're pregnant?"

"What? God, no! I'm not having Alex's pretty little babies. Not yet, anyway. First we have to do the wedding thing. Then I need to be a wife for a while. Then babies. In that order. With years between all those things." She pushes her stomach out further. "I'm just pointing out how much stress this damn engagement party is causing. Now I'm sporting this gross dairy belly."

Charlene pats Violet's tummy, and Violet pushes her in the water, but not before she seizes Violet's hand and yanks her in too. Before I get in, I hit the pool house and grab a bunch of noodles so we can float. I drop my robe on a chair with one of those heating lamps beside it, then sit down on the edge of the pool.

"Seriously. How is this fair?" Violet motions to me.

"How is what fair?" I look down at myself.

"You ate just as much as me. Where's your food baby?"

I run a hand self-consciously over my tummy. "Food baby?"

"Yeah. Food baby. You don't have one."

"Um …"

"Don't listen to her. She's bitchy because of the engagement party."

"And Alex wouldn't put out last night. Don't forget that part." Violet swims over to take a pool noodle. Except she stops right in front of me and grabs my knees. "Holy shit!" She wrenches them apart. "Is that a hickey?"

High up on the inside of my thigh is a large reddish-purple mark. I totally would have brought my bathing suit with the skirt if I'd been thinking. "It's a bruise." Made by Randy's mouth.

"Liar!" Violet sticks her head between my legs and pokes at it. "That's totally a hickey! Did Balls lick your beaver? Did you let Balls ball you?"

"Oh my God! You're the worst!" I'm laughing even though I'm embarrassed, because Violet is the most ridiculous human in the world. I put a hand on her forehead, intending to push her away.

"Uh, Violet?" Alex's deep voice makes us both turn.

Darren's hands are tucked into his pockets, and he's wearing a secret smile. He looks over at Charlene and raises an eyebrow. She does the same in return. What is that about?

Miller's expression is priceless. His mouth is hanging open. "What the shit do you girls do when we're not around?"

"Stop being a pervert, Buck! She has a h—"

I clamp a hand over Violet's mouth.

"I can't watch this. I feel dirty right now. I'm waiting in the car." Miller turns around and walks back into the house.

"Baby, c'mere." Alex crooks a finger and beckons her over.

Violet doggy-paddles to him, and Alex crouches to meet her. His eyes immediately dropping to her floating boobs. His gaze shifts back up. "Is there anything you feel you need to tell me?"

"About what?"

"I don't know; maybe you did some experimenting in college?"

"Oh my God, you're as bad as Buck! Lily has a hickey! Near her beaver!"

"It's a bruise!"

Violet looks over her shoulder at me. "Fine. It's a bruise. Made by Balls' balls slapping on your thighs!"

Alex glances in my direction, his brow furrowed. I take the opportunity to slip into the water and avoid looking at him. I don't need him to know anything about what did or didn't happen with Randy's balls.

Charlene comes to my rescue. "Don't listen to her, Alex. She's giving Lily the gears. And she likes to say balls, although I'm sure you're familiar with her mouth. On yours."

"Nice, Char." Violet turns back to Alex. "Gimme kisses and then go hit some balls with sticks with fat heads."

Alex puts his hands under her arms and lifts her out of the water to her waist. It's impressive. He whispers something to her.

"You can slide your monster cock between them later if you pet my beaver."

Alex grins and drops her back in the water. She goes under and comes up spluttering. "No boob sex for you later! My beaver's hiding in her den for the rest of the weekend!"

"Uh-huh. We'll see about that."

Darren's still wearing that half-grin. He winks at Charlene. "See ya later, sexy."

She blows him a kiss and bites her lip as he saunters away with Alex. Darren's always so quiet. It makes me wonder what the deal is with him.

Violet slides a noodle under her knees and another under her arms. Then she closes her eyes and tilts her head back. "This engagement party is ruining my sex life."

I float on my stomach with a noodle under my arms because my boobs are molehills compared to Violet's mountains. "Shouldn't you be excited about it?"

"Alex is more than excited enough for both of us, and so are our mothers. It's insanity. Whoever heard of an engagement party with a guest list of more than two hundred people?" Violet scratches her arm. "I'm going to do something to embarrass myself and Alex."

"You'll be fine, Vi," Charlene reassures her.

Violet gives her a look. "Seriously? Do you even remember my mom's wedding?"

"What happened at your mom's wedding?" Sunny asks.

"Oh, you know, the usual. I humiliated myself in front of all of my parents' friends."

"I'm sure it wasn't that bad," I offer.

"I told my mom I didn't want to give a speech, because I'm not comfortable getting up in front of that many people. But she was convinced I'd be fine because it was all people we knew." Violet shakes her head. "When it was my turn I got up, tripped over the bottom of my dress, and face-planted into Buck's junk. It set off a chain reaction. He stumbled into the podium and knocked it over, and it landed on the cake! I ruined my mom's wedding."

"You didn't ruin it, Vi. It was just a hiccup," Charlene says.

Vi turns to me and Sunny. "That's not even the worse part! My boob popped out of my dress, and everyone saw it! There were, like, three hundred people at the wedding!"

"There were only seventy-five. It was small," Charlene corrects.

"Well, it seemed like three hundred!" Violet huffs. "The whole team is coming to the engagement party! All of them. And they've all seen me naked. Or parts of me naked. It's embarrassing. What if I have another wardrobe malfunction? What if I say something stupid or talk about Alex's dick, which we all know is highly likely."

Last year rumors circulated that Alex had gotten caught having sex in the locker room with an unknown girl. The claims were never substantiated. We all know the truth, though; Alex got kicked out of a game, and Violet went to see if he was okay. It was close to the end of the third period. The team walked into the locker room right after they finished, or at least that's what Sunny told me.

Apparently Miller and Alex almost had it out right there. I'm not much for violence, but I would have paid to see that fight. I did get to see Miller punch Alex out on national TV, and then I saw Alex return the favor in real life, so that's something.

"Yeah, but you've been around them all a ton since then. I'm sure they don't even remember at this point," Sunny says.

"Oh, they remember all right. That Kirk guy mentions it every time I see him."

"Ick. He's such a pig," Charlene replies.

"Right?" Sunny shakes her head. "Miller says I'm never supposed to be in a room alone with him."

"Why would he say that?" I ask. I have no idea who they're talking about.

"Kirk's one of the guys on the team. He's a dirtbag. He's getting a divorce because he can't keep his winkie in his pants," Charlene explains.

"He's not coming to the engagement party, is he?" Sunny asks.

"Oh, he sure is. Alex didn't want to invite him, but we couldn't very well leave him out since the rest of the team is coming." Violet rubs at a spot on her stomach. "Goddammit! I have hives again. We need to talk about something else." She points at me. "What's going on with you and Horny Nut Sac?"

"Who?"

"Randy Balls. Come on. Spill it. He's clearly had his face in your beaver. Alex is all worried and shit. I'd be jealous if he didn't constantly refer to you as his 'other baby sister' and my rack wasn't way bigger than yours."

I protectively cup my pint-sized boobs. Benji always said they were barely there and I'd better get a good job so I could afford to pay for an upgrade. He loved pointing out girls with more cleavage than me. Violet fills out her bikini top in a way I couldn't even if I wore one of those super-extreme push-up bras. I bought one of those once, and Benji laughed at me. God, he was such a jerk.

"I'm not being mean," she adds after a moment, probably because I haven't come up with anything to say. "Just honest. Alex loves boobs so, so much. He tries to use mine as pillows every night. Maybe he got weaned from breastfeeding too early or something. I don't know. Anyway, what was I talking about? Oh, right. Balls."

She looks at me expectantly.

"There's nothing going on."

"Come on, Lily," Sunny kicks me in the water.

I sigh. "We messed around. That's it. It's not a big deal."

"Liar face!" Violet shouts. "You are the color of a tomato. How was the sex? I hear you were doing it in the bathroom last night."

"We didn't have sex in a bathroom!" I wish I could sink to the bottom of the pool right now. I'm not big on talking about this kind of stuff with anyone but Sunny, let alone people I don't know all that well. I'm a private person. Except when I'm locked in a bathroom with Randy, apparently.

"I'm not judging. I had sex in a locker room, and all of Alex's teammates heard my come moans. Everyone needs a little love now and again. Sometimes it's nice to get laid for the sake of getting laid. Besides, that Benji guy you were with before seems like a real dick. Randy's a perfect rebound bone: he's hot, well built, and can probably screw like a stallion."

Just then, Daisy comes outside in her hot pink bathing suit

with huge flowers on it, putting an end to the conversation.

But maybe Violet's right. I've been looking at this all wrong. As long as I'm smart about it, using Randy as a rebound is exactly what me and my boobs need to forget about Benji for good.

5

RUNNING IN CIRCLES

RANDY

A week after the exhibition game, I'm sitting in a lounge chair close to the pool on Lance's patio back in Chicago. It's been unseasonably warm, but today is likely the last time it's going to be this hot before fall takes me back to jeans and long sleeves. So I'm enjoying the sunshine. Or at least trying to.

Lance invited a bunch of people over. Inevitably, that means bunnies. He's been better about it lately, but he's still Lance, so there's always at least half a dozen hanging around, waiting for someone to throw them a carrot—and by carrot I mean dick.

There's a girl lying on the chair beside me, yammering away about who-fucking-cares what. She won't stop talking. The problem isn't her constant flow of words, which is irritating, but tolerable because I can tune it out. The real issue is that I've slept with her before, and based on the way she keeps edging her lounge chair closer to mine, she has it in her mind it's going to happen again.

I'm not feeling it. Or her. Sure, we got naked, but I didn't call her or respond to any comments on my social media afterward, so the message should be clear. It was what it was, and now it's over. Unfortunately, she's not getting the hint.

I text Miller to see what he's up to. He's been steering clear of Lance's when the bunnies are around. That means he stays for workouts and then he bails unless we're having Xbox wars. Which isn't very often. Lance usually gets antsy after a couple hours and calls in the reinforcements.

Miller messages back almost right away to tell me he's at Waters' Chicago place. That's still weird to me that not long ago those guys were busy breaking each other's noses to defend their sisters' honor. They've worked it out since then, but this hanging out stuff is a new development.

With Miller occupied, it looks like I have two options: stay and let the bunny annoy me, or go home and lounge in my own backyard, minus the pool to cool off in. I have a sprinkler if it's a real problem. Option two holds more appeal than option one, so I excuse myself to the bathroom. Once inside, I grab my duffle and keys from the rack in the kitchen and head for the front door.

"Hey, man, where you goin'?" Lance asks, tucking himself back into his shorts as he steps out of the main floor bathroom. A random bunny appears behind him, adjusting her bikini top. Her eyes are glassy and her cheeks flushed. She looks well taken care of.

"I got a headache. I'm gonna roll out."

"There's lots of cures for headaches here." Lance pats the girl's ass as she passes him. She jumps and giggles, then turns to wait. He lifts his chin in the direction of the pool. "I'll be out in a minute." He waits until she's gone. "Everything all right with you?"

"Yeah. Fine. I'm cashed today. It's been a busy week with getting back into training."

There's a brief hesitation on Lance's part, like he's not sure whether he believes me. Then he slaps me on the shoulder. "I get it. I'll see you tomorrow."

"For sure." He goes back to the pool and his company.

My truck is parked beside a Fiat. I hit the unlock button and start the engine. Then I hear a voice.

"Randy! Can I get a ride home?" It's the girl from the pool.

She's still in her bikini, but she's got a massive purse, or bag, or whatever it's called hanging off her arm. Her legs are like sticks, and her boobs are half hanging out of her top. Her getting into my truck isn't a great idea.

"I, uh, I'm about to run some errands." It's a lame excuse, and she isn't deterred.

"My apartment is, like, five minutes from here. You don't mind, do you? My friends are staying, and I kinda wanna go."

I scratch the back of my neck. "I'm running late already."

"Seriously, five minutes. Please? I don't have money on me for a cab." She drops her head and bites her lip, looking up at me with watery eyes.

"Yeah. Okay. I'll drive you."

She does a little skippy thing and runs around to the passenger side. Her head appears at the window. She really is tiny. Except her boobs. Those are busting out. "Can I get a little help here? It's a long way."

Yup. Here we go. I can feel the regret as I circle the front of my truck. I take her bag and toss it into the cab, then tap the running board with my foot. "Take a step up."

She does as I ask, but she's facing me, so her boobs are right there. It takes an infinite reserve of muscle control not to roll my eyes. After picking her up and dropping her on the seat, I wait for her to swing her legs into the cab. When all she does is give me a blank stare, I hook a finger under the back of her knee and move it so I can close the door.

This is going to be a whole shitton of fun. I hoist myself back into the driver's seat and shift the truck into reverse. The girl, I think her name might be Mary, or Miranda—it's definitely got an M and an R in it—shimmies over. Thankfully the center console is in the way, so she can't get too close.

She practically crawls over it. I don't notice the phone until she kisses me on the cheek and a flash goes off. I put a hand up to stop from being blinded. "Seriously?"

"Sorry! All my pictures from last time were dark. I wanted a better one."

"I'm driving here! And it's nice when you ask first." I try not to be snappy, but the way she shrinks back tells me I'm unsuccessful. Why did I agree to this? I feel like Miller back in the day. This just looks bad.

"Do you want me to delete it?" Her eyes are all wide and sad looking.

Maybe I'm being paranoid. Nothing's going to happen; I know that. "It's fine. I just didn't expect it." I stop at the end of the street. "Where'm I goin'?"

"Oh, right! Duh!" She gives me directions to her place. It isn't five minutes away; it's fifteen according to my GPS, but she's already in the vehicle.

She fiddles around on her phone for a minute, probably posting the picture she took. Once she's done, she drops it on the seat and runs her hand over the dashboard.

"This is a nice truck. Is this the only thing you drive? Do you have a sports car, too? Lance has a lot of cars, doesn't he?"

She couldn't be more obvious if she wore a "*bunny*" sign around her neck. "I have an Audi. And yeah, Lance likes his cars." He has a collection. I'm not sure how he makes things work with all the money he blows, but that's not my issue to manage.

The girl whose name starts with M roots through her bag-purse and pulls out a shirt. I assume she's going to put it on over her bikini. That's not what happens. Instead she pulls the tie around her neck and the one at her back, and the material drops to her lap. I glance at her and then back at the road, holding the wheel tight. I knew driving this chick home was a bad idea.

"What're you doing?"

"Getting changed. You don't mind, do you? My bathing suit's still a little damp, and I don't like the way it feels."

I try to keep my tone even. "Again, I'm driving. You can't be naked in my car."

"The windows are tinted. No one can see." She pulls the shirt over her head. It's almost see-through, but it's better than looking at her nipples. My dick starts to get the wrong idea about what's going to happen here and begins the process of inflating.

Next my passenger shimmies her bottoms off. Now there's naked pussy in my truck. Directly on my seat. She roots around in her bag some more—looking for shorts, maybe. I have no idea. Not like it matters. Normally this scenario wouldn't be a problem, but I've been texting Lily this week, and she's been messaging me back. I'm seeing her next weekend, and based on the content of our texting, I'm almost positive she's willing to get naked and have some fun. She's already made it clear to me and a good portion of my clothing that she doesn't like to share.

Now here's the thing: I don't get into serious relationships. Based on what I've seen happen with my teammates, and my own damn asshole father, all relationships do is cause bullshit.

I travel all the time, and my entire life I've watched long-distance relationships fail. I had a front-row seat to the shitshow that was my parents' ruined marriage. My dad was a professional hockey player—decent enough to be farm team and play a couple pro seasons. But he couldn't keep his dick in his pants when he was away from home.

Apparently I'm exactly like my dad where hockey is concerned, except I'm a better player. At twenty-four, I'm in my sixth season with the NHL. He managed three seasons, but never first line. Still, it's been hammered into me that I'm just like Randy Senior. We have the same personality, the same face, the same skill set, the same style on the ice, the same everything. And I've spent enough time with him to know it's true.

So that means one thing: there's a good chance I'm going to screw someone over the way he screwed over my mom. It might not be intentional, but it'll happen. So I don't get involved. Usually I'll hang out with the same girl for a while, rather than bunny hop. We have fun until it gets too involved and isn't working anymore, and then we part ways and do our own thing.

Most of the time it works out okay. But some girls get invested way too fast. There've been a few bunnies along the way that wanted more from me, but I make it abundantly clear that's not how things are going to roll. It's not my fault they read more into it than they should. There was one who got a tattoo of my face on her tit—and that was after I cut ties. As soon as I see it happening, I bail. I don't want to hurt feelings or break hearts; I just want awesome sex and some sleepovers.

Except that's actually a load of BS, because in all honesty, if I wasn't at risk of fucking up someone else's life, I might want an actual girlfriend. I can see the appeal. But definitely not this chick currently taking up space in my truck.

With Lily, I have to be even more conscious of what I'm doing and who I'm doing it with because she's connected to Miller and Alex. I don't want to mess shit up and make my life or theirs more difficult. She's a lot of fun, though, and she's clearly on the rebound, so I'm thinking we can spend some time getting to know each other without clothes on.

I chuckle at the memory of Lily's expression when she saw my underwear in that bathroom last weekend. I plan to pull them out next weekend to see how she reacts again.

M Girl must mistake my chuckle for some kind of green light to get all up on my dick. She's still pants-less. She adjusts her seatbelt's shoulder strap and leans over as far as she can. Her hand lands on my upper thigh and moves to my slowly inflating, traitor dick.

I glance down and then at her. "What're you doing?"

"I thought maybe I could thank you for the ride."

"By holding my dick?"

"I was thinking more along the lines of a blow job."

I exhale heavily through my nose and move her hand off me. We're less than two minutes from her place now. "I don't really have time for that."

"I can be real fast. I give amazing blow jobs."

I want to tell her that's not something she should be bragging about. I take the next corner a little too fast, almost fishtailing. She slides across the seat and bumps into the passenger door.

"Sorry."

"It's okay." She moves back into position as I turn another corner. I need both hands on the wheel, so she takes the opportunity to slide her hand into my shorts.

Her building is two hundred feet away. I screech to a stop in front—it's a nice place—and throw it in park.

"No!" I bark, gripping her wrist.

Her eyes go wide, and she retracts her hand like she's been bitten.

I close my eyes for a second and breathe. When I look at her again, I'm calm. I've given this speech a bunch of times, so it's nothing new. "Look, you're a nice girl, and we had fun, but the new season's about to start, and I can't get into anything right now. I gotta keep my head in the game, you know?"

"Oh." She wrings her hands.

Shit. I hope she doesn't start to cry. "It's not personal. I need to stay focused." A daylight truck BJ wouldn't be happening with her regardless (still news to my dick), but at least the excuse is mostly true.

"Right. Sure. I understand."

She unbuckles her seatbelt and leans over like she's going for some kind of goodbye kiss. I only spent one night with her. I think we had sex twice. It was decent if I'm remembering right, but I'm not positive. I lift my chin so I get her forehead instead of her mouth.

I pull back and smile. She returns it, but it's got that watery quality again. She reaches for the door, which is when I realize she's still not wearing bottoms.

"Hey."

She stops with her hand on the door, and her hopeful expression makes me feel shitty.

I glance down and get an eyeful of pussy. "You should probably put some shorts on, honey."

"Oh! Oh my God!" Her cheeks flush, and she mutters an apology as she rummages through her bag. It takes forever for her to find her shorts. She jabs her feet through the holes and pulls them up, then jams all the other crap back in.

She opens the door without looking at me. "Thanks for the ride."

There's a thick feeling in my throat. "No problem."

She gets down just fine without any help. She's about to close the door when I notice her phone on the seat.

"Hold up!"

She lifts her head, that same hopeful expression appearing

again. Except she uses the back of her hand to rub at her eyes. I made her cry. I don't think this situation could get any more awkward.

I hold out the phone. "You almost forgot this."

"Shit." She climbs back up to get it. "Thanks. I wouldn't want you to have to come back here or anything."

Any sympathy I might have felt dissolves with the sharp bite of her comment. She backs out of the truck and slams the door. I wait until she's inside before I pull away. As soon as I get home, I check my social media feeds. She's posted the pic. Her name is Marcie. She's also posted this:

RBBRs: Forehead kisses are the worst.

She's referencing a group called the Randy Ballistic Bunny Rejects. Apparently it's where girls I've been with more than once go to swap stories. I stay away from that crap, but I know it exists.

Below the post are a slew of comments from other girls. I recognize quite a few of their names and faces from their profile pics. It's messed up how my rejection is like a rite of passage.

I nab a beer from the fridge, twist off the top, and take a long swig. It's too nice to sit inside, so I step out on my back deck, put on some tunes, and relax. That lasts three minutes. I'm not good at sitting around for long. I also feel shitty about what happened with Marcie.

It's not my fault she romanticized one night, but it never feels good to make a girl cry. I made Lily cry, but that was different, and I think that's been resolved at this point. I pull up her contact. I messaged her a few days ago and got a response that she was at work. I haven't heard anything since. Next weekend will be here soon, so I figure it's a good idea to start a slightly more consistent back and forth. That way I can get a good gauge on whether she's feeling me or not.

What ru up to?

Her message comes less than two minutes later.

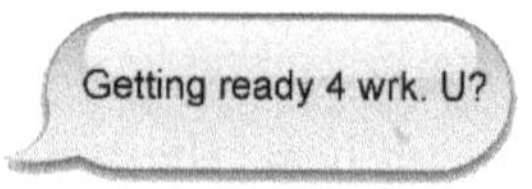

That's all she ever seems to do.

Drinking beer on my back deck.

The next one comes faster. There's a frowning emoticon attached to it.

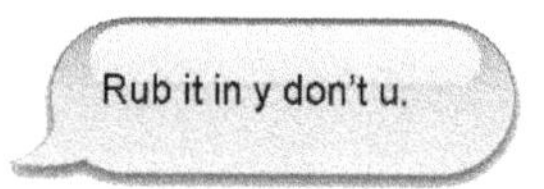

I grin as I type the next message.

I can think of lots of things I'd like to rub on u.

There's a longer break, and I worry I've pushed too far, too fast. I'm about to send a message telling her I'm joking when the dots appear in my feed.

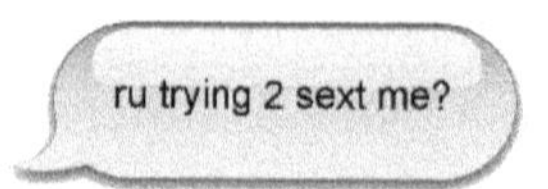

Perfect. This is the exact response I'm looking for.

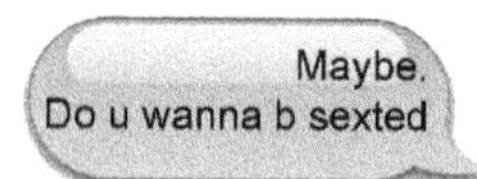

I don't have to wait long for her reply.

I'm about 2 teach a class. Not a good time.

My next message is loaded:

When do u get off?

She either misses the innuendo or ignores it.

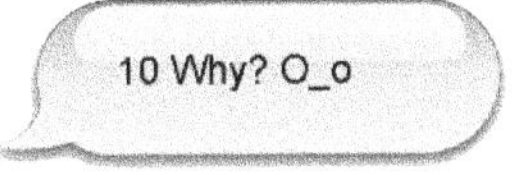

I can wait.

Unfortunately, I drink too many beers and get too much sun, so I end up passed out on my couch much earlier than I intended. I wake up at midnight and message Lily, but I don't hear back after ten minutes, so I assume she's already in bed or ignoring me.

It's cool, though. I have all week to sext the hell out of her in preparation for the weekend.

6

SEXTING 101

LILY

I would like to say I don't wait for Randy's sext messages when I get home from work. But that might be a lie. While I'm hanging out in my room… not waiting… I do what I've been doing since Randy and I first hooked up: I creep him on social media. It's not hard to do. His face is all over the place. His pretty, pretty face and his superhot body.

New ones have surfaced today, including a few of him lounging by a pool in a pair of swim shorts. Even relaxed he has a six pack. There's also one of him with some slutty bunny sitting in what appears to be a car. Her boobs take up ninety percent of the picture. Okay, that's a slight exaggeration, but they fill more of the frame than mine would.

My stomach does this weird drop thing. It's the same feeling I used to get when Benji flirted with other girls in front of me. He did it on purpose to piss me off. He also used to point out all the girls with better boobs than me at the beach. I tried not to let it get to me, but I was rarely successful.

Usually we'd end up having a big fight. I'd break up with him, he'd threaten to hook up with some girl, I'd tell him to go ahead, he'd walk away. Sometimes I'd chase him and cry, other times I'd let him go. He'd always apologize eventually, and we'd get back together. I hated the crying part the most. I don't like to feel weak. Not being with him is so much less stressful.

This isn't the same situation at all. I don't have a claim on Randy; we're doing whatever we're doing. He's been messaging quite a bit, so he seems to have picked up on my decision to give him a try. Casual messing around, I guess. Possibly casual sex, depending on what happens next weekend.

He finally messages me at midnight. I stare at my phone for a good long while, debating whether I want to respond. Violet made a good point about Randy being a fun rebound. Based on all my internet research/stalking I know what's going on between us isn't going to be serious. I think I can handle that. I want to be able to handle it. I've been with Benji for seven years so I have no idea if I can handle it. I'm going to try.

Randy and I have incredible chemistry, and he gives amazing orgasms, but I'm also not interested in being the phone fuck after the bunny fuck. Sloppy seconds are still sloppy, even if they're virtual.

When I get back to him the next day, I make a point of linking to one of the pictures of him with the boob girl, so he knows I'm not an idiot. My phone rings right away. My stomach flips and tries to turn itself inside out as I answer the call. "Hi."

"Are you stalking me?" The hint of teasing in his voice makes the flippy feeling even worse.

Shit. Maybe the social media creeping is getting out of hand. I go with nonchalant. "It's only stalking if I've erected a shrine."

He chuckles. I wonder what that sound would feel like against my vag. "That chick was one of Lance's friends."

"Who?"

"One of my teammates. Listen, I need you to take a picture of your room for me."

His unexpected explanation and request throws me. "Why?"

"So I can see your shrine." I can practically hear his cockiness.

It's my turn to laugh. "I can't. I'm at work."

"Take a picture anyway."

"What's the point if you can't see my shrine?" I bite my knuckle to stop the giggle.

His voice is low. "So I can see you."

Oh my God. Now my girl parts are freaking right out. I made a point of messaging him when I knew I wouldn't have much time to banter. "I'll take one before I get on the ice."

"Promise?"

"Promise."

"I'm looking forward to it. Talk to you soon, okay?"

"Okay."

He ends the call and I stand in front of the mirror in my skating outfit. It's a simple, black, skirted leotard with neutral tights. Nothing spectacular. I hold the camera up high like Sunny does, smile, snap a pic, and hit send without looking at it. I try not to think about the butterfly storm in my stomach. Or the buzz between my thighs.

I toss my phone in my locker, snap it shut, and hit the ice. I have about fifteen minutes to warm up before my girls arrive. After this morning session, I'll spend the afternoon working at the coffee shop, then come back to do an evening class at the arena with the older kids.

Getting next weekend off for the engagement party has been a pain in my ass. I'm working extra shifts at both jobs this week to make up for missing three days. It's hectic, but it'll be nice to have a break. I do a few laps around the ice to warm up.

The sound guy puts on my music, and I practice the routine I'm working on with the girls today. It's simple because they're young, but some of them are so talented. Watching them develop into dancers is as painful as it is inspiring.

I don't have time to check my phone again until I get home that night. I'm exhausted, but Randy's messaged me, so I flop down on my bed and scroll through them.

The first one is a screen shot of the slutty chick's selfie with Randy, but he's pointed out her comment, which I failed to read before because her boobs were my focal point. He rejected her. That makes me feel better than it should.

The next image is a picture of what's obviously Randy's hand down the front of his underpants. It's the pink pair again, with my lovely warning: TINY DICK INSIDE.

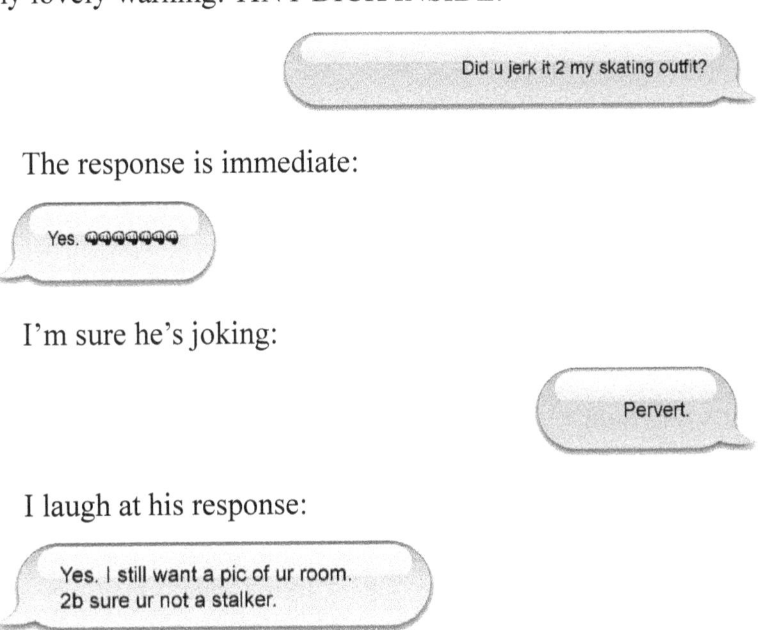

I take off my sweatshirt so I'm wearing a tank and leggings. I search my closet for anything I have that's round. I find golf balls, but those aren't big enough. Eventually I find a set of mismatched tennis balls. I stuff those down my shirt, strike a pose in front of the mirror, and snap a pic from the neck down. I giggle as I press send.

My phone rings. "Hello?"

"You're killing me; you know that, right?"

His deep voice goes straight to my crotch. I flop down on my mattress. "You like my boob job?"

"Don't mess with your boobs. They're perfect the way they are. Especially when they're in my mouth."

His candor throws me, and all I can do is make a whimpery moaning noise.

"You remembering what that was like?"

"No."

"Yes you are."

"I gotta go. It's late. I have to work in the morning."

"How much do you work?"

"A lot. I have double shifts this week because of the engagement party."

"Well, that sucks." There's some rustling in the background and the sound of a door closing. "Where are you staying while you're in Chicago?"

"At Alex's."

"You think you can get a night away from the Waters family while you're here?"

"I don't know. Maybe. Why?"

"'Cause I was thinking maybe we could do dinner or something."

"Uh… um…" That sounds a lot like a date. Or maybe it's Randy's way of enticing me into getting naked: dinner first, then sexing.

"Unless you're all booked up. I know it's gonna be a busy weekend. It was just a thought."

"Can I get back to you on that?"

"Sure. No worries if you can't."

He's so easy about it. I can't decide if that's good or bad until he speaks again.

"One way or another I'll get you alone this weekend, even if I have to lock you in a bathroom."

The naked part is implied.

7

XBOX LECTURES

RANDY

Miller's distracted state is allowing me to kick his ass at Xbox. Also, I'm better at the game than he is. Not that he'll admit that. Either way, the lack of competition is unsatisfying. His phone rings in the middle of a level, and he pauses the game to take the call.

"Hey, sweets! How was the flight? That's good. I can't wait to see you. You think you'll be at your brother's in an hour? Cool. I'll meet you there. Yeah. Yeah. I'm with him now. Oh, yeah?" He gives me a sidelong glance. "Is that right? Okay. I love you, too, Sunny Sunshine."

I shut the game off without saving it and make blow job gestures at him.

"I was beating that level!" He points to the blank screen.

"I smoked you six times in a row," I remind him. "It's not even fun anymore. Besides, I hear you're leaving soon." I don't ask about Lily, though I know she flew in with Sunny. She hasn't gotten back to me about getting together. I haven't pushed either. I don't need to chase girls. If she's not interested, I'll leave her alone. I'll know better tomorrow—unless I get an invite to Waters' place tonight. I'm not banking on that, though.

"I think we need to talk about tomorrow night." Miller settles back against the couch and stretches out an arm.

I pick up my beer. "The Lily situation is under control. I've talked to her since the exhibition game. We're good."

"That's what I'm worried about. What does *good* mean?"

"It means we've talked. We'll be fine with each other." I haven't been totally up front with Miller about Lily, but then, there isn't anything I need to share. We're just talking, and hopefully this weekend we'll be fucking.

"Sunny says you've been sending her messages all week."

"Well, yeah. I'm gonna see her, so I figured it'd be a good idea to make sure we're cool. And we are. So problem solved. She isn't going to try to beat me with a hockey stick or ruin any more of my clothes. You've got nothing to worry about." I forgot that girls talk. Of course Lily's going to say things to Sunny, and she's going to tell Miller.

"Randy, man, we talked about this; you can't screw her around."

"I'm not screwing her around. We're just having fun. She lives in Canada, for Christ's sake. How often can I see her?"

He gives me a look. Sunny lives in Canada, too.

"Yeah, but you guys have a plan. Sunny's gonna move here, and you're all serious and shit. That's not gonna happen with Lily. I'm a rebound. If I think it's going in a direction it shouldn't, I'll back off, okay?"

Miller scratches the back of his neck. "Just don't get too comfortable with her if you're gonna pull the usual routine."

"I never get too comfortable."

"Yeah." He looks like he has more to say, but he slaps his

thighs instead and stands. "I should get going. I gotta pick up a few things from my place before I head to Waters'. Thanks for the hospitality, Balls."

"Anytime you want an ass kicking, you come see me and my Xbox."

As soon as he's gone, I check my phone for messages. Nothing from Lily.

I message Lance to see what he's up to. Turns out he's at a bar, which isn't unusual. I don't have anything better to do, so I call a cab and join him.

I end up staying over at Lance's place, thanks to the drinks we consume. He doesn't bring home bunnies. It's the first time that's ever happened that I can recall, although I've only known him a few months.

Lance and I hit the gym in the afternoon in an effort to sweat out the residual booze. I don't hear from Lily all day, other than one quick text telling me she's in Chicago and she'll see me later. Miller keeps sending me pictures of Waters' mom. She has the most fucked-up hair I've ever seen. It's insane. In the grainy background of a couple shots I can see Lily and Sunny. They're out of focus, but obviously having fun. If I'd gotten an early invite, Lily and I could've found a private place to say hi—naked, with orgasms.

"You need a haircut, bro," Lance says on the way home from the gym, breaking me out of my pornish thoughts.

"There's nothing wrong with my hair."

"That man-bun bullshit has got to go. It looks like you've got a stubby Doberman tail hanging off the back of your head."

I laugh. "The ladies like it."

"Yeah, well, you look like a douche."

On that helpful note, Lance drops me off at my place so I can get ready. He'll swing back around and pick me up tonight since I'm on the way to Waters'. It's not a formal event, but we're supposed to look decent, what with the whole thing being a catered dinner. I put on my favorite Lily-decorated underwear and cover them with black pants and a dress shirt. I'm not dealing with a tie tonight if it's not mandatory, but I pocket one just in case.

By six-thirty Lance still hasn't arrived. He's much like Miller in this regard, so I'm used to him being late, but tonight I'd like to be on time. Or at least close to on time. I sit on my front porch and drum on the arm of the chair. I've already sent him a couple of messages. He assures me he's on his way, and that Tash is the hold up. I don't see how that's possible, as Tash is about as low maintenance as a chick can get. I've never seen her in anything other than athletic gear and a ponytail.

It's another fifteen minutes before they finally get here. Lance is driving his Hummer. It's lime green. He likes to make a statement. Tash gets out of the passenger side, and for a second I don't recognize her. She's in this slinky black dress—not slutty, just fitted. It hugs all the incredible curves of her very toned, very fit body. Her hair is wavy and loose. And she's wearing makeup.

"Holy shit."

She flips me the bird. "Keep your opinions to yourself." She adjusts her dress and touches her hair. "You can take the front seat. There's more leg room."

I shake my head. "No way. You stay put. There's lots of room in the back of this asshole ride."

I hold out my hand, offering to help her back up. She's wearing heels. I'm not sure it's something she does all that often based on the way she grips my arm.

"You're smokin', Tash." I pat her hand.

She gives me the evil eye; then a hint of a smile appears. "Thanks, Randy."

"You better watch yourself tonight, girl. You're gonna need all those ninja fighting skills to keep the guys off you."

"Get in the damn car, Balls. We're already late," Lance calls.

"Calm your tits, bro. That's not my fault."

"It's not mine either," Tash says.

There's something in her tone and the way she looks at Lance. A while back Miller asked if I thought something was going on between them. Now I'm starting to wonder if he was on to something. Lance is giving her the eye—and not the angry eye, but the fuck eye.

I get into the backseat and slide to the middle so I can stick my head between them and be a dick. "So whose fault is it that we're so late?"

Tash looks at Lance, a coy smile pulling at her lips.

He keeps his eyes on the road. "Tash had wardrobe issues."

"If you say so," she flips the visor down and checks her makeup.

It takes thirty-five minutes to get from my place to Waters'. The driveway is packed with cars, and there's some dude in a suit directing us down the street. Lance lets us out and then parks the car so Tash doesn't have to walk a long way in her heels.

I give her a sidelong glance. She does that fidgety thing girls do when they know you're looking at them and they're self-conscious about it.

"What?" she asks.

I shrug. "Nothing. You a little antsy tonight or something?"

"No. I'm fine." She adjusts her dress again.

She's been the team trainer for about two years now, according to Miller. I've only been in Chicago for a few months, so I don't know her all that well. She's good at her job, she pushes us hard, and she's fun to hang out with, but tonight she seems off.

"You wanna wait for Lance or head inside?"

"He knows where we'll be. Let's go." She flips her hair over her shoulder and starts up the driveway.

Waitstaff greet us at the door with cocktails. We each take one and survey the house. It's full of people, but I can see from the front foyer all the way to the open sliding doors at the back. They lead right into the backyard, which is also packed.

"Holy hell, Waters knows how to throw a party." Tash takes a sip of her drink. "Don't let me have too many of these; I'm liable to get up on a table and do a striptease."

"I don't think you'd get too many complaints about that. Except maybe from that one over there." I point to a little old lady sitting on the couch, holding a wine glass with two hands.

"Oh, God. There are grandparents here. I hope the team doesn't do anything to embarrass Violet."

I snort. "Pretty sure she can do that all on her own."

Violet is a riot. She's probably worse than most of the guys on the team with the stuff that comes out of her mouth. I'm not sure if she's a nervous person or half-crazy, but she's entertaining to be around.

As if she hears us talking about her, Violet comes traipsing through the crowd. She's all curves with a tiny waist. She's wearing a red dress. It's one of those wrappy things, so there's a lot of cleavage. Violet's got a huge rack, especially on a body as small as hers. It's hard not to stare.

"Tash!" she yells and waves. There's a slight weave in her

step. When she sees me, she gets the look on her face she always does. I stuff my hands in my pockets and suppress a grin. I already know what's coming.

Violet can't deal with my name. Miller shortens my last name to Balls—it's kind of an inside joke, which he's not allowed to share with anyone or I'll kill him—and her whacked-out brain changed it into something dirty. Although, I guess given my reputation with women, it's not all that far out there.

Violet stops about three feet away from us. She closes her eyes and takes a few deep breaths. The empty glass she's holding shakes. After a few more seconds she opens her eyes and smiles. "Hi, Randy," she says through clenched teeth.

"It's killing you, isn't it?" Usually there's some thrusting action that accompanies the articulation of my name.

"You have no idea. It's guaranteed I'm going to say something embarrassing tonight. So far I've only accidently referenced Alex's dick once."

"Oh, God," Tash stifles a laugh.

Violet holds up a reassuring hand. "It's okay. I don't think my grandmother caught it; she's not wearing her hearing aids. I'm keeping everything crossed that I can control my mouth for the rest of the night, but it's not my strong suit." One of the waiters comes by to take her empty glass. Violet takes a new drink from his tray and holds up a finger so he doesn't leave. She gulps it down in one swallow, hands the glass back, and reaches for another.

"Violet, baby, there you are." Alex comes up behind her and snatches the glass away before she can get it to her lips. "Here. You should try this instead." He folds her hand around the new glass and acknowledges us. "Hey, guys. Glad you could make it.

Natasha, you look stunning."

"Ooooh! What's this?" Violet holds out the champagne flute. The concoction is pink, with little berries floating in it. A toothpick threaded with candies lies across the top.

"Charlene said you'd love it."

Violet takes a sip and smacks her lips. She's definitely drunk. Tonight should be interesting. "This is awesome. You're the best, baby." She runs a hand down his chest.

Alex catches it before it can go too low. "Anything for you, gorgeous."

She leans into him and clutches his shirt, pulling him down. He gives us an apologetic look, and that's before she says, louder than she probably means to, "Tonight I'm gonna ride your dick like we're at the Calgary Stampede."

"Shh," he mutters. "We can talk about that later."

"Right. Shh!" She puts her finger to her lips. "Speaking of riding things …" She lets go of Alex's shirt and points at me. "You might want to find Lily. She is a hot tamale tonight. If I wasn't marrying this sexy piece of ass, and I didn't love his monster cock as much as I do, I might be interested in her. Except she's a girl. So I'm not. But there are a bunch of horny guys who are." She turns to Alex and cringes. "That was too far, wasn't it?"

"Yeah, baby." He nods. "You saw the line and bulldozed right over it."

"I told you this party wasn't a good idea. We need to elope." She guzzles the rest of her drink. "I need another one of these."

"Let me take care of that for you." Alex takes the glass and puts an arm around her. "I'll catch you guys in a bit. Make yourself at home." He steers her away as she grabs his ass.

Tash and I look at each other. "I have a feeling this is going to be an interesting night."

"You can say that again," Tash agrees.

Lance is still missing, so we make our way through the crowd. I'm on a mission to find Lily, especially after Violet's report. Though she's drunk, so she might be exaggerating. I don't see Lily anywhere inside, so I shoot her a text telling her I'm here and ask for a location.

As Tash and I step out onto the deck in the backyard, her heel catches between two boards. I catch her before she can go down.

"Oh, crap! These shoes were a stupid idea."

"You're fine. I got you."

She puts a hand on my shoulder and twists around so she can see what's keeping her locked to the deck.

"Damn it. It's really stuck!" She jerks her foot a couple of times.

"Let me see if I can get it."

Just as I bend down, I spot Lily. She's wearing a little blue dress, her lean legs on display. It reminds me of her figure skating outfits. It's light and flowy, covering everything and not enough at the same time. And fucking Kirk is talking to her. He's a dog.

I hold onto Tash's ankle and tug. Her heel slips free, and her elbow comes up fast. I don't have enough time to react. She connects with my nose.

"Ah, fuck!" I grunt and fold forward.

"Oh, shit!" Off balance from the unexpected freedom, Tash stumbles into me, her drink splashing on my shoe.

I'd like to care, but my face is throbbing, and my eyes are watering, so the drink isn't nearly the issue it would be otherwise.

"Are you okay?" Tash takes my glass and sets it on the deck.

I'm surprised I was still holding it. All I can do is make a groaning sound.

"Do you have words?" She takes my face in her hands. "Randy?"

This time more than noise comes out. "Fuuuuuuuuck."

"I'm so sorry."

I straighten and try to shake it off. "I'm dying."

She laughs, but man, an uppercut to the nose hurts.

"Hey, guys—" Lance's voice permeates the haze of pain. I turn to look at him, processing his confusion as it turns quickly to anger, which he aims at Tash. "The fuck is going on?"

All of the sudden it's quiet on the deck.

Tash rolls her eyes. "Calm yourself, Lance."

He points a hand in my direction. "Why are you all up on Ballistic?"

"I banged him."

Lance seems more upset by this revelation than necessary. "You what? When?"

"Like two seconds ago," Tash replies.

"How's that possible?" He looks from me to her. "You make a pit stop in a bathroom before you came out here?"

"What?" Tash looks confused.

"Huh?" All I want is to lie down with an icepack on my face. These people are crazy.

"You're a real piece of work, Tash. I can't leave you alone for five minutes without you jumping someone."

Tash's eyes go wide, and her mouth drops. Her hand rises in smack mode.

I get in front of her before she can follow through with the bitch slap, which Lance may actually deserve. "That's not what she meant by banged," I tell him. "She elbowed me in the nose, by accident."

"What?" Lance grabs the back of his neck.

Tash shakes her head. "I knew this was a bad idea."

She pushes past him and goes back inside.

"Fuck. Shit. Tash, wait." He goes after her.

Well, I guess Miller called it. There's definitely something going on there. Or was.

8

WHAT'S UP WITH BATHROOMS?

LILY

This creepy dude named Kirk won't leave me alone. I don't know where Sunny went. Or Miller. I scan the crowd again as he goes on and on about how amazing he is. He's old, or older anyway. He's got a few gray hairs at his temples and some creases around his eyes. I think he might be balding, but I can't be sure because I'm a lot shorter than he is. I'd put him in his mid-thirties. But he's not wearing a wedding ring, so I could be wrong about that, too.

Right about now I'd glom onto Momma Two if it meant I could lose this guy. Commotion on the deck pulls my already divided attention away from his monologue. Randy's standing outside the French doors. Oh, God. He looks so, so good. He's wearing black pants and a dark button-down shirt. It's blue—almost the same color as my dress. We match, and we didn't even plan it.

Then there's this tall, incredibly built, very pretty woman with her hands on his face. She looks concerned. He looks—

other than hot—intense. His hand is on her shoulder, and they're close-talking.

I get that feeling—the same one I get when I make a mistake in competition. My whole body heats up and cools down at the same time. My stomach knots.

"I'm sorry." I turn to Kirk, who's still talking. "You'll have to excuse me."

I don't wait for his response. I turn toward the house. Fortunately, I don't have to pass Randy on the way inside since there's another door. I enter through the kitchen and run into Sunny.

"There you are! I've been looking for you everywhere." she exclaims.

Miller's leaning against the counter, stuffing appetizers into his mouth. He's got a satisfied look on his face. I bet they disappeared somewhere to get it on. They've been doing that all day.

"Isn't Randy here yet?" Miller pulls his phone from his back pocket and checks his messages. "Says he got here, like, ten minutes ago."

"Yeah, but he's with some girl." I try to sound like it doesn't matter, even though it feels like someone kicked me in the magic marble.

"What?" Miller's eyes narrow.

The girl Randy was with on the deck comes storming through the house.

I point. "That's her."

"Tash?" Now Miller looks baffled.

"I don't know what her name is, but they had their hands all over each other." I swirl my drink.

"That's the team's trainer," Sunny says.

A hockey player I recognize—his name is Lance, I think—is

right on her heels, calling after her.

"I think maybe there's a misunderstanding, because if anyone's with Tash, it's Lance, not Randy."

Sunny nods. "Totally. Randy's all about you these days."

Miller gives her the eye.

"Isn't that what you said earlier?" She twists her hair around her finger.

"Hey, Balls," Miller's gaze lifts over my head.

"Hey."

His deep voice makes my insides liquid, but not Ebola liquid, sexy liquid. I can practically feel his body heat behind me. Okay, that's not true, but he runs a finger from the nape of my neck all the way to the base of my spine, and I can definitely feel that. My body tightens with anticipation. All the blood seems to get sucked straight into my clit. Just from his finger. I don't get it. Now all I want to do is jump him, even though less than five minutes ago some other girl was touching him.

I take a deep breath and turn. His hair is pulled back in that pony nub he's got going on. Usually I think man buns are stupid. For some reason on him it's sexy.

"Hey, Lily. Not gonna run away from me this time?" His lip curves up in a half-smile.

His beard is so perfect. Just like the rest of him. I want to run my fingers through it. Stroke it. Him. I also might want to ride his face. Again. *Jesus*. What's wrong with me? I realize I'm staring, and he's made a snarky comment. I open my mouth, and all that comes out is a sigh.

His grin gets bigger. Cocky pucker. "I'm sorry, what was that?"

I take a hefty sip of my drink. It's strong, whatever it is. I turn my head and cough. When I look back again, I'm slightly more composed. "I don't see the point since you'll probably follow me anyway."

"There's a good chance." He skims my shoulder with a fingertip. "This is pretty."

"Thanks." The tags are still attached to this dress. They're tucked inside, and the little plastic thing is poking me in the armpit. It cost more than a hundred dollars. I can't afford to keep it, so my plan is to wear it tonight, have it dry cleaned, and return it to the store on Monday. It's dishonest and underhanded, but I wanted to look nice tonight. The last formal-ish dress I bought was for my prom, and that was years ago.

We stand and stare at each other for a while longer, saying nothing. I wish I would have hugged him right away or something, but it seems awkward now. All the messages we've been sending back and forth over the past week make my skin hot. It's so much easier to flirt and threaten sexting when I don't have to look at his face.

"So what's going on with Tash and Lance?" Miller asks.

"Who knows. They're acting all weird. I'm not sure what the deal is, but Tash elbowed me in the face, and Lance misunderstood, and now they're pissed at each other."

"Are you okay?" Sunny asks, seeming genuinely concerned.

"It's fine, just kinda hurt for a few minutes. Thanks for asking." Randy directs his grin at me.

Miller takes a swig of his beer and shakes his head. "I still don't get why she'd be interested in him. He puts his dick everywhere."

"You used to put your dick everywhere," Sunny pipes up. She's not angry, just honest.

"I was never that bad."

Randy lifts an eyebrow. Sunny does the same.

"Seriously. I wasn't *that* bad."

Sunny pats him on the cheek, then replaces her hand with her lips. "It's okay, Miller. I'm just saying, I still gave you a chance even though you were slutty, and look how well that's turned out? People change, or at least the things they want can change."

Miller kisses her fingertips. "I had to work real hard to convince you I was serious about you, sweets."

Sunny bats her lashes. "You did such a good job, too."

Randy makes a gagging noise. "You two are worse than a chick flick. You need to take that shit somewhere else."

"They've been taking it somewhere else all damn day," I mutter into my glass.

Miller and Sunny break apart. "We have not!" Sunny's voice is high, the way it gets when she's lying, or embarrassed.

"It's okay, sweets. Don't feel bad about wanting a piece of this." Miller motions to himself, more specifically his crotch.

"I'll be back in a minute. I need the ladies room." I set my glass on the counter and turn to Randy. "Keep an eye on these two; they keep disappearing."

"And that's a problem why?"

I roll my eyes and head for the bathroom. I need to gather myself. I don't like how territorial I feel about Randy, and we haven't even slept together. I remind myself that this isn't going to be serious. He lives in Chicago. I live in Canada. We're having some fun. I need a break from serious anyway. I deserve this, and I can totally handle it.

I lock myself inside the bathroom, surprised and a little disappointed that Randy didn't follow me this time. I turn on the tap while I do my business, then check my reflection in the mirror. Violet and Charlene had their way with my face. I didn't let them do much, but I'm wearing mascara and eye shadow. I drew the line at lipstick and made do with gloss.

I pull out a package of wipes from my purse and tear it open. It smells like mint and cucumber. Violet gave them to me today and told me to thank her later. I drop my panties, which are edged in lace, and give myself a little rubdown. I want to be prepared for whatever happens, or doesn't, tonight. The mint makes everything tingle.

I toss the wipe in the garbage, wash my hands, fix my hair again, and open the door.

"Took you long enough." Randy steps inside and locks us in.

"What's with you and bathrooms?" I back up until I hit the wall.

He steps in close. "What's with you and always running away from me?"

"I wasn't running. I had to use the bathroom." If I could dig my nails into the plaster behind me, I would. As it is I'm fighting the urge to run my hands over his very hard, very big body. If I arch my back at all, parts of me will touch parts of him.

"I think maybe you were looking for a reason to make me follow you." He braces his forearm against the wall beside my head. His shirt stretches tight over his bicep. God, he's ripped.

"So what if I was?"

"Is that an admission?"

"You've been sexting me all week; what do you need an admission for?" I slide my hands behind my ass so I don't do something stupid, like grab his face and ram my tongue down his throat. Again.

His knee rests against my thighs, looking to get between them. If he does, I'm guaranteed to start dry-humping. I hold them tight together. If he gets in there, I lose this game. I'd really like to be able to control myself until we can make it to a location that isn't a bathroom.

"You're the one sending all the racy pictures." His eyes drop to my mouth.

Game on. "Racy pictures? You mean of me in my skating

outfit?"

"And the one of you fucking up my view with those tennis balls down your shirt."

Cleavage selfies are not my specialty. Especially compared to that slutty bitch's from last week. Not that I'm fixated on that, or anything.

I'm so, so screwed tonight. Any hope of rational decision-making has gone out the window. Not that I was honestly planning on making rational, smart decisions.

The pressure against my thighs increases, so I squeeze tighter. Randy's breath leaves him on a heavy exhale. He smells vaguely of some fruity drink. I tip my chin up; it's as close as I'm getting to caving.

"That skating outfit gave me hours of enjoyment." His mouth descends on mine.

As soon as our lips connect, I part mine and welcome his tongue. I also part my legs and welcome his thigh by grinding on it like I'm pole dancing. Randy doesn't seem to have a warm-up button. He caresses the outside of my leg, reaching the hem of my skirt.

"Please tell me this means we're fucking tonight," he groans into my mouth.

"Uh-huh."

We're rubbing up on each other like cats in heat. I don't even know what the hell is happening. His hands are all over the place: under my skirt kneading my ass, over my dress palming my boobs.

"I need to get you into a bed," he mumbles.

"I have a room upstairs."

"Why are we in here then?"

"Because you followed me like a creepy stalker."

He breaks free from our kiss. "Creepy stalker? Is that what

you really think?"

His gaze is intense. I gauge the tension in his posture and run a soft hand down the side of his neck. "No."

"No?"

I decide now is a good time to be vulnerable. I'm not trying to take advantage of the situation, because let's face it, this man knows his way around a woman's body. My experience is limited to Benji—who I'm discovering wasn't an awesome lay—and the few guys I hooked up with while we were on one of our breaks.

"I'm deflecting."

"Deflecting what?"

"I don't want to be a disappointment."

The hand on my boob stills, along with his knee between my legs. "A disappointment? How the fuck is that possible?"

I cringe. "I don't know why I said that. You make it hard to think." I wish I could stop embarrassing myself.

"You don't need to think about anything other than how good I'm going to make you feel as soon as we get to a bed." He cups my cheek in his palm—it's rough, and warm, and tender all at the same time. "Where's your room?"

I tell him, as best I can, in clipped, nervous directions.

"I'll meet you there in five minutes." He kisses me again, hard. When he's done owning my mouth, he opens the door, checks things out, and sends me on ahead.

9

NO DISAPPOINTMENTS

RANDY

I need a minute to gather myself.

I watch Lily rush around the corner as I adjust my hard-on. Her dress is driving me insane. When I was ten I took a year of figure skating. Me and Miller went together. We thought it was stupid. We could already skate; we didn't need to learn leaps and spins and twirls.

Then we met our coach and stopped thinking it was such a waste of time. Her name was Deanna. She was a hardass, and she was hot as sin. She was probably only seventeen or eighteen at the time, but she was the first chick I ever got a hard-on over, and eventually, she was the reason behind my first wet dream. Lily's even hotter, and this time I get to live the fantasy, not just make a mess in my sheets over it.

Lily is a riot, and she's been dishing it out as good as she can take it all week in our messages. So I came tonight with a preconceived idea of how this would go. And then she drops this little gem: *"I don't want to be a disappointment."*

That's a serious screeching-tires moment. I don't think I've ever slept with a chick—at least not since I was drafted—who seemed at all concerned about her ability to please me, let alone expressed worry about potentially disappointing me.

Most of the time, the women who get in bed with me have zero inhibitions. They get naked and offer themselves up any way I want them. It's a little fucked up, to be honest. Lily doesn't fit into the bunny mold. So I'm having a few reservations about what's about to go down—not enough to back things up, but enough that I need to re-evaluate my strategy.

I don't get how someone who looks like Lily and moves like Lily could have as little self-confidence as she seems to. Unless she's playing mind games. I don't see why she would, though. I also feel like maybe I need to find that ex-boyfriend of hers and beat on him a little. Or a lot. I bet he's directly related to her sometimes shaky self-esteem.

All week I've been fixated on getting to this point: the one where she's naked again. But this time I'll be privileged enough to experience that tight little body from the inside. Tonight needs to be about more than a good time. She needs to come out of this situation feeling like a damn porn star—okay, maybe not a porn star, but she needs to feel sexy. It needs to be good for her. And above all else, it needs to be fun.

Checking the hall again, I turn off the light in the bathroom and head for the stairs, making a right at the top and counting the doors as I go. Waters has a sweet pad in Bridgeport. When I get to the right room, I look over my shoulder to make sure no one else is around before I turn the knob.

"Psst."

I turn and find Lily peeking out of the room on the opposite side of the hall. Oops. At the same time, I hear footsteps. I rush past the stairs, and she grabs my shirt and hauls me inside, closing the door with a quiet click. Then she stealthily turns the lock. I hit the lights.

"What are you doing? I can't see anything!" she whispers.

"Someone was coming up the stairs," I whisper back.

"Oh." Her hands move over my chest. "Who was it?"

"Don't know. I didn't wait to find out."

"Sunny might be looking for me," she mutters as she finds the hem of my shirt and pulls it free from my pants.

"Is that li—"

She mashes her hand over my face and almost sticks her finger up my nose. I lick her palm and feel her nails tickling their way up my ribs. I grasp her forearm before she can reach my nipples, so she rubs her damp palm over my face instead. I grab that hand as well, so now she has none free. Clasping them together behind her back, I drop my chin and bonk the top of her head.

"Ow!" she whispers and proceeds to bite me through my shirt.

In the fifteen seconds or so that the lights have been off, I've grown accustomed to the darkness. Across the room I can make out a set of doors that look like they lead to a closet, and another door I assume is a bathroom. I spin Lily around, let go of her hands, clamp one of mine over her mouth to stop her from ruining my plans, and wrap my other arm around her waist.

She makes angry noises that might be words as I carry her across the room. I shoulder open the door. The slippery tile under my feet tells me I've guessed right and am indeed inside a bathroom. She bites my palm, but I don't set her down until I've got the door closed, and we're once again submerged in darkness.

"What the hell?" She smacks the wall until she finds the light switch, blinding us both. "Was that necessary?"

"You said Sunny might come looking for you. I'm solving problems. You'd think you'd be grateful, but you gotta go and bite the shit out of my hand." I hold my hand up so she can see the teeth marks she's left behind. I'm smiling, though, even if I sound annoyed.

I'm not gonna lie. I think it's kinda hot. I've got a serious hard-on right now.

Her cheeks flush and she ducks her head. It takes all of three seconds for her feistiness to come back. "What's with you and always turning off lights?"

I hit them again and lift her onto the vanity. "It sets the mood."

"And here I thought it was so you could pretend I was a supermodel while we make out," she replies.

I flip the lights back on.

She puts her hands up to cover her eyes. "Knock it off!"

I pry them away from her face. "Look at me." I don't mean for it to come out sounding more like an order than a request, but I want Lily to know, with absolute certainty, that I'm seriously stoked about what's going down here.

"I was just j—"

"You were just what?" I edge my way between her knees.

"Joking." She's barely audible.

"I should hope so." I release her hands and cup the back of her head. "You're fucking gorgeous, Lily."

She blinks like she's been tasered. I lean in and put my mouth on hers. For once it's not a full-on war of the tongues the second our lips connect. Her soft, warm fingers clamp around my wrists, and she makes a small, plaintive noise when I nip at her bottom lip. We make out like that—kissing, me rubbing up on her—for a long while. Every so often I open my eyes and look at our reflection in the mirror.

Lily's dark hair is cut in a bob, so I can see the nape of her slender neck and the arch of her shoulder blades highlighted by the deep V at the back of her dress. It's so low I don't think she can possibly be wearing a bra.

She puts a hand on my chest and pushes, breaking our mouths apart. "You kiss with your eyes open!"

"No, I don't."

"You just were."

"Well, doesn't that mean you kiss with your eyes open, too?"

"You seemed distracted. I was checking to make sure you weren't bored or something."

"Bored?"

"Well, I don't know!" She waves her hand around. "Now I'm self-conscious knowing you're watching me while we're kissing."

I laugh. "I wasn't watching you. Well, not your face." I gesture to the mirror behind us.

She glances over her shoulder. "You were watching yourself? Nice ego."

"Actually," I trail a finger from the nape of her neck down the ridges of her spine to the zipper. "I was thinking there can't possibly be a bra under this dress."

"Oh."

"And I'd really like to find out if I'm right." She sits up straight as I drag the zipper down and shivers as my fingertips brush her skin. "Looks like I am." I kiss the sensitive spot at the base of her neck, pulling the wide strap over her shoulder. Lily's skin pebbles, and I feel the warmth of her exhale on my cheek. She tilts her head to the side, so I close my mouth over the warm skin and add a little suction. Not enough to leave a mark, but enough that she knows I could.

I kiss across her collarbone to the opposite side, repeating the same action, sliding her dress down her arms. Her breasts pop out. I'm about to get excited, because I love nipples. Especially nice ones. I guess it's different for every guy. Some guys like huge tits, some guys don't. Some guys care more about legs, or asses, or other body parts. I like the entire package, and I like things proportional. If Lily had huge boobs, she wouldn't look right. And hers aren't bee stings or anything. She's definitely a woman; they stand up on their own. We're talking a solid B cup. I'm good with that.

And just like every other part of her, Lily's nipples are delicate. Except right now they're covered with Band-Aids. "Uh…"

"Oh, shit!" She covers her boobs.

I pull her hands away and watch her cheeks turn pink. "What's going on here?"

"I didn't want to have obvious nip-ons."

I quirk a brow, and she raises one back.

"Nipple hard-ons."

"Right. I must have missed that lesson in sex ed."

"I'm pretty sure you didn't need any of those lessons," she mutters and picks at the edge of a Band-Aid.

"Want some help with that?"

"I got it." She presses her palm above her chest and tears the Band-Aid off.

I cringe. "Go easy on those."

"It's fine." She pinches her nipple. "See?"

"Don't be so rough. I'm having sympathy pains." I push her hand out of the way and cup her breast, whispering, "Don't worry. I'll keep you safe."

Lily barks out a laugh. "You're ridiculous."

Her laugh turns into a groan when I cover her nipple with my mouth and give a good hard suck. Her hands go to my hair, and she pulls the tie, setting it free. I lick and nibble, then use my teeth on the very tip.

Her fingers tighten in my hair. "Don't you dare!"

I glance up and put the tiniest bit of pressure on her very hard, very pert nipple.

"Randy." It sounds like a warning, but also like maybe she wants me to bite her.

I don't. I kiss the tip and give my attention to the other still-bandage-covered nipple. I'm careful as I peel the adhesive off. Then I go ahead and suck on that one, too. I peek up to check on Lily. Her eyes have that soft, glazed look about them. Her plush lips are parted, and her knees press hard against my sides. I bet if I move in a little closer she'll start rubbing on me.

I lick around her nipple, then do that almost-bite thing again. Her jaw snaps shut, and she shifts her hips.

"We're gonna have so much fucking fun tonight, Lily. You don't even know."

"Oh, I think I might."

I cover her mouth with mine, rolling her nipples between my fingers. I give a little pinch. She shrieks and grips my wrists.

I pull her closer, my lips on her neck, by her ear. "You don't like that?" I bite the lobe and grind my hips against hers.

Any kind of protest dies. Lily latches her legs around my back and does exactly what I expect her to: she starts rubbing on me, all sinew and heat. She takes my face in her hands and pulls me down. My teeth hit her lip, and I taste salt and copper.

"You okay?"

She makes a noise and pushes on my chest, looking around the pristine space. "Seriously. Why do we *always* end up in bathrooms?"

"I have no idea. Let's go get naked on the bed, since that's the reason we left the other bathroom."

"Way better plan."

I open the door and hit the light. Lily turns it back on, so I turn it off again. "We're trying to be incognito here, aren't we?"

"But I can't see anything."

"Your eyes will adjust." I lace our fingers and take a few steps toward the bed. At the sound of voices in the hallway I pause; it's Lance and Tash. He sounds pissed.

"Is someone fighting?" Lily whispers. She doesn't seem too concerned and starts unbuttoning my dress shirt.

"It's Tash and Lance. Apparently they're banging each other," I whisper back. A door slams, followed by the heavy tread of feet moving away.

"The hot chick who was feeling up your face earlier? The one with the rack?" She's on the fourth button.

"Tash doesn't have a rack."

"Everyone has a rack compared to me."

I palm her tits. "See this?"

She glances down. "They were so impressive when I was twelve."

Her nipples peek out between my index and middle fingers. "Your boobs are awesome. You don't have to wear a bra, and there isn't even any silicone keeping them up."

"That's because there's nothing to keep up."

I lean in until our lips are almost touching. "Take a fucking compliment, Lily."

All the bravado drops, and she looks almost innocent. "Sorry.

I'm not used to hearing nice things about my boobs. Benji used to make fun of my lack of chest."

"That guy is a fucking idiot." I'm way out of my usual zone. Bunnies aren't self-conscious. I get now why Miller was so adamant about being careful. That ex-boyfriend of hers has done some damage. My job now is to undo what I can without getting too involved.

As it stands, I'm happy to be Lily's rebound. We can have some fun times before she finds a guy who will give her what she needs, which is more than a good dose of cock.

She unfastens the last button on my shirt and pushes it over my shoulders. Her teeth press into her lip as I pull the cuffs free and let it drop to the floor. She sighs and runs her palms over my abs to my chest, following a path to my shoulders and then down my arms, lingering on the one with the ink.

"I work out."

"Really? I couldn't tell. Your boobs are almost as big as mine."

I grab a pec. "Are you calling these man boobs?"

She cups her own bare breasts and bounces them, then does the same to my chest. "Almost the same."

"That's it. I've had enough of that mouth." I launch us onto the bed, straddle her legs, and run my hands up her sides.

She shrieks and laughs when I find a ticklish spot at her ribs.

I put my mouth next to her ear. "Shh! Someone's gonna hear you and ruin our good time."

She presses her face against my chest, stifling her giggles. I ease her legs apart with my knee and settle between them, my hard-on right where I want it. The easy mood grows heavy, then hot as I smooth my hand up the outside of her thigh, her skirt bunching.

I slide a hand under her ass, feeling satiny fabric. Lily skims my arms with her fingertips, then threads them through my hair, pushing it back so it doesn't tickle her cheeks when I kiss her. We grind up on each other until I'm tired of too many clothes in the way of all the good parts.

I fold back on my knees and Lily sits up, going straight for my belt. I don't stop her. I planned to lose my pants anyway, so there's no harm in her helping out. She gets the buckle undone, pops the button, and unzips me. Before she can stick her hand in my boxers, I back up and step off the bed.

"Where're you going?" Her hands go immediately to her breasts, covering them.

It bugs me that she does that. "Stop hiding your body from me."

Her eyes go wide, and she bites her lip, but she eases her hands away from her chest and tucks them under her legs. "Sorry. It's a habit."

"Because of the ex?" She doesn't have to say anything; the way her eyes dart away tells me what I need to know. "If I ever see that guy again I'm going to beat his goddamn dick off with my hockey stick."

Lily gives a sharp laugh.

Pulling my wallet out, I flip it open and toss a couple of condoms to her.

She catches them and reads the label. "Seriously?"

"Seriously what?" I kick my pants off and lose my socks. I hate sex with socks on.

"Aren't these the big ones?"

"You've had your hand on my dick before, that shouldn't be a surprise."

"Feeling and seeing aren't the same thing."

"You don't think so?" I jump on the mattress before Lily can think about turning on one of the bedside lamps. The blinds let in enough illumination that I can see her without having to fumble around.

"'Kay, I'm ready." I get on top of her and start humping, because I'm stupid like that sometimes. And it's funny.

"What're you doing?" She's giggling again. I like that sound a lot.

"Shh. Not so loud."

I roll us to the top of the bed, so we're stuck in the pillows, push the covers halfway down and roll us back, shimmying around until we can slide under them. I make it so Lily's on top, straddling my hips. The top of her dress hangs loose around her waist, and the skirt rides high on her thighs. I sit up, find the zipper and tug it the rest of the way down.

"Lift your arms, gorgeous."

She raises them over her head, and I pull the dress up, purposely brushing her nipples on the way. I'm extra careful; seems like the dress might be fragile, so I don't want to wreck it.

I'm right about the panties; they're definitely satin, or something like it. There's a delicate lace band around all the edges, and they're pale. Pretty. Soft. Exactly like Lily.

I skim her sides, appreciating the narrow lines and fine curves. She's lean and strong. She's got a four-pack going on under that dress. I stick a finger in the waistband of her panties, pulling them back so I can peek inside. It's dark, though, and I can't see much of anything, so I go in a little farther.

"What are you checking for? You've had your fingers in my panties before; you know what's in there."

I glance up, taking in the smug look on her radiant face. "I've had a whole lot more than my fingers in there." I turn my palm to her stomach and slide my hand over smooth, wet, hot skin. "Feels like you visited your waxer."

"Were you hoping for the natural look?"

She's all snark until I rub her clit. Then her jaw drops, and she drags in a gasping breath. I push her back so she's lying on the pile of covers between my legs with her head near my feet. The elastic and lace of her panties stretch, and a faint tearing sound makes her grab my wrist.

"Don't ruin my underwear! I just bought them!"

Withdrawing my hand carefully, I lean forward and kiss her stomach. "Did you get them for me?"

"No. I needed new ones."

"I don't think I believe you." I suck on her skin as I go lower.

"That's because your ego is as big as your dick." The words come out a little breathless.

"So *now* you admit I've got a big dick?"

"I'd be stupid not to stroke your massive ego with your face where it is."

I laugh and kiss my way down to the lace, then shift her body away from mine so I can stay where I am and her pussy is right in my face. I slide my hands under her ass, forcing her to lift her hips. I lick a slow path along where her panties meet the juncture of her thigh.

Lily clutches my shins through the blankets. If not for the covering of fabric, I guarantee her nails would be cutting into skin. She lifts her hips higher, seeking my mouth.

I slip a finger under the material and circle her clit with my knuckle. She turns her head toward her shoulder and stifles a moan. I keep circling, kissing the inside of her thigh and sucking like I would if my mouth was where my knuckle is.

Lily bends her knees, her toes curling against my ribs. She

hooks her thumbs into her panties and pushes them over her hips. "I don't think we have enough time for all this teasing. Someone's going to notice we're gone. You should probably get in there and do your thing."

I glance up. Her cheeky grin falters a little, and her throat bobs with what could be a nervous swallow, or possibly anticipation. "You rushing me?" I ask.

"I'm just saying." She shimmies her panties down a little farther until they hit my nose. "We can always sneak up here again later. It's not like this is going to be the only opportunity. Right?"

"Here's hoping."

10

DO IT IN THE DARK

LILY

Randy tears my underwear off. Just shreds them with his bare hands. Okay, no he doesn't. I asked him not to. But he does stare at me intently as he removes them, slowly. It's almost unnerving. It's also superhot. I'm so naked. There's nothing but skin and his hands. Shadows move across the wall as lights flicker outside, highlighting all the defined, insanely hot muscles flexing in his arms.

Randy's broad shoulders are right between my thighs, and that mouth of his is about to hit my hot spot. I'm so ready. I'm also a little worried about how fast I'm going to come. Everything's already starting to tighten up, and I've got that familiar tingly feeling going on. It's not from the mint-cucumber wipes, either. I don't want to give him anything else to brag about. He's smug enough as it is.

He smoothes his rough hands over the insides of my thighs. God, that tattooed arm is sexy as hell. I hope those fingers are the ones he puts inside me. Apparently Randy takes me seriously on the time-constraint business; he doesn't bother teasing me any more. Instead, he lifts my ass and drops his head.

I don't know what I expect. Maybe a little kissy-kiss on the lips first, or one of those flat-stroke test licks, or even a nose rub. That sure isn't what I get. Randy closes his mouth over my clit and sucks like he's the black hole of cunnilingus. I have zero control over my body's reaction. I jolt like I've been shocked. And honestly, that's kind of how it feels—like I've been zapped in the vagina.

I bow off the bed, fighting to stay at least a little composed. The last time he did this—against a bathroom wall while I was sitting on his shoulders—I couldn't stop the orgasm from bitch slapping me across the magic marble. Randy lifts me higher and does a crazy swirl thing with his tongue.

I don't have traction anymore; my feet are barely touching the mattress. I find purchase on his thigh and turn my head into the covers so I can groan without letting anyone in the hall know how much I'm enjoying being Randy's dinner, or dessert, or his goddamn sex buffet. His teeth graze my clit as he resumes sucking. I can't handle it. I'm right at the edge, knocking on orgasm's door.

"Holy fu—" I bite the side of my hand to stop all the sounds from coming out. That's when the trembling starts. Every single cell in my body is electrified. I wish there was more light. It's mostly shadow where his head is, and his hair keeps tickling my thighs, adding to the sensation. Not that it matters right now—the entire world goes white. The comforter bunches in my hands. I know I'm writhing around, probably making it difficult for him to keep his mouth on me, but I can't help it. It's the best orgasm I've had in my entire life.

There's movement on the bed that isn't associated with my ridiculous thrashing. Randy's legs are no longer on either side of me, under the covers, preventing me from throwing myself off the bed in my orgasmic zeal. Not to worry, though, now he's right in my face. He swipes the back of his hand across his mouth and then his lips are on mine: hard, demanding, and oh so hot.

I don't even have time to recover. He finds my wet, swollen clit—at least I'm guessing it's swollen based on how much sucking he did—and starts rubbing again. I don't think I've even finished having one orgasm and already he's inciting another. It's insane.

Just when I'm sure I can't handle any more, he goes low and slides a single finger inside me. After two slow thrusts, he adds a second one. I'd say it's unnecessary preparation, but based on the domes he's packing, I think it might be wise to let him finger-bang me. Besides, who am I to say no to yet another orgasm? He breaks our kiss and sits back on his knees. Even with the subpar lighting situation, I can see he's tenting his boxers. And yes, he is using the fingers on the tattooed arm to get me off.

I don't know why it's so sexy. I've never been into tattoos before. Or beards. Or man buns. I don't dislike any of the aforementioned accessories, though the tattoos seem like a lot of pain and a substantial commitment. But all that marked skin makes the ride on the orgasm train that much better. I push up on my arms, hoping to get a better view of what's going on between my legs.

The way Randy's body is positioned makes it more, rather than less, difficult to see what's happening. It's better than no view at all, I suppose. What I really want to do is reach over and hit a bedside lamp, even if it means people will know we're in here. Instead I go for the one other thing I want almost as much as a good visual: Randy's cock. It's awkward getting to his boxers, but I'm determined to put my hand on him while he's got his fingers in me. Then maybe I'll give blowing him a try.

As soon as I touch the waistband, Randy grips my wrist—gently but firmly—and shakes his head. "I don't need the distraction."

"Maybe I do." I try again with my other hand, but he swats it away, too.

"You'll get some of that soon enough." He has this dark, intense look on his face.

Then he curls his fingers and hits that spot I have to work so hard to reach on my own. I give up trying to get to his trouser anaconda and let him give me yet another nerve-shattering orgasm. When I'm done coming, I discover I've been magically repositioned on the bed so my head is on a pillow. Randy runs his hand over the comforter until something crinkles.

He holds up one of the gold foil wrappers. "You still interested in this?"

"Pretty sure that's what I came up here for."

"Are you always this snarky?"

"Mostly." I don't mention that part of it is nerves and being outside of my comfort zone. None of the guys I've been with in the past are anything like Randy. Not as hot, not as well endowed, not as skilled, not as smooth.

"I like it." He pulls the covers over us, cocooning us in cotton, or whatever these extra-soft sheets are made of. "Mostly."

I hear rather than see him tear the wrapper. He must be a master condom roller because he's suddenly between my legs. I don't know how he lost his boxers, but there's just hot skin against hot skin. And latex, of course. Randy runs the head of his cock along my slit a few times.

"I'm goin' in," he whispers.

I laugh, then exhale sharply as the head probes low and he

shifts forward—just the tip, though.

"Okay. I'm in."

I snort.

He pushes in a little farther. "That's all I've got."

I bite his shoulder, or some part of him. I can't see to know since we're still covered in blankets. "Seriously, Ballistic? What'd you do, put your balls inside the condom, too?"

He makes a noise like he's holding back a laugh. "You're not last-naming me while I'm fucking you, are you? That's a no-go, right there." He pushes up on his arms.

"I think you're forgetting I've had my hand on that cock. I know there's more to it than a button in a bush." I wrap my arms around his neck and hook my ankles at his waist. Essentially he's doing a pushup with me attached to his body now. I tilt my hips and, despite being suspended in air, I manage to get him to go a little deeper.

"I don't have a bush."

I'm almost positive he's gritting his teeth. "It's a figure of speech."

"Is it, now?"

I have eighteen years of figure skating under my belt. I'm strong, fit, and limber. I can do things with my body most people can't—including remaining suspended in air for a significant period of time. I'm also heavier than I look. I might be what girls call "skinny," but I'm one-hundred-percent muscle. Okay, not quite, but I have seriously low body fat. And I have zero cellulite. Girls hate my ass. Literally, it's perfect. I got a nice ass instead of nice boobs; it's a fair trade, I guess.

"Okay, maybe it's more of a euphemism, but I'm not sure why that matters. Why aren't you fucking me like you've been talking about doing for the past goddamn month?"

Randy lowers himself until my back hits the mattress again and his chest is pressed against mine. Then he shifts his hips forward. "You mean like this?"

And there it is. The reason for the Magnums. Mother of all things holy, is he ever equipped. I think I might moan. I'm not sure.

"Or do you mean more like this?" He starts to move—filling and retreating, over and over, harder and harder.

"Oh my God." It's definitely more groan than words—not like it matters. I'm sure the way I'm clinging to him is a decent indicator of exactly what I mean.

Randy throws the covers off, which is a relief because I'm getting sweaty under these blankets, and I'm wearing actual makeup. I don't want it to start melting. At least the sheets are dark, so it's not going to stain if any of it rubs off on them. He leans to the left, and the angle is beyond stellar.

All of a sudden I'm blinded by light. Not the light of orgasm, but the light of the bedside lamp. Randy cradles my head, his palm resting at the nape of my neck.

"Now you want the lights on?"

"I want to see your face when I fuck you."

I don't dare close my eyes. Blinking almost isn't an option. Any snarky comment dies when he stops thrusting and starts grinding. *Holy fuck.* I'm not prepared for this. At all. I've never seen anyone look so… primal? Like he wants to… ravage? Consume?

The hand that isn't holding my head skims my hip and hooks behind my knee, drawing it up until it's at his ribs, making him go even deeper. I think I may actually implode when this orgasm hits. I can feel it, traveling through my spine, spreading like electric fingers across my skin. I figure I might as well go one step further and rest my ankle on his shoulder.

And there it is. My cells are grenades. My nerve endings blast like tiny land mines, centered in my clit. The tremor in my body is uncontrollable. It's a whole-system failure. The moan that comes out of me is so loud I scare myself. I'm trying to keep my eyes open, but nothing registers aside from the orgasm.

And Randy keeps going, and going, and going, hips pumping and muscles straining as he holds himself over me. At least I can see again, for now. His jaw is tight, eyes on fire, breath washing over my face in hard pants. He's so close, still watching me. Jesus. This man sure knows how to fuck.

I think I'm fully recovered from the last orgasm, and another one punches me in the clit. His name comes out all garbled. I latch onto his hair, then worry with my lack of control that I'll rip it out, so I hold onto his shoulders instead. I can't rip those off.

His steady thrust turns erratic and harsh, his coordination faltering. His eyes roll up and flutter shut briefly as this sound comes out of him—it's exactly the noise I'll associate with man-orgasms for the rest of my life.

When he opens his eyes again, they're heavy and lust-soaked. He sinks into me, his weight pushing me into the pillows and mattress like he's trying to get deeper inside, which isn't possible because I'm as full up as I can get. Lily's Vagina Emporium is at maximum cock capacity.

Randy's mouth crashes down on mine, his tongue pushing past my lips. I'm not sure if he's having a seriously long orgasm, or he's drawing it out, or he doesn't want to stop, but he's still going. He's changed from thrusting back to a slow hip roll. Eventually he stops moving and breaks the kiss.

He pushes up, the muscles in his arms twitching. "How's it

goin'?" It comes out all gravelly. Even his post-sex voice is hot.

I clear my throat. "Uh, pretty good."

His eyebrows rise. "Pretty good?"

I blow out a breath. It makes his hair flutter around his face. It's almost the same length as mine when it's not up in his little man-bun thingy. I shrug. Well, I try to, but it's not all that easy with the way I'm lying down, my head half sunk between two pillows. "Yeah, pretty good sounds about right. I'd give that a seven out of ten."

"Seven?" It sounds like a vulgar expletive.

Oh, God. He looks pissed. This is way too fun. I should probably stop while I'm ahead, but I can't. "Seven-point-two?"

"Don't kid yourself, Lily. That was a ten-point-oh. No questions."

"You think you're that good a lay, do you?"

"I'm not talking about my performance; I'm talking about yours." He puts his mouth to my ear. "*Oooh, Raaandy.*"

It's actually a decent impression of me, though highly embarrassing.

"But seriously, you had fun?" His fingertips are soft on my cheek.

"Yeah, I had fun."

He smiles, and it's beautiful. "Good. That's what I want. As long as you're having a good time with me. We're just going to have some easy fun, okay? If that changes or, like, the sex drops below nine-point-oh or things start getting too intense or whatever, you let me know."

I think it's already intense, but I get what he's saying without him having to spell it out. We're just enjoying each other, and this—what we're doing right now—is as far as it's going to go. Which I already knew.

A knock on the door prevents me from responding.

Randy opens his mouth to speak, so I do the most reasonable thing I can think of: I grab his hair and bring his face to mine. He still tries to talk, but it's a lot more challenging with my tongue in his mouth.

He doesn't fight me on the kissing. Instead he starts back up with the humping. I'm not nearly as full as I was before—I'm assuming that's because he's getting soft—but it still feels good. I forget there's a reason for the spontaneous making out until another more-vigorous knock startles me.

"Lily? Are you in there?"

Randy pulls away and grins. I put a hand over his mouth to keep him from talking.

After a few seconds of silence Sunny says, "They're about to serve dinner."

Then she's talking to someone in the hall. "I have no idea. I saw her the last time you saw her. I'm calling her phone."

"At least she waited until it was over," Randy whispers from behind my hand.

"Shh!"

He sticks his tongue between my fingers. I snatch my hand away and press my face into his shoulder, biting him to keep from laughing.

All of a sudden my phone starts ringing. I push on Randy's chest, and he rolls off me. I scramble across the room to get it, even though it's too late.

"I know you're in there, Lily! I can hear your phone!" Sunny rattles the knob.

I cut the call, which is pointless. I look over at Randy, and I'm sure my eyes are wide. I don't know what I'm so worried about. It's not like Sunny doesn't know I was planning to do the dirty with Randy. She provided her opinion, which is that I should treat it as a fling, because logically that's what it is—and Randy's confirmed this. I'm good with that. It's not my usual thing, but I'm living a little.

"Give us a minute!" Randy calls out in his still-raspy sex voice.

"Balls?" Miller asks.

"Yeah."

"Seriously? You two couldn't wait until later to bone each other?"

"We were just talking," Randy calls back.

"Bullshit!" Miller rattles the door this time.

"Miller! You're gonna break the handle off!"

"I'm fucking around, sweets."

Randy pulls his boxers up and tucks himself away. I don't get so much as a glimpse of his unit before it disappears. He picks up my dress from the floor, his gaze roaming over my totally naked body. He passes it to me and tweaks one of my nipples while my hands are occupied. I suck in a breath, and he smirks. Then he reaches for the doorknob.

"What're you doing? I'm naked!" I whisper-shout, gripping his arm. The one covered in tattoos. The one with the fingers that were inside me not all that long ago.

"I'm not letting them in. I'm just gonna talk to Miller not through a door."

We're both sweaty. My hair feels damp. It smells like sex and latex in here. Randy's hair is a mess. I'm sure my vagina is all over his beard. He's got scratch and bite marks on his shoulders. Apparently I'm aggressive during sex.

"Well, wait until I have some clothes on, please!" The dress is inside out, and the lamplight doesn't make it any easier to figure out which way around it's supposed to be. Randy turns on the overhead light to help.

"The price tag is still on that," he points out.

"I know. I'm returning it when I get home."

"What? Why? You're smokin' hot in that dress."

"It's not like I'll have anywhere to wear it again."

He reaches over and yanks the tag free. "You can wear it tomorrow night, when I take you out for dinner."

He crumples the tag in his fist and flips the lock, opening the door.

I shove my hands through the straps and pull the top up so my boobs aren't on display. Sunny may have seen them before, but I don't need Miller checking me out.

"Dude!" Miller says. "You couldn't even put on clothes? Sunny, don't look."

"It's not like I haven't seen him in swim shorts before. Oh, wow. You might wanna do—something with …" She makes a sound and then stops talking.

"Where's Lily?" Miller doesn't sound happy.

"I'm right here." I step out from behind Randy—he's broad and tall enough to hide behind. "Can you zip me up?"

"Sure thing." He tugs the zipper, skimming my spine along the way. I shiver at the gentle press of his lips between my shoulders.

Miller makes an unimpressed noise.

"Oh, no." Sunny claps a hand over her mouth.

"What?"

"Your hair!"

"What about it?" I touch the front. It's flipping out instead of under right now, but that's not a big deal. I can always attribute it to the humidity.

“No, the back! Sunny shoves her way past Miller and Randy and takes my hand, leading me to the bathroom. She turns on the light, slams the door shut, and locks it. Taking me by the shoulders, she turns me to face the mirror.

“Oh, shit!” The back of my hair is like a peacock. It gives new meaning to bedhead. There was a lot of vigorous thrusting. The state of my hair reflects that. My skin is flushed, and the rest of my hair has started to curl out at the ends, but otherwise, I don’t look too bad—I don’t think, anyway.

“Everything okay in there, ladies?” Miller asks.

Sunny opens the door and jabs a finger in Randy’s direction. “I’m fixing Lily’s sex hair, no thanks to you!”

He’s already got his pants back on and is shrugging into his shirt. It’s a whole lot wrinkly now. Sunny closes the door and locks it again, then starts finger-combing out the knots.

“Ow!”

“Stop whining and help me! Dinner’s already started, and people are wondering where the two of you are.”

“I bet no one even noticed.”

“Alex did.” She turns on the tap and lowers her voice. “You’ve been gone more than an hour!”

“We have not.”

“Oh, yes. You have. It’s almost eight.”

“No way.”

“Yes way.” Her fingers get caught in my tangled hair, and she struggles to pull them free. “So?”

“So what?”

She lowers her voice even more. “Don’t *so what* me. How was it?”

“Remember how I told you about that spontaneous orgasm I had before?”

"Did that happen again?" She says it way louder than she should.

"Shh!"

She mouths *sorry*. "Did it?"

"No, but it was the same kind of orgasm. So intense. I don't even know how to describe it. God, Sunny, the sex was incredible."

"Better than with Benji?"

"There isn't even a comparison."

"See? I knew a fling was exactly what you needed. Sometimes there's no replacement for hot sex."

"Yeah. Totally." No strings. No attachments. Just a whole lot of awesome orgasms.

11

ALL THE THWARTS

RANDY

Miller's pissed at me. I don't see why. It's not like anyone but Lily's going to sleep on those sexed-up sheets. And no one cares if we go missing. We're not essential to the party.

"Think you can wait until the end of the night before you lock Lily in another bedroom to get your dick wet?" he grumbles as we head down the stairs.

I fasten my cuff and smooth a hand down my shirt. It's wrinkled from being on the floor, but I'm not the focus tonight, so it's doubtful people will notice. "What's your problem, man? Lily says you two have been disappearing all day. If you'd invited me to come early, maybe I could have kept her company."

He grits his teeth. "Seriously, Balls, I'm not in the mood for this right now. Violet's hammered, and we're trying to get her sobered up so she doesn't say something stupider than she usually does. I don't have time to police you and your dick. Lily's like part of Sunny's family. Alex is almost as protective of her as he is of Sunny. You see how you're not helping things?"

"Does he have a thing for her?" A hot feeling shoots down the back of my spine.

"For Lily? No."

"Did he ever?"

"How should I know? That's not relevant anyway, considering he's marrying my sister. My issue right now is that it makes Lily look bad if you're hauling her off to bang her all over the house. Alex won't like it. I've worked way too hard to smooth things over with him for you to go fucking it up by screwing Lily around."

"I've already told you, I'm not screwing her around."

Miller rubs his forehead. "I know you're not trying to, just use a little judgment. You're in Waters' house. He's already stressed. He doesn't need a reason to snap."

Lily and Sunny come out of the bathroom, ending our conversation. Lily looks just as gorgeous as she did before I got her naked and made a nest of her hair. It's still a little tangled, but I can't imagine anyone noticing, other than present company.

Honestly, all I want to do is bail on this party, take Lily back to my place, and fuck her until she has to leave for Canada. She is everything I like in a woman, plus she skates. And she's on the rebound. So I'm nothing but a gateway to the next guy. It's the absolute perfect setup. Miller's getting his balls in a knot over nothing.

Lily's eyes settle on mine. There are questions in them. She probably wants to know what I've been saying to Miller while she and Sunny have been in the bathroom. She holds Sunny's arm while she slips her feet into her heels.

Miller gives me a look, which I ignore. I thread my arm through Lily's. "Ready for dinner?"

"Where's my underwear?" she whispers.

I have no idea. Once they came off I had no interest in putting them back on. "You don't need them."

"But I—"

"We need to get down there. Charlene keeps texting. I think Violet's having a hard time," Sunny says while checking her phone.

"We'll find them later." I squeeze the back of her neck and Lily leans into me, holding my arm as she hums. I don't know what that's about, but I like the way I affect her. I bet I could get hard again right now without much work.

Dinner is going to be so much fun.

I let Lily go ahead with Sunny and follow Miller out of the room. He's still in a mood. I assume he's worried about Vi. Those two are tight for being stepbrother and sister. They're exactly how siblings should be, except they do a lot of sharing. And not the kind you want from someone you're related to.

A huge covered tent with tables and twinkle lights has been set up in the backyard. Everyone's already seated, so it's a bit of a production for us to get to the table assigned to us.

We get a few looks as we make our way through the maze of guests. Lance is at our table when we get there. Tash looks less than impressed right now. She's pushing salad around on her plate and talking to a girl I don't know. The chair beside her is empty, although it looks like someone's been there based on the napkin placement.

I take the seat beside Lance and hold out the other one for Lily. She smoothes her hands down the backs of her thighs as she sits, reminding me that flimsy fabric is the only thing covering that sweet, hot pussy. I tuck her in close to the table and take a seat.

"What've you been up to?" Lance gives me a knowing grin.

"Just gettin' a tour of the house. We miss anything?" I stretch my arm across the back of Lily's chair.

She crosses her legs and pulls her chair in a little tighter, but she doesn't look my way. She's focused on Sunny and her phone.

"Nothing yet, but I have a feeling something's brewing. Waters' girl is hammered." His eyebrows lift, like he's excited for the show.

I check out the head table, not far from us. It's no different than ours. Violet and Alex, along with Darren and his girl, sit with the parents. It's a weird collection of people. Violet's mom looks exactly like she does, just older. They have the same body, same face, same mannerisms. Sidney, Miller's dad, looks a lot like Miller, but with darker hair, and less of it. Violet tries to pour herself a glass of wine, but her friend switches the bottle for a different one. Waters leans in and says something, and Violet gives him a pouty face.

When Waters tips her chin up, I look away. Miller's expressed concern on multiple occasions that this whole engagement party might be a little much for Violet. He says she gets nervous in front of people. There must be a story there, but he hasn't offered to tell it.

Miller pours Sunny a glass of wine. I trail a finger up the side of Lily's neck. She inhales a tremulous breath, and goosebumps rise along her skin.

"Cold?" It's warm for late September, and heat lamps are set up all over the place, but Lily doesn't have much in the way of body fat.

She gives me a strained smile. "I'm fine."

"You want something to drink?"

"It's okay. I can get it." She reaches for the bottle of wine in the center of the table. As she stands, the back of her dress rides up. I stand and move behind her so no one gets a view they shouldn't.

"It's okay, baby, let me do that for you." I put my palms on her shoulders, thumbs smoothing down the ridges of her spine, fingertips caressing her collarbones. Lily drops back into her chair, her fingers brushing along mine, close to her throat. Everyone is looking at me. Or her.

I don't know why it's such a big deal that I'm considerate enough to get my date a damn drink. I pour her a glass of wine, then offer it to everyone else to make a point before I sit back down. Kirk drops down in the empty seat across the table. He drags the chair the blond girl is sitting in closer to him so he can use it as an armrest. She nearly spills her wine all over her dress. Fortunately, it's black, and she doesn't seem to care. He rests his elbow on the back of her chair. He's got pit stains. And his forehead is sweaty.

"You guys get lost in the bathroom or something?" Kirk winks at Lily.

"They were getting the house tour," Tash says, then goes back to chatting with the blonde and ignoring Lance.

I scoot my chair closer to Lily and put an arm around her. It's not that I feel some kind of ownership, or the need to stake a claim, or that we're having a pissing contest; Kirk's a dickface. He's the kind of guy I don't ever want to become.

He's approaching the end of his career. Winning the Cup last year bought him an extra season. But he's pretty much done. Now that his wife has finally left him and taken his kids, he's all about getting the bunny action.

He didn't make a mistake once or twice; he did it all the damn time. Like being away from home was a reason to fuck someone other than the person he married.

I remember the fights my parents used to have when they

thought I was asleep. The nights my dad came home from away games were always the worst. When I was old enough, I could've stayed at Miller's, but then I would've had to leave my sister to deal with it alone, and she was too young. It was a lot of years of listening to screaming matches and tears before my mom finally had enough of the bullshit. I don't see much of my dad. I don't have much use for him. My sister moved all the way to Australia last year for school, so she sees him even less.

Lily's hand on my thigh pulls me out of the dark spiral of my thoughts. I realize I'm glaring at Kirk and give my attention to her. Her smile is tight, questioning. "You okay?" she whispers.

I shift her chair so she's right up next to me and brush my nose against her cheek. She shivers. "I'll be better after dinner's over."

"You're not hungry?" She pokes at her salad.

I don't think she's eaten anything. Based on how lean she is, and how active, and how incredibly flexible, I don't think it's advisable that she misses any meals.

"I'm hungry, but not for this." I stab some lettuce, so I'm a good role model, and shove it in my mouth, chewing slowly.

She spears a lone leaf and regards me thoughtfully. "What're you hungry for?"

"You. Come home with me tonight." I don't consider the words before they're out. I just say them. If she was a bunny, the answer would always be yes.

"I-I—" She removes her hand from my leg. "I can't. What would I tell Sunny's parents?"

"You don't have to tell them anything."

"I've been invited to stay with Alex and his family for the weekend. We have some kind of shopping thing we're doing tomorrow."

"I'll drop you off early, then pick you up later, for dinner."

"Don't you think it's kind of rude to take off so I can have my brains screwed out?"

"Is that what you think I want to do?"

"Isn't it?" She arches a brow.

"What if I just want to talk?"

"In moans?"

I laugh. She's a funny girl. I really do want to screw her brains out, without having to worry about anyone interrupting, or either of us having to be quiet. "If you don't feel comfortable coming home with me tonight, you should at least plan to stay over tomorrow."

"You're determined to get me back into a bed." She stabs another piece of lettuce and takes a bite.

"The bed isn't the most important part; it's the getting you naked again part." I trail a finger across the back of her dress from shoulder to shoulder.

She shivers. "I can't do a sleepover. My flight's super early on Monday. I have to work in the afternoon." She looks at me, her bottom lip caught between her teeth. "You could crash here tonight."

"I haven't been invited."

"No one'll notice."

I spend the rest of dinner trying to get my hand up Lily's skirt while she tries to eat. It's next to impossible because of how close we're sitting together. It's a good thing I'm a lefty and she's a righty, otherwise I'd have to leave more space. She excuses herself to the bathroom, and I think it's going to be the perfect opportunity to follow her out for a quickie, but Sunny goes with her.

I'll never understand why girls have to go to the bathroom in packs. It doesn't make sense. And it's messing with my ability to get back inside Lily. Whatever. I can wait until after dessert. Post-food there'll definitely be an opportunity to disappear again.

Sadly, by the time dinner's over, the girls have all vanished over some Violet-related emergency. Miller, Lance, and I are standing around, drinking beers while we wait for them to figure out what the problem is. Miller keeps getting texts from Sunny and passing his phone to me. Despite the fact that they've been dating nearly six months, Sunny still uses a lot of text slang, and that doesn't work for Miller.

The short forms combined with numbers and missing vowels make the messages difficult for him to read. Most of the time I send him voice memos. It's way easier. He's got a memory like a steel trap if he's told the information rather than having to read it.

"Says something about the moops." I pass the phone back.

"What are moops?" Lance asks.

"Violet can't handle dairy; it gives her problems." Miller hands me his phone again. There are more messages from Sunny.

"Problems?"

"It goes right through her," Miller says.

Lance pulls a face. "That's nasty. Why would she eat dairy if it makes her sick?"

"She does it to punish herself or something. Girls are messed. I don't get it. I also don't understand why she'd eat dairy today of all days. Maybe it wasn't intentional." He rubs his head as I scan the new texts. They keep coming in. The last one is personal, and pertains to activities later in the night, so I message her back and let her know it's me reading because of all the slang. She sends back an *oops* and a blushy face.

"Violet's broken out in hives. Also, Sunny's looking forward to cookie-eating later."

Miller snatches back his phone. "That's not gonna happen if we can't get Violet under control. I wanna know who gave her dairy." Miller looks worried, which has been his expression most of the night. "I think I need to talk to Waters. He's gotta stop pushing the wedding crap on her. They're living together. He needs to back off a little and give her some damn breathing room. She's obviously not ready for this shit." He drains his beer and sets it on the closest table. "I'mma go find him."

"I'll come with you." It's more to keep those two off each other than anything else. Miller's protective of Violet, even though they're not related by blood. He's like that, though, super loyal. He doesn't let anyone mess around with the people who're important to him.

"You coming or staying?" I ask Lance.

He shrugs. "Might as well see what's going on."

Miller gives him a look. "How long's this shit with Tash been going on, anyway?"

"What're you talking about?" Lance gets real busy staring into his beer.

"Romero, come on," Miller says.

"A while."

"You better watch it. Coach finds out he's gonna be pissed," I say, following Miller through the house.

"He won't. Tash is looking for a ride more than anything." He drains the rest of his beer. "She just wants to see what all the hype is about."

He sounds bitter, which is odd, because Lance is probably the biggest player in the league. After Miller got serious about Sunny and we'd go out, he constantly pawned the chicks off on one of us. Lance was always good with taking on more than one. I don't like having my attention divided.

We find Lily, Tash, and Alex standing outside a door at the top of the stairs. Sunny must be in the room. Alex keeps trying the knob, but it's clearly locked.

"What's going on?" Miller asks.

Lily turns; her gaze stops at me for a second, and her hand flutters to her throat. "Violet's not feeling well."

"I know. Sunny's been messaging me." Miller holds up his phone.

"She won't let me in," Alex looks wrecked. His tie is half-hanging off.

"I keep telling you, Waters, you're pushing her too hard. She hates this kind of thing, and you let my mom and yours run with this. Now they're gonna expect something even bigger when it comes to the damn wedding."

"She said it was okay," he snaps.

Miller scoffs. "Do you even know who you're marrying? Do you remember the first time you met her and she flashed every member of the team her bra?"

"She didn't do that on purpose."

I've only heard this story secondhand, but apparently it was epic.

Miller throws his hands up in the air. "Exactly! That's the point. Embarrassing crap happens to her all the time. She doesn't want to be humiliated. She probably thinks this is gonna be exactly like her mom's wedding."

"You mean another wardrobe malfunction?" Lily asks.

"Wardrobe malfunction? What are you talking about?" Alex asks.

I'm wondering the same thing.

Miller's eyebrows rise. "She hasn't even told you?"

"Told me what?" Alex looks somewhere between confused and angry.

Miller lets out a long breath and shakes his head. "I wish she'd damn well learn how to talk about shit." Miller knocks on the door. "Vi, open up. We need to have a discussion about you not telling your fiancé highly important information."

After another minute or two, Sunny finally comes out. "She says she'll talk to you." She's not looking at Alex, though, she's looking at Miller.

"You can thank me later." Miller disappears inside the room.

Waters rubs his forehead. "All we were supposed to do was thank everyone for coming."

"You sure you want to go through with this whole getting-married deal?" Lance asks. "Seems like kinda a pain in the ass."

Tash rolls her eyes. "You're such a dick, Romero."

"You seemed to like it enough earlier," he fires back.

Tash's mouth drops open.

Lily holds up a hand and snaps, "Enough, you two." She turns to Alex. "Why don't you go down and do the thank you? Unless you'd like me to do that on your behalf. Then we can start wrapping things up and get people out of here. That might help Violet be less stressed."

He taps on the door, regarding Lily for a long while. "I wanted this to be fun for her."

She rubs his shoulder. "You can't make everyone happy, Alex. I love your mom, but you gotta rein her in if you don't want Violet to fall apart between now and this wedding."

His head drops and he sighs. "Fuck, I'm a pussy."

Lily laughs. "No, you're not. You're trying to make too many people happy at the same time. Violet has to be priority number one all the time now. Above everything else."

Eventually they manage to get Violet to come out of the bedroom, but she's covered in hives. Alex goes downstairs to deal with the guests, and the girls all huddle in the bedroom to provide moral support or whatever it is girls do when one of them has an emotional breakdown and winds up with hives.

No one seems to question Violet's absence at the party.

Lily messages me a while later to let me know she's staying with Violet. I'm not surprised considering how tight she is with the Waters family. I end up getting a ride home with Lance and Tash. It's awkward; no one really talks. Tash seems pissed, all quiet and brooding in the front seat. Lance drops me off first, which I expect.

I walk up my drive and palm my phone, keying in the code for my door so it's unlocked by the time I reach it. This definitely wasn't how I thought tonight was going to end. I'm glad I managed a little alone time with Lily. And at least I have tomorrow.

I'm on high alert the second I walk into the house. The TV's on in the living room, and there's a body on my couch, shoes hanging off the end. Beer bottles and a half liter of vodka litter my coffee table. One of the bottles has tipped over, and beer drips onto the floor. I'm definitely not in the mood for this. The body on my couch groans and pushes to a sitting position.

It's like I've stepped into a time machine and I'm looking at a much less fit, older version of myself. Without tattoos. Randall Ballistic Senior is crashed out on my couch.

"How'd you get in here?" It's not a friendly greeting, but I don't like my dad much.

"I tried the code from your New York place. Nice pad, kiddo. They're paying you better than they did me." He's slurry drunk.

I don't mention that I'm a better player than he was. "I didn't know you were in town."

He ignores the indirect question. "You're comin' home late." He pushes up and tries to stand, but ends up falling back down on his ass.

I stuff my hands in my pockets. Now I wish I'd gotten an invite to stay at Waters'. "I was at a party."

"And no bunny? You losing your touch?"

"It wasn't that kind of party."

"It's always that kind of party." He picks up a bottle from the table and checks to see if there's anything left.

I go to the kitchen to get him a glass of water and a rag to clean up the mess he's made. It's the story of my dad's life. He's a loser in every sense of the word. Returning to the living room, I mop up the spilled beer and set the water on the table.

He picks up the glass and frowns. "Where's the booze?"

"I don't think you need it." I collect the empty bottles. "Look, you're welcome to stay the night and sleep it off, but I've got plans tomorrow night, so you gotta be gone in the morning."

"I haven't seen you in six months, and that's how you treat your dad? Don't be so damn disrespectful."

"It's one in the morning, and I find you lying on my couch, messing up my house, and you're talking at me about disrespect?"

"I need a place to crash for a couple days. I gotta lay low. Got some business I need to take care of before I head home."

"You're still in Boston?"

"I'm between places right now."

I run a hand through my hair. "So by a couple of days you mean what exactly?"

"A week, maybe two, tops."

I definitely don't want my dad here for the next week, let

alone two, but he's hammered, so discussing it now is pointless. I'd set him up in a hotel, but the last time I did that he racked up a two-thousand-dollar room service bill. Half of it was porn. It's not that I don't have the money to pay for it, it's the goddamn principle. And he's generally a dick.

"Right. We'll talk about it in the morning. I gotta crash. I've got a workout at ten." That's a lie, but talking to my dad in this state isn't productive. It's not that useful when he's sober, either. Looks like the rest of my weekend has gone to shit.

12

FLUTTERY EYED FEAR

LILY

At one-thirty in the morning, I'm back in my room at Alex's huge, nice house. Alone. Violet's hives have finally subsided after a boatload of Benadryl, and everyone else has gone to bed. Probably to have awesome sex. I bet even Violet and Alex are having sex, though she still has a few welts on her face. I'd hate to be that stressed out over getting married.

I change into a pair of tights with a hole in the crotch and one of my T-shirts from high school. They still fit exactly the same since I haven't grown even a little bit since then—not anywhere. I don't have to pull down the sheets because they're already messed up from earlier.

I still can't believe I did that. Well, I can. It was part of my plan, but not quite so early in the evening. I figured it'd be later, like now. I step on something gushy and shriek. Jumping back, I discover the used condom.

"So gross," I mutter to myself. At least he had the courtesy to tie it in a knot so the jizz didn't ooze out and end up between my toes. I snap a picture of it beside my foot and send it to him with a frowny face. I don't get anything back right away, which is kind of a disappointment.

I toss my phone on the bed and rummage through my bag, looking for face wash. I do the nightly routine, still bitter that everyone is getting action now but me. I leave the light on in the bathroom and pull the door mostly closed, leaving a sliver of illumination to guide me to bed. Of course I step on the stupid condom again.

I drop down on the comforter, the empty condom wrapper crinkling under me. I roll over, find it, and toss it on the floor. Now I have that awful spermicide crap on my hands. I should probably shower, but I don't feel like it. I mash my face into the pillows. The scent of Randy's cologne lingers. I close my eyes, tingles starting up as I think about the amazing sex.

Sadly, now I know just how mediocre it was with Benji, and how average his dick seems in comparison. I don't know if all hockey players have giant man rods, but it seems to be the case from what Sunny reports and what I accidentally saw of Alex when I was a teenager.

As I ponder the size of man's most useful appendage, my phone rings. I pick it up, and my stomach does that fluttery thing. It's Randy. Calling me. I let it ring twice more before I answer. "Thanks for the rubbery gift."

"Sorry, 'bout that. I usually clean up after myself, but the interruption made me sloppy. Next time I'll be the good Boy Scout I am."

I try to picture Randy as a Boy Scout. All I get is an image of him at twelve with a beard. "Pretty presumptuous assuming there'll be a next time."

"You didn't have fun?"

"It was okay." I rub my legs together, thinking about how

good okay is.

He laughs. "You're terrible for my ego. You know that, right?"

"If it's anywhere as big as your trouser anaconda, you don't need help in that area anyway."

"Nice backhanded compliment. I'll take it. How's Vi?"

"She's fine now. I think, anyway. It's hard to tell with her. Alex is worried, but then that's kind of how he is. I'm sorry you had to leave."

"Yeah, me too."

"We can still do dinner tomorrow, if you want." I let it hang like it's a question.

"Yeah, about that—"

My stomach sinks, and I get that thick feeling in my throat.

"Something's kinda come up."

"Oh. Yeah. Of course." Maybe Randy lied about my performance being a ten out of ten.

"It's family stuff. Otherwise—"

"You don't have to explain."

"I don't want you to think I'm blowing you off. My dad showed up tonight, and I wasn't expecting him."

My relief worries me. "You don't sound too happy about that. Is everything okay?"

"Yeah. It'll be fine—once he's gone. He's kind of an asshole, and I'm not sure how long I'm going to have to deal with him before he takes off, though."

"I'm sorry."

"It is what it is. I would much rather be taking you out."

"Would it make you feel better if I told you it would've been hard to pull off anyway? We're having some kind of retail therapy tomorrow to make Violet feel better, and that'll probably go all day."

Randy chuckles. "I'd tell you yes, but that'd be me lying. I guess we'll have to try again another time."

"Sure."

"Maybe the next time I play in Toronto or something."

"That'd be fun."

"Don't feel obligated or anything. I'm having a good time with you, Lily, but if it's not, like, your thing, or you think it's getting to be too much, you let me know, okay?"

"Too much how? Like, too many orgasms?" My mouth goes dry, and my hands are clammy.

"Like, it's getting serious or whatever. I don't want to make this something it's not, you know?"

"Right. Of course." I try not to be offended by the reminder.

"Cool." He's so blasé about it. "Sorry about tomorrow. I'll call if anything changes, 'kay?"

"Sure. Yeah." I don't want to get my hopes up.

"Night, Lily."

"Night, Randy."

It's probably better that he can't take me out for dinner. That'd feel too much like a date instead of it being this casual thing where we bang each other on occasion.

I spend all of Sunday shopping with the girls. It's exhausting. Also, I don't have money to spend on frivolous crap, especially since I can't take that dress back anymore. Violet buys us all lunch and splurges on bottles of champagne that cost more than a month's rent. I'm used to being around Sunny's family, but this is extravagant.

Violet refuses to go into any bridal shops. She starts itching as soon as we're within five feet of any store with white dresses. On the way to Victoria's Secret, we pass a kids' store with a window display full of those dolls my cousin is always talking about.

"These are so expensive for plastic," I mumble.

Violet glances at the storefront and starts screaming like she's being murdered. "Oh my God! Why do they exist?" She puts her hand over her eyes and latches on to Charlene. "Get them away from me!"

"What's going on?" I ask Sunny, who shrugs at the freakout.

"Maybe she's really lost it?"

"Stop flailing, and I'll get you away from the dolls."

"Don't say that word!" Violet buries her face against Charlene's shoulder. "Tell me when it's safe."

I'm not sure whether it's comical or not. Sunny and I follow Char and Violet into Victoria's Secret.

"Okay. We're good. It's all bras and panties and sexy things," Charlene assures her.

"No fluttery eyes?" Violet's still covering her face.

"Nope. Not a one."

She peeks between a gap in her fingers, eyes darting back and forth, assessing her surroundings. She drops her shaking hand. "I hate those things. They're so creepy."

"Do—" Charlene makes a chopping motion, cutting Sunny off.

"Let's get you some new bras."

Violet nods. We distract her with a pile of sexy clothes. While she's in the changing room, I ask Charlene what that was all about.

"She's terrified of dolls. I think she watched too much Chucky as a kid. Buck used to torment her with them when they were teenagers. He'd put them by her bed so when she woke up in the morning, one would be staring at her."

Sunny frowns. "That's not very nice."

"They were kids."

Alex calls while Violet's in the changing room, and they have a video chat that everyone is privy to. Sunny leaves the area, uninterested in hearing Alex tell Violet how sexy she is.

Randy doesn't call, and while I'm disappointed, I can't help thinking it's definitely better this way. If I hear from him on a regular basis, it won't feel casual anymore. Some distance is a good thing. Sex is just sex. Feelings don't have to be part of anything.

I fly back to Toronto with the Waters on Monday morning. We have to be at the airport ridiculously early, so I'm bitchy and tired by the time I get home. I'm cutting it close. I have a shift at the coffee shop at noon, and then I go straight to the rink at six. I'm in and out of the house in fifteen minutes, and Sunny drives me to work. I'm on my own to get to the rink after that, but it's not a problem. Busses are frequent and plentiful in this town.

I check my messages on the ride home from the arena at the end of my day. Randy's sent one, checking to see if I made it home okay. I send him a brief reply, but don't invite further conversation.

It's close to midnight by the time I get home. After a flight, a five-hour shift making coffee for stuck-up pricks, and four hours of teaching kids to skate, I'm beat. I hang my keys on the little hook in the front hall, kick off my shoes, and head for the kitchen. I need an unhealthy snack.

I scream at the sight of a man with back hair and a pair of gray boxer briefs gnawing on a chicken bone.

"Who the fuck are you?" I scramble to get my backpack off. My skates are in there. If nothing else, they're heavy, so smacking him across the face will hurt. If I can get them out quick enough, they're a decent weapon.

"Lily!" My mom grabs my bag out of my hand before I can

heave it at the random guy in the kitchen.

"What the hell?" I turn to her, gesturing wildly between them. I realize it's the same guy from last time—the one who caught me coming out of the shower while sporting morning wood. *Shit*. My mom's got a new boyfriend. I wonder how long this one will last.

"This is Tim. He's a friend of mine."

"Why are you in your underwear?" I'm still yelling. I feel like my heart is about to slam right out of my chest. It's then that I realize my mom is wearing her bathrobe. I bet she's naked under there. Gross.

I'm too old to deal with this. I don't need to know who my mom's boning. If Sunny wasn't talking about moving to Chicago, I'd say we should get an apartment now. I don't want to be stuck here, witnessing my mom getting more action than I am. I have enough saved up to front first and last month's rent. I can do it on my own if I have to. My mom's talking while I'm thinking through a plan to move.

"I didn't think you'd be home until tomorrow."

"I told you I was coming back today. It's on the calendar." I point to the adorable kittens rolling around in a flowerbed. In red are the days I'm away. Today is marked with a big H for home.

"I must have gotten the dates wrong."

"Whatever. I'm wiped. I'm going to bed. Nice to meet you, Tom."

"It's Tim," my mom says.

"Night, Tim. Please wear pants in the future."

"Uhhh …"

I don't wait for actual words. I take my bag from my mom and carry it to my room. If this turns out to be more than half a dozen dates, I'm going to have to consider my options. I can't go through another one of my mother's boyfriend cycles. The guys she picks make Benji look like a damn saint.

Over the next week I don't hear from Randy at all. I'd like to say I don't perseverate on this, but I do. And I masturbate often to his pretty face. It's not hard to pull up a pic of him on social media. I creep his Facebook page, but asking him to be friends would take us from casual to something else. We don't want to do that, so creeping is as far as I'm allowing it to go.

September rolls into October, and the leaves turn a lovely shade of red, followed by orange and yellow. Fall's an interesting season. It's beautiful, but all those lovely colors represent leaves choking to death. It's kind of macabre, really.

I slip back into my normal routine: work at the coffee shop, teach skating lessons, hang out with Sunny when I'm not doing either of those things and she's available. Now that training is over and the regular hockey season has begun, Miller can't visit as often.

She's talking more and more about moving at the end of December, after she's finished the course component of her public relations program. Internship placements can be done anywhere, and she's already gone to the program coordinator to discuss options in the States. I don't know that I'd want to up and move my entire life for another person, but then my relationship experience has been limited.

On the ex-boyfriend front, Benji's started calling again. I've come to recognize the pattern. The longest we've ever been broken up in the past is eight weeks—long enough for me to go on some dates; sometimes have meaningless sex I feel guilty about afterwards, and then we get back together. Break up again. Make up again.

I try hard not to respond or encourage him, but I have a box of his crap at my place, and he's got stuff of mine, including my favorite jeans. Seeing him is inevitable. Benji and I have been through a lot together. It was a lot of years, and he was there when I lost my Olympic dream. In the past that's been enough to pull me back to him after one of our breakup fights. But not this time. Among other things, now that I've had much, much better sex—like, the outstanding kind—my position feels less vulnerable. Still, I'd like to avoid him for as long as I can.

Today I'm pulling eight hours at the coffee shop and rushing to the rink to teach three hours of lessons. I'm on hour number six, and there's a lag between customers. It makes the day seem that much longer. My feet hurt, and I'm tired. I'm also cranky.

My phone buzzes against my ass, signaling a text. Since I'm sometimes the manager, I won't get in trouble for checking it, but I try to avoid doing that in front of other employees in case it gives them the impression it's okay for them to do it, too.

I scan the shop, once I'm sure no one is paying attention to me, I slip my phone out. I sigh as Benji's name comes up, along with three new messages. He wants to meet up, presumably to give me my stuff back, but he's vague. I make the mistake of telling him I'm working, so I can't.

Half an hour later he shows up. The counter is a great barrier, keeping him from hugging me. He looks the same as he did the last time I saw him, which was almost a month ago when he stopped by with some girl. I went to the back and made one of the other girls wait on them. He texted a thousand apologies later and said she was one of his coworkers. I know better. He did it to make me jealous.

He's still growing that awful beard, which isn't really a beard. It's a bunch of patchy scruff. It's not attractive. He's wearing a shirt I gave him two years ago for his birthday. He doesn't have a bag or a box or anything with him, but it could be in his car.

"Hey, Lily."

"Hi, Benji."

He stuffs his hands in his pockets. "You look great."

"Thanks." I roll back on my heels and wait.

The awkward silence drags on until his face starts to turn red. "Think you can take a break?"

"I've already taken it."

He sighs, and my toes curl in my shoes, like they want to be fists and punch him in the knees.

"Aren't you, like, kinda the manager? Can't you take one whenever you want?"

"We're short staffed." It's a lie. There are only three people in the shop, and two other people are working with me. One of the girls is in the back checking inventory; the other one is cleaning tables.

Benji glances pointedly at the girl across the shop. "Come on, Lily."

"I can't. It's her break in five minutes. She has to have one. It's unfair otherwise."

"Well, what time do you get off?"

"In an hour. I have to go straight to the rink after that."

"I'll drive you." Benji knows I don't have a car, and that it'll take almost an hour to get from downtown to the rink at the university by bus.

"Fine. Sure."

"Great." He smiles.

I used to find it charming; now it seems more of a leer. He thinks he's going to convince me to get back together with him. He orders a coffee and a scone and takes a seat on one of the couches. He watches me while I work, which I find highly unsettling. I don't feel like doing this with him today. But I suppose now's as good a time as any to let him know this is really over.

At five, I clock out. Benji's right there, opening doors for me, being all sweet. He's good at faking nice, as well as guilt-tripping and manipulating. It's a game he likes to play. I think I'd gotten so used to it after seven years, it seemed normal. But seeing Sunny and Miller together, and even Violet and Alex, I'm getting a much better sense of how dysfunctional my relationship with Benji truly was.

He puts his hand on my lower back, guiding me out of the shop. "You teach at six, right?"

I walk a little faster to get away from his hand. "Yeah." His car is parked in the lot.

Here's an interesting fact about Benji: he dresses like he's homeless, but his family is fairly well off. He drives a brand new Jetta. He didn't pay for it, though. His parents did, just like they pay for everything else.

He hits the button, unlocking it. I grab the handle before he can and slide into the passenger seat. He closes the door for me, his smile wavering a little as he walks around the car. He's back to his grinning, fake-pleasant self by the time he's in the driver's seat.

"How've you been?" he asks, buckling himself in.

"Fine. Good. How about you?"

"Oh, you know. Keeping busy." That's Benji code for boinking other girls, or trying to make me think he has. I don't care if it's true.

"That's good."

He glances at me, lips pursed under his scraggly mustache. He stretches his arm out over the back of my seat as he reverses out of the spot. He nearly hits a customer and has the audacity to flip her off as he pulls out onto the street. I slouch in my seat so she can't see me. It's a ten-minute drive to the campus rink. I'm hoping we can manage not to have a screaming match.

"You know, you can always call me if you need a ride." His fingers graze the back of my neck.

I lurch forward. "Thanks. That's probably not a good idea, though."

"Come on, Lils. How long are you planning to stay mad at me this time? I know I'm not perfect, but neither are you. We had a fight. It happens. It's over now. I know you were mad at me when we were camping, and that's why you kissed that hockey douche. I'll forgive you for that."

This right here is what I'm talking about. This is the kind of crap Benji pulls, putting it all on me. It wasn't always this way. He was a great boyfriend for the first four years—doting, kind, sweet. Sometimes a little too much of all of those things. We were solid until senior year; then there were a couple of bumps and short breakups. Nothing terrible.

Things got rocky after high school. I went to university on a full scholarship instead of pursuing my dream. He went to college to get a diploma in loafing. It was eye-opening to be in classes with other guys who expressed an interest in me. Benji didn't like it; he has insecurity issues. I've realized he used to project them on me by constantly telling me I wasn't good enough. The jabs were subtle at first, but by the end he'd blatantly put me down.

I don't know why I stayed for so long. Maybe I was too scared to have no one other than Sunny, since most of our friends left Guelph after high school. Maybe I was scared I'd end up like my mom, with a revolving door of loser boyfriends. Regardless, it's a cycle that needs to stay broken, for good this time.

"I'm not asking to be forgiven for kissing Randy."

"Fine. Then I won't ask to be forgiven for screwing around on you, either."

"Screwing around on me? Benji, we're not together. You can screw anyone you damn well please. It's none of my business."

He's silent for the rest of the ride—stewing, I guess. I hold my knapsack on my lap, wishing I'd gone with my gut and taken the bus, even if it meant rushing to get to the rink.

Benji pulls up to the front of the arena.

"Thanks for the ride."

"So that's it? That's all you've got to say?" As his anger expands, so does his volume.

"I don't know what else you want me to say. We haven't spoken in two months apart from the time you came to the coffee shop with that girl you apparently work with. We've said all the things we need to say to each other over the years. We should be good at this point, don't you think?"

"Why can't you admit you made a mistake with the meathead? Why are you so intent on becoming your mom?"

And just like that, he makes me feel two inches tall. I take a deep breath, steeling myself against the insults. "Don't bring my mom into this."

"Why? Because you don't like the truth?"

I don't engage; I don't have enough time to battle it out. And I don't want to. "Do you have my stuff with you?"

"Stuff?"

"My things? From your house?"

"I didn't think you were gonna be playing this game with me, Lily. I thought we were gonna work things out."

"Never mind. I gotta go."

I reach for the door handle, and Benji grabs my wrist.

"Let go of me."

He loosens his grip. "Come on, Lily. I'm sorry. I didn't mean that. You know I didn't mean that. I miss you. I'm worried about you."

My phone rings. I slip it out of my pocket. It's five-thirty. It takes a good ten minutes to get changed, and I still need to warm up before the kids arrive for their lesson at six.

"Don't answer that, Lily."

I've about had it with being told what I should and shouldn't do. The screen lights up, the name flashing its alert. Of all the people to be calling at this moment. I wrench my arm out of Benji's grip, open the door, and get jerked back by the seatbelt. I slam my finger on the button and tumble out of the car, landing on my ass in a puddle. It hasn't even been raining, so I'm not sure where the damn wet spot came from. "Thanks again for the ride."

"Come on, Li—"

I hit the green button and bring the phone to my ear, meeting Benji's annoyed gaze. "Hi, Randy." I slam the door, pop up from the ground, and start hoofing it toward the building.

That was probably a really bad idea. Nothing like poking a hornet's nest when you're sitting right beside the hornet. Benji lays on the horn and rolls down the window. I start jogging, not interested in hearing his vitriol spew. My heart crashes around in my chest as I push through the arena doors, leaving Benji to fume.

"Hey, luscious. How's it goin'?"

"Hey. Good. Great. How 'bout you?" I'm breathless, so each word comes out on a pant.

"Excellent. Did I catch you at a bad time?"

"Huh. What? No. Nope. Not a bad time." The unpleasant altercation with Benji is immediately forgotten—okay, not forgotten, but made much less worse by the low, deep timbre of Randy's voice. It makes my girl parts tingle like they've been dipped in mouthwash.

"You sure? You sound out of breath."

"I'm on my way into the rink."

"That's unfortunate. Here I thought maybe I'd caught you with your hand down your pants."

I laugh. "I'd probably get arrested if I did that right now."

"Too bad. It's a nice image." He makes a sound, like a sigh with a hum attached to it. "So I'm guessing you're lying about it not being a bad time."

I shoulder open the door to the locker room. It's empty apart from me. I put my phone on speaker. "I've got a few minutes before I have to teach."

"Awesome. How've you been?"

"Good. You?"

"Yeah. All right. My dad overstayed his welcome; I only got rid of him a few days ago."

"I'm sorry about that. Didn't sound like a good situation."

"It wasn't. It isn't. But whatever. I don't see him much, so I should be good for another six months before he fucks with my shit again."

"I guess that's a good thing?"

"Yeah."

When he doesn't elaborate, I change the subject. "How's the season going?"

"I'm getting used to my new team. It's good even though it's different. You know how it goes—or maybe you don't."

"I can understand that. It's like a learning curve, right? Figuring out how everyone works together and stuff. It's probably like getting used to a new partner for pairs, but with way more people involved." I pull my shirt over my head and kick off my shoes.

"Yeah. That's a reasonable comparison. What're you doing? What's all that noise?"

"I'm getting changed."

"No shit. Are you naked?" I swear his voice lowers two octaves.

"Wouldn't you like to know." Every part of me warms at the memory of the things he did to me the last time we were naked.

"I sure as hell would."

I laugh.

"You're not gonna tell me?"

"You can't see me, so I'm not sure it matters."

"It's the idea, the possibility."

"Fine. I'm naked."

"No, you aren't."

"No. I'm not."

"Too bad. Look, speaking of getting naked, I've got a game in Toronto at the end of the week. We're gonna be there overnight. I can get you tickets, and then you can spend the night with me."

"Wow. Talk about cutting to the chase." I'm not sure what to expect, not having heard from him in weeks. His dad being there may have had something to do with that, though. I'm a little shocked at his boldness, although maybe I shouldn't be. Could be this is just how it works.

"It's at the end of a series, so I can stay an extra night, if you're interested. We can get extra naked. I'll even take you out for dinner like I was supposed to last time."

Oh, God. Hours of uninterrupted time with Randy. A night in a bed with no constraints and no one to walk in on us. Still, I don't want to say yes right away and make it seem like I'm willing to drop everything for him. "I'll have to check my schedule."

"You do that."

"'Kay. I'll let you know as soon as I know."

"Sounds good. I'll make sure my special false-advertising boxers are clean for you."

I cringe, still embarrassed. "You can get rid of those any time now."

"I like them more now than I did before you decorated them."

I won't admit it, but I sort of like that he's kept them. The alarm goes off on my phone, signaling that I need to be on the ice. "I gotta go. Bye, Randy."

"Later, Lily."

I hang up and start lacing my skates. Another dose of Randy is exactly what I deserve for finally getting Benji out of my life for good.

13

PERSISTENCE FOR PAYOFF

RANDY

It's the middle of the third period in New York, and we're down one. It's not always easy to stay in a good headspace during away games. Being on the road means sleeping in beds that aren't mine and a lack of privacy. Miller and I room together in the hotels, like we have since we played rep hockey and had tournaments away from home. Usually Miller's dad would take us since my mom had to work and couldn't afford to take the time off. Once we were teenagers, we went with our coaches.

Miller and I didn't get into much trouble until our junior year of high school. We'd been playing street hockey, and some kid got him right in the face with a puck. Knocked his front teeth out, and a few other ones. It turned out to be a good thing after he got over the pain. Miller had bad teeth as a kid, and a bunch of titanium screws and implants fixed that problem after the accident.

He has to be super careful on the ice now, though. If any of those get knocked out, he'll be wearing dentures until his hockey career is over. Maybe for the rest of his life.

Anyway, he was kinda shy with the girls until his teeth problem was resolved. Honestly, they probably would've been all over his dick regardless, but he's a little sensitive about his perceived shortcomings. Kinda like I am about mine. We all find ways to manage, though.

I'm restless, waiting for my turn to get on the ice. I don't get as much play yet because I'm still getting used to the team and learning how they interact with each other. It drives me crazy. Waters is in a bad mood with the score being the way it is, and the opposition is chippy, making it difficult to keep the puck in play. The refs are lax. It's pissing me off.

Waters ends up getting two minutes for tripping, which gets me off the bench. They switch out a wing for me, and I fly down the ice, ready to take back the puck. I have an advantage tonight. We're playing the team I was traded from in the spring. I know most of the players and how they move. Some of them might be my friends, but in terms of the game and winning, it doesn't make a difference.

I nab the puck from their center, skating wide. I weave through players, my objective clear: get the puck into New York's net. I scan for players close to me. Westinghouse is open and looking for a pass; I send the puck sailing in his direction just before New York tries to steal it. Picking up speed, I make my way toward the goalie, keeping an eye on the puck. Skating around behind the net, Westinghouse trades off right before he takes a hit. I skate around the guy looking to drop me, kiss the puck with my blade, and send it sailing between the goalie's skates.

Scoring against my old team is a fantastic feeling, especially with us being down a player on account of Waters' penalty. Westinghouse and I tap gloves and set up for the next play. I get back pats along the way. I can't keep the grin contained as I face off against my old captain. Nothing beats the high of scoring a goal.

This is the rush I live for, the feeling that I'm invincible. The whistle blows, and the puck drops. I slap it away from NY's center. Westinghouse is on it. He's an awesome wingman. New York gets control, but Miller owns defense, keeping the puck away from our goal.

Waters is back on the ice once his penalty is over, and I'm on the bench, but I'm okay with that. I've done my part. We're tied, and we've got three minutes left in the game. Waters is a bulldozer out there. He's on a rampage, cutting down the ice with the puck, his focus singular. He fakes out the other team, his skating skills so refined he can trip them up without even touching them. The puck sails into the net again with only fifteen seconds left in the game. And we've won. There's no coming back for New York.

The energy is manic in the locker room. There's a shitton of excitement and lots of approval from my teammates. We hit the bar afterward to celebrate the win and eat. The bunnies are all over the place, looking for hook-ups. I take the spot beside Miller.

I'm still waiting on Lily to call me back, so I'm not all that inclined to do the bunny thing. I could definitely use the release, though. I'm edgy and pent up as fuck. I haven't had sex since the engagement party. Normally I wouldn't be opposed to a hook-up after such a long dry run—especially since Lily hasn't messaged in a couple of days—but with her being Sunny's close friend, I need to be sensitive about it.

Lance pulls an empty chair up beside me, turns it around, and drops into it. He looks past Miller to Westinghouse and Waters. "What're you doing here with all the pussy-whipped bitches?" he asks me.

"Classy, Romero." Westinghouse gives him the eye and takes a swig from his beer.

"There've been some interesting rumors floating around out there about you since my engagement party," Waters says.

"Oh, yeah?" Lance spins the coaster on the table.

"You might want to watch yourself a little better," Waters adds.

Lance frowns. "I don't know what you're talking about."

"If you say so." Waters shrugs. "But if Coach finds out, best-case scenario is you being benched. Worst case you end up traded. That'd be a real shame, considering—ego aside—you're a good player." He downs his beer and sets the bottle on the table. "I'm gonna call it a night."

Westinghouse leaves his beer half-full, pushes back his chair, and nods to us. "See you on the bus."

Lance waits until they're gone before he turns to us. "Who the fuck told Waters?"

"Told him what?" I lean back in my chair and glance at Miller, who's checking his phone for the seventy-fifth time.

He looks up and frowns. "Are you talking about whatever's going on with you and Tash?"

"Yeah, man. Did you say something?" His accent comes out. Usually the vague hint of Scottish brogue is undetectable, apart from when he's upset about something.

Miller turns off his phone, which beeps at him, and crosses his arms over his chest. "Why would I tell Alex?"

"I don't know. You two are all buddy-buddy now, soaping each other's backs in the shower."

"Fuck you, Lance. He's gonna be my brother-in-law. I'm dating his sister. I don't have much of a choice unless I wanna make my life more difficult. Besides, he's a good guy. A weirdo, but that's not much of a surprise considering he's with Vi and all."

"Well, someone said something to him." He spins his bottle between his palms. "It's not like it's a big deal."

"If you say so, but you should be careful. Tash can't be banging the players she's training, if that's what's going on." Miller's phone rings, so he checks it. "I gotta get this."

It's obviously Sunny. He takes the call and covers the receiver. "I'mma head up to the room. See you guys later."

Lance watches him leave. "Do you think I should be worried?"

"Miller's got a point. It's not professional. It makes her look bad."

He pounds back the rest of his beer. "I think I'm done for tonight."

"Yeah. Good plan. It's gonna be an early morning." The bus leaves at nine, and the drive from New York to Toronto for our next game is about eight hours plus stops. We'll be on the road all day.

Lance and I go our separate ways. When I get to the room, Miller's in the bathroom talking on his phone. I key in my passcode and find a new message from Lily.

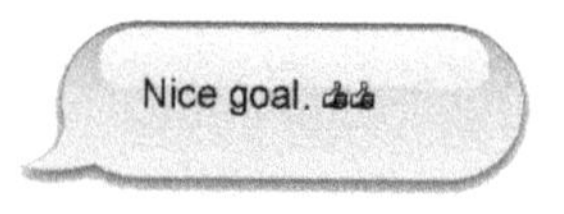

It was sent more than an hour ago. I'm surprised I missed it. I shoot her a message back.

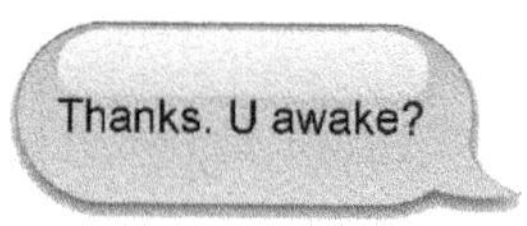

I lie down on the bed that isn't covered in Miller's discarded clothes and wait for a reply. We'll be in Toronto by tomorrow night, and I want to know what my plans are going to be.

I've already booked a better room than the ones we usually

stay in during away games, just in case I need privacy. I'm hoping. My plan is to require privacy as much as I possibly can in the short time we'll have.

I take off my shirt and lose my pants, dropping them on the floor beside the bed. I'm tired. And in need of release.

My phone vibrates with a message.

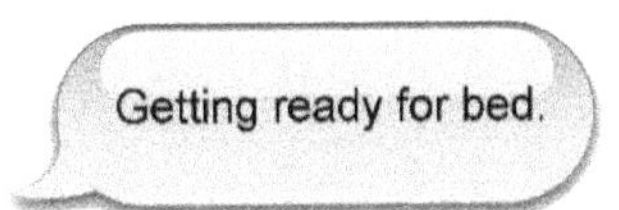

I fire one back.

I get one a few seconds later of her empty bed. It looks small. Not big enough for the things I'd like to get up to with her.

I don't wait long for her curt reply.

I grin.

The inchworm dots appear.

An image follows. She's wearing a paper bag over her head

with holes punched through for her eyes. I love that she doesn't automatically send me naked pictures. I hit the call button. She answers on the first ring. It's late. After midnight.

"You can beg all you want. I'm not sending a picture."

"I have a ticket for the game on Friday. I'll deal with no picture if it means I'm going to see you."

"About that—"

I get this sinking feeling low in my gut. It's not something I'm used to. Girls usually bend over backward, literally, to get what I'm offering. I brush it off and roll with it. "You don't wanna come?"

"It's not that. I have to work. I can't get out of my shifts."

"Call in sick."

"I can't."

"Sure you can. It's easy. You pretend you have the flu, and you call in. Then you come to the game. Then we get naked, and I make you come."

She snort-laughs. "You make it sound so appealing. I wish it was that simple."

"I've already got a room booked. I can rent a car and drive you back the next morning to wherever you have to be."

"You already booked a room? Wow. That's presumptuous."

I can't tell if she's offended. "It's wishful thinking, not presumption. Come on, Lily. I had a lot of fun last time, didn't you?"

"Well, yeah, but—"

"But what? I've been looking forward to getting you naked again. We can even fuck in the bathroom, since that's our thing."

This time I get a real laugh out of her. "Oh my God, are you always like this?"

"Pretty much. So you'll call in sick. I'll email you the ticket."

"I'd love to, but I've already asked for the time off, and it won't work. I teach lessons that don't end until eight-thirty on game night, and I teach again the next morning."

All the excitement over my plan fizzles out. "What about after your lessons in the morning?"

"I have a shift late in the afternoon, too."

"You work too much." I don't intend to sound pissy.

She's snappy in return. "I don't have a choice."

"Sorry. That was assholey." I run a frustrated hand through my hair. "I just wanna see you. What time are all your shifts the day after?"

"I teach skating from seven until eleven-thirty in the morning. My other shift is from five to ten at the coffee shop."

"And after that?"

"I go home to sleep and get up for a nine a.m. shift at the rink. Then I work at the coffee shop again in the afternoon."

I blow out a breath and scrub a hand over my face. "Fuck."

"I'm sorry, Randy. It looks like it's not going to work out this time. Maybe when you're back in Toronto, if I plan far enough ahead and you still want me to come to a game…" Her voice goes soft at the end.

"That isn't for, like, another month."

"Oh."

At least she sounds disappointed. "We'll figure something out," I tell her.

"Yeah. Sure. I should probably go. I have to be up in less than six hours."

"Right. Okay. I'll talk to you soon."

"Good luck on Friday. Night, Randy."

She ends the call. I bang my head against the headboard and swear.

Miller comes out of the bathroom, butt-ass naked. "What're you doin' up here? And why're you banging your head?"

"Lily's not coming to the Toronto game."

He half-smiles before he neutralizes his expression. "You get blown off?"

"She's gotta work—unless that's an excuse."

Miller tosses his phone on the bed and scratches his leg, right beside his balls. "It's probably not an excuse. Sunny's mentioned that she works a lot. Pulls doubles all the time and stuff."

"You gonna put on some boxers or something." I keep my eyes on the blank TV screen.

"I'm airing out."

"We're not in the locker room."

"You know, Balls, you can do it, too. No one gives a shit that your junk's a little wonky."

"Fuck you, dude."

"I'm not being an asshole. I'm serious. The scars make you gangster."

"I don't need a therapy session about this."

Miller's sensitive about his dyslexia; I'm sensitive about my junk. But then, almost losing half of it as a kid can do that to a guy.

"I was there, man. I saw it all happen. You're not the only one who has nightmares about it."

"Drop it, *Buck*." I rarely ever call him by the nickname asshole kids gave him in grade school, so he knows I'm serious.

He holds up his hands. "Consider it dropped."

Back when we were kids, we used to play hockey on the pond down the road in the winter. We never wore helmets or cups or anything; we were just goofing around on the ice. Sometimes we'd join games with older guys—teenagers who played rep looking to get scouted to the minors. Miller's dad was always on the lookout for new talent.

Once we were playing with them and I stole the puck—even

then I was better than most kids. It was one of the perks of having a pro dad. He knew guys who could train me the way I needed in order to make professional hockey a career. Anyway, some kid didn't like it and decided to put me in my place. It got a little rougher than it should've, and I ended up with a skate to the groin.

Vascular appendages bleed a lot. Emergency surgery repaired the damage, but the end result was pretty fucking disturbing. My dick looks like it belongs to Frankenstein. I was off the ice for a few months while I recovered. Dick stitches are not fun, especially with the whole onset-of-puberty deal, when erections are spontaneous and uncontrollable.

Everything still works, obviously, but there are residual sensitivity issues, lots of scars, and a bend that otherwise wouldn't have been there. The upside: I still have all of my dick, instead of half of it. But I don't swing free in the locker room because I don't like answering questions, or making people uncomfortable.

I shut down those unpleasant memories and go back to quizzing Miller about Lily's job situation. "She teaches figure skating. Doesn't it pay well enough? Why does she need a second job?" It's seriously interfering with my ability to see her.

"There's financial stuff goin' on there. I think she helps out her mom. Sunny's mentioned a couple of times that things are tight. She's got school loans and stuff. Her dad's a deadbeat. I think he was pro hockey, and he got her mom knocked up and bailed."

"That's seriously shitty." It also sounds kind of familiar.

"Right? She was, like, prepping for Olympic trials but the money wasn't there to support her, so she had to drop out."

"How do you know all this shit about her?"

"Because Sunny's my girlfriend, and we talk as much as we

fuck."

Interesting. When I talk to Lily, it's mostly me sexting her, or joking around about stupid shit. If things were different, I could know all this stuff, too, without having to ask Miller.

He nabs the remote and turns on the TV, flipping channels until he gets to the highlights from tonight's game. "Maybe it's not a bad thing she can't come to Toronto."

I glance at him, waiting for an explanation.

"Come on, Randy. You gotta know it's not gonna end well. It never does."

"What's that supposed to mean?"

"Nothing. Never mind. Forget I said anything. Oh, shit." He points at the screen. "That was a serious screw up by Cockburn. I think he tries that move every damn game, and it never works."

I get sucked into the highlights and picking apart the other teams' mistakes—how they could have managed a breakaway better, who missed what goal, who's making the best plays—but I don't forget what Miller said about things ending badly. And it irks me, because it's true, and I don't want it to be.

14

SWEET BALLS

LILY

I'd like to say I go to work the next evening and don't take it out on my girls that I'm missing a hockey game and an opportunity to see Randy. That would be a lie, however. I almost make one of them cry. That's when I rein in the snap-itude and stop pushing them.

I have the sound booth guy put on some upbeat music, and we freestyle it for the last fifteen minutes of class. They have a training schedule to keep and moves to learn, but sometimes it's important to skate for pure enjoyment. Also, I'm struggling to focus, knowing I could've been at the game that's now almost over. Even more important is the fact that instead of sleeping in my crappy double I might've been able to sleep in a sweet hotel bed with Randy. Or not sleep. At all. And now I have to go home and deal with my mom and work in the morning.

I'm bitchy.

And maybe a little sexually frustrated. Or a lot.

I berate myself for not having a backbone all the way home.

I should have pushed harder for the time off. I never take days. Ever. Then I check my messages to see if Randy's sent me anything. He hasn't, but Sunny's sent me fifty pictures of the game. Half of them are blurry. Most of them feature Randy on the ice. They don't make me feel better.

I'm sure my not being able to come to the game means I've shot my chance of ever getting back into his bed, or whatever bed is available. Or bathroom. Guys have short attention spans. I'm sure he'll be all over some bunny tonight as a result.

I put my phone on airplane mode and hide under the covers. It takes forever to fall asleep, so I roll my marble until I come, then finally pass out.

My mood does not improve the next morning. During my bus ride to the rink, I check Randy's social media like an obsessed stalker. All the pictures are of him with Miller and Alex. No girls except Sunny and Violet. I hate how relieved I am. And jealous. I also hate how preoccupied I am with the fact that Sunny hasn't messaged me since last night, and I have to work all day today instead of spending it naked with Randy.

Damn it.

There goes my mind.

I spend the next four hours on the ice pretending I love teaching kids how to spin and twirl and be as awesome—if not better—than I was a couple of years ago. Most days I love what I do. Today I'm still bitchy. I wish I wasn't. The kids can sense my mood like a pack of wolves. I stay on point, though, because last night I wasn't, and I can't have two bad days in a row.

By the time I get to my older girls, I'm more focused. Which is good, because they're all about competition, and they need me to stay on them. At least one girl is destined for the Olympics.

She's got the financial backing to make it, so I push her. It's hard to watch them sometimes, knowing my lost dream is something they can have and might not want.

I'm in the middle of showing the girls the last of the new routine when they become distracted. I run through the moves, finishing with the toe loop, but they're not looking at me. Instead they're focused on the stands.

I stop to see what has them so flustered. My stomach flips. There's a man who looks distinctly like Randy leaning against the boards. He lifts a hand and waves. My girl parts swoon.

"Oh my God!" one of my girls whisper-shrieks. "Is that Randy Ballistic? From Chicago? Why's he here?"

"I'll be right back," I mutter and skate down the ice toward him.

The girls are freaking out. I guess I am, too, except I'm better at managing myself. At least on the outside. I stop in front of him, a small spray of ice puffing out from under my blade. A grin makes his eyes crinkle. He has a tiny dimple up near his left cheek. I want to press it, like it's a button that will undress him.

"Hey." I play it cool, propping a hand on my hip and cocking my head to the side. It would work well if I wasn't huffing from exertion. "What're you doing here?"

"Surprise." He does half-assed jazz-hands while looking me up and down.

I feel naked. And hot. And sexually frustrated. "It sure is." It comes out sounding all raspy, like I've just had an orgasm.

His lip quirks up. I want to lick it off his face right after I smack it. Or his ass.

"I figured if you couldn't come for me, I could come for you."

The innuendo is intentional. I ignore it. For now. "How'd you know—" I shake my head. "Sunny told you I work here?"

"She gave me directions last night."

"It's a miracle you made it." I snicker. Sunny is not the go-to girl for directions. Sometimes she gets lost coming to my place.

I glance over my shoulder; the girls are twittering in a little cluster. They're making their way closer. One of the girls steps in front of the others. She clamps onto her friend's arm with wide, starstruck eyes.

"You've been recognized. Get ready for the fangirling."

Randy waves to the girls. They burst into giggles. I give him a look. "You shouldn't encourage them."

"Why not?"

One of the girls finally takes it upon herself to skate over. She glances at Randy and then me, wringing her hands together, then playing with the end of her long ponytail. "Miss LeBlanc, um… should, uh…" She glances at Randy again. "Should we practice one more time or get changed?"

I look at the clock. It's almost eleven-thirty. "Oh! You girls can get changed."

"Okay." She nods frantically and then gives Randy the side-eye again.

"Unless you all want to show Randy your routine. He's not a figure skater, but he plays hockey for Chicago."

"Oh my God!" She looks over at the other girls, who are pretending not to watch us, and screeches, about six inches away from my ear, "You were right!"

I cringe at the excited squealing. For the next ten minutes, Randy's bombarded by thirteen-year-old girls. He's sweeter than maple-butter tarts while he signs things like binders, notebooks, and backpacks that the girls retrieve from the locker room.

Then their parents show up and do the same thing. The moms are the worst. Especially the pretty ones. They put their hands on his arm and simper compliments. It makes me want to barf. It also makes me want to boob-punch a couple of them. I pretend to keep busy checking my clipboard. After a while it's clear they're not going anywhere, and I still need to get changed—and shower now that Randy's here. Usually I do that at home as the locker room showers are questionable.

I'm a little concerned about what the plan is going to be. I don't have a car, so I would've taken the bus home, but I don't want to take Randy there for a multitude of reasons. My mother will not approve. Also, the underwear guy has been over a lot. He puts on sweats now, but he walks around shirtless quite a bit. It's unpleasant.

I shoulder my bag and start toward the locker room. Randy grabs my wrist. "Just wait a minute, 'kay?"

"I'm going to change."

"Is anyone on the ice after this?"

"There's another class in less than half an hour."

Randy frowns. "That's too bad. I wanted to watch you skate."

"Some other time. I'll be out in a few." I leave him with the parents. He's used to dealing with this kind of attention, and he doesn't seem to mind it.

As soon as I'm in the locker room I call Sunny, but her phone goes to voice mail. I get her message about chi-cleansing and karma being her friend and wait for the beep.

"I can't believe you didn't warn me that Randy was coming here! I didn't even shave my girl parts, and now I'll have to… I don't even know. It's not good. My situation is dire here. My garden needs to be pruned. No, not pruned, sheared. I'm mad at you until further notice! God, he's so hot," I tack on at the end.

I hang up and debate calling again to apologize. It's not that bad. I definitely need to give everything a onceover with a razor, but it's not a jungle or anything. I toss my phone in my purse and rummage through my bag. I don't have conditioner or soap. I don't even have a towel, which sucks, but options are limited. I can't leave here without showering. Luckily, I have shampoo and a razor. It's old, with rust marks, but it'll have to do.

I turn on the water, take off my skates, and strip. I'm ripe after four hours on the ice. The water feels fantastic, so I stand under the spray for a few seconds, enjoying the heat. I try to keep my hair out of the water as much as possible so I don't have to mess around with it. I squirt some shampoo on my hand and rub it all over my vag. My legs need doing as well, but the crotch is most important. I've got some growth from my last home-waxing job.

The razor is super dull. It's terrible. I can't believe how little hair it removes on the first pass. I go over it several more times and get most of it, but it could definitely be smoother. I move on to my legs; they're just as bad, and I make almost no progress. I might as well be using a butter knife.

I'll get Randy to stop at a store on the way to wherever we're going. I'll have to fix my fuzz problem before he sees me naked. I give up on my legs, which are now red in the spots where I've razored them.

I use the shampoo to wash the rest of my body and dry off with one of my spare leotards. It's highly ineffective. I get the biggest areas, but I'm still damp, which makes getting dressed a pain. Everything sticks. And I don't have one of my nice bras, just an old sports bra. It's been washed so many times it's gray instead of white.

As excited as I am to see Randy, I feel totally unprepared, aside from the fact that my girl parts are moist. I pull on my sweats—the only thing I have other than my work clothes—and they smell like burned toast. I check my reflection in the mirror; I look like a street person.

Holes pepper the knees of my pants. If I look close, I can see skin through a pea-sized tear at my hip. I hope Randy doesn't notice. After the sports bra and the old University of Guelph shirt with bleach stains on it, I pull on my hoodie. I'd like to say this is an improvement over my T-shirt. It's not. I finger-comb my hair—no brush, of course. I'm a hot mess today.

I jam everything into my bag, aware that I'm taking a long time. I half expect to find Randy waiting for me in the hall. I'm actually a little surprised he didn't end up in here with me. As I round the corner to find him, I run into someone I definitely don't want to see.

"Benny!" I step out of the way before we end up in a head-on collision. Benny is Benji's older brother. They're only a year apart, and they could almost pass for twins. I have no idea what his parents were thinking naming them something so similar.

"Hey, Lily. How's it going?" He's laden with heavy-looking boxes.

"Uh, good." I look over his shoulder, past him. "I didn't know you were still working here."

"I picked up a couple of shifts this week 'cause they needed some help. You look—" He glances at my horrible outfit. "Well."

"Thanks. You, too." This is so awkward.

"So I'm guessing it's done for real this time with Benji, eh?"

I knew the question was coming. I haven't seen Benny since before the camping trip.

"Yeah, it is."

He nods. He looks like he's about to say something, but his walkie goes off. "Shit. I gotta go. They need these upstairs, like, ten minutes ago. Guess I'll see you around." He gives me a weak smile and hurries off.

I heave a sigh of relief that there wasn't more to that

conversation. Eventually I'm going to have to get my stuff back from Benji, but that's not my concern right now. There's a seriously hot hockey player waiting for me.

Randy's still talking to parents when I return to the rink. Now he's discussing something with a dad whose son, who can't be more than eight, is staring up at Randy like he's a god. I totally understand the feeling from a very different perspective.

Randy smiles at me, then looks back at the dad and kid. "It's been nice meeting you, but we gotta head out. You keep it up, buddy, and I'll see you in the pros in a few years, hey?" He holds out his fist, and the kid bumps it, his smile toothy.

Once they're gone, he turns to me. "Wanna get outta here?"

"Sure."

He slips a finger under my backpack strap and lifts it from my shoulder. "Let me take that for you."

I've got two bags and a purse, so I let him be a gentleman. That's the heavy one anyway, and it's sweet of him to offer.

"You guys played amazing last night. That was an awesome goal you scored."

"You watched?"

"I saw the highlights reel. I was at work until late."

"Right." He nods. "I wish you coulda been there. We woulda had a good time last night." His grin is lascivious.

I hold in a shiver of anticipation. I sure hope today we get to have the same amount of fun, although I assume the post-win high must make for some incredible sex. Fingers crossed I get to enjoy that sometime in the future. Casually, of course.

"Do you have a car here?" Randy asks as he opens the door.

I'm hit with a chilly gust of wind. Late October brings the colder temperatures. I should've brought my winter jacket, but I'd figured it would warm up today, not get colder. "No. I planned to take the bus."

"That works out well." He jams his hand in his pocket and pulls out a set of rental car keys, twirling them around his finger.

"Sure does."

I follow him to a Jeep with seriously tinted windows. He unlocks the door and helps me in. He doesn't even try to feel me up, although there are kids and parents in the parking lot, so that might be why. It's chilly inside, but at least there's no wind. Randy tosses my bag on the console, then climbs in and turns the engine over. Country music blares through the speakers.

He rushes to turn it down and blasts the heat, wearing a sheepish grin. "Sorry 'bout that."

"Country, eh? I didn't figure you for the type."

"No?" He frees the tie from his hair, then gathers up the fallen strands, pulling it back into a little nub. "What kind of music did you think I'd listen to?"

"I don't know. Pop? Dancy stuff."

"Really? Huh." He moves my bag to the backseat. "Why'd you think that?"

"I don't know. You're always at the bar, and that's what they play there."

"I'm not so big on the bar scene lately." Randy digs around in his back pocket and tosses his wallet on the seat next to him. "You don't have to work until five, right?"

"Right."

He stretches his arm across the headrest and fingers my hair. It probably looks like crap. Much like the rest of me. "So we have a few hours to kill."

"Yup." My stomach is doing all sorts of acrobatics. It feels like there's an entire amusement park inside there, and I'm on all the craziest rides. The one I want to get on is sitting right beside me.

"You wanna go get something to eat? You must be starving." Now he's drawing lines on my neck, or something. Tiny pleasure currents are being radio-signaled through my body. They'd be attached to a satellite in my underwear—if I was wearing any. I'm not very focused on his words. Instead I'm staring at his mouth.

"Lily? You wanna go for lunch? My treat."

I snap out of my vagina-induced trance and look down at my outfit. "Sure. We can hit a drive-thru or something."

"Drive-thru? I was thinking an actual restaurant."

And I'm thinking about how tinted the windows are, and how roomy the backseat of this Jeep is. He hasn't even tried to kiss me yet. What kind of casual-sex business is this?

"I can't go to a restaurant dressed liked this—unless you want to hit a crappy diner. Then I'll fit in with the bums and potheads. We've got lots of those downtown."

He looks me over. It lights all my special parts on fire. "You look great."

I glance down at my old hoodie and my pilly, holey sweats and then back up at him. "You didn't take a hit last night, did you?"

"What? No. Why?"

"You do see what I'm wearing, right? I can't go out in public like this. Especially not with you looking all—" I motion to his hotness.

"Me looking all what?"

I give him the cut eye. "Are you seriously fishing for compliments? Like you don't already have a huge hockey-star ego. You need me to stroke it now, too?"

His tongue peeks out to touch the scar on his top lip, the one

I like to run my tongue across before I stick it in his mouth. I am so sexed up right now. I need to get a razor and fix my forest-style legs. Beyond that, I need to make out with this man again. I'm so busy thinking about what I want to do to him, I almost miss his snappy response.

"I have things that need stroking more than my ego."

I shouldn't want to launch myself at him for being such a cocky bastard, but I do. I manage to keep it together enough not to offer to eat his cock for lunch.

Instead I fire back with some snark, because it's more acceptable. For me. "Would you like me to leave you alone for a few minutes so you can take care of that?"

Randy grins. "I'm good. I can wait until after lunch. Why don't we stop at your place and you can change, if it isn't too far."

Nothing in Guelph is far away. Everything is twenty minutes, give or take. But there's no way in Satan's hairy ball sac I'm letting Randy see where I live. I'm not ashamed of my apartment—but I know exactly how much a professional hockey player makes a year. It's a lot of money. Randy wears nice clothes. His underwear is expensive—I ruined them knowing this. And I bet he drives a sweet ride with leather seats.

I don't need him to know my life isn't as easy as his. Then he might feel like he needs to "save me" or "take care of me" or something like that. It'll make things weird. Well, weirder than this casual-sex thing that apparently includes lunch dates. I need to learn more about how this works.

If I start telling Randy about my life and the crappy stuff, it'll be less about having a good time. I don't need that either. Also, I have no idea if my mom's at home, and she definitely cannot meet Randy. Ever. And the fact that I'm almost twenty-two, have finished university, and still live with my mom is another reason we won't be stopping to get me a change of clothes, even though I could use one.

I make a face I hope is convincing. "I live on the other side of town. It takes forever to get there. Plus there's construction, and you'd have to go the long way around. I'm not even that hungry."

Randy taps on the headrest beside my ear. "We could go back to my hotel room and order room service."

"You have a hotel room?"

He shrugs. "I figured maybe you'd wanna hang out again after your other shift, so I got a room."

"Hang out? In your hotel room?"

I can't tell whether his grin is sheepish or smug. "We could have a sleepover, with a naked pillow fight and everything."

"Those are my favorite!" I clap my hands together and bounce in my seat.

"Awesome." His smile widens. "Mine, too."

But seriously, if he wants to have a naked pillow fight with me, I'm all over that. After my legs are shaved.

Randy fiddles with his phone and the GPS, and we hit the road. I'm super nervous. This is different than spontaneous bathroom make-out sessions followed by sex. This is planned. On his part.

I ask him to stop at a Shopper's Drug Mart, the Canadian equivalent of a CVS. I buy a three-pack of the nice razors, soap, oil for my sensitive parts, deodorant, gum, a Listerine pocket pack, a toothbrush, a pack of those insanely huge condoms he uses, a hair brush, and some candy, just because. If they sold underwear, I'd be all set. I pass the Depends and consider, for a second, if they're better than going commando. No. Never.

Maybe I can wash my dirty pair in the sink and let them dry overnight.

Oh, God. I'm having a sleepover with Randy. I doubt there'll be much sleeping. I rush back to the Jeep, my purse filled with important junk.

"Got what you needed?" he asks as I climb back in the passenger side.

"Yup."

"Awesome. Let's hit the hotel." The way he says that, combined with the way he's looking at me, makes me think room service is going to be last on the to-do list.

Guelph isn't a big place. It doesn't boast much in the way of quality hotels, so the best he can do is the Hilton, but Randy's managed to secure the nicest room. It has a huge king bed and a couch I'm not sure we'll need, considering the bed is enormous and there's a TV on the wall across from it. We can watch while we take breaks from our sex-a-thon.

The second the door closes, Randy has me pressed against the wall with my face in his hands. His mouth crashes down on mine, tongue sliding along the seam. He groans, the sound deep and needy. Sweet mother of wet vagina, these sweats are going to need a wash after we're done.

As is typical with Randy, his knee goes between mine, and he immediately starts with the slow hip circles. If I don't stop him, he's going to take off my clothes. I'd be totally cool with this if I didn't need to manage my leg issues first.

I push on his chest. He backs off right away, steps out of my personal space, and exhales a harsh breath. "Shit. Sorry."

"It's fine. I mean, I've kinda been waiting for that to happen. It took you long enough to kiss me. I figured you'd have at least tried to make out with me in the car, or go for a boob grab. I just need to use the bathroom."

"I can come with you if you need help holding something."

"That's a nice offer, but I can handle this on my own. I'll only be a minute." I pick my purse up off the floor where I dropped it, thanks to the brief hump-off.

"I'll be waiting." Randy adjusts his erection, in case I'm confused about what he'll be waiting for.

I close the door, lock it, and turn on the fan, but it doesn't work. Damn it. How am I going to be incognito about this if I don't have a fan? I turn on the water and dump out the contents of my purse. The package of razors is adult-proof, so I have to fight to get it open. I don't know why they make them so hard to get into.

I finally get a blade free and strip out of my clothes. I think my best plan here is to shave and come out of the bathroom naked. That'll save me issues with my lack of underwear and ugly sports bra. It's not my style to be that forward, but I seem to have issues with keeping my lips and other body parts to myself where Randy's concerned, and we did come back to his hotel room for the express purpose of sexing, so why not be brazen about it?

Randy's clearly already been here and set up all his stuff. He's a tidy guy based on the organized line of man products. I take a peek in his small black case, checking for shaving cream. Bingo! He has one of those pint-size travel containers. I shake the contents and squeeze it into my palm. I check out my legs before I lather it on. The old razor I used at the rink has left streaky red marks on my shins.

I'm almost afraid to check out my vag, but she doesn't look quite so massacred, thankfully. We can turn out the lights (of course), and hopefully it'll be too dark to see what I've done to my legs.

Randy knocks on the door. “Everything okay in there? It’s been more than a minute.”

“Everything’s fine.” I reach over and flush the toilet. “I’ll be right out.”

Two minutes later he knocks again. “The water’s been running for a long time. You sure you’re okay?”

“One more minute!”

I manage to get the right leg done and only nick myself twice. I’m halfway through the other leg when the door swings open.

“What the hell? Is this Groundhog Day?” It’s exactly like the first time we met, except totally different, because back then I didn’t want to have sex with him.

He looks me over. “What are you doing?”

“Performing a voodoo ritual. What does it look like I’m doing?”

I consider covering my nakedness, to be modest, but Randy’s already mentioned he’s a fan of me unclothed, so I don’t bother. He shoves his hand in his pocket and does some rearranging. So I’m thinking the fact that one of my legs is covered from ankle to knee in shaving lotion isn’t a big concern.

“Are you using my shaving cream?”

“Maybe.” I drag the razor up my leg and nick myself again.

“Is this why we stopped at that store?” He gestures to my pile of crap.

“I wasn’t expecting to see you. I figured you’d find a nice, willing bunny and get yourself good and laid last night. The last thing I anticipated was you showing up at my work looking to spend the afternoon naked in your hotel room. My legs were unfit for viewing or touching.”

“I’m sure it wasn’t that bad.”

"I assure you, it was that bad." It wasn't that bad.

He takes a step closer. The bathroom is spacious, but he's got long legs, so he's right up on me. "I'd like to point out that I offered to take you out for lunch; it wasn't all about getting naked on my end."

"You're the one who started humping on me the second the door closed."

"You're the one who suggested we come here in the first place."

"I did not! I suggested a drive-thru!"

He takes the razor from me and frowns. "What're you doing to my legs?" He touches a spot where blood has welled.

All my parts get excited at the possessive reference. "They're *my* legs, and I was in a rush thanks to all your knocking."

He sets the razor down and he lifts me onto the vanity. The porcelain is cold on my ass. A wave of goosebumps breaks out across my skin.

"What're you doing?"

"Helping out." Randy pulls his shirt over his head and drops it on the floor on top of my discarded pile.

His eyes stay on mine as he rests his palms on my thighs, above my knees. I don't particularly care if we have sex while I'm still covered in shaving lotion, but it'll be messy. Not that there isn't a shower right here. His eyes drop, and he gives my thighs a squeeze, fingertips digging in. I check myself out. He's focused on my vag. It looks fine, no stray hairs making a mess of things.

I have a nice vagina when it's taken care of. It's this pretty shade of pink, and only a tiny glimpse of clit peeks out to say hi. When I'm really turned on, obviously everything's a little more prominent. Like now.

His eyes lift, heavy with lust, or need, or just plain old desire. Any which way I look at it, he's turned on. The alternative would suck a lot. For a few seconds I think he's going to drop to his knees and stick his face between my thighs. Which would totally be welcome. Instead, he releases his grip and lifts my shaving-cream-covered leg.

Randy rests the sole of my foot against the center of his chest. I'm a little confused until he picks up the razor. I try to pull my leg away, but he grips my ankle tightly.

"You don't trust me?"

"To weed-whack my forest?"

That grin of his makes my toes curl. God, he's sexy. And I'm naked, totally on display for him. When did I become such a whoreburger?

"I'm good at shaving. I bet I'll do less damage than you have."

"You don't even shave." I point to his beard.

"I sure do shave, and trim, often." He shows me the side of his neck and the perfect line where his beard ends and skin begins.

"Just be careful."

He presses a kiss to my ankle, where there isn't any shaving cream. Then he touches the blade to my leg and slowly skims away the lotion. With the arm with the sleeve. I won't lie. It's kind of hot to have this huge, badass-looking, tattooed hockey player shaving my leg for me.

He goes over my shin first, then lifts so he can get the back. "You're flexible, huh?"

"It's all the figure skating."

"I love the figure skating."

I laugh out of embarrassment.

"Seriously. It's sexy. I would've liked to watch you. Maybe I can tomorrow before I leave."

"If you want. I teach at nine."

"That's kinda early for a Sunday."

"It's better than the six-am ice time for hockey."

Randy nods his agreement and makes another pass with the razor. Finishing up, he tosses it in the sink and holds a washcloth under the warm water. He then runs it over my skin, washing away anything left over.

"I think I did a nice job." He presses another kiss to my ankle. "Don't you?"

"I think you did great. Thanks for not cutting me." It comes out all breathless.

He lowers my leg and fits himself between my thighs. Sadly, he's still wearing pants, and a belt, so getting him to the same state of undress as me is going to take more than a quick tug.

He slides his fingers through my hair and tilts my head back. He doesn't go right in for one of those all-out tongue-war kisses. Instead his lips touch the edge of my jaw, then my chin. It's nice, sweet, unexpected.

I close my eyes and wait for his lips to reach mine. I can feel his breath wash over my face; it smells like cinnamon gum. I feel the faintest brush of lips and then… nothing. My eyes pop open. He's not in my face anymore. Instead he's on his knees.

He pulls me forward until I'm teetering on the edge of the vanity. It makes a faint creaking noise. I hope whoever installed it did a decent job of attaching it to the wall. I don't have time to worry about it. Randy bites the inside of my leg and sucks hard. At my gasp, he releases. Then he nuzzles my thigh, his beard tickling the already sensitive skin.

He stays like that for a few long seconds, his back expanding and contracting with deep, heavy breaths like maybe he's trying to stay composed. I have no idea. All I know is he's sexy as hell on his knees in front of me.

I pull the tie, setting his hair free. Wet kisses bring him closer to where his mouth will provide the most pleasure. The first clit lick is soft, followed by a tentative circling of his tongue.

I moan. It's loud, or maybe it sounds a lot louder than it actually is because we're in a bathroom—again—and the acoustics are killer. His eyes lift to mine, and he does that sucking thing. Sweet lord. I can't even imagine how much practice he's had eating pussy.

He disengages long enough to say, "Not as much as you'd think."

"I said that out loud?" I make a face that's probably unattractive. I'm not sure if I should apologize for that comment or not.

"No, I can read minds."

I squeeze my legs together, and he chuckles. "I'm surprised you haven't come already."

"If you stop talking smack and start licking, I'll get there a lot faster."

"Like this?" He flat-tongues me.

I almost fold forward, but I'm too close to the edge of the vanity, and I'll topple over if I do. Instead I grip his hair with one hand and brace my free palm on the counter. I'd like to lie back, but the taps are behind me. He sucks my clit, following with a teeth-graze.

And the show's over. I come so hard I'm sure brain cells start dying. I'm moaning his name and bucking against him. The vanity makes an accompanying sound. I'd like to get off of it, but I don't have control of my motor function, so I'm relying on Randy to keep me from breaking it while I come all over his face.

He must realize we're putting too much pressure on the counter. Suddenly I'm not sitting anymore. I'm standing—well, that's untrue. Randy's got one arm around my waist, keeping me from dropping to the floor. This time when he kisses me it's the kind I've come to expect from him: demanding, hard, dominating.

I don't even have the ability to fight back with my tongue. I'm still shaking. My muscles are still contracting, like they're grabbing for the dick that isn't there, yet. I fumble around, searching for his belt so I can either return the favor, or we can get down to it. It takes me a few tries to get the buckle undone, but I'm determined when necessary. I manage the button and the zipper as well.

Before I can get my hand down his pants, Randy spins me around. He presses his hips against me, the zipper digging into my ass cheek. He clamps his tattooed forearm across my chest and nibbles from my shoulder to my neck, meeting my spaced-out gaze in the mirror. "Wanna watch me fuck you?"

All that comes out is a whimper.

That smirky grin appears for a second. "I wanna watch me fuck you."

I manage words this time. "Sounds like fun."

Now I get a real smile. "I like fun." He slaps a condom on the counter. "Open that for me?"

"Sure thing, Captain Ballistic."

"I hate it when you last-name me." He bites my shoulder.

"Sorry, *Randy*," I say it all sweet and breathless, like I imagine the bunnies do for him.

Tearing the wrapper, I push the latex ring up. "I can put it on if you want."

"I got this." He shoves his pants down but doesn't bother taking them off. He's still got one arm clamped across my chest. He doesn't let go as he plucks the condom from the wrapper and rolls it on one-handed. I don't understand why he won't let me do it, but his skill is impressive nonetheless.

Once the condom is where it should be, he unbars my chest and runs his hands down my arms. His lips are on the nape of my neck as he presses my palms against the vanity.

I glance over my shoulder, hoping to get a look at… something. He nudges my cheek with his nose. "Keep your eyes on mine, baby."

I glance up and get caught in his hot stare. Holy mother of all things moist, he's got one hell of a smolder going on. Randy keeps one hand on top of mine and grips his cock with the other. Spreading my knees, he bends, and then I feel it: the head of his cock gliding over my clit. I glance down as it disappears from view. And then he's pushing inside me—slow, controlled. It's so, so good. Scratch that. Good doesn't cut it. It's more magical than Oz.

I arch, pushing back, seeking more. And I sure as hell get it. He buries himself completely on a deep exhale.

His eyes flutter, and he groans. "So fuckin' good."

"Totally agree."

He runs a palm up my spine, fingers curling around the back of my neck. I'd consider it a highly dominating action if he didn't knead my tight muscles. He follows this up by using my hair to pull my head back. Not hard, just firmly. Then he presses the softest, warmest kiss below my ear. There's no way to know what's coming next.

"Ready, baby?"

"Uh-huh." I'd nod, but he's still holding my hair.

His smile sends a shiver down my spine and a shot of *holy shit* to my clit. He angles my head to the side so he has access to my mouth. This time it's the battle of tongues two-point-oh. I fist his hair. The harder I grip, the harder he kisses. He's still not moving, though. I'm ultra cock-filled, but without the friction, there's no way to reach the land of bliss.

Randy breaks the kiss on a grunt, and the fucking commences. It's a no-holds-barred, fuck-me-until-the-little-bottles-of-shampoo-fall-over-and-roll-onto-the-floor experience. And the entire time his eyes are on mine—apart from the occasional split-second glance down as he eases out and pushes in super slow. Just to keep me guessing, I suppose.

I'm close to coming. A few well-placed rubs and I'll free-fall into orgasm outer space. The problem is, I'm afraid to lift my hand with the way Randy's pounding into me. The only reason I'm still upright is because he's holding my hips and my arms are acting as support beams. Unsteady ones, but I'm managing. For now.

"Randy?" It comes out fairly coherent in spite of the vigorous pounding.

"Yeah, baby?"

My clit practically lights itself on fire. His voice is straight-up sex shooters.

His next thrust is gentler. "You need me to slow it down?"

I shake my head. "I need to come."

"You sure fuckin' do." He releases one hip, and I nearly face plant into the sink. His wide palm covers my sternum, his thumb and forefinger spreading across my collarbones. He pulls me against him. His other hand slides down the back of my leg, hooking under my knee. I have no idea what his plan is, but he's basically responsible for carrying all of my body weight.

I hold onto the back of his neck so I have an anchor. I'm standing on the ball of one foot. I can see the latex ring at the base of his cock in the reflection. And his balls. They're pulled up tight. There's also a long, pale scar on the inside of his thigh.

That's definitely not my point of focus, though. This position is almost reminiscent of a figure-skating pose. Except we're naked and his massive, fabulous cock is inside me, which definitely wouldn't happen on the ice.

Randy's one coordinated man, because he's able to roll my marble and hold me up while still thrusting. It's insane. And hot.

So of course I come. It's the apocalypse of orgasms. I moan so loudly I have to cover my mouth with my hand. Otherwise I'm concerned anyone walking by in the hall might think I'm being murdered.

Randy stops with the magical genie clit rubbing and moves my hand away from my mouth. "No fuckin' way. I wanna hear you come as much as I wanna watch. Make those fingers useful."

I'm not sure whether to be a snarky bitch or even more turned on. I'm mostly the latter. "People might hear me."

"Like I care who hears you."

He shifts until my knee rests on top of the vanity. Then he reaches over and slams the door. "Now you can make all the noise I want."

He guides my hand between my legs, encouraging me to take over the rolling of the marble. It takes me all of half a minute to have another orgasm. He goes back to the aggressive, heavy thrusting, and I keep rubbing and trying not to scream his name or feed his ego more than I already have.

I don't know how it's possible for him to pick up speed, or momentum, but he does. The vanity starts to creak with each frantic thrust. I come again and give up the marble rolling, bracing a hand on the mirror instead. I'll definitely leave a juicy handprint behind. Which I'm sure Randy will love.

"Fuck. Fuck. Fuck." His head drops against my shoulder, and he bites his way across my neck. "All night long, Lily. I'm gonna be inside you every fucking minute you're here with me."

"Sounds like a good time." I say, and then, because I can't help myself, "But it'll probably get a little awkward when we're sleeping."

"So fucking cheeky." This time he uses more teeth, and I gasp. A smile tips his mouth, but it's brief. He's too close to coming to make more jokes.

He circles his hips, and the hand splayed across my chest comes up a little higher, resting below the base of my throat. "Your mouth, Lily. I want it."

I turn my head and he kisses me, going deep. His other hand drops low, cupping me. He makes the same sound he did last time he came. So I fall down the rabbit hole again with him.

We're both breathing like we've been running from the cops. And we're sweaty. I'd be grossed out, but I'm too orgasm-saturated to care.

Randy carefully lifts my leg down from the vanity. I attempt to use the counter to help brace myself, but we've definitely done some damage. It's pulling away from the wall. And it's on an angle.

I hold on to his arm. My legs are seriously unsteady after that thorough fucking.

"Look what you did." I push the vanity with one finger, and it wobbles.

"Look what I did? Look what *you* did." He jiggles it. It sounds like drywall chunks hitting the floor. And possibly a tile.

"Stop! You're going to make it break! How will you explain

that?"

"Why am I explaining it? It's your fault."

"My fault? How is it my fault? You're the one who busted in here on me. How did that happen anyway? I locked it! Were you some kind of juvenile delinquent as a kid? Are those your prison tats?"

He laughs.

"Stop!"

He takes my chin between his thumb and finger, tilting up. "You're so cute I can't even stand it."

"I am *not* cute." I push his hand away. He lets go, turns around, and pulls up his pants. He's all tucked inside and hidden away when he swings back around, though his boxer briefs sit low and his pants are still undone.

He's got what could possibly be an appendectomy scar, but it seems like the wrong place for that. He tosses the used condom in the garbage. Then reaches around me to turn on the tap, pinning me against the vanity.

"And you're also sexy, so you shouldn't be too upset about being cute."

"Cute is for pink tutus and puppies, not grown women."

"Mmm. I see." He finishes washing his hands and takes my face between his wet palms.

"Ah! What the hell, Randy!"

He doesn't answer, just kisses me while he smiles. I stop fighting against him and go with it, even though he's making my face wet. He leans in, and the vanity cracks loudly. "You can't tell me that was anything but ten-out-of-ten sex."

"Probably even eleven. I need a shower."

He gives me some space. "I'll order us some room service."

"You don't want to join me?"

"Another time. I'm hungry, and you gotta be starving."

"But you're all sweaty."

"I'm used to being sweaty; plus I'm totally happy smelling like this."

He pats me on the ass and turns on the water. While I wash my hair he peeks through the curtain and reads me the menu. It's already two by the time I'm done with my shower. I have nothing clean to put on, so I use one of the robes the hotel provides for guests who rent the nice rooms. I find Randy lying on the bed, watching Sportsnet.

He's still shirtless and wearing jeans. He pats the bed. "Come hang out with me."

I lie in the mound of pillows, and he slides an arm behind my back, pulling me close. It's comfortable, which is a little unnerving. I get all cozy along his side and close my eyes. I'm so tired. Having two jobs is exhausting, as is multiple orgasms and awesome sex.

I must nod off, because suddenly Randy's all up in my face, using my boobs to shake me awake. I open my eyes with a frown.

He's smiling. "Food's here!"

"Nice."

We sit cross-legged on the bed, and I devour the entire personal pizza he ordered for me. It was only six slices. "I'm so full." I lean back against the pillows and rub my belly through the robe. "And sleepy again."

"So catch a nap."

I check the clock. It's already three-thirty. "I have to leave in an hour."

He frowns. "And you're off at what time?"

"Not until ten."

"You should call in sick."

"I can't do that."

"Why not?"

"Because I'm not sick."

"So? Come on, call in." He crawls up my body and lies to the right of me. "I don't have another Toronto game for a month, and I doubt you can get a whole weekend off to come to a Chicago game."

I run my fingers through his hair, debating.

"You can nap, and then we can use the rest of that box of condoms." He traces the edge of the robe and pulls the tie free. "I promise it'll be more fun than work." He parts my robe and circles a nipple with his fingertip. It pebbles under his touch.

I shouldn't call in. I should work my shift, but he's right, I can't logically coordinate the time off with both jobs, and there's no guarantee he'll still be interested in another month. This could potentially be my last opportunity to have seriously uninhibited sex.

I sigh. "Okay."

"You'll call in?"

"Yes."

"I'll get your phone." He rolls off the bed and jogs to the bathroom. He returns with my purse and my bag of goodies from Shopper's. He holds up the box of condoms I purchased. "You're a regular Girl Scout, aren't you?"

"It's Girl Guides in Canada."

"Good to know. You better call work quick. We have twenty-three condoms to blow through tonight. We have to get started on that right away."

I wait until Randy turns the volume down on the TV before I call. Once I'm on the phone with my boss, he runs his hands up my shins. When he reaches my knees, I kick at him. He grabs my legs and spreads them apart, pulling me down the bed.

I mouth for him to stop, but he pulls me in tight, grinding against me. He's already hard. I can both see and feel him through his jeans.

"I'm so sorry. I know. It must have been something I ate. I got takeout last night, and I've been sick all day." I cough to cover my groan when he rubs against my clit. "I thought I'd be over it by now, but I don't think it's a good idea for me to work around food if there's a possibility I'm contagious. I should have called earlier—Yes, of course. I'll call tomorrow and let you know. 'Kay, thanks. I'm sorry again."

I hang up the phone. "You couldn't have waited until I was done before you started with the humping?"

"What fun would that have been?" He takes my phone and tosses it on the bed, then lies on top of me.

"I thought I was supposed to nap."

"Fuck first. Nap later."

"You're insatiable."

I pull his mouth down to mine, and the only words I manage after those are moans of affirmation.

True to his word, Randy keeps me up most of the night. I'm naked the entire time, and the only reason I get out of bed is to hose down or use the bathroom.

He orders wine and cheese and fruit for us to snack on between sexings. I don't think I've ever been this indulged in my life—not with sex or attentiveness.

Randy has some interesting sex habits I can now cross-reference with his bunny groups: he always starts with the covers on, and then we lose them later. He likes the lights down in the beginning, and then he likes to be able to see me when I come.

He's also a little weird about me touching his cock. I have

no idea why, but any hand-job action is short-lived and always while the lights are down. And when I offer to go down on him, he tells me some other time since he'll taste like latex.

I'm not about to ruin all the awesome orgasms and sex we're having by asking personal questions, so I leave it alone.

It's after five in the morning by the time we finally finish a box of condoms, save one. I need at least three solid hours of sleep or I'm going to be a mess at the arena. Randy slips an arm under my pillow and pulls me to him. I'm naked, still, and so is he, but I have no more energy left for sex. My vagina will fall off my body. He seems to be done—for now—so this time when I fall asleep, I'm not awakened by his mouth next to my ear, asking me if I wanna have more fun yet.

15

JUST A RIDE

LILY

Eight comes horribly fast. I cut my alarm and look over at Randy, still out cold. His full lips are parted, his tattooed arm thrown out to the side. There's a hockey scene captured on his forearm, and a Toronto emblem, as well as the one for New York. It's still too dark for me to make out the rest.

I leave him where he is and tiptoe to the bathroom. My hair's a mess. I look like I've been boned from here all the way to the North Pole. And not freshly either—in a used well and ridden like a cheap hooker kind of way. I also smell like a big, huge pile of sex. I take a quick shower and call a cab. I don't want to wake Randy up to have him drive me in.

I put on my crappy jogging pants and hoodie, thankful that I have a spare skating outfit in my locker. There's nothing I can do about the lack of underwear, since I forgot about washing them, but I've dealt with worse issues.

I pack my bag in a rush, knowing I'm cutting it close. I debate whether or not to leave without saying goodbye. I decide I don't want to. I wouldn't like it if Randy did that to me. Although I'm a girl, and we're different.

I creep around to his side of the bed. My plan is to whisper a goodbye and thanks, but I note the tented sheets at his waist. He's asleep with a hard-on. I lift the soft cotton carefully, but I'm disappointed to find he's got his boxers back on. It's like the damn Loch Ness monster. Everyone says it's real, but they've never seen it to prove it.

I reach under the covers, ready to sneak a peek, but Randy snatches my hand. "If you want it, all you have to do is ask." He pulls me down and rolls on top of me.

"I was saying bye. I have to leave for work."

He nuzzles his face into my neck and gives me a couple of humps through the sheets and my clothes. "No. Don't go."

"I have to."

"I wanna fuck some more."

I laugh. He's all groggy and uncoordinated—aside from the hip grinding. That's very coordinated. "I called a cab. I have to leave, like, two minutes ago."

"I'll drive you in."

"You're not even conscious."

"My dick is. He'll drive."

I push on his chest, but he's not budging. "If I'm late I could lose my job."

He stops grinding and rolls off me. "Now I have to deal with this alone." He pats his hard-on.

"Just go back to sleep; it'll go away."

"What time are you done?"

"One, but I work a shift at my other job at four."

"I'll come get you."

"Don't you need to go back to Chicago?"

"I'll fly or something." He shoves his hand down the front of his boxers. "See you at one, luscious Lily."

"Whatever you say, raucous Randy." I turn to leave.

"Wait."

"Hmm?"

He taps his cheek lazily. "I wanna kiss before you leave."

I lean over and plant one there, then drop another on his lips. "Thanks for all the fun."

"Anytime."

Since he was half-asleep when I left this morning, I don't really expect him to show up at my work. So when he arrives at eleven-thirty with coffee and a bag and sits in the stands, all the butterflies in the world take up residence in my stomach.

We had an insane amount of sex. I've never in my life used an entire box of condoms in one night. Three, maybe, but never more than that. All my muscles ache, but the pain isn't something I mind.

At the end of the lesson, I skate over to Randy. He looks fresh, cleaned up, and a whole lot less disheveled than I did this morning. "I brought you something." He passes me the bag.

I take a peek inside. "You bought me clothes?"

"I figure we only have a couple of hours before you have to go to work, and you'd want something fresh to change into. I guessed at the size. I know your dress was a four at the party." He jams his hands into his pockets.

A guy remembering a dress size seems epic. "That's sweet, but you didn't need to do that. I have my work clothes. I was going to change into them."

"Well, I thought I could take you out for lunch, since that didn't happen yesterday."

"You don't want to go back to your hotel?" I'm sort of being cheeky, sort of not.

"I had to check out." He rolls back on his heels. "The backseat of the Jeep is spacious, though."

I can't tell if he's being serious. One of the parents comes over to ask me a couple of questions, and of course, another mother recognizes Randy and starts freaking out. She's got to be almost forty, and she's definitely undressing him mentally. I know the look. Lucky for me I don't have to work to imagine him without clothes. Well, except for one part.

I head to the locker room, shower, and put on the new clothes. He's good at guessing. He's also got expensive taste. A pair of gray leggings, a pretty shirt dress in royal blue, and a new pair of very lacy, very delicate panties cost over a hundred and fifty dollars, according to the price tags. The receipt isn't in the bag, so there's no way to return them.

Randy takes me to a nice restaurant. Everything is expensive. Benji and I didn't go out on dates very often. If we did it was to see some local hipster band. He'd eat sweet potato fries and complain about his parents not putting enough money in his bank account. It was annoying, but he always paid for me, so I never said anything. He liked to hold things like that over my head so I'd feel like I owed him something. He also liked to manipulate by digging at my insecurities. It set us up for inequity, and that doesn't work for me. I don't think it works for anyone.

Randy just seems to want to go out for a nice lunch. He gets a beer, and I get a glass of wine even though I have to work in a few hours. I'm starving, making lunch that much more amazing. Probably because of all the sex.

We get dessert, and not to share because I want my own and so does Randy.

"You work a lot, huh?" he says as he shovels a mouthful of peach pie into his mouth. His dessert choice is ironic.

I got the fried banana and ice cream. Also ironic.

"Yeah. I finished school in April. I'd like to work on a masters in physiotherapy, but the program's expensive, so I need to save for a while. I've worked at the coffee shop since high school. There aren't any full-time skating-coach positions unless I move to the city, so I do both for now."

"A masters, huh? So you're smart."

I shake my head. "Not really. I mean, I guess for science and stuff I'm decent. I had to work hard to keep my scholarship. School wasn't a breeze or anything."

"So do you have a place close by? We have more than an hour before you have to go to work." He's got that look on his face.

Right now, more than ever, I wish I had my own apartment. Or one I shared with Sunny so I could take him back there for one last sex-and-orgasm marathon before I have to go to work and he has to leave for Chicago.

"I, uh… um… I don't live on my own."

"You have a roommate?" We're sitting beside each other, not across the table. His arm is draped across the back of the seat, and he keeps running his knuckles down either side of my spine, from my hairline to the collar of my shirt. I can feel it right in my magic marble. Which I would love for Randy to roll again.

"Uh, yeah."

"Do you think she'll be home?" Now he's running a single finger back and forth along the collar of my shirt. That he bought for me. So I didn't have to deal with wearing dirty clothes. I'm also not wearing a bra since all I had was my ugly, ancient sports one.

My nipples are hard and obvious through my shirt. He's noticed. He touches the scar on his lip with the tip of his tongue. I can almost hear his thoughts. And he's got an obvious rod in his pants. It's angled toward my vagina like a directional arrow. That helps with the mind reading.

"I don't know. Sometimes she works odd hours." It's not a total lie. My mom's job isn't always predictable, and some days she works from home. Plus it's a Sunday, so who knows what she could be up to.

"Well, she won't mind if we come back and use your room, right?" He leans in and puts his mouth to my ear. "You can always bite a pillow if you're worried about being loud."

I picture the scene that might require me to do that. Any one of the many positions from last night would definitely qualify.

"Why don't I pay the bill and we can get outta here?" Randy nuzzles my neck, and my clit lights up like it's the Jumbotron flashing a winning score. I'd like to jump him right now. At this table. Regardless of the audience.

I have to tell him the truth. I can't risk bringing him back to my apartment on the off chance my mom is there.

"Unless you're not interested." It's meant to come off as sarcastic, or cocky, but there's a waver in his smile, and what might be a little insecurity.

I'm experiencing a high level of embarrassment. It's almost as bad as the first time I met him—naked, with my fur burger on display—or worse, the limbo period of time after I defaced his underwear and before he ate me out in the bathroom. "It's not that I'm not interested; it's just that—" I try not to make a scrunchy face, but I can tell I'm unsuccessful.

"Last night too much for you?" Again with the humor/sarcasm.

There's no way to say this that isn't going to be horrifying, so I blurt, "My mom is my roommate."

Randy cocks his head to the side. I say a little prayer. It goes something like this: *Dear God, It's me, Lily. I've probably done this three times total in my life, and you never seem to be online when I am, but it'd be super awesome if you clubbed Randy over the head so he doesn't remember this whole episode. Thanks.*

It doesn't work. Instead Randy gets the look I'm used to by this point: half cocky asshole, half hot bastard. "You live with your mom?"

"I'm saving for an apartment." It doesn't matter how good the reason is, I still feel losery.

I'm highly aware that this generation, us twenty-somethings, sometimes stay at home longer than what was normal in the past, thanks to the cost of education and the fact that jobs aren't as easy to get. There's also that sense of entitlement thing some people have going on—like Benji, who's more than happy to ride the free train as long as possible. That's not why I stay. Mostly I'm there to keep an eye on my mom when her relationships inevitably fail. And anyway, Sunny and I had a plan, which isn't going to happen now that she's seriously considering Chicago. Unless I go with her. That's looking more and more appealing all the time.

"So it's you and your mom, then? No other roommates?"

It's a roundabout way of asking a personal question. We haven't had many conversations about family, apart from what he's said about his dad. But then, we've been too busy getting our sex on for much talking.

"Nope. No other roommates."

He nods, pensive, but doesn't push for more information. If we start talking about serious stuff, a last round of ride-the-dick won't happen.

"There's a bathroom here."

I've already considered it. I won't tell him that, though. "So classy."

"We could always find one of those by-the-hour hotel rooms."

"That's the worst idea ever in the history of ideas, Randy. I'd rather do it in the back of the Jeep than a hotel room that looks like a Rorschach test under a black light."

Randy laughs. "Backseat it is then."

I'm not sure if he's kidding, but he gets the check, and we walk out to the Jeep. I still have an hour and a half before my shift, and he doesn't seem to be a in a rush to leave, so I suggest we go for a drive. We park in the middle of nowhere on a trail that leads to who knows what. Apparently Randy is totally serious about the backseat, because I end up with my pants off and my shirt pushed up with him inside me again.

By the time we've finished round eight million of our sex marathon, I've got twenty-seven minutes to get to the coffee shop. I change into my uniform in the backseat with Randy's help—which mostly consists of fondling and some gropes—and he drives me to work.

I'm nervous about goodbye. I don't know what to expect. This isn't like any of our previous sexual encounters. He parks the Jeep in the lot and turns to me. My hands are clammy. I'm not going to see him again for at least a month. It's probably a good thing, preventing me from getting attached, or too comfortable.

"I had a lot of fun with you, Lily. Definitely ten-out-of-ten fun."

I'm still nervous, but his joking makes the tension dissipate a little. "Me, too."

His answering smile makes my panties want to climb into his pocket. "We'll do it again next time I have a Toronto game? I'll hold on to the other box of condoms until then."

I bite back a laugh. "As long as I can get the time off, sure."

"Great. I'll send you a message with the date so I can get in you again."

I roll my eyes. "I better go. My shift starts in ten, and I plan to make out with you for at least five minutes before I leave this car." I don't wait for him to lean in. I unbuckle my seatbelt and plaster my mouth to his.

He holds on to the back of my neck while we kiss. It's not frantic, because we both know it's not leading to anything more, but it still makes my toes curl and points below light up. We break apart after a few minutes, both of us panting.

He exhales a long, slow breath. "I'll walk you in and get a coffee for the road."

"Sure. Okay."

Randy gets out of the Jeep and comes around to help me with my knapsack full of clothes that smell like sex. The Jeep also smells like sex, and I'm positive I do, too. He opens the door of the café like he's being all chivalrous. Except he pats my ass.

I stop inside the door. What in the serious shit? Sitting at one of the tables is my mother.

Here's the thing, my mom almost never comes to visit me at work. Most of the time she doesn't pay attention to my schedule. Not that she needs to. I'm an adult; I can manage my own life. Usually we try to stay out of each other's business. So I have no idea what would bring her here, today of all days. She's not alone either. She's got a guy with her. His back is to me, so I have no clue who he is, or why in the world she'd have a coffee date at my work.

My first instinct is to push Randy back out the door. But the damn bell has chimed, alerting everyone in the shop to our arrival. My mother looks up before I make any kind of pre-emptive move in one direction or another.

She smiles and waves.

"Oh, shit."

"Some crazy customer?" Randy runs his fingers through the back of my hair, catching a few knots along the way. I didn't even think to check it before I got out of the Jeep.

"That's my mother. I don't know what she's doing here."

"Oh. Shit is right. Is that your dad?"

"Nope. My dad's a dick. I haven't seen him since never." I don't mean to impart that massive boulder of baggage truth.

"Huh. Well, my dad's a dick, too. So we have that in common." He pushes me forward. "We should go say hi."

"I'm so sorry."

"It's cool. Just don't moan my name or anything when you introduce me."

"Your ego is its own country." I take a couple of halting steps forward, figuring out what I'm going to say.

"Lily bird!" my mom gets up, her eyes darting behind me to Randy and then back, clearly wanting some kind of introduction.

I'm pretty sure telling her he's the guy I'm casually boning who provides the best orgasms I've ever had isn't going to fly. "Hey, Mom, so weird that you're here right now. This is my friend Randy." I motion between them. "Randy, this is my mom, Iris."

"Randy. Hi! So nice to meet you." She sticks her hand out.

He shakes it with the one that's been inside me in the past hour. "Hi, Iris. Looks like I'm surrounded by all the most beautiful flowers."

It's a super cheesy line—like, poutine with double cheese and extra gravy—but my mom giggles like she's fifteen. I roll my eyes, and Randy flashes me a grin.

"Holy shit!" the guy with my mom yells.

I'd almost forgotten he was here, thanks to the shitting of my pants over introducing Randy to my mom. At least she hasn't recognized him as anyone important yet.

"Randy Ballistic?" Dude shoots up out of his chair and thrusts out his hand.

"Hey." Randy takes it, and the guy—who I now realize is Tom, or Tim, or whatever his name is, all I know is I'm glad he's wearing more than underwear this time—gives him one of those over-enthusiastic handshakes.

He continues to pump Randy's hand so much that I almost expect Randy's mouth to open and water to come splashing out. "Iris, do you know who this is?"

My mom lifts her shoulders in an apologetic shrug.

"This is Randy Ballistic. He's a new forward for Chicago. He used to play for New York. That game on Friday was killer. You really showed your worth to the team."

Her smile freezes. "You're a *hockey* player?" Her tone makes it sound more like he's committed a heinous crime.

"Uh, yeah. It's cool if you root for Toronto. I won't hold it against you. I used to play for them, too."

"Um, I'd love to chat, but I have to start my shift." I wave behind me to the counter, where no customers are currently waiting.

"I need to use the ladies' room," my mom says through gritted teeth. She threads her arm through mine, gripping hard as she steers me toward the back of the shop.

"A *hockey* player, Lily? What is wrong with you?"

I can't deal with her now, so I need a cover story—one that's plausible and no one can refute. "Relax yourself, Mom. He's a friend of Alex's. I stayed at Sunny's last night, and Alex was home visiting. He brought a couple friends with him. Randy was on his way out the door and offered me a ride."

"Oh, I'm sure he did."

"Mom. He drove me to work. He's nice."

She stares at me hard for few seconds. "They all seem nice at first."

I love my mom, but sometimes her hypocrisy is frustrating. "I need to start my shift. Is this Tom guy going to be at home when I get there tonight?"

"His name is Tim. Maybe. Probably. Why?"

"Can you please make sure he's wearing more than underwear outside of your bedroom?"

She gives me a pinched look.

"I gotta go. I'm supposed to be working already."

"We'll talk about this later."

"There's nothing to talk about, Mom. It was just a ride." I mean that literally and figuratively.

My mom goes into the bathroom, and I drop my bag in the manager's office and rush to get my apron on so I'm out before my mom is finished in the girls' room.

Randy and Tim-Tom are still talking. Well, Tim-Tom is talking, and Randy is nodding. Tim-Tom follows Randy to the counter and stops yapping long enough for Randy to order a coffee, one of the specialty kinds.

My stomach is in all kinds of knots. I need Randy to leave before my mom comes back, but based on Tim-Tom, that's not likely to happen. I pass the coffee to Randy, along with a bag of cookies, and I try not to let him pay, but he keeps shoving the money at me.

He covers my hand with his, blatantly ignoring Tim-Tom's rambling. My mom shows back up at the same moment Randy kisses me on the cheek and whispers, "Thanks for all the fun."

My mom shoots laser beams from her eyeballs. At least we're in public and she can't make a scene.

16

TRAINER TROUBLES AND OTHER PROBLEMS

RANDY

I miss a training session because I don't get back to Chicago until late on Sunday. After dropping off Lily I stopped in to see Michael, the kid we held the exhibition game for back in September, before I caught a flight home. Miller had been to see him yesterday, like I figured he would. We can't be this close and not visit. I talk to him on Facebook and stuff, but it's not the same as face to face. It's hard to see a thirteen-year-old sick like that, but his treatment is going well, and surgery is scheduled for early December.

I've ignored my phone since I left Toronto for Guelph. More like I turned it off. I have seven messages when I turn it back on. Three are clearly speech-to-text-recorded from Miller because some of it doesn't make sense. The rest of are voice mails. I only have to listen to one to know he's stressed.

"Dude. You need to call me. Shit's about to go down. Coach is pissed. I mean pissed. You have no idea. Where the hell are

you? We have a team meeting at eight tomorrow. You better not miss it or you're gonna be benched. You might be anyway for missing today."

That's early for a game day. It's already after eleven. I've just walked in the door after my flight back from Lily Land. Calling him to find out what's going on will probably kill the buzz I'm still riding.

Instead, I throw some food in the microwave and send Lily a message while it heats.

Back in Chicago. I'd rather b in u.

We used an entire box of condoms. All twelve, with the last time in the Jeep. That's a record. I've never had that many consecutive hard-ons in a row and been able to finish every time.

If that keeps happening, I'm going to develop some kind of addiction problem. To her. I glance down. I'm hard. Again. And everything is hypersensitive after so much action in such a short period of time. I'm almost inclined to pull a Miller and walk around naked to keep the friction at bay. If I end up having to whack it tonight, I'll need some kind of lube to prevent it from being unpleasant.

The microwave beeps, so I take the plate out, burning my fingertips. I search for a dishtowel or something and take my meal into the living room so I can watch sports highlights. I also call Miller on the off chance he's still awake. I should probably know what I'm walking into in the morning.

He answers on the third ring. "Fuck you for calling me this late, asshole."

"What's going on?"

"We have a meeting at fuck you o'clock in the morning, and

a game tomorrow, night, and you're calling to ask me what's going on? Screw you, Balls. You'll find out in the morning." I get dead air.

I'd call him back, but he sounds pissed. Miller's usually a level guy. He wasn't exactly happy about me swinging by Guelph to visit Lily. He didn't so much say it as I could tell by his attitude.

I check my messages again, even though my phone hasn't beeped. Lily's definitely asleep. I'm sure I wore her out this weekend. She kept up, though. It's hard to find someone who can manage my sexual appetite. I kinda wish she lived closer.

Since there's so much time between seeing each other, I should be able to stretch things out a little longer than usual with her. Which is fantastic since the sex is out of this world. Plus she's not clingy. Usually after a marathon sex-fest like the one we had, the girl is texting me nonstop, asking about the next hook-up. Lily's not like that. I appreciate it, and I don't. Her lack of communication makes me second-guess how well things went and how she's feeling about it.

I scrub my hands over my face and vow to stop fixating on Lily and start wondering what I missed at our training session this afternoon. I'm probably in trouble for that, but I'm sure Coach'll understand my flight delay—which didn't actually happen, but I'm pretending did.

I give Lance a try, but I get his voice mail. I don't leave a message. I try one last person. I hit the call button and regret it immediately. Waters and I aren't all that tight yet, but he seems to like me well enough. As the team captain, he might be willing to give me the information Miller isn't.

I'll be lucky if I'm not waking him up. I second-guess myself and am about to end the call when someone picks up. "Horny Nut Sac, why are you calling my fiancé's phone at this hour?"

It's Violet. I'm not sure whether I should be relieved.

"I'm sorry."

"You've been inside a Canadian haven't you?" she asks.

"What?"

"You're apologizing, and you don't even know for what. You've definitely been inside a Canadian."

"I don't—"

"If you tell me you don't know what I'm talking about, I'm going to kick your ass."

I decide there isn't any reason to lie about this situation. Also, there's no way Violet can kick my ass. "Miller left me a message and said some shit had gone down. He's not answering his phone right now, and I don't want to go into tomorrow's meeting blind."

"You boned Lily."

I have no clue why this matters to Violet. She's not close with Lily, at least not that I know of.

"I don't see how that—"

"Matters?" She doesn't wait for me to answer. "You don't see the importance of you banging your bestie's girlfriend's bestie? Seriously, Balls, I thought you were smarter than that."

"Smarter than what? How do you even have this information?"

"Honestly? I live with Alex. Sunny's his sister, and we're girls. We talk. In detail. Sometimes too much."

"It's not a big deal. I'm a rebound. Me and Lily are having some fun."

"If you say so, Balls. Anyway, if you want to know what the real issue is here, you should probably talk to Romero or Tash, but I doubt either of them is answering the phone right now."

"What happened with Lance and Tash?"

"Nothing good. You'll get the full report in the morning. I'm tired, and my fiancé is already passed out, so I'm gonna go snuggle up to him and get some sleep. Good luck tomorrow."

I'm ten minutes early for the morning meeting. I'm tired and on edge because I don't know what's going on. Most of the team is already there, and I find Miller sitting beside Waters. They're deep in conversation, both of their knees bouncing hard. I drop down on the bench beside Miller.

"Nice of you to show up, Balls."

I ignore the shot. "What's going on? Where's Lance?"

"He better get here soon," Waters says. He's in a foul mood. Most of the time he's not bad to deal with. But when he's pissed it's advisable to stay out of his way.

"I think he's fucked either way already," Miller mumbles.

"I told him to watch himself, but he didn't. Now he's screwed the entire team," Alex replies.

"What happ—"

A whistle blows, and everyone stops talking. Coach stands in the middle of the room with Lance and some new guy. Coach tells Lance to take a seat, and he drops down on the end of a bench. He rests his elbows on his knees and clasps his hands together, keeping his eyes down.

A few whispers break out, and Coach clears his throat, silencing the room. "This is Evan Smart, the new team trainer. He's been training professional athletes for the past seven years. He's got a great track record, and we're happy to have him on board. Whatever he says goes. You will work with him as a team. If there's a workout scheduled, you will be there. Unless you have some kind of injury, or a life-and-death situation you have made me and Evan aware of in advance, you'll be at training. Everyone understand?"

There's a murmur of acknowledgement.

"Anyone who misses a training session without notifying me and Evan will be benched for a game." Coach gives me a hard stare. "Ballistic, you missed yesterday, so you'll be warming the bench tonight."

"Yes, Coach. Sorry, Coach." Arguing would be a seriously bad idea, based on the somber mood in the room. Also, the fact that Tash has been replaced is a shock.

Coach sighs, lifts his hat, and runs a hand through his thinning hair before replacing it. "All of you will take home the team rules and regulations book and read it over, so I can be sure you understand what they mean. There will be a test. If you guys are gonna act like you're in high school, I will treat you like you're in high school. I'd like you to pay particular attention to the fraternization policy with support staff. He looks to Lance. "Romero, you're on a three-game suspension."

Lance glances up and gives him a curt nod. The muscle in his jaw tics. "Yes, Coach."

Coach claps his hands together. "Get yourselves suited up and on the ice." When Lance doesn't move, Coach snaps his fingers. "You too, Romero. You might not get to play, but you sure need to learn how to be part of this team if you want to stay on it."

"Yes, Coach. Sorry, Coach."

"Anything else you want to say, Romero?"

He shakes his head. "No, Coach."

"Then get moving."

The room is quiet as we get ready for the pre-game skate. I have questions, but I can't ask them right now. Practice isn't easy. We're all off, and it shows in the way we play. I don't have much faith that we'll be able to pull it together for the game tonight.

Lance takes off afterward without talking to anyone. I wait

until me and Miller are alone before I ask any questions. "How'd Coach find out?"

"They were going at it in the locker room. Coach was the one who walked in on them, so Tash got let go, and they brought in this new guy."

"Shit."

"Yeah."

"How's Lance?"

"Not good. He's not answering calls. I think this has been going on a lot longer than any of us realized. Tash's career is shot—at least in terms of working with any pro team." He stops in front of his car and spins his keys around his finger.

"This is a clusterfuck."

"Yeah, man. He's lucky he's not getting traded. He's gonna have to watch his ass from now on. Coach is seriously pissed. Tash's been the team trainer for two years. These guys had a routine down, and now they gotta get used to a new one. There can't be anymore bullshit like this or we're gonna have more than new-trainer issues."

"That's kinda hypocritical coming from you, huh?"

Miller scoffs. "Even I knew better than to get all up in the staff." His phone beeps. "Hold on." He takes the call and walks away from me, his voice low. I can tell its Sunny since he calls her sweets.

I'm thinking it might be a good idea to stop by Lance's later, if he still isn't answering calls. He's not good when he's upset. He has a tendency to fly off the handle. And drink too much. I want to make sure he's not face down on the bathroom floor or anything.

I send him a text while I wait for Miller to be done talking to Sunny. He's doing a lot of pacing. I hope things are okay there. The last thing I need is more chick drama with my teammates.

There's already more than enough to last me a year. This is one of the reasons I'm wary about relationships; they mess with people's heads.

I see it happen with my mom every so often. I think she's tried to date a couple of times, but after the way my dad fucked her over—and sometimes still does if he feels like being a real asshole—she doesn't trust men. I can't blame her, either.

I scroll through my messages. I've got nothing from Lily. I get this twinge in the back of my neck. I rub it, but it doesn't go away. It should be good that she's not texting the day after. It means she's not making this into more than what it is.

I pocket my phone when Miller turns around. "Everything all right?" I ask.

"Yeah. Fine. Sunny's just worried. I guess she talked to Violet and got the story from her. Now they're talking to Tash, and she's all upset. I still don't get why they'd be banging in the damn locker room." He blows out a breath. "This situation is seriously messed."

"I'm gonna stop by Lance's to check on him."

"Good plan. I'll come with you."

"Food first, though?"

"Damn right."

We hit a buffet and carb load so Miller's ready for the game tonight; then we drive to Lance's place. We have the code to get in, but the safety latch is on, so we can't get through the door. It doesn't matter how long we ring the doorbell; he's not answering.

"I'mma scale the fence," Miller announces.

"That's probably not the best plan." Lance's fence is one of those wrought-iron jobs, covered in ivy with pointy things on top.

"It'll be fine." Miller ambles over and jumps up, catching

two posts. He plants his feet on the bars, but he's wearing skater shoes, and they don't have traction. Miller's also a big guy. He's beefy, like defense usually are, and he's got a good thirty pounds on me, maybe a little more. I have to work hard to bulk up at all, and if I don't watch it, I end up dropping all the weight I put on over off-season as soon as we start hardcore training.

He struggles with a couple of attempts, and I watch, biting back a laugh. "Want a boost?"

"Like you can lift my ass. I'll boost you over."

"No fucking way. You see how pointy that shit is?" I motion to the sword-like tips. My balls get achy just thinking about being near those.

"You'll be fine. Seriously, Balls, those aren't razors attached to the top."

He's right. I know that. But I'd rather boost him, even though I'd likely strain something. He laces his fingers together and bends down far enough for me to use them as a step. I can't argue. He'll razz the shit out of me. He knows I have irrational fears regarding the state of my balls.

Or maybe they're not irrational considering how I almost lost them, and half my dick, when I was eleven.

"Fuck you, Buck," I mumble and put my foot on his hand bridge. "I hope I stepped in dog shit."

"I'll wipe it on your ass when I hoist you over."

"You do, and I'll kick you in the face."

"And I'll taint-punch you, so we'll be even."

"Just boost me, asshole."

"On three."

"Yeah."

Miller counts to three and launches me up. I manage to get my foot on top of the rail.

"Nice work! Now up and over." He grabs my ankle.

It's easier said than done. There's maybe six inches between the iron bars, or whatever regulation is so kids can't climb through or get their heads stuck. It doesn't give me a lot of room for maneuvering. If I don't have one of those spikes close to my balls, the other's almost up my ass.

"Dude. Seriously. I will knock your fake fucking teeth right out."

He lets go and steps back, which would be fine if I was prepared, but I'm not, so I almost end up spiking myself on both sides. There's a lot of profanity, but eventually I make it over the ten-foot fence of death and land in Lance's garden, crushing his flowers. Not that he'll notice or care.

I hold onto my balls out of habit as I pop up. "Fuck you, Butterson."

"Why are you pissed at me? I helped your ass over."

"You know what, when you almost lose half your dick, you can be lackadaisical about this shit. But until then you need to be a little more fucking sensitive."

"Lackadaisical?" Miller grins. "Have you been hanging out with Vi lately? Or Waters? Do you even know how to spell that?"

"I hate you." I stalk in the direction of the patio doors. They better damn well be open.

I stop at the gate and unlatch it so Miller can get in. Then I continue my irritated stalking. I pull on the door handle, half expecting it to be locked, but it slides easily.

"Oh, shit." Miller's behind me, surveying the same scene I am.

It's not good. Clearly our friend has lost his mind based on the state of his living room.

"Lance? Buddy? You here?" I call. I have to step over a broken something and around a bunch of other smashed shit to get through his living room.

"You sure you're ready for this? He's gonna be messed."

Miller follows behind me, shaking his head.

Lance has had a meltdown. They're epic on the ice; off the ice they're destructive. I check the kitchen and then the rest of the main floor and come up with nothing. We don't take off our shoes on our way to the second floor—there's too much broken glass. Music is playing up there. Heavy, angry stuff.

I pause at the landing. There's a lot of shit in the hallway. Girl clothes. Some nice underwear. And a lot of holes in the walls. And more broken glass.

Lance isn't a bad guy. He's actually a decent person under all the bullshit and fighting, but he's got a complex. No one knows why, or what he's trying to prove, because as much as he invites everyone to his house to party, none of us is close enough to know why he does the things he does. All I know is his relationship with his family back in Scotland isn't good. The rest of them are in Connecticut, and he doesn't see them much, either.

Miller goes ahead of me. "Romance? You up here?"

Lance stumbles out into the hall, his shoulder slamming the wall. He's holding a bottle of booze, and his knuckles are bloody. He's definitely responsible for all the holes in the walls, not that there was any other possibility.

Miller rushes him and grabs the bottle before he loses his grip. Lance points an accusing finger at us. "Why didn't anyone warn me?" Weaving into the wall, he stumbles toward the bathroom. He doesn't quite make it to the toilet, but at least he hits the sink.

Getting him sobered up for the game tonight isn't going to be fun.

Over the next couple of weeks, Miller and I keep an eye on Lance. He's not going out to the bars, and he's not throwing parties, which is a surprise. I figured he'd for sure bunny-fuck his way out of his funk, but he's not interested in anything—apart from training and booze, anyway. After his three-game suspension, I was sure he'd get himself in shit on the ice, but he's managed to keep it together for the most part. He still leads for penalty minutes, but at least he's not picking fights as much.

I haven't heard from Lily at all. It should be a good thing, but it kinda bugs me. I decide I'll be the one to break the silence when I realize our next Toronto game is coming up. This time I want her at the game, and then in my bed for the rest of the night. Unfortunately, the game's not at the end of a series, so I don't have time to stick around. But at least we can have the night—and breakfast or something before I fly back to Chicago.

Lily answers on the fourth ring. "Hello?" Her voice is raspy, like it was when I woke her up in the middle of the night—repeatedly—to get back inside her.

"Hey. I wake you up?"

She makes a noise that isn't really a word.

"I'll take that as a yes. You want me to call you back tomorrow?" I don't want to, but I figure I should give her the option since it is kind of late. I don't even know if she wants to talk to me. Maybe after last time she's not all that interested. Although considering how into it she was, I'd be surprised.

"No, it's fine. I can sleep later. How're you?"

I laugh at her mumbling. "You musta been out cold."

"Musta. What time is it?"

"Eleven."

"Wow. I've been out for hours." The words are clearer now, no longer running together with the heaviness of sleep.

"Working too much again?"

"Still. Yeah. Nice goal last game."

"You saw that?" I grin.

"The highlights, but yeah. How's the new trainer? Sunny told me what happened with Lance. It's kinda soap opera-y, eh?"

"Yeah. I guess. We're all adjusting." There's a few seconds of silence, so I decide to throw it out there. "Since you mentioned games and scoring goals, we'll be in Toronto in a couple weeks. Wanna come play with me?"

"You wanna see me again?"

I put her on speaker phone. "Well, yeah. I'm gonna be local. Why do you sound so surprised?"

"I don't know. I haven't heard from you since last time." She's all quiet.

"You didn't message me either."

"Well, I don't know how this works. I figure it's supposed to be all casual and stuff."

Sometimes I forget this is different. She's not a bunny. "You can still message me and send me pictures of yourself. I like naked ones the best." I adjust the pillow behind my head. "In fact, I think you should send me one right now."

"I'm not sending you naked pictures. They'll end up on the internet."

"I promise I'll keep them to myself." I don't expect her to send me naked pictures, although I've had plenty of women do that.

"Still no."

"You can't blame me for trying. I guess you'll just need to come to my game so we can get naked in real life afterward." Several memories, including the sex in the hotel bathroom, make my dick spring to life.

"I don't know, Randy. I think I'm still recovering from last time."

"Three weeks later?"

"We used an entire box of condoms." Her voice goes a little soft, like maybe she's reliving some of it, too.

"I remember. It was fantastic. We should definitely try to break that record this time."

"What makes you think I want to do you again?"

"Do *me* again? Oh baby, I'm pretty sure it was me doing you, not the other way around." She huffs, and I laugh. "If I say you did me instead of the other way around will it help me get you naked again?"

"Maybe. When's the game?"

"Not this Friday, but next."

"Let me check my calendar." Silence follows, and then several seconds later, "Randy?"

"Still here. Waiting for a naked pic."

"Still not happening. I have some bad news."

"Don't tell me you can't come." I don't like disappointment.

"I can come just fine. I think you should know this by now."

My voice lowers. "I sure fucking do, and I have plans to make it happen repeatedly in under two weeks."

"That sounds fun, but I won't be able to make the game."

"Because of work? Just call in sick."

"I would, but we have a holiday performance, and that's our dress rehearsal. I can't miss it. You could always do what you did last time and come to Guelph."

"I can't. We have a game on Sunday in Chicago. I have to fly back with the team."

"Oh."

"Fuck." I run a hand through my hair. "I wanna see you."

"You mean you want to get me naked."

"That, too."

"Well, Sunny's been talking about moving to Chicago, and Alex has already put in an offer on a house for her, so it looks like I might have a reason to come out your way sooner or later."

"Miller mentioned that."

He's more than mentioned it. He's counting down the days. He's got Sunny's work placement all set up so she can finish college here instead of in Canada. He's already looked into what it takes to get her citizenship and everything. At first he thought he could have her run the foundation he set up, but it's way more involved than any of them realized, so between him and Alex, they managed to secure Sunny something in a non-profit organization.

"I'm kinda surprised she's not moving in with him, what with how whipped he is," I add.

"She will eventually. She wants her own space for a while. She keeps trying to convince me to move out there with her."

"You should. That'd be way more convenient for me." I'm half-kidding. I'm also all-the-way hard at the idea of having access to her more often.

Lily laughs. "I'm all about making it more convenient for you. I'll get right on packing."

"Seriously, though, how hard is it to get a work visa?"

"I have dual citizenship, so that's not really an issue."

"For real?"

"Yeah. My dad didn't give me much, but he gave me that."

"So it's perfect, then; you move out here with Sunny, and we can get naked all the damn time. It'll be awesome."

"Except for the fact that I won't have a job."

"You teach skating. This is Chicago. People are insane about hockey here. Everyone wants to be pro, and most take a year of figure skating to build ice skills. I bet I could make a call and get something lined up just like that." I snap my fingers. Then I consider the idea of Lily in one of those little skating skirts with prepubescent boys drooling all over her. They won't be the problem. It'll be the dads.

"Alex has already offered to do that."

I get that feeling in the back of my neck again. "Then you should do it."

Lily laughs. "I don't know."

"What isn't there to know?" I have no idea why I'm pushing this so hard. Maybe it's because I haven't had sex in three weeks and I was totally banking on having lots of it next Friday. With Lily. I think I might be developing a slight problem—not that it matters since I won't be getting what I want.

"It's not like Sunny's going to stay in that house forever. I give her six months tops. Or maybe Miller will move in, and I'll have to find my own place. Besides, I don't really know anyone in Chicago."

"That's not true. You know Alex and Violet and her friend—the one who's with Westinghouse—and most importantly, you know me." My voice goes low as I stick my hand inside my pants and adjust my hard-on. "Think about all the fun we could have, Lily."

"Oh, I'm very familiar with all the fun we could have."

"Then you should definitely consider it. I mean, how awesome would it be if we could have bathroom sex in houses, as well as hotels and arenas."

"We could've had bathroom sex at Alex's."

"True, but the bed was so much better. *Fuck*. We need to stop talking about sex in bathrooms."

"Why? Is it stressing you out?"

"It's making me hard."

"You should send me a picture."

"I'm hanging up and calling you back." I seriously have no idea what's wrong with me. It's not like I can't take care of this shit on my own. Or I could hook up with some random and get relief, but then I'd have to deal with Miller and possibly Waters getting on my case.

"What? Why?"

"I want to video call you."

"Video call me?"

"Yeah. You cool with that?"

"Yeah. Yup. Uh-huh."

She hangs up before I can.

17

HANDS IN THE PANTS

LILY

I throw my phone on the bed and run to the mirror to check my reflection. I'm wearing a camisole and a pair of shorts. Sexier would be better, but there's no time. I drop my pants and check out my panties. They're horrible. My phone's already ringing. I accept the call, then rush back over to my dresser and yank open the top drawer with all my underwear.

"Hey. Gimme a second." I'm not sure what exactly Randy has in mind, but if we're going to have video-phone, mutual-masturbation sex, I need to be wearing nicer panties. I also make sure my door is locked and find my headphones.

"Why am I looking at a ceiling?" Randy asks.

"Just hold on."

"Oh, I'm already holding on."

A rush of warmth floods my body, settling low in my stomach. All Randy has to do is speak, and I feel it right in my magic marble. He's a human aphrodisiac. I root through my undies until I find the pair he bought me. I check my girl parts. I took care of business yesterday, so everything's a thumbs up there. So are my legs. After Randy-bathroom incident number four, I've been way more regular about shaving them.

I smooth out my hair, turn on the lamp on my nightstand, and turn off the light over my bed to help set the mood. Then I get an idea.

I was Jason for Halloween this year. It's an easy, inexpensive costume: a mask and a blue jumpsuit. It's also not slutty, which is one of the things that bugs me about that particular holiday. It's like a license to dress like a hobag and then get all militant about guys who do the ass-dickrub in bars. I don't go out on Halloween if I can avoid it, especially not in a university town like Guelph.

I rummage around inside my closet for the mask.

"What's going on over in Canada?" Randy asks from his spot on my bed. If only he was here. And my mother wasn't in the living room watching some stupid TV show with Tim-Tom. He seems to have become a new permanent fixture.

"I'm just getting ready for you!" I call back.

"I seriously hope that means you're going to be naked."

I slip the mask over my face, take a deep breath and pick up my phone.

"Hey." I can see my own image in the small video box on the right side of the screen. All Randy can currently see is my horror-movie-inspired face.

"Fucking shit, Lily. Are you kidding me with this?" He sounds distressed.

I smash the phone against my chest to muffle his voice and burst into a fit of giggles.

"Seriously, Lily. That is not a sexy look."

"What about this?" I hold the phone out farther so he can see the rest of my outfit. I lost the shorts when I changed undies.

Randy groans. The sound makes my nipples hard and all my sensitive places tingle. "You need to take that mask off. It's seriously freaking me out."

I toss it on the floor, then drop down on the mattress, holding the phone back up to my face. "Better?"

He's lying on his bed, shirtless, his tattooed arm tucked behind his head. God, he's built. There's so much arm and chest and sexy going on, it's hard not to sigh. His hair isn't pulled back and it's shorter, reaching his cheekbones instead of his chin. He's trimmed the beard. I remember how that felt between my thighs the first time he ever went down on me. He's gorgeous.

"You need to show me that whole outfit you've got going without the mask," he says in that gravelly voice that makes my girl parts light up like a Christmas tree.

I scan my body with the phone, then bring it back up to my face. "That's all you're getting."

"If you lived in Chicago, I'd be at your place in a hot minute."

"Would you now?"

"Definitely. So you should give serious consideration to moving here." He lifts his head and runs his hand down his chest, following the action with his phone. He's wearing one of the pairs of defaced underwear. He has a serious hard-on. I can see the ridge of the head through the blue cotton. "Just imagine, Lily, all this could be yours, as often as you want it."

He slides his hand into the waistband of his underwear, and I moan. I can't help it. I know what he's hiding under there and how it feels to have it inside me. Repeatedly.

He moves the phone back up to his face before I get a glimpse of anything good. Well, apart from his seriously hot body. "You like that?"

"I like it better when your cock isn't confined by stupid things like underwear. I also like it better when it's inside me, rather than hundreds of miles away in a bedroom I can't get to."

"You see how solid my argument is, then?"

"I saw how solid something was. At least it looked solid. Unless you stuck a dick-shaped rod in your underwear. You should show me again."

"I'll show you mine if you show me yours." He grins and his tongue peeks out to touch the scar on his lip.

"I already showed you mine."

"Not without something covering it. You want more of me, you need to give me more of you." He's got that damn smile going. It drives me crazy.

"I'm not getting naked on video. How do I know you won't screenshot it?" I ask.

"How'm I gonna do that with my hand in my boxers?"

I stare at his hot face and notice his arm is moving. In a very rhythmic way.

"Are you jerking off?" It's comes out all low and breathy.

"Wanna help me out if I am?"

Now here's an interesting fact: I've never had phone sex, let alone video phone sex. Based on Randy's comfort level, I'm guessing he's done this before. So as hot as this is, I'm feeling a little out of my element.

"I'm messing with you, Lily girl. I just wanted to see that gorgeous face of yours so it's fresh in my mind for later."

"Later as in after you hang up?" I squeeze my thighs together. Pressure builds as I imagine him stroking himself with the same aggression he uses when he gets me off, over and over again.

"Yeah. That's the plan, anyway."

I have a feeling that wasn't his plan at all, but I'm obviously nervous enough that he's backtracking. I wish I had the balls to follow through right now. I bite my lip, considering it.

"I'm gonna let you go so I can take care of things. 'Kay, Lily?"

"I'll do the same over here." My hand is already creeping down into my panties. In my head I say, *or we could do it together*.

"Let me know how that goes." His eyes are heavy and his chest rises and falls faster. "Night."

"Maybe we—" I say, but he's already hung up. "Fuck. Shit." I had the chance for phone sexy times, and I ruined it by not being adventurous enough. What's wrong with me? I could've watched Randy come. I could've said dirty things to him. Except I've never dirty-talked unless, *oooh, fuck me harder* and *that's so good* count. I don't think they do.

I decide to do something either really bold or really dumb. Probably both. I stick my hand down the front of my panties and slide two fingers inside. Then I snap a picture, but only of my hand in my panties. And I send it to Randy.

I want to take it back as soon as I've done it. This is how people end up famous for having their girl parts splashed all over social media. But my face isn't in the shot. No one can actually prove it's me. Well, Randy could prove it, and possibly Benji because he's seen all my parts up close—although he was never much of a magic-marble licker, so maybe not. He was more of a stick-it-in-and-pump-until-it's-done guy.

I stop thinking about Benji, because he's an asshole and not someone I care to imagine while my hand is in my underpants. I get a message back from Randy a minute later.

I see how it is. Now ur not feeling shy.

It's followed by an image. It's not a dick pic, but it's close. Randy's wrist peeks out of the waistband of his underwear. He's clearly fisting his cock, and the head is peeking out as well, just a little tiny bit. It's mostly in shadow, but it's there.

Talk about missed opportunities. I get myself off to that picture. It doesn't take long, so I go for round two. Once I'm sated, I pull on a pair of sweats, unlock my bedroom door, and peek into the hallway to make sure it's clear before I hit the bathroom and wash my hands.

I'm so disappointed I won't get to see Randy next weekend. Maybe if I could get the car for the night I could drive to Toronto and meet up with him afterward. It doesn't hurt to ask.

The next morning I find my mom in the kitchen with Tim-Tom. He's wearing plaid pajama pants, and he's shirtless. I don't need to see his bare, hairy chest first thing in the morning. Or ever.

I make some mindless chitchat for a few minutes to appear social even though I'm not in the morning, especially with the smell of old sex in the air and Tim-Tom giving my mom the goo-goo fuck eyes.

"Do you think you'll need the car next Friday night?" I ask, swishing the teabag around in my mug.

"I work next Saturday morning at seven."

"What if I could have it back by then?" I'm working on being super nonchalant.

"Don't you have some skating thing on Friday night? Aren't your girls performing?" She glances at the calendar. It's marked with a huge red square, as is Saturday, since that's the day of the performance.

"Yeah, but Sunny invited me to Toronto, and I thought maybe

I could go after."

"What's in Toronto?"

"Isn't Chicago playing Toronto? That game's gonna be fantastic," Tim-Tom pipes up.

I hate him.

"Is this so you can see that boy? The one with the tattoos?"

"I already told you, he's a friend of Alex's, and he was dropping me off."

She sets down her mug. "He kissed you!"

"On the cheek!"

"In front of me. I bet if I hadn't been there his tongue would have been down your throat."

"He's a hockey player, not a tacky, classless asshole."

"I'm sure that's what he wants you to believe."

I put my hands up to stop her. "Never mind. Forget I asked."

I'm not in the mood for another lecture on how dirty professional hockey players are. I've already had more than one since the Randy introduction. My mother's assumption is that he only wants one thing, and once he gets it he'll toss me aside like a half-eaten taco. She didn't use that exact analogy, I don't think, but I stop listening almost as soon as she starts in on me.

She's not exactly wrong. But the point is, I also only want one thing from Randy, and that's his awesome dick inside me. But I can't tell her that. She thinks I need a break after Benji. He's still calling, and that worries her. He's sent a few texts and left a couple of voice mails, but they were predictably him: the words were sweet, and the tone was not.

Looks like I'm out of options where seeing Randy is concerned. I'm sure he'll get bored of chasing me soon and end up banging a puck bunny. Not that he isn't already doing that. I just haven't borne witness to it through social media—yet. It's bound to happen. I can't be the only person he's screwing, seeing as there's so much time between screw sessions. And that's part of casual fun, right? I could screw someone else, too.

I don't want that to bother me. But it does. A lot. Maybe if Benji hadn't been such a horrible boyfriend, I wouldn't be at risk of getting attached to the first guy who's remotely nice to me.

18

UNMADE BEDS

RANDY

We're in Toronto, we won the game, and I should be naked in my hotel room with Lily underneath me. Or on top of me. I checked in twice more to see if anything had changed, but she couldn't find a way to make it work. Today I got a picture of her in her skating getup. I don't know why, but those little skirts make me so fucking hard.

So instead of being balls deep inside that sweet, hot pussy, I'm sitting at a table in the bar with Lance. He's past the moping phase now, or at least he's acting like he's past it. He's taking bunnies home or back to hotel rooms again. And because they know that, a couple of them have found their way to our table. Lance bought them drinks, which means I feel obligated to stay and chat.

Maybe I should have gone to Guelph tonight. I could've cabbed it, called her, booked a hotel room for a few hours, then cabbed it back in time for my flight out in the morning. But I didn't. So I'm here listening to these girls talk and talk about how much they love hockey.

The one sitting beside me is wearing a low-cut top and lots of eye makeup. I think her eyelashes might be fake, or they're just insanely long. She keeps moving her chair closer until she's almost in my lap, then she puts her hand on my arm.

"Wow! Your art is amazing! Where do you get it done?"

"I go to this place in downtown Chicago." I'm used to handsy chicks. Normally it doesn't bother me, but I'm in a bad mood. I wanted Lily this weekend, and I don't get to have her. I'm bratty.

"Really? I have friends in Chicago! I've been thinking about getting some new art, and I'm looking for someone good. What's the place called?"

"Inked Armor. They're booked out, like, six months to a year in advance, and they don't do walk-ins. I see this guy Hayden. He's a master artist. Moody as fuck, but all his work is amazing."

"Oh. Wow. Good to know." She nods like this means something to her. "So …" She bites her lip and gives me what I suspect is supposed to be a coy smile. "Do you have any other ink you're hiding?"

I fight an eye roll. "I only have the sleeve right now."

"Does it go all the way to your shoulder?" Her fingertips slide under my cuff. She's trying to segue, and I'm too preoccupied with the fact that she's not Lily—and why that matters—to assess what's coming.

"Yeah. It's a full."

She leans in until her breasts press against my arm and her lips are at my ear. "Maybe you wanna go back to your room and I can show you my ink?"

Miller's long gone with Sunny. Waters and Westinghouse are bromancing it up in their room since their girlfriends are back in Chicago. There's no one here to give me any grief about hooking up. Lily and I aren't a thing. I haven't seen her in more than a month, and she's not falling all over herself to see me. It shouldn't be an issue for me to bag a random and release some of the pent-up tension I've been carrying around since last goddamn month.

It shouldn't. So I don't know why I stall instead of saying yes right away.

"It's okay if you have a roommate. I'm not shy." She bats her abnormally long eyelashes.

"I don't have a roommate."

"Great. So I can have you all to myself." She hooks her purse over her shoulder, looking at me expectantly.

Lance has his arm around the other girl, his hand resting near her tit. He looks at me, then at her, then back at me. "You out, Ballistic?"

"Uh, I don't—" I should feel something other than conflict, like maybe some kind of reaction in my pants, but there's nothing. Not even a hint of hard-on happening.

Lance eyes her again. "You check your messages lately?"

I don't know why he's asking me that. I've got this weird feeling in my stomach like I drank too much. That could explain the lack of action in my pants, except I've only had three beers. That's nothing. I can drink at least six before I start feeling it.

I reach behind me for my jacket and feel around in the pocket for my phone. The girl who thinks she's going to get naked with me puts her palm on my thigh and squeezes. "You can check your messages on the way to your room, right?"

I ignore her and her wandering hand and look at my phone. I checked it a couple hours ago after the game on the way to the bar, but I had nothing—not even a good luck message from Lily, which kind of sucked. Now there are fifteen new messages, all of which have appeared in the last half hour. I don't know what the deal is with the reception here in Canada. Miller warned me it can be wonky sometimes. It's weird, like this country creates some kind of phone limbo.

Some of the messages are from Miller—but his contact is all screwy, coming up as a number instead of his name. Several are from another number that's vaguely familiar. The girl beside me is still talking. Her hand's still on my thigh. I move it off because it's distracting. "Gimme a minute."

I skip the messages from Miller and check the other ones.

"Fuck." A horrible feeling slams into me like a puck to the groin. "Fuck, fuck, *fuck*." I scrub a palm over my face.

The girl puts a hand on my arm. "Is everything okay? Why don't we go upstairs?"

"Can you back off?" I'm way loud. And angry. For a lot of reasons I don't understand.

She blinks a few times, her caterpillar eyelashes fluttering. "What's your problem?"

My phone beeps with another message:

I gotta go." I push my chair away from the table. "I'll get you for the drinks tomorrow, yeah?" I say to Lance.

"Sure thing, Ballistic. You okay?"

"I don't know yet."

The girl, who's clueless, stands up like she's ready to come with me. I hold it up, prepared to shut her down, but Lance grabs her by the wrist and pulls her close. "He's got shit to take care of. You can stay here with us, gorgeous."

She's does that blinking thing again, but seems too stunned or maybe confused to argue. Lance pulls her down in the chair beside him. I owe him one.

Grabbing my jacket, I make my way to the exit. I don't want Lily to see Lance with the girls. Nothing happened, but that doesn't mean I don't feel like shit about what might or might not have if I hadn't gotten her messages. I hit the call button and bring the phone to my ear.

"Hello?" her voice hits me in stereo.

She's standing in the lobby, close to the elevators. She's wearing a skirt, and her legs are bare. Her shirt has a sheen to it—fitted, pretty, soft. My cock jerks like it's been electrocuted. I cross the room, punch the button for the elevator, and slide an arm around her from behind.

I lower my mouth to her ear. "You came."

She gasps, and her phone drops to the carpeted floor. "You scared the crap out of me!"

She turns around and puts her hands out as if to push me, but I tighten my grip around her, crushing her to my chest.

"Seriously, why didn't—"

I don't give her a chance to finish the question. I tilt her head back and take her mouth. It's already open, so I don't have to fight to get my tongue inside. She tastes sweet, like she's been eating candy. She stops trying to push me away and holds on to my shirt. I don't give a shit that we're in the middle of the lobby and I've got my tongue down her throat. I may also have my hand on her ass.

I hear my name and see the flash of a camera, reminding me that while I'm fine with this PDA, Lily's picture posted all over the bunny sites—with me groping her—isn't going to go over well with Waters or Miller. It's more Waters I'm concerned about.

I move my hand to her waist and break the kiss, pressing my forehead against hers. "Hi."

"Hi back," she says breathlessly.

"You came."

"Well, not yet. But based on this greeting, I probably will soon." Her laugh is shaky, laced with nervousness maybe, or uncertainty.

The elevator dings. I scoop up her phone, take her hand, and pull her inside, slamming my thumb against the *close door* button repeatedly before anyone else can get in with us. We narrowly miss having to share the space with another couple. As soon as we're alone, I press the button for the twenty-second floor. Then I cage her against the wall with my arms.

"I didn't think you were coming." I don't mean to sound pissed, or like it's an accusation, but I think I do. I don't get what the hell is happening, or why I'm feeling so messed up. It's not like we're a thing. She's not my girlfriend. I'm the guy she's fucking, or being fucked by, every once in a while.

"Neither did I." She swallows hard.

Her hands are on my chest, those gorgeous, dark brown eyes locked on mine. Her full lips are parted, breath still coming fast.

"I'm really glad you did." I lean down, intending to kiss her, but the elevator dings. A group of guys joins us, forcing me to back off.

Lily drops her head and stares at her shoes. She's wearing navy flats. The toes are scuffed. The cuff of her jacket has a string hanging from it, and one of the buttons is missing. She's carrying what I'd call a girl-sized duffle bag. It's worn out to the point that it looks like it's going to fall apart.

She never talks about money with me, but then most of our conversations don't include a lot of personal facts. Based on my discussions with Miller, I have a feeling the two-jobs thing is about more than saving for school. There are loans for that.

She had to take a cab to get here, and that cost money. Which I have lots of, and clearly she doesn't. But she's never said anything about it, ever. Maybe she doesn't trust me, or she's embarrassed. Both of those possibilities bother me. Normally this isn't something I'd be concerned with, but it's just that making things easier for Lily would make things easier for me.

It's about more than that, though, if I'm honest. Lily's almost-absence tonight nearly caused me to make a choice I wouldn't have felt good about. I'm not even sure I wanted to feel good about it. I want to say I wouldn't have done it, that I wouldn't have brought that girl up to my room and fucked her. But I don't know if it's true, and for some reason that's messing with my head.

I put an arm around Lily's shoulder and pull her to me because one of the guys keeps looking over at her, and I don't like it. I glare at him, and he drops his gaze to the floor.

Thankfully, the next time the elevator stops we can get off; otherwise I'm liable to start something I shouldn't. I'm really worked up, and I don't think it's going to get better until I'm inside Lily. I shoulder-check the guy on the way out because he's an idiot and won't move to make it easy for Lily to get past him.

Taking her hand, I guide her to my room. I jam the card in the door and glance over my shoulder. She's standing behind me, fidgeting nervously with the frayed strap of her bag. Her eyes go wide when she looks at me, probably because of my expression. I imagine it's fairly fucking intense. "I hope you weren't planning on getting any sleep tonight."

"And here I thought we were gonna have a little snuggle and a nap." A wavering smile pulls at her perfect, luscious lips. Her words are meant to be snarky, but her voice is soft. "Of course I don't plan on sleeping," she adds. "What the hell would be the point of me coming all the way here for that?"

This is what I need. Confirmation that she's here for one reason and one reason only: To get fucked.

19

ALL THE FIRES IN THE WORLD

LILY

I take three steps into the room and jump at the sound of the door slamming shut. I turn to find Randy latching the safety. He advances on me, and I take a cautious step back. I don't know why—okay, I do. His eyes are fiery with lust, but for some reason he looks angry. Also, his hands are balled into fists. He must notice me staring at them because he flexes and releases them a couple of times, then rolls his head on his shoulders. I'm not sure if I'm the reason for his current state, but there's something exhilarating about having a man like Randy look like he's about to lose control. It's also a little unnerving.

I have to pee, but I'm thinking he's not going to be interested in letting me go right now. I back into the wall, and he stops coming at me when we're six inches apart. His warm, minty breath washes over my face.

"I tried to call you this afternoon, and yesterday." His words are heavy, dropping like boulders.

"I called back. And messaged."

"Canada screws with my phone."

"We're like that. Passive on the outside, messing with everyone on the down low." I'm nervous, more than I've been before with Randy. I can't read his mood, and I showed up unexpectedly.

He looks so good right now. He's wearing a pair of black dress pants and a white button-down, the top two buttons undone. His red tie hangs loose, and his sleeves are rolled up to his elbows. The ink drives me nuts.

Looking at him is like being punched in the face by Medusa. He's the kind of beautiful that makes women turn into mindless, sex-crazed puck bunnies. I get it now. I've had this man inside me. He can fuck like a champion.

It's the reason I Ubered here. I have to leave in five hours, and I'm positive Randy's not kidding about getting no sleep tonight. I don't care. I can deal with being tired. That's what coffee and energy drinks were created for.

My gaze flips up to his, and I get trapped there. I feel like I'm locked in a room with a panther, not a man. He leans in a little closer and his tongue glides along his lip, the skin glistening in the dim light. I notice, once again, that all but the bathroom light is off. He's always setting the mood. I act on instinct and pounce. Literally, like a cat, I jump him.

I thread my fingers through his hair, and they go easily this time since it's held back by nothing. It's thick and gorgeous and dark. Holding on to the back of his neck, I propel myself up, our lips colliding, teeth clashing.

Randy grips my ass and presses his hips into mine, pinning me against the wall. I always end up pinned against something. Beds are the nicest since they're soft. He groans and starts rocking his hips, like he's planning to fuck me right through our clothes—not that I'm wearing many. My legs are cold thanks to the stupid skirt. I forgot to pack leggings, but I wasn't stopping home to get a pair.

He palms my ass with one hand and cups the back of my head with the other. At first I think it's to protect me from any kind of banging. But he curls his fingers in my hair and tugs my head back. It's not gentle, but it's not rough either.

I lift my chin, and his mouth descends on my throat. His lips are so soft; his teeth make me shiver. "I need you naked. Now."

"I'm not stopping you."

He carries me over to the bed, which is a relief. I've been on the ice all day and a prone position is much preferred. So is a mattress over a wall. Randy finds the hem of my shirt and pulls it over my head. His eyes dart to my chest. I bought a new bra two days ago when I started toying with the idea of cabbing it here.

"This looks new."

"I haven't worn it much."

"Does it still have the tags attached?" He slides a finger under the strap at my back and kisses along the lacy edge.

"Haha. Why don't you take it off and find out."

He looks up at me, still wearing that fiery expression. With one easy flick he opens the clasp. I make a noise that turns into a moan when he noses the cup out of the way and immediately sucks a nipple into his mouth. *Oh God.* I'd forgotten how good it feels to have his hands and mouth on me.

Okay, no I hadn't. But I've been trying to forget for the past four weeks, because I'm not so sure I'm managing this casual thing all that well.

I've been dying to see him this entire time, aching for the feel of him on me, around me, in me. If it was just the sex, I'd be okay, but it's not. I think I might actually like him—as a human being. A person. A man. If he didn't live in another country, I might want to date him. And that's a bad thing to want, because Randy doesn't date. I know this.

When my mom wouldn't give me the car for the night I was pissed—and maybe a little relieved. But then I started thinking about it. And Randy. And how this might be the last time I get an opportunity to be naked with him. He seems into these encounters we have, but he could strike me from his list at any time. The sex is amazing. I didn't want to end up regretting not having it again. Just in case. Which is pathetic, but I'm not going to focus on that right now. Instead I'm going to focus on the feel of Randy's mouth on my nipple.

I'm also going to work on getting him naked. I shove my hands under his shirt until I reach his pecs. I give his nipples a little tweak—but not too hard, because I'm not sure how he'll react. Reversing the motion, I run my nails down his tight stomach. His whole body does this vibrating thing, like he's on some weird radio frequency, and he breaks the suction. "Your nipples. Fuuuuck."

It's not much of an explanation. He sits back on his knees and works on getting his shirt off. He doesn't bother with buttons, just yanks his tie over his head. I go for his belt buckle, but he gets there first. He's just as aggressive with that as he was with the shirt. He pulls it free, and it snaps against the comforter.

I eye the belt. He's still holding it. "I don't do spankings."

"What if I do?" He slides it ominously along his palm.

"Then you can pass that over, and I'll do my best not to feel bad about smacking you around with it."

Some of the heavy mood dissipates, and Randy cracks a smile. "Don't worry, luscious Lily. That's not my thing. Hair pulling is a totally different story, though."

"I like the hair pulling."

"I know." He pops the button on his pants and slides them

over his hips, kicking them off.

He's not wearing his favorite underwear, maybe because he wasn't expecting me. Before I can shove my hand into his boxers and get a look at Nessie, he flips my skirt up. I'm rewarded with one of his amazing groans. My vagina claps her pretty lips, and my magic marble lights up like we've won the million-dollar prize. Sexing with Randy is almost that good.

"You bought these for me." He's not asking, he's telling.

I'd lie, but it's pointless. Also, acknowledging will likely get me what I want faster. Which is his cock inside me. "I did."

"I promise I won't shred them with my teeth, but I really want to." Randy shakes his head and looks down at my crotch like it's a dessert he's dying to eat, but can't. Which is ridiculous, because he can have it whatever way he wants it. Well, almost any way. I'm not down with him trying to stick his whole damn hand in there, or any weird things like produce.

He runs his hands slowly up the outside of my thighs, taking a few deep breaths. He's muttering to himself a little. Maybe it's a pep talk.

"Everything okay up there?" Again, I'm going for snark, but I'm still a little discombobulated by how intense he's being, so it's more breathy than sarcastic.

"Everything's fuckin' fantastic." He bites his bottom lip and exhales a couple more heavy, deep breaths. His fingertips slip under the elastic.

I whimper when they don't stay there, but glide back down to my knees. I part my legs, giving him lots of room to get all up in there with whatever he wants—fingers, tongue, dick. Any of them are welcome at Lily's Vagina Emporium.

On the next upward slide, I do the bridge to encourage him, lifting my hips off the bed so my pussy is closer to his face. I'm beyond caring about how worked up he was in the elevator, or how his jaw was doing that tic thing every once in a while. Now he seems better. Maybe my near nakedness calms him, like a sedative.

I toss my bra over the side of the bed and push my panties over my hips, but Randy covers my hands with his, stopping me.

"Not yet."

"But I—"

"I'm savoring, Lily. It's been thirty fucking four days. Thirty-four days since I've licked that pretty pussy of yours. Been inside you. Made you come. Don't rush me."

All it takes from him are words to get me close to the edge. I wonder if this is normal. I don't think so. He's like a snake charmer, except it's orgasms he's charming out of me rather than reptiles.

On the next pass, he breaches the elastic. He flips his hand and drags a single knuckle along my slit. I'm shaking like a crackhead looking for a fix. It's insane. I bite my lip to stop all the words from coming out. A few random whimpers escape, but I keep the stilted phrases like "fuck me" and "oh God, I want to come so bad" and "I'll be your sex slave forever if you'll continue to make me orgasm like this for the rest of my life" inside my head. Instead of saying any of those things, I moan his name and continue with the random noises.

He shifts my panties to the side. I'm not sure why he doesn't take them off—it'd probably be easier—but as long as he keeps rubbing my clit, I'm fine with how awkward this must be for him.

His erection is poking at the safety hatch of his boxer briefs. If my arms were longer, and I wasn't already on the cusp of coming, I'd try to get a hand on it. Randy takes care of the problem by sticking his free hand down the front at the same time as he pushes two fingers inside me.

I release one of those high-pitched, helium gasps. All I want to do is throw my head back and let go, but I can't take my eyes off his hand moving in quick, aggressive strokes behind his underwear. Why won't he shove them down so I can see better? I can't even manage the words to make that happen.

I notice that scar again. The one on his hip—cutting a straight line along his perfect skin and deep V. His hand shifts, and I get a glimpse of cock head. His fist, his big fist with his long fingers and the gorgeous tattoo that covers the back of his hand, is tight around the base. The head—*oh, God*—is thick and shiny and slick. And glistening, even though there isn't much in the way of light to reflect off the wetness seeping from the tip. He's getting off on getting me off, which is so, so sexy.

I know enough to realize Randy is a rare, special breed of man, which may be part of the reason I keep coming back for more. He abandons the cock stroking. Keeping my panties pulled to the side, he curls his finger and lowers his head. His mouth is on me, and I'm lost, lost, lost… spiraling down and floating up. It's the most amazing delirium.

As soon as my senses and vision return, he removes my panties and settles one thigh between mine. I'm naked. He's not. Those stupid boxers are still in the way. He rolls his hips, his erection pressed hard against my stomach. I want all of him between my legs. I want that hot, hard cock pushing inside me.

He's propped up, basically doing a one-armed plank on a soft mattress. He splays a hand out over my stomach, easing upward and stopping between my breasts. His palm rests below my sternum, and his thumb and index finger spread across my collarbones.

He's back to looking intense. "I'm so glad you're here." He drops to his elbow and bites along my shoulder, his warm, wet tongue on my skin.

I skim his arm, following the contours of muscle over his shoulder. "I'm sorry I didn't let you know earlier."

He makes a noise, neither positive nor negative, and finally shifts so he's between my legs. All his weight settles over me. "All that matters is you came in time."

"In time for what?" Uneasiness flutters in my stomach. I can't hold onto it, though. I'm too consumed by the feel of him.

His tongue runs up the side of my neck, and he bites the edge of my jaw. He palms my breast, making a plaintive noise. "In time for me to get inside you."

His fingers glide through the hair at the nape of my neck, and he cradles my head, kneading the back of my skull. Propping himself up on one arm again, he lifts his head, his breath leaving him in hard, sharp pants.

Dim light filters through the crack in the bathroom door, creating a pale line on the other side of the room. That and a tiny gap in the blinds provides enough illumination for me to see his heavily shadowed face. His jaw clenches, and he swallows thickly.

I place a palm against his cheek and feel the muscles jump under my touch. "Are you okay?"

He turns his face toward my hand. "Yeah. No. I don't know. I just thought… you weren't coming, and now you're here. I really needed you here."

A terrible, dark feeling takes root, fear pushing its way into my vocal cords, making the words tremble. "Well, I'm here now, so that's good, isn't it?"

"Yeah. I almost—I can't—" He drops his gaze and bites the fleshy part of my palm. All the blood in my body rushes low as he shifts against me.

The knot in my tummy moves up to my throat. "Randy?"

He brings his other hand back to my sternum and presses the

heel down, his thumb sweeping back and forth against the base of my throat. "I need to be inside you right now, Lily."

The desire seething behind his eyes and the tightness of every muscle in his body makes me want to ask more questions. But I don't, because something tells me I shouldn't. We're keeping things light. "Then that's where you should be."

I bring his mouth to mine. The kiss isn't a soft, slow reunion. It's desperate and intense. Randy's tongue sweeps my mouth, and his hips move hard between my legs. His back ripples with a shiver as I push his boxers down. He lifts his hips to help make it happen, and when he settles against me, his cock glides over my clit.

Randy breaks the kiss. His nose brushes mine, his breath washing over my lips. He keeps grinding against me, bare and wet and slick from his mouth and my orgasm. "I just wanna be with you." His entire body is shaking. "I just wanna be in you." He keeps rolling his hips. It's rhythmic and relentless and *oh, God I want*.

As delirious as I am with need, there's something in his words, in his expression, in the way he's aggressive but tender, that makes my skin prickle. I don't understand what's happening, but everything is shifting, turning on its axis.

"Then be with me. Be in me."

I stretch my hand across his lower back and push down to add more friction. On the next roll he goes low, and the head nudges my entrance. He hesitates. It's understandable. Sex without a condom is a dangerous and slippery slope. It indicates both stupidity and a belief that this is more than two people banging on occasion. I'm concerned it's becoming more than that for me. Worse is that I want it to.

I'd like to blame my lack of protest on something other than hormones and desire. I'd like to say I tell him we need to stop because it's obvious something is very wrong and this is a terribly not-smart, bad idea. But I don't. Because I'm an idiot, lulled into false security by taking the pill.

No protection with someone like Randy is stupid. Idiotic. He's slept with a legion of women. But in the moment, it feels *oh so good.* And the look on his face as he eases in a little farther makes it impossible to say no to what's happening between us.

His mouth drops open, and his brow furrows as pain merges with euphoria. His hands tremble against my cheeks and his eyes roll up. He exhales in a rush, dropping his face to my neck.

"Condom," he says.

He's off me in a flash, sweeping the floor for his pants. The sudden loss of his warmth makes me shiver and close my legs. But I don't argue with his thinking. The rustle of fabric accompanies a few choice words of frustration. He must find what he's looking for, because there's a soft thud and the distinct crinkle and tear of a condom wrapper.

A few seconds later he turns back to me, tapping my knees in a request to open for him. I comply, my gaze fixed on his wrapped cock.

"Look at me, Lily."

"I am."

"Up here." He snaps his fingers, then eases between my legs once more.

There's no slow transition. He pushes inside, his jaw going slack, eyes glazing. He drops his head, soft hair tickling my cheek. I rest my palm on the back of his neck, adjusting to the wonderful fullness. Randy's lips part on my shoulder, his tongue sweeping along the skin. Warmth is replaced by the hard press of teeth. And then he starts to move.

He angles my hips up off the bed as he grinds into me. He bites harder until I whimper, and then he kisses his way over my neck, all teeth and suction until his mouth is on mine, taking until my breath is almost gone.

It's hard and fast. He kisses me with frantic need, groaning into my mouth. Sliding his arms under my shoulders he sits back so my ass rests on his thighs. He moves me over him, watching his cock sliding in and out, over and over. I glance down, wanting the same view.

Again I note the thick, pale line traveling all the way to his groin. I have to wonder what kind of surgery he had to acquire that. But then he commandeers my mouth again and begs me to come. I fall into the pool of desire, basking there while he swallows my moans. Randy whispers that he's going to make me come again and again until it's the only thing I can do anymore.

20

ALMOST TRUTHS

RANDY

I'm fucking Lily like it's the last time I'm ever going to have sex. That's kind of how it feels. I almost thought about going bareback. Okay, not almost. I totally thought about going bareback with her, but then I'd have to explain about blood tests and how I never go bareback with anyone, ever—not even in high school when guys made notoriously bad decisions by saying things like they couldn't feel anything with a condom.

That's a load of shit. Guys can feel fine through latex. Does it mute the sensation a bit? Yeah, sure. But that's not a bad thing considering how fast I'd blow if I wasn't wearing one. At least when Lily's involved.

I don't know what it is about her. I don't know why I'm so hung up, but I do know there's still a whole storm of conflict going on inside me over that stupid girl at the bar. I almost told Lily before I got inside her, which probably would have screwed things up—screwed the screwing. I stop worrying about things that didn't happen and focus on the feel of Lily around me.

She's moaning my name and clawing at my back and shoulders. She's about to come. The wave of goosebumps and her increase in volume tell me that. I reach between us and pinch her clit. Lily throws her head back and cries out. If I had a free hand I'd skim the long, smooth line of her throat. But I'm keeping her from falling backward on the bed right now. I want her close.

Threading my fingers into her hair, I grip the satiny strands, forcing her chin down. Her eyes are fluttering up, her low sound of desire pushing me closer to the edge. Her pussy contracts around my cock, so I rub her clit until she covers my hand in a silent request to stop.

I keep one hand fisted in her hair, the other I press against her sternum. I move her over me, harder, faster until the entire universe comes to a screeching halt with the force of my orgasm. It's like a goddamn hurricane, blasting through my body, blowing me apart.

When I'm done coming, I press my face into her neck. She's sweaty, but she smells sweet. She pushes her fingers through my hair, over and over.

"Randy? You okay?" she whispers.

I shudder and shake my head instead of nod like I'm supposed to.

"What's wrong?" She strokes down my back.

I don't know how to feel about her gentleness. I want it. I like it. I'm not used to it. I hold her tighter. "There was a bunny at the bar."

Her whole body goes rigid. It's understandable. I'm still inside her. I don't know why I feel compelled to disclose this.

"She wanted to come back to my room with me."

Her reply is quiet, reserved. "You don't have to tell me."

It almost sounds like she's pleading with me not to. But I

can't stop.

"Nothing happened. I turned her down. Then I finally got your messages." My face is still buried against her neck. "And then you were here, and that's all I wanted."

Her voice wavers. "I'm glad I could come, then."

I lift my head and take her face in my hands. "Me, too."

I don't tell her the things I want to: that I haven't been with anyone else since we messed around at Alex's cottage. That was months ago, and we didn't even have sex. I don't tell her how I think about her all the time and have to stop myself from texting her on a daily basis. Or that for a minute I considered sleeping with that girl in the bar because I was angry she couldn't make tonight work. And I don't tell her that my almost-actions have freaked me out because they're another way I'm like my dad. I don't say anything about how I want this to be more than just fun, but it can't be because I'm too much like my father.

One night Lily won't be there to save me from making the wrong choice, and I'll do to her what my dad did to my mom. I don't want to be responsible for wrecking anyone's life but my own.

So instead I kiss her, grab another condom, and do the thing I'm supposed to. What we've agreed on. I keep her up all night, providing endless orgasms.

At five forty-five in the morning, she calls for a ride. She looks exhausted. She has dark circles under her eyes. I've left a bunch of hickies on her chest—at least it's not her neck. I pull on a pair of sweats and a shirt while I watch her dress. Then I decide I want one more quickie. I bend her over the dresser, flip her skirt up, pull her panties down far enough that I can get inside her, and make her come again. Once I'm finished straightening her up, I follow her out into the hall.

"You don't have to come down with me; I'm okay on my

own."

"I know. I'm not."

"Oh." She looks confused, which is understandable since I haven't explained anything.

In the elevator, I pull her against me and rest my cheek on top of her head. I'm gonna be grumpy later from lack of sleep. I don't care right now, though.

Once we get to the lobby I walk her to the front doors.

"I thought you said you weren't coming out," she says.

I shrug, holding the door open, and follow after her. There's a small sedan with a guy leaning against the hood. I open the passenger door, toss her bag inside, and usher her in. She looks a little disappointed, until I slide in beside her.

"What're you doing?"

"Coming along so I can have more time with you."

"You're crazy. Aren't you leaving for Chicago this morning?"

"Not until later. I'll be back in plenty of time."

"Don't you need sleep?"

"I'll do that on the ride back, and on the plane. C'mere." I hold an arm out, and she snuggles into me. I pull her onto my lap and stretch out on the backseat.

I know this is a problem. I want to do more than just have sex with her. I want to make the problem worse. "You should move to Chicago."

She laughs. It's tired-sounding and only half awake. "Alex bought Sunny a house last week. She's moving in over the holidays."

"You should move then, too. Think of all the free orgasms that would come along with that."

I get another laugh. She snuggles in closer. "I'm orgasmed out right now."

"I'd be able to dole them out regularly instead of all at once if you lived closer."

"Sounds nice. I'd still need to find a job, though."

"I'm happy to make a call. Like I said before, there's a lot of opportunity in Chicago for skating instructors. You're amazing on the ice—like, Olympic ability."

She makes this noise, like a huff.

"It's true."

"I almost went to the trials," she says quietly.

"Almost? What happened?" I hope she'll tell me more than Miller did.

"It's an expensive sport, like hockey. My dad stopped paying child support, and the money wasn't there for training, even with sponsors."

"Shit, Lily. That's just—" Losing her chance because of finances seems criminal.

"Shitty?"

"That's not really a strong enough word. What would it take to get you back in?" I wonder what kind of strings I could pull to make it happen for her.

She laughs and lifts her head. "I'm too old, and I don't do pairs anymore. It would take years to get back to where I was. Plus there's still the money."

"Can't you get it out of your dad? Where is he? Want me to hunt him down?"

She laughs. It's breathy and embarrassed now. "You can probably look him up in the hockey rosters. He played for the NHL. My mom was a one-night stand who ended up pregnant. She kept me, and he bailed."

"What's his last name?"

"Head. He played for North Carolina for about five years. He was good, but not great—third string. Last time I heard, he was living on an island somewhere, and he'd blown most of his money—hence the lack of payments."

"That doesn't make it okay." I'm angry that her potential was squandered.

"Not everyone gets to live their dream, Randy." Her eyes are soft when she looks at me. "Don't feel sorry for me. I have more than a lot of people. We're almost at the rink. You should kiss me until we get there."

I sleep all the way back to the hotel. I have just enough time to get packed up and meet everyone at the bus.

Miller shuffles over, drops his bag, and sighs. "I need some serious sleep."

"Yeah." I'm not capable of full conversations with words and stuff.

"I can't wait until Sunny's in Chicago permanently," he mumbles.

"Not long now." I stuff my hands in my pockets, thinking about the conversation with Lily in the car.

"Just a few more weeks. How was your night?"

"It got a lot better when Lily showed up."

"Definitely a better option than the bunny I took off your hands," Lance says.

Miller looks at me, his expression stony. "You were gonna bunny fuck?"

I shoot Lance a look. "No. She was persistent and couldn't take a hint."

Miller pinches the bridge of his nose. "You need to watch yourself, Balls."

"I'm not gonna make your life more difficult, Miller. Lily came to get balled. That's it."

He takes a couple of deep breaths and runs his hand through

his hair, making the short strands stand on end. "It's not my life I'm worried about. I'm too tired to deal with this right now." He leaves me standing there and gets on the bus.

I don't bother to sit next to him since we've got lots of room. I take a seat near the front. I try to sleep all the way to the airport, but I can't. All I can think about is what might've happened if Lily hadn't shown up.

Last night I was just jacked up, but today I know why.

I jam in my earbuds and cue up the thirty second video I made last night when Lily fell asleep on me. Then I set it on repeat.

It's not only about fun anymore. Not for me anyway.

21

THE BOOT

LILY

The door to my room is locked, and my mom is yelling at me through it. And pounding. If she breaks her hand, I'm not going to feel bad.

Okay, I'll feel a little bad, but this is ridiculous. I'm an adult. I get to make my own decisions, whether they're good or bad.

I didn't tell her I went to see Randy after dress rehearsal last night. The hickies and bite marks decorating my chest gave it away. I didn't notice them, being extra exhausted from my night of stellar sex, until my mom loudly pointed them out.

I shove a bunch of clothes in a bag and call Sunny. She's hard to hear over my mother's lecture-yelling.

"What's going on? Is that your mom?"

"She found out I went to see Randy."

"And she's freaking out this much? Wow."

"Can I come crash at your place for a few days?"

"Of course. Want me to pick you up?"

Sunny's such an awesome friend. "That'd be great."

"I'll be there in fifteen. Should I come up?"

"Probably not."

"Okay."

I end the call and keep shoving clothes and things into my bag. I can't get to the bathroom for my toiletries, but I can always come back later. I open the door and step back in case my mom decides to come flying in.

She props her hands on her hips. "Where do you think you're going?"

"To Sunny's. I'm gonna stay there for a few days."

"Oh, no you're not! That girl is nothing but trouble for you. I should never have let you hang out with her when you were teenagers. I should've seen this coming. This is totally my fault. You're turning in to one of those brainless hockey sluts!"

I get my dramatic flair from my mom. I hope I'm not this bad. "Brainless hockey slut? I'm not a puck bunny, Mom. We're hanging out."

She points at my chest, even though it's now covered. "Hanging out *naked*!"

"I'm an adult. If I decide I want to hang out with someone naked, I can. I'm having fun."

"Fun? *Fun*? You're having fun?"

The parroting is getting annoying. "This conversation isn't productive, and you're being a total hypocrite. Sunny isn't a bad influence, and not all hockey players are bad guys. Alex is engaged, and Sunny's boyfriend is probably the sweetest human being on the face of the earth."

"That's two out of hundreds! Thousands!"

"I can't believe you. Do you even hear what you're saying? Do you even realize how ridiculous this is? It's not like you've been an excellent role model." I gesture to Tim-Tom sitting on the couch. He's wearing pajama pants and that's it. As usual.

"Don't you own any shirts?" I call.

He looks down at his bare chest.

"Don't talk to Tim like that!"

I decide it's better to leave than say something I'll regret. "I gotta go. Sunny's picking me up."

"Fine. Go! Leave! Just don't go getting yourself pregnant and ruin your life like I ruined mine." She sucks in a breath, clamping her hand over her mouth like she's trying to push the words back in. "I didn't mean that, Lily."

When she reaches out, I step back, away from her touch, her apology. In that moment, she gives credence to all my insecurities—that I'm not enough, that I'll never be wanted, that I'm not worth the effort to love. Her regret is a mark I can't erase.

"That's the unfortunate thing about words, Mom. Once you put them out there, you can't take them back."

She tries to grab my wrist as I push past her, but I yank it free.

"I don't want you to make the same mistake I did."

"Which mistake is that? The one where you got pregnant, or the one when you decided to keep me?"

"You're the best mistake I ever made, Lily."

"But I'm still a mistake." My phone buzzes in my pocket. I check the message. It's Sunny. "My ride's here."

She doesn't try to stop me from leaving. Which is good. I'm close to tears, and I hate it when my mother sees me cry.

Two hours later, Sunny and I are lying on her bed. We're halfway through the magnum of white wine we picked up at the store. We're both tipsy since neither of us are drinkers. We've also gotten into her dad's cookie stash.

Robbie Waters is a chemist. He works for a marijuana lab

perfecting strains for medical use. He does a lot of "testing."

I've ugly-cried, and Sunny's shed sympathy tears. It's one of the many reasons I love her; she's the best, best friend in the world. She'll laugh with me, cry with me, get as angry as she can with me—which isn't very angry, but the thought is always there.

"Do you want to know what I think you should do?" Sunny asks as she lifts her legs straight up in the air and lets them fall toward her head. Her toes hit the mattress behind her, and her legs are still straight. She's more flexible than I am, and that's saying something, because I'm damn flexible. I can practically fold myself in half backwards.

"Take up yoga so I can have super-bendy sex like you and Miller?"

"That's one thing you should do. Except you can't have sex with Miller, or me. You can have sex with Randy, though." She's definitely drunk.

I smack her ass.

"Ow!" She flips out of her pose and rolls on her side. "I think you should move to Chicago with me."

"We've already talked about this. I don't have a job there."

"But it would be so easy for you to get one. Alex says it won't be a problem to find you a spot as a skating coach, and the money would be way better than here. Plus you get paid in US dollars, not Canadian ones, so if you decided to move back here, your savings would be worth more."

"I like my job here." Though I don't love it like I used to. Lately I like it less and less.

Sunny takes a lock of hair and rubs the end of it over her lips. It's something she's always done when she's thinking, or nervous. She did it a lot at the beginning of her relationship with Miller. I still feel bad about the way I judged him before I knew him. He really is so, so good to her.

"I'm going to say something, and I don't want you to get mad at me for it, okay?"

I laugh. "I'll do my best."

"I know you love working with those girls, but Lily, I don't know if it's the best thing for you. Sometimes I think it makes you as sad as it does happy. It's such a reminder of what you missed out on."

She's right. Teaching skating in the same arena where I used to prepare for competitions hurts sometimes. Maybe it's because I get further and further away from my dream while these girls get closer. "It's a big decision."

"I know, but sometimes change is good. I love your mom, and she loves you—despite the things she said—but it's kinda like me and my mom, you know?"

I nod. I do know. Daisy is loads of fun to be around, but she's got archaic ideas about how relationships work. It never occurred to her that Sunny would want a career and all the other things women in the twenty-first century strive for.

"At the very least, you should take some time off work and come with me to Chicago over the holidays. See if you like it."

"I can't do that." It's an automatic response.

"Why not? You're allowed to take a holiday, Lily, and frankly, you need one. You've been working two jobs for the past three years, and until April you were in school full-time as well. You need a break. Miller's off from the twenty-third to the twenty-eighth. Your girls have a break from skating then anyway, right?"

There's always a two-week break between sessions this time of year. "Yeah. I still have the coffee shop, though."

"There's no reason for them not to give you time off, and if they won't, you should quit. You shouldn't be killing yourself over the measly twelve dollars an hour they're paying you."

She's right. Again. It's just that I've worked there for a long time, and it's familiar. But I guess that's the crux of the problem. It's how I've always done things. I stayed with Benji because he was familiar and I knew what to expect, even if it wasn't good. I keep living in the apartment with my mom partly because I feel like she needs the help financially, and maybe emotionally, but also because it's what I'm used to, and the same with working at the arena and the coffee shop.

I'm boring and predictable. Except where Randy's concerned. With him I do things I never thought I would in a million years. Like let him eat me out against a wall in a public bathroom—with a locked door, but still. Or take Uber all the way to a hotel in Toronto so we could get our freak on for a few hours.

"Plus Randy'll be around."

"He rode all the way to Guelph with me this morning."

"What? But didn't they fly out today?"

"It was early. He wanted to come for the ride, and then he went back to the hotel."

"No way! He is so into you." Sunny sits up and spills her wine all over herself and the comforter.

"He's so into sex with me, you mean." I won't admit out loud that I'm digging him more than I should. Especially if I'm considering moving to Chicago.

Sunny gives me a look. "You are so coming to Chicago with me. Alex says the house will be ready by then, and we're doing all the celebration stuff at his place, and you need time away from everything. So you're coming. It's decided. I'm deciding."

"Just like that. You're the boss of me, eh?"

"Yup. That's right." She puffs out her chest. "See how assertive I can be?"

I toss a pillow, and she deflects it.

There's a knock at the door. Andy, her Great Dane, jumps up

from his spot on the floor. Titan, her little Papillon, pricks up an ear but doesn't move otherwise.

"Come in," Sunny calls.

Daisy peeks her head in. Well, it's more like just her face because her hair can't fit through the crack. "Just checking to see how you girls are doing." She eyes the bottle of wine. "Oh. Looks like you're doing just fine." She holds out a bag of sweet potato chips. "You could probably use these if you're planning to finish that off."

Daisy invites herself into Sunny's room to hang out with us. Neither of us minds. Daisy's a great mom, even if she's a little backward. Her dating stories about Robbie are hysterical. Plus, staring at her hair is always fascinating.

It's well past midnight before I stumble down the hall to the spare room. I could sleep with Sunny, but sometimes she tries to spoon. I also want to check my messages. Not that I expect to have one from Randy. He's unpredictable with his communication.

I pull the covers back and slip under them. My stomach does a stupid little flip-flop over the three messages from him.

The last message wasn't sent that long ago, maybe twenty minutes. I'm drunk enough that calling him seems like a great idea.

He answers on the second ring. "Hey." He sounds like maybe he was sleeping.

His gritty voice wakes all my corresponding parts up. "That's quite the pitch."

"Are you sold?"

"So alluring." There's a little slur to my words. Randy picks up on it.

"Are you drunk?"

"Nope."

"You totally are."

"Sunny and me might've had a little wine. I'm staying at her place for a few days." I don't know why I tell him this. It's completely irrelevant.

"Everything okay?"

"Yeah. Fine. Anyway, I'm coming to see Sunny's new place over the holidays."

"You mean you're coming to see my bathrooms?"

"Those, too."

"We're gonna have a sleepover."

"So far sleepovers with you haven't included much sleep."

"How long you gonna be here? A couple days? A week?"

"Sunny said something about the twenty-third to the twenty-eighth, but we might stay longer. I don't know yet."

"You're not spending Christmas with your mom?"

"We're not exactly seeing eye to eye on things right now. And she's probably spending the holidays with Tim-Tom."

"Who?"

"Her new boyfriend."

"Is he the reason for the dissension?" Randy asks.

"Part of it." Why can't I lie like normal people?

"What's the other part?"

"My not coming home last night."

"You're in trouble for not coming home? Are you lying about your age or something? Are you really seventeen and you just look older because you wear makeup that looks like you're not wearing makeup?"

I snort. "It would explain my mostly prepubescent body."

"Don't talk shit about your body. I fucking love your body. Especially when you're naked and I'm on top of you, and even more when I'm inside you. Shit. Now I'm hard. Again. You'd think after last night and this morning I'd be done with the hard-ons."

"Your dick giving you problems?" This is easier than conversation about my family. All his attention isn't because he wants to date me. We just have insane chemistry, and he wants to fuck a million orgasms out of me.

"My fantasies about you are what's giving my dick problems. If you move here, they don't have to be fantasies; I'll get to live them out all the damn time. Then my dick wouldn't be such a problem for me."

"If I was there I'd put your dick on lockdown." I have to pause and choke back a laugh. "In my vagina prison."

"How soon can you get here?"

"Not for another two weeks."

"Damn it. Prison never sounded so cozy before."

"I'll keep him locked up the entire time I'm in Chicago, if you want. We might actually get thrown in real prison, though, if we have to go out in public. And it might make our friends uncomfortable."

"Miller and I are pretty open. I'm sure he won't mind."

I blush and snicker. "Anyway, it's late. I should go."

"Because you have to work in the morning?"

"Yup."

"'Kay. I'mma go whack off to the pictures I took of you while you were sleeping last night."

"Lies! I didn't fall asleep."

"You totally did. For about ten minutes. Night, Lily girl. I'm looking forward to spending time in pussy prison."

Less than a minute later, I get a text. It's a picture of me with my head on his chest. I'm definitely asleep. And we're both naked. My hand is curled up under my chin, my lips are parted, and my hair is damp near my forehead. Randy's smiling, and his stunning, honey-colored eyes are on the camera.

Another message comes from him:

look at how gorgeous ur

My tummy flutters. He's such a flirt and a charmer.

Another message comes in. This time it's a video. It's exactly the same scene as the picture, only not a still frame.

With his eyes still on the camera, he drags a fingertip down my cheek. "Lily, Lily, Lily, wake up for me."

I moan in my sleep, but lift my head toward his voice.

"Come on, baby, open your eyes for me."

I watch my lids flutter, another soft sound escaping. Randy's not looking at the camera any more, he's focused on me. "There you are. Didn't I tell you? No time for sleeping tonight."

"No time," I murmur.

"That's right. Where am I supposed to be right now?" His voice is whisper quiet, his chest rising and falling faster as I lift my head, blinking blearily up at him.

My lips curve into a coy smile. "Inside me."

The video goes blurry when his mouth finds mine. His groan is the last thing I hear before the screen goes blank.

I'm so turned on right now. And a little mortified. But mostly turned on. Holy hell. Randy made a video while I was sleeping. He could use it for blackmail. Except that doesn't make sense. I have nothing he wants. Apart from my vagina prison.

I think that was the third time we had sex. Or the fourth. I lost track after a while. They were all amazing. But the one time he was really sweet. So soft. Gentle. It was different. He put me on top. It's all so hazy, and now I'm really sexed up.

I get another text:

I can delete those if u want, but I wanted u2cu how I cu.

I should tell him to delete them. Definitely. But I don't. Instead I send one short message back:

It's ok. U can keep them. Just 4u tho.

He response is quick:

No one sees u naked but me.

I slip my hand under the covers and between my legs and watch the video over and over until I come.

I don't want to read into things, but all of this—Randy's messages, the late-night phone calls, and now this video—feels like something dangerously real.

22

SKATES ON LACES OUT

LILY

Four days after my fight with my mom, she shows up at Sunny's. I've been ignoring her messages. The second we see each other, we both burst into tears. Thankfully, no one's home to witness the epic display of girliness. We sit on the couch in the Waters' living room, cross-legged, facing each other.

"I'm so sorry, Lily."

"I know you didn't mean it." I smooth my palm over my shin. I'm wearing the leggings Randy bought for me.

"But I said it, and I shouldn't have. I can't take it back, and I wish I could because as strong as you are, I know it hurts you to feel like a mistake." She tucks my hair behind my ear. "You might not have been planned, but you've always been the best choice I made. The only thing I regret is not being able to give you more. I don't ever want you to feel like you aren't wanted."

"I know you love me, Mom." I hate these kinds of conversations. They're hard. Emotional. They make me feel worse and better at the same time. "It wasn't your fault he didn't want either of us."

I spent years sending my dad letters, school pictures, birthday cards. The only response we ever got was the child support check in the mail. By the time I was ten, I'd given up.

She strokes my hair, her eyes full of remorse. "I did a terrible job picking good father figures."

"Robbie's always kinda filled that role, anyway."

"I didn't mean what I said about Sunny, either. I know she's been an amazing friend to you. And the Waters family has been so important. I know with Sunny moving to Chicago and you breaking up with Benji it can't be easy."

"Benji and I were done long before that relationship ended."

She nods. "I know. I could see that. He hadn't been good for you for a long time."

It's funny how easy it is to see something falling apart from the outside. "I wish you would have said something. Maybe I would have kicked him to the curb sooner."

She gives me one of those smiles. "You know that's not true. That had to be your decision, uninfluenced by me or anyone else."

She's right. "I'm going to help Sunny move into her new place in Chicago over the holidays." I trace the piping on the edge of the couch, waiting.

"I can't say I'm surprised." She props her cheek on her hand. "Are you considering moving there, too?"

"Sunny wants me to."

"What do you want?"

"Change, I guess? Something new. Alex can get me a job teaching skating lessons. One that pays well." I wait for her reaction.

"He's a nice boy."

"He's not a boy anymore, Mom. He's getting married."

"Hmm. This is true. Your hockey friend will be there? Randy?"

"Not at Sunny's, but he'll be around when he's not on the road."

"So you'll see him?"

"I don't know. Maybe. It's only casual, Mom. It's not a relationship. I'm not looking to get serious right now, not after Benji." The words don't feel like the truth.

My mom sighs. "You're being safe?"

"Of course." I think about that one time we almost weren't. Pill or no pill, it would have been a bad choice.

"Okay."

"Okay? That's it? No lecture?"

My mom laughs. "You're almost twenty-two. I can't tell you what to do anymore. Just be careful with your heart, Lily. Don't give it to someone who doesn't deserve it and won't take care of it."

Even though my mom and I work things out, I decide to stay at Sunny's for a little longer. Her parents are away at a conference, and it's almost like living on our own. I'm treating it as a trial run, sort of.

Randy and I message back and forth over the next couple of weeks. He sends lots of dirty texts and sometimes even voice memos. Those are my favorite. I often listen to them during marble-rolling sessions. I also put in my ear buds and replay the thirty-second video.

I manage to get two entire weeks off work. I don't think I've taken more than two days off in a row in the past three years. I'm not sure how I'm going to deal with the freedom.

Sunny keeps trying to sell me on moving to Chicago. I'm

starting to think it's not a bad idea. Benji's resurfaced as the holidays approach. Which sort of makes sense. We haven't been apart for any significant celebration in the past seven years.

Part of me thinks I should miss him at least a little. But I don't. I'm too excited for sleepovers at Randy's while I'm in Chicago. He's mentioned several times that I should stock up on sleep while I can.

I help Sunny pack up her bedroom, and we send the moving truck two days ahead of us. All her stuff will be there by the time we arrive by plane on the morning of the twenty-third. Miller, Alex, Randy, and Darren won't be back from their away game on the other side of Canada until later that night. They're at the end of an away series, so I'm banking on them being tired—not that it's going to stop me from jumping on Randy as soon as I have the opportunity.

I'm a little concerned about my level of excitement. Feelings aren't supposed to be involved, and I know I'm supposed to tell him when they are, but I'm not brave enough. I don't want him to end this. Sometimes I convince myself he must have feelings too, but I know his pattern, and he's been very clear with what he's said, no matter how he acts. Anyway, I will have to deal with it, but I want this week with him.

Sunny and I take my cousin Brett to visit Michael before we leave for Chicago. His surgery was successful, which is the best gift any of us could have asked for. Miller and Randy have plans to visit him in the new year, the next time they're in Toronto. With a little more recovery time, they're hoping he'll be back on the ice soon, doing what he loves most.

Violet picks us up at the airport driving a crazy vintage sports car. It's bright orange with stripes. She gets out and hugs us enthusiastically. Her huge boobs mean she has to lean in a lot.

"Oh my gosh!" Sunny exclaims as Violet struggles to find a

way to open the trunk. "I can't believe Alex lets you drive his car!"

Violet sticks her head through the window and fumbles around. The trunk pops open. "I suck his gigantic dick on the regular and don't even complain about the gag reflex or the potential lock jaw. He lets me do anything I want."

"Wow. You must be really good to get that thing in your mouth," I say, then realize how that sounds.

"You've seen it?" Violet asks. She eyes me up and down, like suddenly I'm competition.

"By accident when I was a teenager."

"Oh." Violet nods and relaxes. "I can only get it in, like, halfway, but it's the head that counts—and the tongue action."

Sunny hasn't said anything. I'm assuming it's because we're talking about her brother's penis and Violet putting it in her mouth. She twirls her blond hair around her finger and tilts her head. "I can get almost all of Miller's peen in my mouth, but I don't have a gag reflex, so that helps a lot."

"Okay." I clap my hands together. "What's the plan? Where are we going first?"

"The house, of course!" Sunny says.

"Hell, yeah! We're picking up Charlene on the way." Violet swoops back into the driver's seat.

Sunny and I get in the backseat, and after half an hour we stop at a very cute condo building close to the lake. Charlene comes running down the front steps and jumps into the front seat. "Are you trying to get Alex to take back the ring?"

"What?" Violet gives her a look.

"Why are you driving The Colonel?"

"It's not The Colonel. I've renamed her Maxine, and Alex doesn't know I'm driving her." Violet waves her hand around in the air. "He's not going to be home until late, so it's fine."

"I thought you said he lets you do whatever you want," I say.

Violet glares at me through the rearview mirror. I'm not scared of her. She's all words and no actual bite. She flips her ponytail over her shoulder and opens her mouth to speak.

"Anything *except* drive this car. Didn't you scratch it last time?" Charlene asks.

"That was *not* my fault! That fire hydrant came out of nowhere." Violet turns around and points a manicured finger at us. "Do *not* say anything to Alex about me driving this car unless you want me to sneak dairy into your dinner tonight."

"I'm not a vegan. Only Sunny is."

"And that would be a terrible thing to do, Violet. I haven't eaten anything that comes from anything with a face in five years." Sunny crosses her arms over her chest.

"I wouldn't really do it. I'm just saying, don't tell Alex or he'll be pissed, and then he won't give me naked beaver licks, and those are my favorite."

"Violet!" Charlene smacks her on the arm.

"Ow! What?"

"Sunny's here! She doesn't want to hear about her brother licking your beaver."

"My *naked* beaver."

"No one cares if your beaver is naked or if it has a Mohawk or if you let it grow in for Movember," Charlene says.

I say nothing. I'm thoroughly entertained.

Sunny's not even paying attention. She's too busy checking her phone for new messages. "Boo! Their flight doesn't get in until five. Oh, wait. Maybe it's two. Miller gets that mixed up a lot. Can someone else check?"

"It doesn't matter what time they get in. We already have plans for tonight," Violet says.

"Plans?" Sunny and I ask at the same time.

"We're having a girl's night in and sending the boys out for a few hours."

"But they're just getting back."

"There's a game on tonight, and they're playing the team next week. They're going to sit in front of the TV for three hours and talk strategy like they always do. I'm not interested in listening to that crap. So the plan is this: the guys come home, we send them to the pub while the game's on—"

"Or Darren's since he lives down the street," Charlene interjects.

"Or Darren's. Wherever has beer and better food. They come back after the game, and we can all disappear into bedrooms and enjoy some alone time."

Sunny raises her hand.

"You don't have to raise your hand, Sunny. You're free to speak anytime," Violet says.

"I haven't seen Miller in two weeks. I'd like to have some alone time before he goes out to the pub. Or Darren's."

"No alone time before the pub," Violet says.

"What? Why not?"

"Because that's what they expect. Look, I know you're all excited about moving here, Sunny, and you're super in love with Buck, or Miller, or whatever you want to call him, but trust me; you need to make him wait for it."

"She's right." Charlene nods her agreement.

"I only have a little more than a week here, so I'm not sure what the point is in making Randy wait," I say.

Violet comes to a stop at a red light and points at me. Her nails are really nice. "You especially need to make him wait."

"I don't see why."

"Because you need to make sure he gets that you're not at his whim, that your beaver is a snowflake and should be treated as such."

She's not even making sense now. I stop arguing and let her rant. A few minutes later we pull up to the sweetest house I've ever seen. It's two-stories of white clapboard with adorable gardens lining the front porch. Two solar panels are attached to the roof. The backyard is modest in comparison to her parents place in Guelph, and there's no pool, but a dog run has been installed, and a small glass greenhouse sits at the back of the property.

Sunny cries. Violet pats her back and steers her inside, where we pop a bottle of champagne and take a tour of the four-bedroom home. It's cozy and exactly the kind of place Sunny loves. Live plants inhabit every window, and dog beds are set up in the living room and Sunny's bedroom, which has been outfitted with a brand new four-poster bed with a sheer curtain. It's romantic and gorgeous.

"There's no way Alex picked out this stuff," Sunny says through a fresh round of sniffles.

"Buck helped out, and so did Charlene and I, because you know how boys are." Violet's smile says it all.

"How did you find the time to do this?" Sunny can't stop the tears.

Violet hugs her again. "Alex hired someone to decorate. All I did was oversee the furniture decisions and make sure everything didn't end up Chicago team colors."

"You guys are the best."

When Sunny stops crying, we resume the tour. In the bedroom at the far end of the hall, I lose the battle and join the emotional breakdown brigade. Turning to Sunny and Violet, I motion to the room, but I don't have words, so I keep gesturing, hoping they'll get what I'm not able to say.

"I wanted to be prepared for whatever you decide," Sunny

says softly. "And you need a room here no matter what."

"Where did you get all these?" Along one wall are skating pictures. Of me. As a teenager on the brink of moving from competitive to Olympic trials. I never did, of course, but the images are beautiful—movement captured in still form.

"My mom used to take them all the time." Sunny rubs my back and puts an arm around my shoulder. Her smile is sad. "I don't want to do this without you."

Being here in this gorgeous house, knowing Sunny's staying and I have to go back to Guelph at the end of the holidays, makes me seriously evaluate my options.

"Okay. This is way too premenstrual for me," Violet says. "We need more drinks!"

"Totally!" Charlene agrees.

We end up spending way longer than we intended to at Sunny's new place, partly because we polish off the rest of the champagne. Violet only has one glass, but she's paranoid about driving Alex's car, so we hang around in Sunny's living room while Violet caffeinates herself and the rest of us keep drinking.

It isn't until everyone's phones start pinging that we realize it's late afternoon.

"Oh, shitballs!" Violet jumps to her feet. "We gotta go! The guys are already on their way back to the house!"

Charlene, Sunny, and I chug the rest of our drinks and leave them on the coffee table.

"Why is winter so painful? Why are there so many zippers!" Violet says as we scramble around each other, trying to get our boots on.

"Our bags are still in the trunk," Sunny says as we climb into the backseat.

"You're staying at Alex's tonight anyway. We're all gonna be too drunk to go anywhere."

"But I wanna sleep in my new bed."

"They'll be plenty of opportunity, trust me." Violet pulls out and tears down the street.

She's a freaking menace on the road. Sunny and I white-knuckle it all the way to Alex's. I get a text about halfway there. It's from Randy:

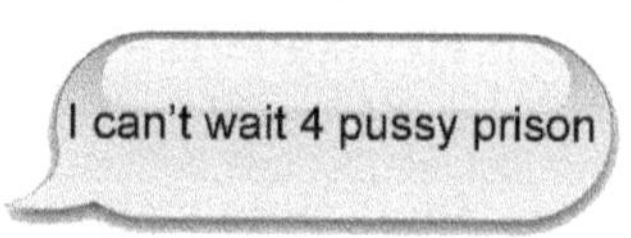

Other phones start dinging ten minutes later. Sunny checks her messages. "They're already at Alex's, Vi."

"Fuckerdoodles."

"I can always tell Alex I asked you to pick us up in the fun car," Sunny suggests.

"He won't believe you, and I can't lie."

I'm actually kind of interested to see how this is going to play out. Alex has a temper sometimes. I can't see him getting super pissed about the car, but then maybe it's a bigger issue than I realize. Or Violet's being dramatic. Either option is possible.

We pull into the driveway, and Violet hits the button for the garage. She creeps in, checking the side mirrors a million times. The car jerks as she hits the brakes repeatedly, inching forward until she taps the garbage can in front of it.

She puts the car in park and cuts the engine. Shrugging out of her coat, she flails around. "I'm so sweaty." Then she opens the top two buttons on her black-and-red plaid, fitted button-down shirt. "Watch how it's done, ladies."

Alex opens up the door to the garage as Violet gets out of the car. "Hey, baby!" she exclaims. "We totally lost track of time. I'm so glad you're home!"

She runs over to him. It's awkward; she's got her shoulders back and her chest pushed out. She nearly trips up the three steps on the way to meet him as he comes down. She falls into him, throwing her arms around his neck. She's practically popping out of her shirt.

"Hi, baby." Alex isn't looking at the car anymore. His eyes are right where Violet wants them. He runs his hands down her sides and stops at her ass.

Maybe they've forgotten we're all here.

I look at Charlene and Sunny. As usual, Sunny's focused on her phone. Charlene is grinning. I open my mouth to ask a question, but she puts her finger to her lips, signaling for me to wait.

Violet kisses the bottom of his chin, because that's as high up as she can reach, even on tiptoes. "I missed you."

Alex makes a noise, but dips his head and kisses her lips. "Me too. I hate being gone more than a week." He rubs his nose against hers. It's so sweet I want to gag. "You know I don't drive The Colonel in the winter, baby."

"I changed purses and couldn't find my keys. I'm sorry." Violet pushes away from him and his eyes go back to her rack. "Oh, the buttons on this shirt are the worst. I'll put these away until later." She winks.

"I can help." Alex sticks his finger into her cleavage.

Charlene gives me a raised eyebrow and slams her car door shut. Alex jumps, like he's just realized we're all here. "Hey! Hi!" He jams his hands in his pocket and turns to the side. It doesn't hide what's happening in his pants. He untucks his shirt to cover the issue.

There's a flurry of action and hugs, then Alex yells out for a hand bringing bags inside. I get as far as the hallway before I'm tackle-hugged by Randy. He lifts me right off my feet and buries his face in my neck.

"Hi." I giggle-moan at the feel of his beard and his lips parting against my skin.

"I can't wait to go to pussy prison," he murmurs in my ear.

And just like that, I'm ready to get undressed and take him. Except we're standing in Alex's hallway, and our friends are here. Randy spins around and for a second I think I'm going to end up against a wall. Instead he carries me down the hall.

Everyone's staring. Lance is slack-jawed. Miller's got a frown going on, and Alex's expression matches. Darren cocks an eyebrow.

"No way, Balls!" Miller shouts. "You and Lily aren't allowed in bathrooms together!"

Randy doesn't listen. He sidesteps through a door. It's not a bathroom, though; it's a laundry room. He tries to shut the door, but Miller's leaning against it. He makes Alex look small and Randy skinny, which he's definitely not.

Randy leans back, his arms straining. "I need a little something right here." He sets me down and taps his lips.

I push my fingers through his hair. It's grown out in the past two weeks, hitting below his cheekbones. I rise up on my toes and press a soft kiss to his mouth.

"Seriously, Balls, can't you wait, like, five minutes?" Miller asks.

"I'm just saying hello, and I'm looking for a little privacy to do that." Randy gives the door a hard shove with his shoulder. Miller shouts and Randy turns the lock. "And now we have some."

His smile holds anything but humor as he lifts me up and sets me on the dryer. It's the perfect height. I part my legs and scootch forward so I can feel his hard-on. And he's definitely hard. Randy leaves wet kisses on my neck as he cuts a path up to my mouth.

"You're terrible."

"I know. We don't have to stay here long—like fifteen minutes, and then we can go back to my place where we can play until you have to go back to Canadia."

Miller knocks on the door. Or maybe it's Alex. I don't care. All I know is Randy's tongue is in my mouth, looking for something to tangle with.

"Why're you wearing pants? They're so inconvenient," he complains.

I laugh into his mouth and wrap my legs around his waist. He's dry-humping the hell out of me, and the seam of my jeans is hitting the right spot. Like that time in the bathroom at the exhibition game, I get that shimmery feeling—the one where I'm sure if we keep going I'll probably come. Randy finds his way under my shirt. Tickling along my ribs, he slides his finger under my bra until he reaches my nipple.

"I seriously need you naked. It's not even funny."

I keep rubbing up on him, grinding harder. I'm whimpering and yanking on his hair. Randy breaks the kiss to look at me. "You're gonna come aren't you?"

"Uh-huh."

He gives me that smile I used to love-hate and now I just want to suck off his face. With my vagina. "I should be inside you for that."

That's all it takes—and the friction, and the way he pinches my nipple. The orgasm slams into me like a linebacker on crack. It's a toe-curling, mind-numbing, full-on quiver attack. I try not to make a sound, because there are people on the other side of the door—and if I can hear them they can certainly hear me—but I fail. It's a high-pitched moan that includes Randy's name.

I'm not even close to being over the crest of it when the door bursts open. All my muscles are locked like I've been dipped in liquid nitrogen. Randy doesn't even bother to look at them, his focus is singular: me.

I bite my lip, a whole-body tremor making my eyes roll up.

"Oh, wow." That's Sunny.

"Is she—" Charlene starts.

"Oh, definitely," Violet interjects. "Check out her toes."

The commentary kills the end of the orgasm. I glance over at the three of them gawking at us. Randy seems totally unfazed. In fact, he's smug as fuck.

"Um. You should stay there. Both of you." Sunny holds her hand out to the side. Lance collides with it, and she pushes him back. "All of you."

Violet fans herself. "I feel like I just watched porn."

"Close the damn door!" I finally croak, collapsing against Randy's chest.

He's laughing. I'm so mortified I could die.

"Kinda pointless now, don't ya think?" Violet asks. "Seven minutes in heaven is up, Balls. I hope yours aren't too blue right now. Either that, or you need a change of pants, and I need a drink." She turns away. "Alex, baby, can you make me those shots I like? The ones you call panty removers?"

When I look back, Sunny has her hair twirled around her finger, and she's brushing it across her lips. Randy helps me off the washing machine. I slide down the front of his body and feel his hard-on against my stomach. I don't know how he can still be so smirky. He pats my ass as we step out into foyer. Thankfully, most of the crowd has already moved on. It's only Miller and Sunny. He gives Randy a look, then puts an arm around Sunny's shoulder and guides her down the hall.

My face feels like I have the worst sunburn in the world. I'm usually a private person. Private about sex, about my life, about pretty much everything, so knowing all these people heard me in the throes of ecstasy—because that's exactly what it was—is the pinnacle of embarrassing. Randy picks me up and sets me on a stool at Alex's breakfast bar, then he hugs me from behind. I don't know what to think about all this affection. Apparently neither does anyone else, because it's not me getting weird looks—despite my loud orgasm—it's Randy. Maybe I'm not alone in thinking this thing between us doesn't seem totally casual anymore.

Alex makes us all shooters, which we drink. Then the guys have beers, and Violet offers us cocktails or wine. Since we've already been drinking wine, we decide it's safest to stick with the same thing. I feel a little bad for Lance, since he's the only one without a girl—not that I'm Randy's girl or anything. Even if it feels a little like I am.

Violet mentions her plan to get rid of the guys. There's some serious protesting, mostly on Randy's part, but also from Miller. Violet whispers something to Alex, and his eyebrows rise. He slaps his thighs and stands up. "All right, guys, guess we're going out to watch the game since the girls are watching *Magic Mike Two*."

"It's XXL," Violet corrects.

"I don't like your friends very much right now," Randy mutters in my ear.

"I'll be here when you get back." I pat his cheek and get off the stool.

He gives me a look. "No sleep tonight."

"It's totally overrated."

Once they're gone, we order takeout, change into comfy clothes, and get back to drinking wine.

A little while later, Violet's sprawled out on the floor, rubbing her belly after plowing through an entire box of chicken balls. "I hope these digest before Alex gets back, otherwise I might have to backtrack on the blowy tonight."

Charlene snorts. "Nothing screams sexy like puking on a dick."

"Has that happened to you?" Sunny asks, eyes wide.

"No. Thank God." Violet pulls a face. "But it might if my stomach doesn't settle down soon. You don't think there was dairy in any of this, do you?"

"It's Chinese food. I don't think they do dairy," Charlene replies. "You ate too much."

"I totally did." Violet nods.

"Once I choked on Kale's hair," Sunny says. Her nose crinkles. Anything related to her ex-boyfriend, Kale, warrants that reaction.

Violet props herself up on an elbow. "You mean a ball hair?"

"Ew. No. I never would have put Kale's balls in my mouth. They were way too hairy."

"So, like, you mean his bush? Didn't he trim?"

"No. I'm talking about shaft hair. It got caught in the back of my throat. It was so gross."

Talking about Kale makes me think about Benji and his similar lack of grooming in the dick department.

"Hold the phone." Violet puts out a hand. "He had shaft hair. Like hair on the *shaft* of his penis."

"Uh-huh." Sunny nods. "Miller's so good about maintenance, though. I don't mind sucking on his balls at all."

Violet spits out her wine. "Can we not talk about Buck's balls?"

Sunny shrugs. "I'm just saying. It's nice. And Miller loves

blow jobs. He says I'm awesome at them, and he always eats my cookie afterward because he appreciates it so much."

Charlene is laughing so hard she's curled in a ball holding her stomach. Violet looks a little green, but I can't tell if it's because she ate too much, she's had too much to drink, or because Sunny's talking about blowing Miller. Again.

"What about you, Lily? You like sucking on Balls' balls?" Violet's snickering so much that her wine sloshes over the side of her glass and lands on her boobs. She frowns and rubs at it, then looks up at me expectantly.

"Uhhh..."

"Come on, you don't have to be shy. We've all watched you come," she adds.

I guess it's meant to be encouraging. Mostly it's embarrassing. There are lots of things I've shared with Sunny over the years, but a front-row seat to my orgasm wasn't one of the things I ever intended to put on the list. I puff out a breath. "Well… uh, I've never given him a blow job."

Everyone goes silent. I lift my eyes from my glass to find them all staring at me. I gulp my wine.

"How have you managed to get away with that?" Charlene asks.

"It's not like I haven't offered, he just… I don't know… Maybe it's not his thing?" I have no idea what to say to this.

"Not his thing? Every guy likes blow jobs." Violet seems mystified.

Charlene and Sunny both nod in agreement.

I lift one shoulder and then down the remaining contents of my glass. I jump up off the couch. "I need more wine. Anyone else need more wine?"

"We need to talk about this," Violet says.

"I think we all need more wine," Charlene says. "Especially if Violet thinks we need to talk blow jobs." Charlene puts a hand on Sunny's. "I'm sorry for the things you're about to hear. I know they pertain to your brother, and it's probably going to be disturbing. I have the name of a great therapist if you happen to need one later."

"I'm sure it'll be fine. Alex and I are close, and Violet does this every time we hang out. I'm used to it."

Charlene gives Sunny another sympathetic hand pat and sits back in her chair, her eyebrows raised in my direction. "So, like, do you mean he hasn't come in your mouth? Is he more of a pearl necklace kind of guy?"

Sunny raises her hand. I think it's an unconscious reaction. "Um. What do necklaces have to do with blow jobs?"

I'm grateful she asks the question, as I don't have the guts to.

Violet looks from me to Sunny and back again. Then she glances at Charlene. "You know what a pearl necklace is, right?"

Charlene rolls her eyes. "Of course."

"Just checking." Her gaze flips back to me. "Are you two telling me you're unfamiliar with pearl necklaces?"

Sunny and I nod. I feel like we've been missing out on a lot over these important, formative years when sexual knowledge and discovery peak. Sunny's clearly rectifying that now. So it's just me, all by myself, with my casual-sex hockey friend who apparently doesn't like blow jobs. Which I now suspect is weird, along with some of his other sexual quirks—like lights off and covers on. Why does he want to cover up all that hotness, anyway?

Violet grins. It's a horrible, devious smile on her beautiful, evil face. She twists her ponytail around her hand. "You get the guy's jizz all over your chest and throat."

I must make a face.

"Don't knock it 'til you try it. Alex gets so excited when I let him come on my boobs. Then he goes down on me; it's awesome. And sometimes I'm too sore to deal with the monster cock. Also, jizz tastes awful, so letting him come all over my chest is a decent option."

Sunny's horror is understandable. I can't blame her. That's a lot of information about Alex she didn't need.

"So I'm guessing Balls isn't a pearl necklace kind of guy. Hmm. Maybe he thinks he'll choke you with his dick if the rumors are true." At my lack of confirmation or denial, she continues. "Based on his issue after your make-out session, I'm guessing it is." She taps her lips with a sparkly finger. "It's considerate, if you think about it—the not wanting you to choke on his dick part."

I shrug. "But you don't think it's normal for a guy not to want a blow job if it's offered?"

I'm met with more silence and stares. Violet pulls out her phone and starts typing.

"What are you doing?" Charlene asks.

"Calling Alex."

"What? Why?" I rush to stop her, but she rolls over the back of the couch. It'd be graceful if she didn't land on her ass.

She pops back up, grinning. "Hey, baby!"

She has him on video, so we can all hear and see him. "Are you drunk?" he asks.

"You bet your Super MC I am. When you guys get back from your fun night, my beaver's gonna devour your wood, like whoa."

"I don't think my sister needs to know that."

"She doesn't care. Anyway, I have a question."

"Fire away."

"Do you like blow jobs?"

"Uhhh…"

"It's not a trick question. Answer yes or no. Do you like blow jobs?"

"Of course I like blow jobs."

"Great. Thanks. Give the phone to Buck."

"But—"

"Do it and I'll lollipop your dick later."

There's some chatter in the background, then Buck's face appears on the screen. "Buck. Quick question. Do you like blow jobs?"

"Fuck, yeah. Sunny's mouth is the best." There's a loud noise. "Fuck! Waters, get off me!"

"Put Lance on the phone."

There's some more clattering and loud noise before the phone is finally passed to Lance. Violet has to calm Alex down by pointing out he's a hypocrite to get mad at Miller for liking BJs.

Lance's strawberry-blond hair pops into view. "You don't even need to repeat the question. The answer is definitely yes. I'd give up pizza for the rest of my life if I could get a daily blow job."

"Good luck finding a mail-order bride to fulfill that dream. Put Darren on the phone."

Darren shows up next. Violet asks the same question. Darren's wearing that dark, secret smile again. "Charlene can answer that."

"Awesome. We already know you love to pearl-necklace my bestie."

I glance at Charlene, who's blushing. "What is it about the quiet ones?"

"You have no idea," she says with a similar devious grin.

Violet rolls her eyes. "Pass the phone to Balls, Mr. Grey."

There's a round of snickers. I don't even want to know if that's a joke. I step out of view so Randy can't see me, but I can still see him.

"Balls." Violet punctuates his name with a single hip thrust. "Do you like blow jobs?"

His hand comes up to run through his hair, his forearm and biceps flexing. "They're all right, I guess."

"They're all right? All right? Are you telling me that having a woman's lips wrapped around your cock while you fuck her mouth doesn't do it for you?"

Randy goes sideways for a second before Alex's face appears on the screen. "Violet, baby, you can't say things like that to other guys. Ever. Not ever. 'Kay?"

We hear Buck laughing in the background.

"Is this about your Frankenweiner, Ballistic?" That sounds like Lance.

"Shut the fuck up, man!" There's a loud crash. "That's under the damn cone."

"Hey! You're gonna get us kicked out!" Alex yells. His face reappears. "I gotta go. Ballistic and Romero are about to rip each other's heads off. See you in a bit, babe." The screen goes blank, and everyone looks to me.

Violet raises a brow. "Frankenweiner?"

I shrug. "I don't know what that means."

"Well, you've seen his dick, right? Does it look normal? Is it massive like Alex's? I mean, he's monstrous." She hold up her arm and points to her wrist. "Thicker than this, that's for sure."

"Violet." Charlene kicks her.

"What?"

"Sunny's here."

"What does that matter? I'm sure she's accidentally seen his junk at some point. I mean, I know what Buck's looks like, even though I don't want to." Violet's drunk. She gets louder as she gains momentum. "Besides, didn't you go into Alex's room and steal his condom stash, Sunny? You gotta know he's packing a massive cannon—not to mention all the years he spent in spandex."

Sunny just shrugs.

"Anyway, it's not Alex's dick that matters; it's Randy's. Back to that. So, what's so Franken-y about it?"

They're staring at me intently. "I-I don't know."

"What do you mean you don't know? Is the head a weird shape? Oh my God! Does Randy have a dick piercing?"

"He doesn't have a dick piercing." I would've felt that.

"Too bad. I've heard those are awesome. So what's the deal?" She gestures for me to continue.

I shrug. "I've never seen it."

I get three blank looks in response.

"It's always dark."

"Dark? Really? Huh. But you've, like, held it, right?"

"Well, yeah, of course."

"So did it have nodules or a serious curve?"

"Nodules?"

"You know, like the nuts and bolts that stick out of Frankenstein's head—that kind of thing."

"There aren't any nodules. He's definitely circumcised, though."

"Hmm." Violet taps her lips. "Too bad about the foreskin; it's super fun to play with. Sunny, you should text Buck."

"Why?"

"Because him and Balls have known each other forever. Buck has to know what this is about."

"Why do you care?" Sunny asks. "Maybe it's personal. Maybe Randy's sensitive about it."

"He's a guy. How sensitive can he be?"

"Some of them are very." Sunny doesn't immediately pull out her phone.

Violet looks around the room, seeking support. "Seriously? I can't be the only one who's curious about this. Here you've got this smoking-hot hockey player, a legend in the bunnysphere—sorry, Lily, but it's true—and Lily's his fuck buddy, and she hasn't even seen his dick. She hasn't wrapped her lips around it and gagged a little when he gets excited and goes too deep."

"We're not fuck buddies."

"You're boning him, yes?"

"Well, yeah—"

"Your beaver eats his wood?" At my silence she waves her hand around her crotch. "Less than three seconds after you walked through the door, he pulled you into my laundry room and did some magic voodoo to make you come fully clothed."

"We're just having fun," I say lamely.

"So you're banging, but you're not dating."

"Yes. No. But we… I—"

"That's the twenty-first-century definition of a fuck buddy. Don't feel bad about it. It doesn't make you slutty. I mean, shit, you spent seven years dating that Benji douche. You deserve a fuck buddy, or seven." She thumbs over her shoulder to Charlene. "If anyone's slutty, it's this one. She had three FBs going at once our last year of college."

Charlene shrugs. "It was a phase. I'm way past that now."

"Anyway." Violet turns back to me. "So you've only had

sex with the lights off, you've only ever had your hand on his dick, and he doesn't like blow jobs. Doesn't anyone else find this odd?"

"I find it weird," Charlene agrees.

"Maybe he's shy," Sunny says.

"Uh, have you read any of the stuff girls say about Balls?" Violet asks.

"You know I don't look at social media. It creates problems," Sunny replies.

"True. But some of it has merit." Violet ponders while sipping her wine. "How big is his dick? I know what the bunnies say, but they all like to exaggerate."

"It's big."

"Like, hammer of death big?"

"Um, we use the gold condoms, not the regular ones."

"Well. That's, uh …" Violet nods her approval. "High five, girlfriend." I high five her. "So he's packing, and I'm assuming it works fine."

"We used an entire box of condoms the last time he came to Guelph." I might be a little braggy about this.

"Holy shit. Over how many days?"

"One."

Violet puts her hands on my shoulders. "Does your beaver have super powers? Is it made out of titanium?"

"Um, no."

"That's insane. How'd you manage walking the next day?"

"Carefully."

"Okay, so let's line up the facts and see what we know."

"This is like the game of Clue, but about Randy's penis," Sunny says.

"Exactly!" Violet exclaims, clapping her hands together. "So once the wood is sheathed, lights come on and covers come off. No blow jobs, but no issues with longevity, and he's hung. Do I have all this right, Lily?"

"Pretty much." Individually, those things didn't seem too odd. But now, talking about it with the girls—particularly Violet and Charlene, who seem to have a much broader wealth of experience in this department—makes me wonder exactly what the deal is. All together, Randy's sex quirks add up to a big WTF.

"Is there anything else you can think of that might provide clues as to what the real issue is?" Violet asks.

"Oh!" I sit up straight. "He has a scar. It looks like it could be from an appendectomy, but way low, and it seems like he had a butcher for a surgeon. He has another scar on the inside of his leg. I saw it once—never mind, that part doesn't matter."

"So he has scars near the wood, eh?" Violet taps her lips again.

"Above the wood, and below, but that doesn't mean one is related to the other."

Sunny's on her phone. She looks up and says. "Hockey accident."

"Why would you think that?"

"'Cause that's what Miller just said. I messaged him about it. He won't give me details, but he said it's from a hockey accident, and Randy doesn't like to talk about it."

"Wow. That must've been some accident if he ended up with a nickname like that," Violet says.

"That's a pretty awful nickname," Sunny says.

"I'm sorry, Lily. I wouldn't have made a joke out of it if I'd known Lance was being serious and not just a jerk." Violet actually looks taken aback.

"It's okay. I mean, I'm curious, too. I didn't realize it was something so—"

"Sensitive?" Sunny says.

"Yeah." Now I feel bad, too.

"Well, mystery solved, I guess." Violet has recovered. She rolls off the couch and opens a set of cupboard doors. "We should play Scrabble!"

"I hate Scrabble," Sunny complains.

"We'll play partners," I offer.

"And we'll make it dirty. Only pervy words allowed." Violet sets the game up on the floor because the coffee table's too full of stuff.

Sunny's first word is *hoor*. No one says anything about the spelling.

At midnight, the guys finally roll in—well, almost all of them roll in. Lance is absent. I assume he picked up a bunny and went back to his own house. Randy's the last to come in. He stands at the back of the group, hands shoved in his pockets. He glances at me, gives me a small, strained smile, and then his eyes dart around the room.

I'm drunk, so I don't have much of a filter left, but he looks uncomfortable.

Alex surveys the living room. The coffee table is covered in empty wine bottles and half-eaten bowls of chips and popcorn. Bits of food litter the floor. The Scrabble game is still set up and covered in dirty words.

"What'd you girls do tonight?" Alex leans over Violet and kisses her forehead. Then he adjusts her tank top so she's not flashing so much cleavage.

"We talked about dicks and blow jobs. The usual." Violet wraps her arms around his neck and tries to get one foot hooked around his waist, but she's sloppy drunk. "You should take me upstairs so I can show you a new trick."

Alex laughs. "Shh, baby, inside voice, remember?"

"That wasn't a whisper, eh?"

"Not even close," Miller says from across the room. He stretches and makes a big show of yawning. "Sunny, you wanna come snuggle with me?"

She glances at me, as if she's afraid to leave me alone. It's not like she needs permission. I'm hoping whatever's going on with Randy's dark mood can be fixed by some vagina prison.

Two by two, everyone heads upstairs to bed. And then it's me and Randy. And for some reason it's awkward. Maybe because everyone's a couple, and we're not. Maybe because of the conversation earlier in the night, or Violet's mentioning it the second the guys walked in the door.

I unfold my legs and push up off the couch at his approach. As soon as he's close enough, I hug his waist. He's stiff. And not in his pants. His whole body. I slide a hand up his chest and around the back of his neck. He doesn't resist as I pull him down. I don't go in for a kiss; instead I bring my lips to his ear and whisper in what I hope is my sexiest voice, "Wanna go to prison?"

He skims my side, butterfly-wing soft. He turns his head so his cheek brushes mine. His voice is a hoarse whisper. "Yes, please. I've been waiting all night for prison."

There's heaviness in his words, like the joke between us has something darker tied to it. I take his hand and lead him up the familiar stairs to the same room where we had sex for the first time. Randy hits the lights as soon as we're inside and the door's locked. I don't try to turn them back on. We move toward the bed, and as soon as we're a foot away, he grabs me from behind and dive-bombs us onto the mattress.

I shriek and giggle, then sigh as his lips find my neck. "Did you have fun with the girls tonight?" he asks.

"Uh-huh. Did you have fun with the boys?"

"I woulda rather been here with you. Or at my place with you."

"You're here with me now."

His hips are pressed against my ass. I can feel him, but he doesn't seem hard. At least I don't think he is. I can't tell through all the unfortunate layers of clothing, and he's not doing his typical grind. I try to flip over under him so I can see his face, but he presses his hips into me, keeping me face down. Now I can feel him. He's *definitely* not as excited as usual.

He sits back on his knees, straddling me, and slides his palms under my shirt. His rough, hot hands glide heavily up my back. He gives my shirt a tug, and I raise my arms over my head so he can take it off.

The next thing I feel are his lips at the top of my spine, followed by the press of his cheek between my shoulder blades. It's intimate and sweet and confusing. I don't know what's going on tonight. We started out with such a bang—or at least I did—and now I feel uncertain about everything. He kisses a path down my vertebrae and back up, one hand curled around my shoulder, his thumb brushing up and down along my nape.

I should be enjoying this soft, unhurried contact, but it's unusual, and being around three women in highly defined relationships makes it glaringly obvious that's not what I have. Or it's not what we've said I have. At this point I'm lost because my previous relationship had very little of this involved. It shouldn't matter. I should just enjoy it, but I'm not used to this kind of undefined status. The longer we keep it up, the harder it is to keep my emotions separate.

I push back the worries about what's coming after this holiday and focus instead on being with him while I can.

"Randy?" I crane to look at him, but all I get is a view of his tattooed hand in my peripheral vision.

"Mmmm?"

"Let me up."

He freezes. "What?"

"I wanna turn over."

He hesitates. And sighs. Then he rises enough that I can flip over under him. I'm super quick, sliding out like a snake before he can trap me again. He looks worried, and for the first time ever, vulnerable. Maybe if I get naked first, he'll want to follow.

I shimmy my pants over my hips, then follow with my panties. Now I'm naked, and he's still fully dressed. His eyes are on me, hot, needy. This is the Randy I'm used to—the one who's more animal than man in bed. I can work with this.

I get up on my knees, mirroring his position. Except I'm more than six inches shorter than he is, so I'm staring at his chest. His shirt-covered chest. I remedy that problem, drawing it up over his head. He takes over when I get to his shoulders, pulling it off and tossing it over the side of the bed. I'd like to move right in on the belt, but I'm thinking that'll make him jumpy. Also, it's hypocritical of me to think I can forgo the foreplay, since Randy makes sure we get it every single time.

I run my hands up his chest, circle his little man nipples with my fingernails and follow with my lips. I'm rewarded with one of his deep groans. *Nice*. He must like this a lot. While I distract him with my mouth, I manage to get his belt undone. I carefully flick the button on his jeans and drag the zipper down.

I look up, fingertips brushing the head of his cock through his boxers. "Can I take these off?"

Again, there's hesitation. Eventually he nods, and I push his jeans over his hips, leaving his boxer briefs on. He tries to pull me down on top of him, but I straddle him and put a hand on the center of his chest. Circling my hips, I lean in slowly and brush my lips over his. "Randy."

He skims my sides. "Hmm?"

I'm not much of a dirty talker. I've never felt confident enough to pull it off. I'm going to try now, though. "I want your cock in my mouth."

Randy stills, and his eyes flare with panic. "You don't need to do that." It comes out all gravelly.

"I know, but I want to." I bite my lip. I'm definitely feeling less than confident with the way he seems so uncertain. I'm not sure how I'll feel if he rejects me.

"It's really not nec—"

"Please?" If someone ever told me I'd beg to give a blow job, let alone to a professional hockey player, I would've laughed at them. Before it was curiosity that had me wanting to perform this act, now it's a genuine desire to return all the favors.

Randy glances over at the bathroom where light filters through, cutting a line across the bed. When he doesn't say yes or no, I start kissing a path down his throat, going lower, stopping at his nipples before I continue to the mysterious beast in his boxers.

I reach the waistband and peek up at him. His expression is tight, a combination of anticipation and what appears to be terror. I can't understand what would be terrifying about getting head, unless sharp teeth are involved. I kiss the pale scar a few inches from his left hip and push his boxers down.

He's maybe semi-hard. Every other muscle in his body is locked tight. His hands are balled into fists at his sides.

"I don't know if this is a good idea." He grits his teeth and closes his eyes, exhaling a long breath.

"You think me sucking you off is a bad idea?" I'm glad it's dark, because I'm blushing at my own words.

Randy groans.

I drop a wet kiss on his scar. Instead of pushing his boxers farther down, I brush my nose along the length of his semi-hard erection through the material. When I reach the head I press my tongue against the cotton and suck. Randy's abs tighten, and his hands flex by his hips.

I repeat the same series of motions, eventually slipping my fingers into the pocket to touch him. This time he doesn't protest as I push the waistband down a little farther and follow the scar. It stops abruptly a few inches from his pelvis.

"Lily." Randy reaches for me.

I take his hand before he can take mine. I bite his knuckle, then kiss it, licking his finger—mimicking what I plan to do to his cock. If he'll let me.

"Please, Randy?" I lay my cheek on the damp fabric, right over his erection.

The noise he makes is pained, but he slips his thumb into my mouth, so I swirl my tongue around it. I push his boxers down again until the head peeks out. Keeping my eyes on his, I kiss the tip.

Randy exhales a shuddering breath, and his eyes flutter closed. I do what I did to his thumb, swirling with my tongue. At the shift of his hips, I cover the head with my mouth, applying the gentlest of suction.

"Oh, shit."

I pop off. "Is that okay?"

Randy nods.

"I can do it again?"

"Yeah. That'd be great."

I repeat the same kiss, swirl, suck pattern a few times before I ask, "Can I take these off now?"

His expression is heartbreaking. It's obvious he wants to say yes, but he's afraid to. Someone must've done or said something awful to him. His lids close in what looks like resignation, so I whisper, "Eyes on me, baby."

They flip open, locking on me as I slowly move his boxers over his hips. I put my lips to his skin and keep the connection. Randy's semi-hard erection jumps on his stomach.

I glance down. Even in the dim light I can see very clearly the scar that cuts across his lower abdomen There's a two-inch gap on his stomach where the scar ceases to exist.

And that's when I notice the very pale, very significant scar slicing a line across the center of his cock. My eyes flip back up to find him staring at me intently. It's like he expects me to freak out or something.

I'm not going to lie, my stomach twists. I'm not repulsed, though; I'm stunned. This injury was caused by a skate. And based on the damage, I'm going to have to assume Randy's lucky to have everything still attached to his body. It's a damn miracle it still works.

Returning my gaze to his, I grip his cock and press a soft kiss to the top of the scar on his hip. I don't have to look at it to feel it beneath my lips. I keep kissing until my chin bumps his cock. Then I glance down.

I don't want to think too much about how horrible it must have been. The line across his cock looks like a frown. I press my lips to it, and Randy shudders. "Does that feel okay?" I whisper against the soft skin.

"Yeah." Randy clears his throat. His hands are fists again.

This time I part my lips and stroke the shaft with my tongue. Randy grunts, which I take as a good sign. His cock throbs in my hand, growing a little.

I keep kissing, moving from base to tip. Circling the head with my tongue, I make my way back down. The frown has become a straight line. He's harder now, too.

On my next trip up, I take in the entire head. He keeps growing, getting harder with each shallow stroke. I pop off and lick around the head, then down the shaft again. I think he might be fully hard now. He feels pretty damn solid.

I take him back in my mouth and keep going until the head hits the back of my throat. Randy shoves his hand in my hair. I pause and meet his hot gaze.

"Okay?" I ask with a mouthful of cock.

He seems to understand. "So fucking good," he rasps.

I smile as much as I can with a dick in my mouth.

23

REVERSE BLOWJOBOLOGY

RANDY

Lily's mouth is bliss. Those luscious lips are stretched around my cock, and she's sucking like a goddamn champion. I can't take my eyes off her as she lets me guide her.

She moans, and the sound vibrates through my body. I keep going—deeper, harder, faster—and she doesn't seem to mind one bit. She strokes the shaft and cups my balls. The sensation is way more intense than I ever remember it being, although it's been a lot of years since I had a blow job, so my memories are vague at best.

I'm getting close to coming, faster than usual. One of the perks of having nearly lost half my dick is that I can go for a long time thanks to some loss of sensation. But right now, watching Lily's mouth makes everything hypersensitive.

"Lily, baby, I'm gonna come soon." I figure I should warn her so she can make a decision about where she wants that to happen.

Her gaze flips up to mine, and she takes me deeper, sucking

harder. I can't take it anymore. The orgasm checks me to the boards. I shudder violently with the sensation. Lily swallows, God bless her, which makes it even better.

When I'm finally done, she slowly eases off. The cold air is a shock. Lily runs a gentle finger across my cock. She must be touching the scar, because the sensation is muted.

She giggles.

"What's funny?"

She rests her head on my hip. "Did you know when you're soft your scar looks like a frown, but when you're hard it's a smile?"

"What?"

"The scar makes your cock look happy when it's hard."

I bark out a laugh.

She crawls up my body and kisses me on the cheek. "Thanks for letting me do that."

"You're thanking me for letting you blow my fucked-up dick?"

"It's not fucked up."

"It sure isn't pretty."

Lily cocks her head to the side. "Says who? It makes you super badass."

"You think?"

"Mmm-hmmm." She circles my nipple with her fingertip. "That must have been so painful."

"It was."

"You don't have to talk about it."

"It's fine. It's an old hockey injury. We were kids messing around on the lake. I got into it with a guy a couple years older than me. I wasn't wearing a cup, and, well, I almost had my dick decapitated."

"That must've been awful. How old were you?"

"Eleven."

"Oh, God. That would be traumatizing."

"I was pretty scared I was going to end up with half a dick."

She snorts. "Your half is most people's average."

"I'm glad I have all of it."

I run a hand up and down her spine, thinking about how things went down after the accident. "Surgery was brutal. My mom stayed at the hospital the entire time 'cause my dad was away. He only came to see me once, and he freaked out. He was less worried about my feelings about the injury and more concerned about how it was going to impact my ability to play hockey. When I got out of the hospital, my dad had moved out."

Lily lifts her head from my chest, her disgust almost soothing. "What?"

"It wasn't because of what happened." I look up at the ceiling. I don't know why I'm telling her this, but I want to. "He had a hard time not putting his dick where it didn't belong when he was away. I think my mom had had enough. My accident was a good reason to finally put an end to it."

"I'm so sorry. That must have been tough."

"He was away a lot, so I didn't see much of him, anyway. Things were a lot less stressful once he was out of the picture." I put my arm around Lily and roll her over so she's under me. I don't know how this conversation got so serious, or why I feel compelled to tell her all this personal shit. It's not something I usually do, but then, blow jobs are also unusual. "We're supposed to be having fun, aren't we?"

"I thought we were having fun." She runs her fingers through my hair.

"We should have more." I cover her mouth with mine. Then I make her come with my mouth before I get inside her like I've wanted to for the past two weeks. Usually I keep my eyes on hers when I come, but this time I have to bury my face against her neck. It's just too much.

The next day I hijack her from Waters' house and take her back to my place. We spend the entire day screwing our brains out. Lily blows me in the shower and again in the living room while I'm trying to watch sports highlights. I feel like I'm making up for all the missed years of BJs in one week.

I don't get to keep her the entire time she's here, which sucks, but the time we do have is awesome—and we're not always naked. Although, we are naked a lot. Two days before I'm scheduled to leave for the next away game, I get a message from Miller saying Waters booked ice time, and we need to get our asses in gear. And to bring Lily along.

We're in bed. Lily's lounging on my chest, flipping aimlessly through channels. She's naked. As is my preference.

"You brought skates with you to Chicago, right?" I ask, skimming the contour of her hip. The thought of her in one of her skating outfits makes me instantly hard. I tent the sheets.

Lily pulls the covers off my dick, and he springs free, sticking straight up. Well, mostly straight. I've got a curve from the scar.

"I have a spare pair at Sunny's. Why?" Lily circles the head with her fingertip, watching it jump. She thinks my scar is sexy. It's interesting how one person's reaction could change my perspective so quickly. She kisses from my neck to my chin.

"Because we're going skating."

She pauses in her mission to get her tongue back in my mouth. "Why would we do that when we can get our exercise here? We're supposed to be fucking our faces off."

I chuckle. "Waters scored a couple hours of ice time today. Miller and Sunny are gonna be there. It'll be fun to do something other than get naked."

"Naked is the most fun."

"We'll do that again later." I attempt to roll off the bed, but Lily throws her leg over mine.

"Fine, but we're already naked, and you're hard, so we should do something about it before we go anywhere. Otherwise you'll embarrass yourself with this."

She strokes me a couple of times. I nab the box of condoms from the dresser and shake one out on the bed. Lily tears it open and rolls it on. I flip her over on her back, get inside her, and make her come like I always do.

Afterwards, we get dressed. I convince Lily to wear one of her skating outfits because I think they're hot. We're about twenty minutes later than we should be getting to the rink. But Waters rented it for two hours, so we've got plenty of time. Miller told me Waters wants to teach Violet how to skate, and he figured this would be the only way it would happen.

When we get there, Waters and Westinghouse are already on the ice with Sunny and Charlene. Lily's quick to get her skates on and hit the rink. Violet's sitting on the bench with Miller, who's adjusting his skates.

"Hey, man, you're late." He gives me props. "Once Vi gets the hang of things, we're gonna play girls against guys."

Violet snorts. "On a cold day in hell."

"You'll be fine. It's easy. You're marrying a hockey player. You have to learn how to skate."

"Aren't there skates with double blades on them? Can't I learn on those?"

"Those are for toddlers, Vi. They don't make them in your size." Miller pats her on the shoulder. "You'll be fine. Come on. Let's do this."

"Give me a minute. I'm psyching myself up."

"That's what you've been saying for the last twenty."

"This takes a lot of psyching, Buck." She taps her temple, then motions to her feet. "I'm wearing a set of blades. On my feet. It's dangerous. Someone could die."

"No one's gonna die."

"I could lacerate someone."

Miller looks at me and cringes.

"Maybe we should all wear cups," I say, *mostly* joking.

"It might not be a bad idea." Miller looks back at Violet. "I'm sending Waters over here to get you if you're not on the ice in two. He's being super patient, Vi. You're probably hurting his feelings."

"Whatever. Nothing a BJ won't solve."

Miller points a finger at her face. "That's your overshare for today. No more freebies."

"You won the overshare contest today when you told me your dick is chafed from too much Sunshine cookie."

"You two realize I'm right here, listening to this."

They both look at me.

"And your point is?" Violet asks.

"Just letting you know it isn't a private conversation."

"Miller will pay for your therapy bills." She turns back to her brother. "See? I used your real name. Give me five more minutes. Then I'll come out."

Miller shrugs, steps out onto the ice, and is gone. I sit down on the bench so I can adjust my laces. Violet's got hockey skates on instead of the figure skating kind. Lily waves as she skates past us, doing a little twirl and a jump.

Violet frowns. "Seriously. I have no idea how she does that."

We watch her make her way around the rink, leaping and spinning. She's graceful and smooth. It's exactly the way she is in bed. I fucking love it.

"You're thinking about having sex with her," Violet whispers. "I can tell."

I glance at her. "Why would you think that?"

"Your woody." She points at my crotch.

I glance down, even though I'm not hard.

She starts laughing. "Oh my God, Balls. You're the funniest." She punctuates it with one of her hip thrusts. She's been managing not to do that as much lately.

I shake my head and lace my skates. "What's your beef with skating?"

"I don't have a beef. I'm uncoordinated. I can't even do yoga without falling on my face. I don't know why Alex thinks I need to learn how to skate. I'll probably commit accidental manslaughter and end up in prison. They won't even have a library, and if they do they'll only carry the classics and none of the smutty books I like to read for fun. Not that I'll want to read smut with no dick around. See why this is a bad idea?" She crosses her arms over her chest, eyeing everyone on the ice.

They're in the middle of the rink. Miller's disappeared somewhere. All of a sudden music blasts through the sound system.

Sunny claps her hands. "Oh! Alex and Lily, remember that routine you used to do?"

Lily and Waters share a look. I don't like the hot feeling in my neck. They laugh.

I can't hear the rest of the conversation over the music, but Lily and Waters face off against each other. It looks like they're getting ready to drop the puck, but then they start talking, moving their feet in little stilted circles, making hand gestures.

"What's going on over there?" Violet asks.

"I'm not sure." I remind myself that Lily and Waters have known each other their whole lives. They're like brother and sister, kinda like Miller and Violet, except hopefully not quite as open.

Waters holds out his hand and Lily takes it. They skate down the ice. Together. She doesn't look at me when she passes; her eyes are glued to Waters' as they start in on a routine. I glance at Violet, who's looking at me with something like panic on her face.

I check the ice again. Waters is definitely rusty. He's an awesome skater, but he's been in pro hockey for the past six years, so the whole light-on-his-feet business hasn't been much of a priority. But he's still more graceful that most of the guys on the ice, and now I get why.

By their third pass, they've found their rhythm. Lily skates circles around him and does this incredible spin thing. Then things get serious. They've got their hands on each other. His are on her waist and hers on his shoulder. I'm not all that excited about them touching each other.

Their faces are close, and she gives him a nod. I don't know what it means until Waters lifts her in the air. Her body arcs in this perfect pose. A slapshot of emotions hits me. I'm suddenly sad all over again that she lost her chance at the Olympics. She would've been amazing. I'm in awe because she's damn well gorgeous. I'm also irrationally pissed that Waters is touching her. I recognize the emotion as jealousy. I don't get to think too much about that, though, because suddenly Violet is elbowing my side.

"Maybe you should get out there. Go get your girl."

"They're doing some kind of routine." I reply evenly, though I feel some level of panic.

"Notice how intimate this routine is. Note how good they are at it?"

"That's probably because they've done it a million times."

"So you don't have a problem with the way they're touching each other, then?"

I glance at her to see whether she's serious. She looks it. "Do you?"

"They grew up together, so it's probably fine, right?" She watches them for a few seconds before she asks, "Does Lily bone like she figure skates?"

I open my mouth to tell her I'm not at liberty to say, but she cuts me off with a wave of her hand. "Never mind. I already know the answer to that question. Guys like you don't go back for repeat sexing if isn't stellar. I bet she fucks like a goddamn prostitute on steroids. I bet her pussy is like Fort Knox. Do you think she ever crushed on Alex?"

"I doubt it."

"Do you know for sure?" she asks.

The real answer is I don't. I'm guessing. And I've already mentally asked myself that question. I open my mouth, but Violet goes on one of her tangents.

"I need to take stripper dance classes so I can move like her. Lily may have small boobs, but she could get a boob job to have ones like mine and try to seduce my man."

"That's not going to happen and Lily's boobs aren't small."

She gives me another one of her looks as she stands up and wobbles on her skates.

"It won't. And they're nice."

"Nice and small. There's nothing wrong with that." She puts a hand on my shoulder and stares me right in the eye. "Don't think for a second that I buy you not caring about what's going on out there, Balls." She grimaces but doesn't even thrust once. "I see how you look at her. I was there when you dry-fucked her in my laundry room, and I saw the expression on *your* face when you made her come. You want to pretend all you're doing is buddy-fucking, go right ahead, but I see through you like watery jizz. Now help me get on the ice so Alex can show me how to skate." She clutches my arm. "And I'm glomming onto you, just so you know, not because I want him to be jealous, but because I'm pretty sure I'll fall flat on my face otherwise."

I cock a brow.

"Okay, I want him to be a little jealous, but not worried I want to bone you or anything. Because I don't. Now help me."

"Don't worry. I got you." Violet comes maybe to my shoulder, if that. I thread my arm through hers. There's no way to avoid brushing the side of her boob; it's that big. I pretend it's not happening.

I step out onto the ice first and direct her to hold on to the ledge until she gets her footing. "You've never skated before?"

"I've skated. I was a kid. All I remember was that I didn't like it, and I hurt myself, and my mom didn't make me do it again. I avoided sports. I did math camp instead. Oh, and cooking classes because I love eating."

Once she gets both feet on the ice, she freezes.

"Okay. Time to let go," I tell her.

"Of you?"

"No, the wall."

She does what I tell her, but her attention is divided between me, the ice, and Lily and Waters. He misses catching her this time, and she stumbles, ending up in his arms. They're laughing, and Sunny's clapping again. If I had a free hand and a camera ready, it'd make a great picture. Except I don't want pictures of her and Waters.

Then Violet flails, and her feet go in two different directions. She really is the most uncoordinated person I've ever met. Maybe her boobs throw off her center of gravity. She grabs me with both hands, kicking me in the shin with one of her skates in the process. It hurts, but I've been kicked way worse, so I try not to make a face or anything. I grab her under the arms as she shrieks and tries to get her skates under control. All she succeeds in doing is kicking my feet out from under me.

I roll to my back as we go down, making sure she's on top so I don't crush her when we land.

Waters puts Lily down, shooting me a dirty look. "Baby, what're you doing? I would've come to get you!"

"I want you to spin me around like that!" She turns back and gives me a devious smile. Her voice drops. "Just so you know, I was totally fucking with you. I'm not worried about Alex and Lily. He and I are solid. But your response told me everything I already knew. It's pretty damn obvious Lily's more than just your fuck buddy. Maybe you should man up and do something about it."

I'm about to laugh that off when Waters skates over and helps Violet up, Lily right behind him. Violet smirks as Alex holds her against him, and Lily gives me a *holy shit* face, coming to a stop beside me as I push to my feet. Her cheeks are pink, and she's breathing heavy.

She presses her body flush to mine. "Are you okay? Violet's a menace."

"I'm fine. You looked good out there." I won't admit that I didn't like Waters' hands on her, or that Violet may be on to something.

"Thanks. Alex and I used to practice together sometimes. Come on, I'll teach you some moves." She circles me, urging me to follow her. And I do.

We spend the next hour on the ice. Lily's incredibly talented. Between her and Waters, we finally get to the point where Violet can make it around the rink without falling. She still has to hold on to someone, but at least she isn't landing on her ass.

After skating we go to an all-you-can-eat buffet restaurant. It's the only way to go with hockey players; unlimited options and no cut-off point is the best.

Lily and I end up being invited back to Waters' place, which means no sex until later. And I'm okay with that. It's a good day, even if it's not the naked kind.

I pull into Waters' driveway. We've managed to get here first, so we have to wait for them to show up. I play with the lock of Lily's hair that's flipping out instead of curling under. It always seems to do that. "Can I ask you something?"

"The answer is no. Sunny and I have never experimented with each other," she says immediately.

I choke on a cough. "Where the hell did that come from?"

"Now you're imagining it, aren't you?"

I laugh. "There's no right answer to that, Lily."

"Maybe you like the idea of me and Violet better. Her boobs are huge, and we're closer to the same height."

"Jesus."

"Sorry. I'll stop. You had a question."

"Does that mean you've thought about experimenting with Sunny?"

"Ew. No way. She's my best friend. Violet maybe, because of her boobs. Okay. Question. Shoot."

It takes me a few seconds to remember it. It's a decent segue anyway. "You ever have a thing for Waters?"

"Alex?"

"Yeah. Like when you were a teenager—you ever crush on him? You know, hook up with your bestie's brother or whatever?" I try to come off as casual, but I'm pretty damn sure I fail, based on Lily's expression.

"Did I ever have a crush on *Alex*? Oh my God, no! He was such a dork in high school. I mean, he was always really nice, but so, so nerdy. I can't even tell you. Why?"

I shrug. "Just curious."

"Just curious? Is this because of the skating thing?"

"You guys seemed to know how each other moves. I figured maybe you knew more about that than just what he was like on the ice."

"I grew up with him, and Sunny's my best friend. I never would have gone behind her back like that."

I nod like I get it. Mostly I'm relieved. And I recognize that's not necessarily a good thing—much like the jealousy this afternoon when they were on the ice. It means I'm getting attached. Comfortable. I'm not exactly sure why that's happened.

I told her to tell me if things got too intense, but I have no idea what to do with myself.

24

SLAP SHOT TO THE HEART

LILY

I've spent the majority of my time in Chicago with Randy, apart from the actual holiday and the hours during which he has practice or training sessions. We have such a great time together. And not just the sex, which is still so, so amazing. But this week we've spent as much time in a group as we did alone. He and Sunny get along great. Violet's almost stopped thrusting when she says his name, and him and Alex and Darren and Miller are hilarious to be around. I'm still trying to figure out Lance.

It's New Year's Eve. Sunny and I are sitting in her living room, painting our toenails. Charlene and Violet are putting on blue eye shadow and acting like assholes.

"Alex says he can get you an interview for a coaching position, if you want it," Sunny says.

I stop painting and sit back, wiggling my toes. I've been thinking about this all week. I want desperately to take her up on the offer; I'm worried it's for the wrong reasons.

"Your mom'll be fine without you. It's only an hour-and-a-half flight. You can go back anytime you want."

"I know." Sunny's right. This Tim-Tom guy actually seems decent, apart from the shirtlessness. He owns a small gym, he's nice to her, and she's happy—happier than she's been in a long time. She met his family at Christmas. There's talk about her moving in with him. I know she'll say it's okay for me to tag along, but it's time to get out.

"Then what's holding you back? Not the messages from Benji, I hope."

"Your douchey ex?" Violet asks.

"Yeah, that's the ex, and no, he's definitely not a factor in the decision." Benji has sent several texts and left a couple of voice mails over the past week. I sent one text back, because I'm not a total cold-hearted bitch, but I don't miss being with him. I still have to give him his things back, though at this point I'm not sure I care about mine. It'd be easy enough to drop his junk off at his house and be done with it. I've already got closure.

"Okay. Good. Just checking." Sunny draws a tiny little champagne flute on her big toe in silver. She's incredible at painting pictures on nails.

"Can you fix mine when you're done?" Violet lifts a foot. There's nail polish everywhere but on her toenails, it seems.

"Of course. Do you want it to match the crazy you're putting on your face?" Sunny asks.

"Yes! I can't wait to send Alex pictures of what he's missing tonight." Violet grins, and she has red lipstick on her teeth. She's wild at the best of times, but tonight she's more so than usual, with Alex and the boys being at an away game. We all would have gone, but they're flying back tomorrow, so we decided to delay the official celebration. Sunny and Alex's parents also came in for the holiday, and there's been more wedding talk. Tonight Violet and Charlene decided to re-create the pre-wedding makeup test run Daisy suggested. There are bottles of Aquanet on the table. Sunny says Violet's not allowed to use them because they're aerosol and bad for the environment.

"So is it because of Randy, then?" Charlene asks.

All three girls stare, waiting.

"No."

"Liar!" Violet points at me.

"Randy isn't the reason I'm not sure."

"He might not be *the* reason, but I bet he's *a* reason," Violet replies. "Your last name is LeBlanc, right?"

"Yeah." I'm not sure what that has to do with Randy, but then Violet doesn't often stick with one train of thought.

"Is that your mom's or your dad's last name?" she asks.

"My mom's. I've never even met my dad. There's no way I'd take his last name." I don't mean to sound bitchy.

"You've never met your dad?" Violet asks. "Wow. That's crazy. Me neither."

"Really?" I ask.

"For reals." Violet nods. "Apparently he's a jerkwad. My mom says it was a whirlwind romance. I think it means she had a slutty phase and decided not to give me up for adoption."

"Wow," Sunny and I say in unison.

"It's no biggie." She shrugs. "My mom raised me on her own."

"Just like Sidney raised Miller," Sunny says. She gets this wistful look in her eyes. "It's like fate brought your parents together."

"Actually, I think he accidentally stole her coffee one day, and that's how they met, but yeah, they love each other," Violet agrees. "So what's the story with your dad?"

"He was a pro hockey player, and my mom was a bunny who got pregnant." I shrug. "He paid child support until he didn't anymore."

"Wow. How's your mom feel about you boning an NHL'er?" Violet asks.

"She doesn't get an opinion on that, considering," I reply.

"Fair enough," she says. The three of them go quiet for a few seconds. "Wait! So you've never met your dad, and isn't Randy's dad some ex-NHL'er who couldn't keep his dick in his pants? Aren't his parents divorced?"

"Uh, yeah."

"Holy shit!" She sets her glass down and grabs the edge of the coffee table. "What if you two are related? And not like me and Buck—all step-sibling and stuff. Like, it would be weird but okay if we hooked up, but you'd be for-real brother and sister. We could make a reality TV show out of this."

"Randy's dad isn't my dad."

"How do you know?"

"Because his name isn't on my birth certificate."

"What if it's a fake?"

"Violet, you're being an asshole," Charlene says.

"My dad's last name is Head," I say.

"What's his first name? Dick?" Violet asks.

"Actually he goes by Richard."

"Are you serious? Your dad's name is Dick Head?"

"If he went by Dick, yes."

She's silent for a few seconds, then she starts laughing hysterically. "Oh my God, that's priceless." When she calms down a bit, she holds up a finger. "So if you and Randy ever got married, your name would be Lily LeBlanc Balls. Lily White Balls!" She falls over laughing.

I want to find it funny, but I can't. Instead I'm sad. "Yeah, that's never gonna happen."

We get super hammered and ring in the New Year with

champagne. I get two messages at midnight: one from Benji telling me he misses me and another from Randy saying he wishes he was inside me. I can't pretend it doesn't make my chest ache when I realize all over again that that's where this whole thing starts and finishes.

Turns out Alex doesn't give me a choice about whether or not I'm doing the job interview. He sets it up for me and tells me when I'm disgustingly hungover that I'll need to be at the arena the following morning.

Randy and I spend the majority of New Year's Day in his bed. I'm not in very good shape, so we don't have much in the way of sex. Instead, I drink ginger ale, and we cuddle. Things feel off. Or maybe I'm off because I'm hungover.

The next morning while I'm getting ready for my interview, I spot Randy's defaced pink boxers on the bedroom floor. I snatch them up and shove them in my bag while he's in the bathroom. I don't know why, or maybe I do. This week has been amazing, but this thing with Randy is getting too big. I want more than he says he has to give.

Alex picks me up to take me to the interview, and Randy tongue-fucks the hell out of my mouth before he lets me get into the car. I have to go home tomorrow—possibly to pack up my things—so he's taking me out for dinner tonight. Which, to me, sounds and feels like a real date. I didn't mention that to him.

"I know it's none of my business—" Alex says as we pull away.

"It's just casual."

"You're sure about that?"

"I'm sure. I wouldn't move to another country for a guy, Alex. I was with Benji for seven years. I'm having some fun, and Randy's a fun guy." The words sound flat.

"And he feels the same way."

"Yeah. He feels the same way." I poke the fuzzy dice hanging from the rearview mirror.

"You're sure about that, too?"

I think about the message from New Years. And about how deep I've gotten myself in. I'm going to get my heart ripped out. "Yeah. I'm totally positive. Can we talk about something else? Like this interview? I feel unprepared."

Alex drops the subject and tells me what to expect at the arena. It's been a long time since I've done an interview. I'm legitimately nervous, but I must do okay, because they offer me the job on the spot. Randy's plan to keep me to himself is overruled as a result, and we end up going out for dinner to celebrate with the whole group. It's almost a good thing, because now that I know I'm moving to Chicago, I have to do something I've been holding off on.

After we eat, Sunny and Miller go back to his place, which gives me and Randy the entire night to ourselves at Sunny's. It will be my place, too, in three weeks. That's how long I have before I start my new job, in my new city.

Except I don't want to move here and keep doing what I'm doing with Randy. I'm not good at casual. I know that now. I keep seeing how in love Violet, Sunny, and Charlene are. I can invite him in tonight, but it's not going to help anything. I'm still going to feel the way I do, and I'm still going to be just the girl he fucks. Like a champ. It's the perfect scenario for someone who isn't me. I should have told him this wasn't working for me ages ago, but the sex part was working so well I didn't want to. I think I'm going to throw up.

Randy parks in front of the house and cuts the engine. Unbuckling his seatbelt, he starts to open his door and then realizes I'm not moving. He cocks his head. "What's up? Why you still sittin' there? I bet I can have you naked in, like, under a minute once we're inside. Unless you're feeling like street sex is more your speed tonight."

I half-laugh, but the twist in my stomach makes it sound fake.

His grin drops.

I look down at my lap, exhaling a deep breath. I should have stopped this as soon as the fun started to turn into feelings. But I didn't, and now I'm sitting here, choking on my words because I don't want to say them. I have to.

"You okay?" He reaches out, brushing my hair from my face.

I want to lean into that touch. I want to wrap myself around him and never let go. But if I keep doing this with him, he's going to break my heart. Well, that's already happening, but at least I have some control over this decision.

I beat down the desire to jump him, which I know now isn't just because he's super amazing at sex. We have a connection when we're naked, and when we're not. It's more than orgasms; I'm falling in love with him.

And not just the unclothed parts of him; it's his sense of humor, his sweetness, his generosity. It's everything. But it's only a matter of time before he does to me what he's done to every other girl before. He'll get freaked out and cut ties. I know it's coming. We're getting too close. It's becoming too real. He has to feel it, too.

This road ends like one of those old Bugs Bunny cartoons: there's a sheer cliff I'll drop off of eventually. Only I won't pop back up and brush away the dirt as if nothing happened. If I do this now, the fall won't be as far.

As least that's what I tell myself when I say, "I don't think you should come inside."

He spins his keys on the chain. "You wanna come back to my

place instead?"

"I don't think that's a good idea, either."

Randy frowns. "Why not?"

My throat feels tight, and my stomach starts to roll. The amazing dinner I ate feels like it wants to make another appearance. "I don't think we should do this anymore."

He scratches the back of his neck. "What?"

"This." I motion between us. "I don't think it's working."

His shoulders tighten, and a half-smile appears. "You're not enjoying the multiple orgasms anymore? I thought we were having fun."

He's hitting me with sarcasm, and for once I don't dish it back. "We were."

"So what's the problem?"

I've caught him off guard. I've caught myself off guard, too. Only after I got the job did I truly realize I've been fooling myself. All I could think was how living in Chicago would mean more time with Randy. But not just in his bed—with friends, on dates, hanging out. All things that aren't on the table. Or they aren't supposed to be. I fiddle with my purse and give him back his words from the start of this thing we've been doing. "This isn't just fun for me anymore, Randy."

"I don't get it." He smoothes his hands down his thighs. "I thought you had a good time this week."

"I did. I—" I take a deep breath. I don't want to cry in front of him. I don't want to be weak. He told me what this was. It's not his fault I wasn't honest with him before now. "That's what this was supposed to be, right? Just fun. It feels like it's getting too… serious. And I can't—"

"Too serious?"

I wring my hands, unsure what to do with them. "I should've said something sooner."

"What are you talking about?" He sounds irritated.

"I can't move here and do this casual thing with you."

"Why not?"

"It's not just about the sex for me anymore."

"But I'm your rebound." His confusion makes me sad.

"I can't make the feelings go away, Randy." I look at him—at his gorgeous face, at the panic and the anger—and I know I'm right. It was only a matter of time. At least I didn't humiliate myself and tell him I'm in love with him outright.

"You were supposed to tell me if it was getting to be too much." He runs his hand through his hair, his frustration obvious. "I don't understand. You just got out of a seven-year relationship. This was supposed to be simple."

"I didn't mean for this to happen. I'm sorry I didn't say anything. I didn't want things to change. Maybe we could see—"

He cuts me off before I can finish the sentence. "I can't be your boyfriend, Lily. I almost screwed some chick because you couldn't make a damn game."

"But you didn't. And that was—"

His anger is a wave rising. I don't know if it's directed at me or himself, but his words hit me like shattering glass. "The only reason I didn't was because you showed up. I *will* fuck you over. Is that what you want?"

"No, Randy. That's not what I want."

He jams the key in the ignition and starts the truck. "Then I guess this is it."

"I guess it is. I'd say we could still be friends, but I'm not so sure that would work out very well." I leave off the rest, which would go something like this: *because I'm in love with you, and I'll pine over you and cry if I see you with another girl.*

"Probably not." He's staring straight ahead.

"If I left anything at your place—"

"I'll give it to Miller to give to you. He'll be over here all the time."

"Okay." I open the door and go to get out, but once again I've forgotten to unbuckle my seat belt, so I jerk back.

Randy reaches over and jabs the release with his thumb. He's still not looking at me.

I lean over and press my lips against his cheek. The sensation is electric. He freezes. I pull away before I make any more bad decisions, like inviting him inside for one last naked session. Or stripping in his truck. "Bye, Randy. Thanks for the ride."

"All of them, or this one in particular?"

It's a shot. My heart feels like it's made of sandstone, and it's crumbling into dust inside my chest. None of my breakups with Benji ever felt like this.

"All of them, except for this one," I say.

I slip out of the truck. Randy waits until I've unlocked the door to the house. Then he takes off down the street without so much as a parting wave.

I step inside the empty house and lock the door behind me. Randy's absence feels like shards of glass buried in my chest. I don't make it past taking my shoes off. I sit down on the floor, put my face in my hands, and cry.

25

FUN IS NOT MY MIDDLE NAME

RANDY

I drove home on autopilot. I don't remember stopping at lights or pulling into my driveway, but I'm sitting here, staring at my front door, so I must have obeyed the rules of the road. Otherwise there'd be cherries flashing in my rearview.

I cut the engine, but I don't move. My truck still smells like Lily, so I wanna stay here a little longer. I don't get what happened. I replay Lily's time in Chicago in my head, trying to figure out where I went wrong—how I missed the signs. Or maybe I didn't miss them at all. Maybe I decided not to see them because that would mean admitting I want more than I can have.

I was such an asshole to her.

I sit here until I can see my breath and start to shiver. Trudging to my door, I put my thumb to the keypad and turn the knob. The first thing I do is pour myself a generous shot of vodka. I have to fly out at seven-thirty tomorrow morning for a game. The last thing I should do is get drunk to manage whatever just happened. But I'm feeling shitty about this, so alcohol is the numbing agent of choice.

I get good and shitfaced and watch that little video I made while visiting Lily in Guelph, when I woke her up in the middle of the night for sex. I don't watch it because I want to jerk off. I mean, yeah, it makes me hard—even as wasted as I am—but it's the way she's so unguarded. She's looking at me like I'm more than just someone she's passing time and exchanging orgasms with. I knew even then that it was more than what it was supposed to be, and I let it keep happening. Because I wanted it. I wanted her. And now I don't get to have her at all.

Pounding on my door echoes the awful feeling in my head. I peel my eyes open and groan.

"Balls! We gotta roll!" It's Miller.

I push up off the couch, and the world spins so much I fall forward over the coffee table. I don't have great coordination, and my reaction time is shot—probably because I'm still drunk, and I've been shocked awake. I hit the floor with my face and taste blood.

It takes me a couple of tries to get my ass back up. I stumble to the foyer, fumble with the lock, and throw the front door open, almost hitting myself in the face.

"Oh, shit. What happened?" Miller looks over my shoulder like he expects someone to be behind me. Maybe the person responsible for my bloody lip.

"I fell." I lean against the wall.

Miller frowns. "Are you drunk?"

"You woke me up."

"You smell like booze."

"I'm fine."

Miller's phone starts ringing. He glances at it, then at me.

"Get your shit. We need to be at the airport. You should be ready to go."

I try to walk, but it's not working. I smash into the wall.

"Seriously, Balls, what's the deal? Sweets, can I call you back? What? She's what? I don't understand; she should be here, not there—"

I know they're talking about Lily. I turn and walk down the hall, knocking a picture to the floor.

"I'll call you back in a few... I love you, too, Sunny Sunshine."

I'm unnecessarily jealous of their relationship. I know exactly how *not* easy it is to be a professional hockey player dedicated to one person. I've watched Miller struggle with Sunny. I've seen Lance almost destroy his career. I've witnessed the impact on my own mother and sister. But right now, all I want is someone to fight for, and I've messed that up, too.

I make it to my bedroom and grab my duffle bag. My hockey shit should be in the garage. I hope. All I need are clothes. Miller isn't behind me like I figured he'd be. He shows up a few seconds later with a glass of water and pills.

He holds out the glass and his palm. "Drink this, and take these."

I do what he tells me. Then I look around my room. Evidence of the past week is everywhere. Three empty boxes of condoms litter my nightstand. A half-empty bottle of lube has fallen over and dripped on the carpet. My bed is unmade. My room smells distinctly of sex and Lily. I can still see the look on her face when I told her I'd fuck her over. That devastation is exactly what I don't want to cause someone.

Miller snaps his fingers. "Dude, we gotta go."

"Right. Yeah." I nod, but I'm still not moving.

Miller shakes his head and shoves three pairs of pants, three shirts, a suit, and a couple of ties into my bag. Then he goes to my dresser and tosses in some extra boxers and socks. A pair of Lily's underwear must have accidentally ended up in there, because he tosses them on the bed. "Get changed, Balls. You smell like a bar. They won't let you on the plane if they know you're drunk." He passes me a pair of boxers, then goes to my closet and picks up a pair of jeans off the floor.

I have to sit down to make it happen, but I manage to get changed into fresh clothes. I pick up Lily's underwear from the comforter and shove them in my pocket. I don't know why. But I need them.

Miller forces me into the bathroom and makes me brush my teeth. Once I have my wallet, he ushers me back to the foyer. I have to brace myself on the wall to get my feet in my shoes.

He shoves my jacket at me, shaking his head, and pushes me out the door. I climb into Lance's ridiculous Hummer and sprawl out across the backseat. I check my pockets for my phone, but it's not there. "Wait. I don't have my phone. I gotta go back in."

"I've got it." Miller tosses it at me. I try to bring up the home screen, but it stays blank.

"Took you two long enough. What was the hold up? You catch Balls doing what he does best?" Lance puts the vehicle in gear.

"You wanna tell me what happened? Sunny called me freaking out about Lily," Miller asks.

I close my eyes, undecided as to whether keeping them open makes the nausea go away. "Lily broke up with me." The car jerks to a stop, and I fall off the backseat onto the floor. "The fuck, man?"

"*Broke up* with you?" Lance is looking at me like I've told him aliens really do exist.

I manage to get my ass back on the seat. This time I buckle myself in. "Or I broke up with her. I don't know. She said she didn't wanna see me any more."

"I thought you two were just having fun." There's a bite to Miller's tone.

"We are." I shake my head. "Or we were. Last night she said it wasn't fun anymore. That it was getting, like, serious. So that's it. It's done."

Miller and Lance exchange a look. Miller turns so he can see me. "So you're telling me Lily's the one who ended things?"

"She initiated it. Yeah. I dropped her off after dinner, and I was gonna spend the night, or as long as I could, but she said I shouldn't, and that she didn't want to see me any more, and that was it. Can we not talk about this right now?" I drop my head against the seat and close my eyes again. I'm leaving out a lot of details, but talking about it doesn't make me feel good.

Neither of them says anything else, so I keep my eyes closed. All I want is to fall asleep again and shut off all the thoughts in my head, the roll in my stomach, and these brutal feelings I don't know how to manage. Before Lily, as soon as things started to get intense, I bailed. But with Lily it was intense like that right from the beginning, so maybe it took longer for me to realize what was happening. Or maybe that's an excuse.

"Hey, sweets. Yeah. We're on our way to the airport. Uh-huh. We got 'im. He's still drunk," Miller says.

"I can hear you, Butterson. You know that, right?" I crack a lid.

He flips me the bird. "Balls says she's the one who cut things off."

"You wanna find a different way to word that?" I mumble.

Lance barks out a laugh. Miller slaps his arm.

"Sorry, bro, you know I didn't mean it like that." Miller goes back to talking to Sunny. "I don't get it. Why's she so upset if she's the one who ended it?" Miller's silent for a long time, during which Sunny's distressed voice filters through, but her words are lost in the sounds of traffic. "Oh. Right. Okay. I guess that makes sense. Sure. I love you, too. I'll call you when we land."

Miller ends the call. "Women are confusing."

Lance snorts. "They're vicious is what they are."

I don't say anything, because what is there to say? It's probably better we ended it now anyway, especially with her moving to Chicago. I'd want to see her all the time, and I'd try to be her boyfriend, and I'd ruin it by messing around with someone else. It's the whole apple-and-apple-tree scenario.

By the time we get to security, I'm feeling my hangover. I've got the sweats, and I think I'm going to hurl. I'm not very steady on my feet either. I take off my jacket and shoes and throw them into one of the bins. I follow with my belt and phone. Then I empty the contents of my pockets, starting with my wallet.

I check for change and find Lily's wadded up panties. It's the pair I bought her when I surprised her in Guelph. She looked so good in them. And out of them. I rub the soft lace between my fingers.

Lance is behind me. He elbows me in the side. "Balls, put your souvenir away."

"It's not a fuckin' souvenir," I growl.

He puts a hand on my shoulder. "Keep it together, man."

I toss the panties in the bin and push it down the ramp. The security chick gives me a look, but I'm too morose to care. I wait while the guy pats me down, and then collect all my stuff, shoving the panties back in my pocket before anything else.

I don't talk to anyone on the plane ride, mostly because I feel like a bag of shit, physically and mentally. I'm grateful for the hour of sleep I manage. The nap makes me feel marginally better. By the time we land, the nausea has passed for the most part, but all the other shit is still there.

As soon as we get to the hotel, I hijack the bathroom and shower to get rid of the booze smell. Miller's lying on his bed, watching sports highlights. "Your phone's been going off."

I check it, but it's not Lily. It's my mom, wishing me good luck in the game. I feel guilty that I didn't see her more over the holidays, especially since my sister didn't come home, but I was with Lily. I guess it's a good thing I didn't invite her to meet my mom.

"Not who you wanted it to be?" Miller asks.

"Nope." I toss my phone on the bed. I should call my mom, but I don't feel like talking to anyone. I rub my chest, annoyed by the weird ache.

"You could call her, you know."

I drop down on the mattress and lie back against the pillows. "What would be the point? I can't make this something it isn't supposed to be."

"What does that even mean?"

"She said she wasn't having fun anymore, end of story." I don't want to tell him what I said to her. How shitty I made her feel. How I blamed her when it was my damn fault.

"She say why she wasn't having fun?" Miller asks.

"She said it was getting too intense. Look, I'm in a shitty mood. I know you're trying to help, Miller, but talking about it makes me feel worse. I just wanna focus on strategy for the game, okay?"

"Yeah, sure. I'm gonna shower, and then we can go get something to eat with the team."

I'm sitting on the bench, waiting for the whistle to blow so I can get on the ice and get out some of this aggression. We're down one, and Waters has something going on with his shooting arm. He's been rubbing his shoulder every time he gets off the ice. As soon as it's my turn, I rush down the ice after the puck.

I put all my focus into getting close to the net. Westinghouse is parallel to me. I pass the puck, but one of the guys from Colorado manages to trip him up with a dirty move and gains control. He doesn't keep it for long, though. Miller's got things under control, and manages to get the puck back.

I camp out in front of the net, knowing if Miller can get it back to Westinghouse, he'll pass to me. Colorado's defense knows this, too. Number sixty-three is on me, nudging me in the back with his stick. I'm not in the mood for bullshit tonight.

I get behind him and give a little shove back. He elbows me, so I shift my foot between his and nudge the back of his knee, setting him off balance. We go down together. I wait until he grabs my jersey before I take hold of his. As we fall, I flip us.

When I'm on a slick surface with blades on my feet and I'm going down, there's one essential rule: always be on top. He's spitting obscenities, pissed because I pulled a shady move. But he's been a problem all game. My plan isn't to fight, though. All I want is to get him off my back. But he starts swinging, so I don't have a choice but to deflect.

He grabs my cage.

There are very few things that really make me angry on the ice. Chippy playing is one of them. Asshole defense is another. And cage-grabbing makes me see red. I hold his helmet with both hands, pinning his head to the ice. I keep trying to get traction, but he's still holding on to my cage with one hand, and trying to punch me with the other, so my feet keep sliding out from under me.

It takes three tries for me to get up. The crowd is going crazy. Colorado fans are screaming at the refs to do something.

Chicago fans are just as wild. I shove off the guy as the whistle blows. I'm not surprised by the penalty, but at least Colorado gets one, too.

"Nice ice-hump there, Balls. That'll look awesome on the highlights." Miller pats me on the shoulder on my way to the penalty box.

We end up losing the game by one. At the bar some chick offers to make me feel better. She has dark hair like Lily's, but it's longer. Her lips are red, and her boobs are bigger. Her eyes are blue. I could try to fuck out some of the anger and whatever else is going on inside me, but I think it'll have the opposite effect.

I decline and head up to the room instead. Miller's already there. He's lying down, doing what he always does after a game: watching the highlights.

"Check this out." He points to the screen.

There I am, ice-humping the guy from Colorado. No wonder he was so mad. "He was being a dick; he deserved it."

"Not arguing with that."

Miller rolls out of bed and ambles to the bathroom. I shrug out of my suit and drop it on the floor, too lazy to give a shit. I check my phone, but I don't have any new messages from Lily. Normally after a game she sends me one.

I pull up her contact and call her. It rings a bunch of times and goes to voice mail. I close my eyes at the sound of her voice, telling me to leave a message at the tone.

I take a deep breath after the beep. At first I consider hanging up, but then I figure she's going to know it's me from the number, and all I've done so far is pervert breathe. Miller comes out of the bathroom as I start talking. "Some girl wanted to fuck me tonight. She looked kinda like you. Well, only her hair, but not even—"

"What the hell is wrong with you?" Miller smacks the phone out of my hand.

"I'm leaving a message."

I try to grab my phone, but Miller shoves me out of the way. I slam into the night table, and the lamp falls over.

"About banging some other chick?" he yells.

"I didn't fuck another chick. That's the point!"

Miller nabs the phone and puts it to his ear. I tackle him to the floor, and we wrestle, me trying to get the phone while he tries to punch buttons. He puts a hand on my face. "Stop being an idiot, Balls. I'm trying to delete the message."

"I'll delete it." I elbow him in the ribs and finally get my phone, but I must hit the wrong button because I don't get the option to delete or send. "Shit."

"Don't tell me you sent that." Miller pushes me off of him.

I lie on the floor, panting. "I think I sent that. Should I message her and tell her to delete it without listening to it?"

Miller shakes his head. "You know, I thought I was hopeless with relationships, but you make me look like goddamn Einstein. I'mma call Sunny."

"What good is calling Sunny gonna do?"

"She can at least talk to Lily." Miller punches away at his phone, brows furrowed in concentration. "I'm getting voice mail." He waits a few more seconds. "Hey, sweets. I'm guessing you're asleep. If you get a chance, can you call me? Randy left a stupid message for Lily, and it'd be better if she didn't listen to it. Love you. Can't wait to come home …" He lowers his voice so I can't hear the rest.

I decide it's probably best if I message Lily since Miller can't get a hold of Sunny.

If u get a msg from me can u delete it?
It came out wrong.

I don't hear back from her.

Sleep sucks. In the morning I have a message.

You're not mine, so u can fuck whoever u want.

This isn't a conversation I want to have over text. I try to call again, but it goes to voice mail. I don't leave another message since the last one sucked my balls.

Once I'm back home, I drop my shit at the door and head for my bedroom. All I want is to lie down and smell Lily. It's weird, and maybe a little messed up. But the housekeeper's been by, and the sheets are fresh. The clothes Lily left behind are folded in a neat pile on her side of the bed.

The damn chest ache is back. I rub the spot, hating the phantom pain.

That's when I realize what I'm feeling is heartbreak. I'm always worried about hurting someone else; I never thought about myself. And it's my own damn fault.

But trying for more with Lily will only end up causing her pain in the end.

"Why don't you go see her while we're in Toronto if she won't answer calls?" Lance is currently kicking my ass at NHL Hockey on Xbox. Granted, I'm not trying very hard.

"There's no point." It's been two weeks, and I've heard nothing from her.

He beats me for the third time, so I toss the controller to Miller. "You're up." I must throw it with more force than I intended because it hits him in the throat.

"Seriously, dude." Miller rubs his neck.

"Sorry."

"You're worse than a PMSing teenage girl right now."

"I'm not that bad."

"Uh, yeah, you are. You've had penalties every game for the past two weeks. You're almost as bad as me," Lance says.

He's right about that. I've been way more aggressive than usual. I almost got ejected from the last game for fighting. "Seeing Lily isn't going to change that."

"You can't know until you try," Miller says. He's been on me to work shit out, but there's nothing to work. Lily hasn't messaged me again since I left that voice mail, and I don't have the balls to try again. I don't know what I was thinking doing that in the first place. She'll be moving to Chicago soon, but it's not like I'm going to run into her all the time. Unless she's at games. Then I'll want to talk to her when I should really just leave her alone.

According to Sunny, Lily's flying to Chicago next week. Alex didn't want her driving in a U-Haul in the middle of January, so he's having her stuff shipped to the house. I hate that I'm jealous of a guy with a fiancée.

"It's not like talking about it is gonna change anything."

"How do you know that?" Miller asks.

I run a frustrated hand through my hair. "Because it was supposed to be just fun and now it isn't for her."

"Can you explain that?" Miller asks.

"It was getting too serious," I summarize.

"For who?" Miller scratches his week-old beard.

We've been over this before. I don't see why we're having the same conversation again. "For her."

"So all she wanted was dick?" Miller asks.

"Well, yeah. We had a conversation right at the beginning about it being just fun and keeping things light."

"Can we back up a second, because I'm still confused. Sunny

says Lily's a fucking mess over this. I don't get why she'd be so upset if she was only in it for the dick."

"I'm her rebound. I didn't think it was going to turn into a case of the feelings."

"Am I the only one here who's acknowledging that you've been talking about Lily like you two were in a relationship?" Lance asks.

"No, we were—"

"Just having fun. We know." Lance rolls his eyes.

"Well, what else could it reasonably be with her all the way in Canada and me traveling half the year? Besides, she just got out of a seven-year relationship—"

"From the sound of it, that relationship was over long before that," Miller says.

"It's not like it matters. It's better this way. Ending shit was smart before I could ruin it by doing something stupid." Shit. I am teen-girl PMS-y.

"What are you even talking about?" Miller asks.

"She's moving here, and I'm gonna want this to be something it can't be." I think it should be clear by now who I am.

"You mean a relationship?" Miller presses. Lance is staring at his Xbox controller.

"Yeah."

"I don't get why it can't be exactly that, especially with her moving to Chicago. That's way easier to manage than her living in Canada. I would know. It seems like that's what you want."

"Yeah, but I'm gonna fuck her over eventually."

"How can you know? They replace your balls with crystal ones? Can you see into the future?" Miller looks extremely unimpressed.

"That's what my dad did. He fucked my mom over. Repeatedly. I don't ever want to do that to another person. I don't wanna hurt someone like that."

"You're not your dad," Miller argues.

"I'm exactly like him."

"No, you're not."

"Yes. I am."

"Uh, dude, I grew up with you. I know what your dad's like, and while you might look like him and you might play hockey like he did—except better—that's where the similarities end. You've spent your entire life trying *not* to be like him. You'd never do to another person what he did to your mom. You're a better person than he is."

"I almost screwed another girl the last time I was in Toronto. The only reason I didn't was because Lily showed up."

"You wouldn't have fucked her," Lance says quietly.

"You don't know that. If you hadn't said something, I wouldn't have checked my messages, and I would've taken that chick up to my room."

"Doesn't mean you would've fucked her. I wouldn't have let that happen," Lance replies.

"I don't see how you would've been able to stop me. And that's the point, isn't it? I don't have the ability to be with one person."

"You've never even tried to know," Miller fires back. "You always cut out when it starts getting real—except you didn't do that with Lily."

"Look how well that's worked out! And when she told me how she felt, I told her I'd fuck her over. Why the hell would she want anything to do with me after I said something like that?"

Lance is shaking his head now, but still looking at the floor.

Miller runs his palms over his thighs. "Look how much I screwed up with Sunny at the beginning, when I was still going to parties and there were all those pictures and shit. We had fights, and we talked it out. We got over it and made it work. You can't know what the deal is with Lily unless you see her and talk. And if she's not on the same page anymore, well, at least you tried rather than sitting here on your couch, making everyone around you deal with your fucking misery."

He's not wrong. And that sucks.

"We've all seen you with Lily," Lance chimes in, the hint of Scot gets thicker as he continues. "There are feelings there. On both sides. Don't let someone else's bad choices be the reason you give up something that could be good."

"He's got a point," Miller says.

I can't believe I'm about to take relationship advice from Lance.

26

PINING: NOT JUST FOR TREES

LILY

I'm not a piner. I don't sit around and wallow. Well, I never used to sit around and wallow. But that's what I've been doing between packing and training a new coach. She's fantastic, and she'll do an amazing job. But leaving my girls is hard. I've worked with some of them for a long time, watched them become beautiful skaters. The change should be good, though. *Will* be good. When I stop pining.

I keep having moments of sheer panic in which I envision myself driving over to Randy's, knocking on his door, and begging him to hold me/fuck me/love me. The middle scenario isn't the most prevalent. Shocking, I know.

I keep going over my decision to move and reminding myself I'm actually doing it for the right reasons now. The whole point of ending things with Randy was so I'd have some perspective, and to ensure I didn't make a huge life choice based on wanting something I can't have. I still want it, but at least I'm not pretending and holding on to something that wasn't even real any more.

In the end I can't say I'm moving for *all* the right reasons, but I do know I never want to get back together with Benji, and living in a big city will definitely be an experience. Besides, my mom's moving in with Tim-Tom, so I'd have to find a new place to live, one way or another.

I lay my suitcase on my bed and flip it open. It's new. I bought it two days ago on a shopping expedition with my mom. She's okay with the move. She's not even getting on my case about the whole Randy situation—although that may be due in part to my epic fits of snot-sobbing since the end of having fun.

Things I've learned about myself in the past six months: I'm not cut out for casual sex. My sometimes bitchy exterior is my Lego armor against how sensitive I am. If I'd been this insightful prior to falling for Randy, I might have come out of this with a little less angst. Or maybe not. There were a lot of mixed signals, I'm coming to realize. He was the one who insisted it be "fun," but that week with him in Chicago… I can't help feeling it wasn't just me. Regardless, it's over, and I'm sad about that.

I neatly pack my suitcase, starting with my socks. I discover I have a lot of socks, and half of them are missing their partners. It seems rather karmic, considering. Fucking karma. Such a bitch sometimes.

I put on some music—emo, of course, to match my constantly fluctuating mood—and move on to my underwear drawer. Half my panties need to be replaced because they're old or falling apart. I still have the ones Randy bought for me over the holidays.

We didn't so much exchange Christmas presents as we exchanged underwear. I'm missing the pretty blue pair with the lace, but I have the pair of his pink boxers I vandalized—a parting gift to remember him by.

It's a little creepy-stalker, but I'm okay with that. I'm also guilty of creeping his social media accounts and trolling the puck bunny/hockey hooker groups. So far there are no reports of Randy going ballistic (ha) on any new bunnies. It's a terrible form of torture, waiting for it to happen and break me all over again.

At the knock on my door, I stuff Randy's underwear under a pile of socks. "Come in."

My mom pokes her head in. "How's it going?"

"Good. I'll be done with this in a bit, and then I can help you with the kitchen." I close the empty drawer. I feel something wet on my face and realize I'm crying. Again. Emotions blow dick. Randy's badass scarred dick. Thinking about that definitely doesn't stop the tears.

My mom folds me in her bony embrace. We're both lean, so it's nothing like hugging say, Randy, who's all hard lines and muscle and man, and—*shit* I really need to stop thinking about him.

My mom strokes my hair, like she used to do when I was little. It's soothing. "Is this because you're moving away from me, or because you're still sad about your hockey boy?"

"I don't know. Both I guess." I sniffle. It's rather pathetic.

She lets go and takes my face between her hands. Her smile is sad. "He's an idiot not to want you."

"He wants me, just not the way I want him." I try to stifle one of those horrible snot-sobs. I'm unsuccessful.

"You're sure about that?" she asks softly.

"He made it clear from the beginning it was only ever going to be casual."

"Feelings can change, Lily."

"His haven't." I think about that phone call, the one about the girl at the bar who looked like me. In a matter of hours he'd been looking to replace me. "He said he'd fuck me over, eventually."

My mom sighs. "Sometimes when people are scared of what they're feeling, they push people away."

"Maybe. I don't know. He hasn't tried to call me lately, or text. I think it's just done."

She gives me another bony squeeze. "I won't tell you there are plenty of fish in the sea, even though there are. And you'll find the one who's right for you, at the right time."

It doesn't feel like I'm going to find another fish right now. I sniffle. "You probably shouldn't since you turned forty and the verdict's still out on Tim-Tom."

"It's Tim, honey, and he's good for me."

"Tim-Tom has a nice ring to it, though."

My mom laughs, and then grows serious. "I know I made a lot of mistakes along the way, and a lot of bad choices, but I want you to know I have no regrets when it comes to you. Well, that's not true. I wish I could've given you more. You deserved so much more than you got, but I did the best I could—"

She chokes on the rest of the words. Which is probably a good thing. My mom and me, we don't have these deep, heartfelt conversations, likely because we both end up ugly-crying.

I pat her back. "You did great, Mom."

"I'm sorry about the hockey boy."

"His name is Randy, and me, too. The sex was really great."

"I definitely didn't need to know that."

"I've seen Tim-Tom's woody."

"I think we should have a drink."

I follow her out to the kitchen where she pours me a glass of wine, and we watch the hockey game. Toronto is playing Chicago. Randy's beard is beautiful. He looks fantastic. And he scores a goal. My phone buzzes about half an hour after the game ends. I won't lie; my entire being wants it to be Randy—from my hair follicles to my Vagina Emporium.

It's not.

It's Benji. I dropped his stuff off a few days ago. It went slightly better than I'd expected. He tried to convince me I was making a mistake by moving to Chicago, and that we should get back together. I pointed out that it definitely wouldn't work with me moving. He got mad and then cried. It could've been way worse. But in my haste to leave, I forgot my box.

I groan and check the message. He's letting me know Benny is stopping by in the morning with my stuff.

There's some relief in not having to deal with him directly again. We have a lot of history, and I'm a little sad that this is how it's ending, but I'm also aware that I'll be back, and sometimes time and distance makes it easier to be friends. Who knows if that will ever happen with us.

I go to sleep with my suitcase taking up half my bed, and I wake up to my phone going off. It's Benny. I forgot to set an alarm.

"I'll be right down," I tell him.

I pull a hoodie on over my tank top and shove my feet into my slippers. They're huge and cumbersome, but at least they're warm. Sunny got them for me for Christmas. I don't bother checking my reflection in the mirror before I go down. Frankly, I don't give a shit what I look like.

I close my eyes for the ride in the elevator. I have a headache. I only had one glass of wine, but it was a big one.

Benny's car is parked in front of my building. I pad across the snowy sidewalk in my moose slippers. I'll need to set them on a vent to dry, but I don't want Benny to offer to bring my stuff up.

He gets out of the car. He's got a beard going on. It's neater than Benji's, but when they both have one, they could pass for twins. He raises a brow at my outfit. "Looks like I woke you. I could've met you at the door."

"It's fine. I needed to get up anyway. Lots of packing to do." I don't have much left, but it's something to say.

"So you're moving to Chicago, eh?"

I shove my hands in the pouch of my hoodie. "Yeah."

He nods. "Getting out of Guelph will be good for you."

"I think so. How's Benji?" I don't ask because it feels obligatory; I'm honestly concerned, especially since he's sent Benny in his place.

Benny shrugs. "You know how he is. He needs to start figuring out his life. You moving on might actually end up being a good thing for him, too."

We leave the rest unsaid. Benji needs to do some growing up. "I hope so."

"Me, too." He sighs. "Let me get your stuff. I gotta get to work, and the snow's making it hard today."

"Yeah, of course." I'm relieved he can't stay and chat. Also, it's freezing out, and my feet are going numb.

He opens the passenger door and pulls out a banker's box. It's stuffed with mostly useless crap. There's a prom picture of me and Benji sitting on top. We broke up that night after one of the guys on the football team asked me to dance and Benji flipped his lid. It's amazing how seven years of memories can be reduced to one cardboard box.

I tuck it under my arm and give Benny an awkward side-hug. It's while I'm doing this that I notice an SUV driving by on a slow roll. Snow squeaks under the tires as it comes to a stop beside Benny's car.

The man in the front seat makes eye contact as I disengage

from Benny. I feel like I might be hallucinating, because it sure as hell looks like Randy. He starts rolling again, like he's about to leave. Which doesn't make sense if he drove here all the way from Toronto.

I'm in pajama pants with moose on them, my moose slippers, and a hoodie with stains. I haven't brushed my teeth, and it's damn well freezing out, but there's no way he's leaving before I find out why he came all the way here. If it's him. Otherwise I'll be embarrassed by what I'm about to do.

"Sorry, Benny, I gotta—" I drop the box in the snow, make wild flailing gestures, and start running. It's as slippery as a pool of lube, but I'm determined to catch the guy before he blows the stop sign. I hope I'm not losing it and it's actually Randy.

Thankfully he's driving cautiously due to the heavy, unplowed snow. I've never been so grateful for poor city maintenance. He comes to a halt at the stop sign at the same time I throw myself over the hood. I grab hold where it meets the windshield and look up to find Randy's stunned face staring back at me.

Sliding off the hood, I wrench open the passenger door and heave myself inside. I decide to play it cool. I pull the door shut and lean against it, going for casual even though I'm breathing like I've run a marathon, my shirt is soaked from the snowy hood, and I'm wearing moose slippers. "Hey."

Randy looks like sex rolled in bacon and dipped in maple syrup. His hair is seriously fucked. It's longer again, but it's not pulled back, and half of it is hanging in his face. His beard is all beardy, and all I want to do is wrap myself around him.

"Do you have any idea how dangerous that was?" He points to the hood and then to me.

"You were driving away." I say in breathy defense.

"Are you back with that douche?" Randy jerks his thumb in

Benny's direction, except Benny's already in his car, so Randy's motioning to an empty space.

"That's Benji's brother, Benny. They look a lot alike with facial hair. And no, there's no way I'd get back together with him."

"His brother's name is Benny?"

"His parents are jerks."

"Obviously."

We stare at each other for a few long seconds, in which time I consider all the ways to get naked.

Randy taps the steering wheel, and I stop mentally undressing him so I can listen to his words. "So things are finished with him?" he asks.

"Yeah. Totally finished. Benny was dropping off my stuff from Benji. It's easier than seeing him. I mean, I can manage seeing him, but he can't manage seeing me. He still wants to get back together, and I don't, so it's awkward." Kind of like this conversation.

"That's good. You can do better than that dickhead." He chews on the inside of his lip while nodding slowly.

"He's insecure."

"Doesn't give him the right to treat you like shit or belittle you."

God, he's sexy, and the way he's talking reminds me of when I first met him at Alex's cottage. He was so cocky, and then he defended me, and I rammed my tongue down his throat. I can't believe that was almost six months ago. I can't believe I'm in love with him, and he's sitting here, and I have no idea why.

"So, what brings you to Guelph at eight o'clock in the morning?" I ask, again going for casual.

Randy stretches his arm across the seat. "You."

Well, that's direct. "I… uh…"

"I don't wanna not see you anymore." He blurts it right out, like word vomit.

"Um …" I have no idea what that means. If he's here for a booty call, I think I might punch him. I will not have casual sex with him, even if I want to.

He runs his hand through his hair. "Sorry. Last night was long."

"I watched the game."

"Yeah?"

"You've been racking up the penalty minutes lately."

"I've been in a bad mood. Happens when the girl I want to be with breaks up with me 'cause I'm not fun anymore."

Talk about laying it all out there. "I didn't say you weren't fun anymore. Wait. Break up with—"

"You said it wasn't fun for you anymore. Isn't that the same thing?"

It's actually very, very different, but I'm still getting my head around the "break up" comment. I need to say something. I can't look at him, so I drop my gaze to my lap. Shit. I am not dressed for this conversation. I bet my hair's a mess. This is the most fail reunion ever. If that's what it is.

"Lily?"

"The sex didn't stop being fun—"

"I'm glad my fucked-up dick is useful." He sounds so bitter.

I look up at him. "I love your fucked-up dick."

"Not enough to want to ride it any more, though."

I'm angry that he's come all this way and we're still just talking about the sex. "Your dick isn't fucked up, and this is about more than sex, Randy!" I shout. I don't mean to, but this conversation isn't going in a helpful direction, and now all I can think about is riding his dick.

A car honks its horn behind us. Randy rolls down the window and gives the person the bird. It's Benny.

"We're sitting at a stop sign." I point to the red octagon.

Randy puts on his blinker and turns the corner. He drives around the block before he pulls over in front of my apartment building and puts on his hazards. He strokes his beard, his expression pensive. "I thought I was just gonna be your rebound. I didn't expect it to turn into something else."

I go back to looking at my moose pants. "Look, maybe I should have said something long before I did, but casual sex doesn't work for me, and you've made it clear that's what you do."

Randy frowns. "So you're not good at casual, and that's all you thought this was."

"Yes." Finally, I think we're getting somewhere. I sigh and shove my hands between my knees. "Everything was fine at first when I kind of hate-liked you, and you were eating at the Vagina Emporium in public bathrooms. Then you started taking me out for lunch, and you bought me clothes and joked about me moving to Chicago. Spending time with you over the holidays changed things—it seemed like it changed things for you, too. It started to feel like something else, but you'd told me it wasn't."

Randy stares straight ahead, gripping and releasing the steering wheel. "Was it all the talk about you moving to Chicago?"

"You joking around about me moving isn't the issue, Randy."

His jaw tics. "I see." His chin drops to his chest, and he closes his eyes. "What if what we were doing wasn't just casual?"

"I think the word *casual* needs to be banned from the rest of this discussion. Can you please explain what you mean?"

"So, like, what if we're doing what we were doing, but with

feelings."

"Most people call that a relationship, Randy."

He bites a nail. He looks like a cornered animal.

"If you can't even say the word, it's not something you're ready for."

"I can say it."

"Then do."

"Relationship." He's still chewing on his thumb, so it comes out all garbled.

I don't know whether to laugh or cry. My stupid eyes decide for me and start to water. I hate crying. "I can't—" I reach for the handle.

"Wait!" Randy grabs my wrist. It's the first time he's touched me since I got in the vehicle. His skin is warm and rough. It's still electric. My heart aches so badly, and my magic marble is going crazy.

He licks his lips and swallows hard, eyes darting to me and away. "Look, my whole life everyone's compared me to my dad. How I look, how I talk, how I act, how good I am at hockey—I'm just like him. And he ruined my mom with all his dicking around. She's never gotten over it and my sister moved halfway around the world to get away from him. I don't ever want to do to someone else what he did to them, and to me. I don't want to put anyone through that."

The pain this has caused him is clear in his eyes, in the rigid set of his shoulders, in the tremor in his voice. This man, so confident on the ice and in bed, is floundering in the face of feelings.

I sweep my thumb across his knuckles. "You don't have to repeat the same mistakes, Randy. You're your own person. You control your actions."

He says quietly, "I haven't been with anyone but you since we fooled around in the summer. No one."

"No one?" I'm kind of stunned. Okay, I'm a lot stunned.

"There was that one girl at the bar who kept touching my arm, but all I could think about was you, and then you showed up. I was so relieved and terrified at the same time because I knew I was your rebound. I think I wanted it to be something else even back then; I just didn't realize it yet. Or I didn't want to see it." He exhales a long, slow breath. "I shouldn't have reacted the way I did when you brought up how things were getting intense, but you said you'd say something if it got to be too much, and you didn't, and neither did I, and I panicked."

"I see that now."

"I don't know if you still have those feelings, or if what I said made them disappear, but I still want you. I mean, I want to be with you—and not just for sex. If this is moving too fast and you need this to not have a label, we can do that." He pauses, his eyes wide, and then he shakes his head. "That's not true. I want a label. I want to be in a relationship with you."

"A relationship?" I sound like an idiot. I'm still reeling over the fact that we often went more than a month without seeing each other, and he wasn't screwing bunnies. I mean, of course I'd hoped he wasn't with bunnies, but I didn't expect exclusivity, what with it being casual—or not, apparently, on either side.

"Yeah." He nods once.

"You haven't been with any bunnies since the summer?"

"Not one."

"Why?"

"Because I only wanted you. Sorry, I mean want, present tense."

"Wow. You went weeks at a time without pussy."

"I jerked off a lot."

"I bet." I glance down at his crotch. He's definitely got some happy going on down there. He's still holding my wrist, and his thumb brushes back and forth over the skin, soothing, warming. "So you want to date me?"

"No, I want you to be my girlfriend."

"You're going for the big-gun label, eh?"

"Go big or go home, right?" He tugs me toward him. "So? You want to give it a shot?"

"Okay."

"Okay?"

"Yes. Definitely."

His smile makes my heart all melty. I don't realize he's coming in for a kiss until his mouth is almost on mine. I slide a hand between our faces so he gets my knuckles instead of my lips. "I haven't brushed my teeth yet."

"I don't really care."

"My mouth tastes like cheese dick."

"How do you know what cheese dick tastes like?"

"You've seen Benji. His beard matches his balls." I'm pretty sure I ruined what's supposed to be our first official couple kiss by talking about my ex's ungroomed ball sac.

Randy pulls a face. "That's fuckin' nasty."

"Sorry, pretend I didn't say that."

"Too late."

He pulls a pack of mints from his pocket, pops one out, and pushes it between my fingers and into my mouth. I chew it a couple of times, rub all the little minty bits over my tongue and swallow. Water would be good, but since I don't have any, I'll have to manage. I drop my hand. "'Kay. Ready."

Randy gives me that sexy grin that makes my panties want to

crawl off my body and into his pocket. Except I'm not wearing any. All my girl parts get tingly as soon as he cups my face in his palms. He smoothes his thumb along the contour of my bottom lip, wiping away a mint crumb. Then he leans in.

I can't help myself. I still don't understand what it is about him, but all I want is to hump all over him the second he starts touching me. I immediately shove my tongue in his mouth and moan. His laugh is muffled by my tongue thrusts.

Whatever. It's been a couple of weeks, and I've been all mopey and heartbroken. Now I'm sexed up and excited. I have a boyfriend—a hot one, with a badass happy-face dick. I hold on to the back of his neck and stroke him through his jeans.

He's hard, and I want to feel that between my legs since now it's mine. Exclusively. I kick off my floppy slippers and get ready to either straddle him or pull him down. Both will work fine.

The knock on the window reminds me we're in a car, and it's eight in the morning, so there's no cover of darkness. We're also parked in front of my apartment building. I separate my face from Randy's, ready to flip off whoever's interrupting our make-up make-out session. Except it's my mom.

So instead of swearing at her with hand gestures, I roll down the window. "Hey, Mom."

She presses her hand against her chest and heaves what appears to be a relieved sigh. "For a second I thought that was Benji."

"Uh, no." I gesture to Randy. "As you can see, definitely not Benji."

My mom looks him over as he wipes his mouth with the back of his hand. "No. Definitely not."

Randy waves. "Hi." His face is beet red.

"Mom, you remember Randy. Randy, you remember my

mom, Iris." Wow. Talk about awkward.

"Of course I remember Randy. What a nice surprise. You two should go inside. I know the apartment's a bit of a mess, but it's cold out."

The way she phrases it doesn't give us much of an option, so Randy cuts the engine, surreptitiously rearranges his hard-on, zips his jacket, and gets out. My mom gives me a kiss on the cheek. "Nice to see you again, Randy. I hope this means we'll be able to catch up another time."

"Where're you going?" I ask.

"Work, honey. It's Monday."

"Oh."

"You two behave yourselves." She pats Randy on the arm and leaves us on our own.

Randy picks up the box I dropped when I chased after his car and tucks it under one arm. I thread my fingers through his.

He follows me to the elevator. We're the only two people in it, so I take advantage of the situation by tongue-fucking his mouth again. Randy pulls me against him via my ass, doing what he does best: the clothed humping. We pry ourselves away from each other when the elevator dings. The door slides open, and I take his hand again, dragging him down the hall. I'm all thumbs with the key, struggling to get it in the lock.

"Let me do that," he murmurs.

I let go, and he takes over, sliding the key in the lock and easing the door open. As soon as we're inside I'm on him again, pulling at his jacket, trying to unzip his pants.

Randy puts his hands on my shoulders. "Lily."

"Winter sucks for layers."

He pushes me back. "Do you hear that?"

"Hear what?" I yank his belt free from the clasp.

He puts his hand over mine, as if that's going to stop me. "That."

I don't hear anything, so I go with snark. "It's the sound of my pussy crying for your cock."

Randy laughs, then groans as I pop the button and slide my hand inside his boxers, finding him rock hard. "There's water running."

I pause, still holding his dick, and listen intently. "Shit."

"Who's here?"

"Tim-Tom.

"Who."

"My other boyfriend."

Randy's expression goes dark.

"Sorry. Sorry, that was a terrible joke. I'll never, ever say anything like that again. It's my mom's boyfriend. I thought he went home last night." Still holding Randy's dick, I tiptoe down the hall and peek around the corner. He has no choice but to follow.

The water's still running, so we can definitely make it to my room without Tim-Tom knowing we're in here. I let go of Randy's man rod and motion to the door across the hall from the bathroom. I tiptoe stealthily, and Randy clomps across the parquet floor with his boots on. It's smart not to leave evidence of his presence behind, apart from wet boot prints, that is.

I pull him into my room by his jacket, lock the door, and frantically undress him. "What're you doing?" he asks.

"Getting you naked. What does it look like?" *Like, duh.*

"Your mom's boyfriend's here."

"So? They bone while I'm here all the time. We'll be quiet. If I get loud you can put a hand over my mouth; I kinda like that."

He stands there blinking at me like maybe I've gone a little crazy, so I pull my sweatshirt and tank top over my head and push my flannel moose pants down over my hips. And voila, I'm naked. It does the trick. Randy shrugs out of his jacket and takes off his hoodie and T-shirt. I shove his pants and underwear down his thighs and drop to my knees.

"Look at him! He's so happy to see me, grinning like a fool."

Randy laughs and inhales as I trace the scar with a gentle finger.

I don't bother with a warm-up. It's unnecessary and a waste of time. All I want is to lube up his cock and get it inside me. The best way to accomplish that is by slobbering all over it. Or putting as much of it in my mouth as I can and sucking, whichever sounds classier.

I lick along the shaft and engulf the head. I look up as I take more of him in. Randy's mouth drops open, and his hands go into my hair. I hold on to his ass, and he cradles my head. I suck as if blow jobs are an Olympic event, and I'm going for the gold medal.

"Holy fuck, Lily." Randy puts a hand on the wall to steady himself.

His knees buckle at my loud slurping noise. Guys are so funny about having their cock in a mouth, and based on Randy's previous experiences, I'm turning into his blow-job goddess.

All my hot spots are lighting up like a Vegas slot machine when Randy fists my hair and pulls me off. A string of saliva connects the head to my bottom lip. From my perspective it's gross, but Randy's a guy, and for whatever reason, they seem to like all the suction sounds and bodily fluids.

He bends over me, panting, muscles straining. His cock is inches from my face. He's still holding the wall with one hand and my hair with the other. I won't lie. It's superhot. I may be on my knees, but I'm definitely the one with all the power. I run my hands up his thighs and bite my bottom lip, being coy. I trace the white line across his hip, then sweep a single finger all the way down the shaft, over the smiley scar, to the tip. Randy's eyes roll up, and he shudders.

"Are you going to fuck me now?" I'm saccharine sweet about it.

He pulls me up by my hair and crushes his mouth to mine. Oh, man. This is going to be some serious get-back-together-now-I'm-his-girlfriend sex. He must forget that his pants are still around his ankles, because he stumbles and has to shuffle to the bed. We fall in a heap on the mattress. My comforter is a rumpled mess, and I didn't even bother to put my suitcase on the floor before I went to bed last night, so I had to sleep on an angle.

We slither-flop up the bed so half our bodies aren't hanging off the end. Randy's heavy on top of me. His cock is nestled in tight between my legs. And of course, he's already started with the wet-humping.

At this point I've stopped being surprised by how quickly he makes me come. I think it's just the way we are together. With the next roll of his hips, the head rubs my clit. I dig my nails into his ass and arch. He slips low. The head breaches the Vagina Emporium's front door.

Randy breaks the kiss, and we do the stare off. We don't need actual words to convey the question we're both silently asking. Is it okay? Can we do this without a condom? He hasn't had sex with anyone else in a long time.

"I'm clean." Randy cringes, embarrassed. It says more than his reassurance. "I'll get a condom."

"It's okay."

"You're sure." He sinks in a little more.

"I've been on the pill forever."

Randy's hands are on my face. He goes deeper, maybe testing out whether or not I'm serious. I don't stop him, so he keeps going. His groan is loud and low. "Don't judge me if I come fast."

"As long as I come before you do, we're good."

"No promises."

His back expands and contracts with every breath. He's definitely not in control. His entire body is trembling. I lock my legs around his hips and skim his cheek with my fingertips. "Hey."

His eyes flip up to mine.

"Be with me."

He releases a sharp exhale and starts to move. It's not some gentle, let's-make-love bullshit. It's hip-slamming, bed-creaking, full-out make-up fucking. There's no way we're being quiet. I'll be surprised if we don't break my bed. Thankfully, I don't need it in Chicago.

We can't kiss because the pounding is too vigorous. All I can do is hold on while he goes ballistic. It's awesome. I come twice and bite the shit out of his shoulder. We're rocking the bed so much my suitcase falls to the floor with a loud crash.

Randy slows down with the knock on my door. "Everything okay in there?" It's Tim-Tom. I guess he's out of the shower.

"It's fine. I dropped my suitcase!" I call.

Randy's face is buried in my neck, and his shoulders are shaking.

"Need any help?"

"Nope. I'm good! Thanks, Tim!"

"Okay. I'm going to work. See ya later."

Randy circles his hips, slow and tight, while we wait for Tim to leave, but even after the door closes he doesn't go back to the vigorous, intense pounding. Instead he stays close and kisses me deep. When he comes, it's like he's trying to climb inside my body and stay there forever.

I run my hand down his back, smiling at the shiver I create. Randy lifts his head from the crook of my neck, eyes soft and warm. "That was a lot of fun."

I laugh and touch his lips, brushing over the scar. "It sure was. We should do it again."

EPILOGUE

COUCH CONFESSIONS

LILY

Three months later

I drop down on Randy's couch and throw my legs over his lap, cradling my snack bowl.

He leans over and peers inside. "What the hell are these? Why're they red?"

"They're ketchup chips."

Randy makes a face. "Ketchup?"

My mom sent them in a care package. I love living in Chicago, but there are a few things I miss about Canada. Ketchup chips are one of them, my mom is another, and maple-flavored bacon completes the list.

I pop one in my mouth and make a sound similar to the one I make when Randy's face or fingers or incredibly amazing cock is between my legs. "They're so good."

He stares at my mouth, watching while I chew. I swallow, then take a sip from the glass of cider he's poured for me. It's my favorite kind—not too sweet, with the perfect level of dryness. As soon as I put my glass down, he lifts the bowl out of my hand, sets it on the coffee table, and tackles me, taking me down to the cushions.

He's got some serious skills with the way he's able to get his knee between my legs without me even realizing it until I start auto-humping. He cups the back of my head, his fingers pressing in. I don't know why it makes me so hot; it's like he's holding on so I can't get away from his mouth. Not that I'd want to.

He presses his lips to mine, sniffing. He backs off, giving me the funky eye. Then he goes in for another kiss, a little longer this time. He sucks my lip, running his tongue along it, and pulls back again.

"Ketchup?" he says.

"They're the best."

Randy resumes kissing me, and this time he slips his tongue into my mouth. After a few seconds of exploration, he breaks the kiss and shakes his head. "Nope. I don't like it. You need to brush your teeth. That tastes like shit."

He's still got a knee between my leg, and he's kind of thrusting against my pelvis. I can feel his hard-on. He can't be all that negatively affected by my bad breath.

"Just try one." I reach over and pluck a chip from the bowl, bringing it to his mouth.

He leans in and sniffs again, his nose wrinkling.

"Eat it."

"I'd rather eat you."

"Pretty sure ketchup-chip breath is better than vagina breath."

"That's debatable. I love the way your pussy tastes."

"Like I'm made of maple?"

"Exactly."

"Open your mouth." I press the chip against his bottom lip,

but he keeps it closed. I keep pushing until the chip breaks and crumbles in his beard and onto my chest. A few crumbs tumble into the V of my shirt.

"Oh! Look at that. Your shirt's dirty now; it needs to go in the laundry." He shoves his hand under my top and pulls it over my head. I'm braless, as is normal when I'm at home—his or mine.

"I thought we were going to watch a movie."

"We could make our own." He waggles his brows, his grin devious. "I need a new one for next week."

Randy leaves in the morning for a series of away games. He'll be gone for ten days. It'll be our longest separation since I moved to Chicago. We spend most of our free time together. It's almost a good thing he has to travel; otherwise I feel like we'd be immersed in just each other, all the time. This way I get to hang with Sunny, Violet, and Charlene.

Randy pulls his shirt over his head so we're matching in our level of nakedness. Then he settles between my legs. Instead of tongue wars, he brushes his lips softly over mine. "When I get back from this series, I want to talk about you moving in."

The change of topic throws me, having gone from hating on ketchup chips, to wanting sex, to this. "You mean to live with you?'

He licks his lips and nods. "Miller's gonna put his condo on the market at the end of the season, which means he'll be moving in with Sunny, so you should move in here."

He's so matter of fact. "Because it's logical or because you want me here?" I ask.

"Option two. Unless you're not ready." He props his chin on his fist, looking a little unsure of himself.

"You're positive you want me and my ketchup-chip breath in your space all the time?"

"The ketchup-chip breath I'll deal with if it means you're here all the time." He drops a warm kiss on my lips. "Do you know what makes away games bearable?"

"Video phone sex?"

Randy smiles. "That's number two on the list. Number one is knowing you're going to be here when I get back."

"It's super awesome when I answer the door naked, isn't it?"

"So awesome. Except that one time Lance was with me."

I cringe. "He got an eyeful." All I was wearing was a ribbon around my throat, tied in a little bow. After Lance left, Randy made me put the ribbon back on, and we had intense bathroom-vanity sex. He does *not* like that Lance has seen me naked, at all.

Randy makes a sound, like a growl. His version of territorial is sexy combined with vulnerable. "So you'll move in, then?"

"End of the season?"

"Or whenever you're ready. No pressure, though."

I cup his face in my palms and bring his mouth to mine. "I love you."

He smiles and grabs his phone from the coffee table, then sits back on his knees. "Say that again, please."

"I love you."

He passes the phone to me, and I hold it up, recording the broad expanse of muscle and ink. He's so stunning.

"You're the most beautiful thing in my life," he says.

I shiver as he yanks my pants down and tosses them to the floor. I ignite when he lowers his head and puts his mouth on me.

Everything about my relationship with Randy is intense, from the sex to the way we love each other. I keep waiting for the newness to fade and the emotions to temper, but they haven't. Being with Randy is like the first and last bite of my favorite dessert: it's full of giddy anticipation and blissful satiety.

I don't know if we'll always be like this, or if things will settle with time and familiarity, but for now, we are ravenously in love.

NYT and USA Today bestselling author of PUCKED, Helena Hunting lives on the outskirts of Toronto with her incredibly tolerant family and two moderately intolerant cats. She writes contemporary romance ranging from new adult angst to romantic sports comedy.

Find more books by Helena Hunting
by visiting helenahunting.com

Lightning Source UK Ltd.
Milton Keynes UK
UKHW022232040321
379798UK00005B/554